Letters
OF THE ~
CLOTH

— A   N O V E L —

R O B E R T   L U P I N A C C I

The Library of Congress has catalogued the paperback edition as follows:
Lupinacci, Robert
Letters of the Cloth/Robert Lupinacci– 1st Edition p.cm
ISBN: 9798731913027

Book design by Daniel Yeager
Cover photo by Robert Lupinacci
Author photo by Noah Bailey

This book is dedicated to...

Lori ...

... for her love and unwavering support.
I love being me when I'm with you.
My life without you is like dancing
without the music.

Mackenzie, Aman, Noah,
and Rebecca ...

... you taught me how amazing it
feels to be loved, and how
rewarding it feels to love you..

All those who perished in the
Holocaust, all those courageous
souls that helped some survive, and
all those caring *people of the cloth*
who advance honor, integrity, and
social action through churches,
synagogues, mosques, and spiritual
institutions everywhere, every day.

Those selfless souls who lost their lives,
innocence, sanity, and humanity on
wars' battlefields.

Contents

PART I

CHAPTER 1

The Victrola

The Victrola belonged to Giuliana Luciari. So did one of the 6-year-old boys dancing with her in the piazza. Marcello. Marcello duplicated his mother's every step, gesture, move, and expression as she led him and his friend and dancing partner, Chiano Pratto, through the intricacies of American Swing dance. Every afternoon, after teaching formal ballroom and classic ballet to the children of Roman aristocrats, Giuliana returned home to a humble piazza near the Roman Ghetto to teach her own children and neighbors to dance. Her Victrola preserved the sanity of a community impinged by war, and enabled Giuliana to pursue her passion to dance and teach dance.

She moved effortlessly, with athletic power, meticulous precision, and a silky, fluid grace that accentuated the Victrola's every note. Her inner verve emerged from perfectly shaped, sharply defined, crimson lips. Her slender, distinct nose, liquory brown eyes, and shiny waves of cascading chestnut brown hair rewarded the sun for finding her. An intense, yet understated simplicity within her evoked an allure impossible to ignore. Men and women alike were hard pressed to merely see Giuliana, or simply look at her; she commanded one to stare, especially when she danced.

Somehow, Giuliana weaved the choppy steps of Swing dance into cohesive elegance. Her lithe button-up sundress flowed in sync with her lean length. Brilliant red sandals completed her simplicity's magnificence in a natural fusion with her Italian beauty's magnetism. But Giuliana's most impressive features, qualities, and abilities– even her purpose– appeared more evident, even amplified, through Marcello.

Marcello was a chiseled replica of Giuliana's perfect form. Her warm spirit and vigor shined through his eyes like admiration flickering from diamonds. Marcello's movements were instinctively graceful and athletic. Music's glee radiated from his sinewy body, as his animated being cast a sprawling net of influence, a charismatic ether, even though he was just six. The glowing light of his being shined deep into destiny's unknowns, illuminating his path with optimism and resilience, and by way of some mysterious social proxy, he lit the same path for his best friend, Chiano. These two dutiful and inseparable friends, born three days apart, and living across the hall from each other ever since, cultivated a compelling union that was recognized by all, discounted by none; they were a duo of one.

Giuliana's devout husband, Vieri, manned the Victrola, keeping it wound and loud. The Victrola meant as much to Vieri as it did to Giuliana: being a gifted and skilled woodworker, Vieri painstakingly reconstructed the tatty Victrola that he found in an alley into an instrument of beauty and deep sentimental value. He restored its wooden base, refashioned its wooden horn, polished the brass tone arm, crank, back bracket, and reproducer with artistic patience and pronounced care. The Victrola was a neighborhood icon that united and inspired its residents during dire times, and in some small way, connected this tiny corner of Rome to the rest of the world. The Victrola thrived at the core of the community and the heart and soul of the Luciari family. It brought the gift of music to suffering people and a modest means to Giuliana. It warmed every soul that ever gathered around it to sing and dance in an enduring and endearing pursuit of happiness amidst a cradle of suffering.

It was October of 1943. Rome was occupied by hostile Nazi troops arresting innocent Jews and sentencing them to Hitler's death camps. The world was teetering between fear and courage, and shock and understanding, but music and dance supplied a temporary antidote to the indigence imposed on horrified Roman Jews and righteous Christians dodging Hitler's wrath. For the innocent victims unsuspectingly pleated into the path of Nazi destruction, the Victrola provided comfort and inspiration like faith inspires hope.

American Swing music's incomparable, spirited melody, rhythm, and beat gushed from the reconditioned Victrola. Music rained unsullied happiness over the piazza's stone buildings that housed small shops and apartments shrouded in plants and laundered clothes pinned to drooping laundry lines. American Big Band and Swing music temporarily released these humble Italians from adversity's unrelenting domination. Neighbors and merchants routinely stopped what they were doing and stood in their doorways to watch Giuliana, Marcello, and Chiano dance. Neighbors placed whatever small offerings they could at the base of the Victrola to show their appreciation: hunks of bread, cheese, fruit, buttons, an occasional coin, a cigarette, candy, and notes of thanks. Shoppers stopped to soak up moments of delight, provisionally preserving innocence, and protecting the Roman spirit from the prowling sprawl of war.

As Giuliana spun, twisted, and stepped through a raucously enjoyable Swing dance, Marcello and Chiano aptly mirrored her every step, every gesture, her every movement.

"I taught you well, miei dolci ragazzi," my sweet boys. Their proud smiles and visceral happiness shined a festival of simple pleasure on the piazza. They fell into the very rhythm and melody that was Giuliana. As the Victrola needle vibrated through the grooves of a record, bringing music to life, Giuliana embedded the joy of song and the elation of dance into the essence of Marcello's total being. After giving the Victrola a brisk wind, Vieri joined in, dancing with Giuliana.

"Look at them, Vieri," Giuliana said, motioning to Marcello and Chiano, their smiles, laughter, and dancing filling the piazza with joy. "Will our love and nurturing help these innocent 6-year-olds overcome the horrors of war?"

"The only thing we can do, is to do everything we can do," Vieri said in his simple wisdom. A measure of Giuliana's happiness faded into the quiet of her mind as they continued to dance. Vieri waved for Chiano's father, Lucio, to join in the dance but he opted to clap and dance on his own– apparently hearing a different beat than the others, but he clapped and danced, nonetheless. Lucio and Vieri were as inseparable as their sons, Marcello and Chiano, all their lives. Lifelong friendships were essential and the norm as the way of life in Rome.

Giuliana's brother and Catholic priest, Father Salvestro Frischetti, skillfully played the drums– on the tiny shoulders of his two nieces, Marcello's twin sister, Gaia, and their younger sister, Mia. Father Frischetti– known affectionately as Uncle Sal to the children– pulled Gaia and Mia into the frolic and whirling of Swing sweeping through the piazza.

A happy and resounding clapping spread through the small group gathered, stopping time, denying the turmoil of war, securing this moment of joy. For the moment.

Like a siren in the still of the night, Chiano's older brother, Dario, frantically bolted around the corner screaming, "I nazisti stanno arrivando! I nazisti stanno arrivando! The Nazis are coming! The Nazis are coming!" Vieri stopped the Victrola. The piazza's gleeful cheer crashed into terror's wall and fell silent. Lucio grabbed Chiano and Dario and scurried his two sons toward an open doorway leading to apartments on upper floors. Chiano broke from his father's hold in a river of adrenaline and ran back to Marcello. His eyes, wide. His speech, quick. He and Marcello hugged with a mature sense of knowing the moment's gravity. Chiano took a marble from his pocket and handed it to Marcello.

"You keep mine, and I'll keep yours," Chiano said.

"Deal," Marcello agreed. Marcello pulled a marble from his pocket and they swapped marbles. They shook to honor the trade with their special handshake: three shakes down followed by three claps of their hands, followed by a thumbs up and tapping on each other's heart. Chiano raced back to his father who was waiting nervously at the doorway. He stopped and looked back at Marcello. They waved anxiously to each other, unsure of what was to come, but assured of their lifetime bond. Lucio scooped Chiano into the doorway and looked back to lock understanding eyes with Vieri. They held their gaze, peering into each other's souls. Lucio blew Vieri a kiss and touched his heart. He charged into the doorway's shadow, frantically urging his sons up the stairs.

In a well-practiced routine, Lucio and his sons pulled open an ingenious opening that Vieri had crafted into the ceiling of a closet. A rope ladder fell from the opening and they climbed into the attic crawl space and huddled together in a far corner, cowering, retreating behind an imaginary shield. They heard the bustle and panic in the street below as everyone who was jovial just a moment ago was now scrambling in panic, tripping over their own fear and uncertainty as they fled. Doors slammed shut. Footsteps scampered over the cobblestones in a cadence of near hysteria. Lucio and his sons huddled closer together in a corner of Vieri's tiny attic.

"We'll be alright. It's going to be alright," Lucio promised, more rotely than assuring. The chaos continued in the piazza below. Then fear got closer. They heard footsteps on the stairs they had just climbed. "It must be Vieri and Giuliana," he thought. Lucio crawled to the eve of the attic where an opening in a vent enabled him to look down onto the piazza. Vieri and Giuliana were packing up records near the Victrola, which was perched on a café table. The footsteps got louder. Closer. And closer. Seconds later, the secret ceiling opening slid open. "I nazisti stanno arrivando," Lucio's older son whispered. "Loro sono qui." They're here. The indistinct sound of hands grabbing the rope ladder and feet struggling to climb its rungs sent jolts of terror through Lucio and his sons. He pulled his boys closer to him and prepared for whatever the worst was to be.

Then, like a refreshing wave soothing the parched shore, relief washed over them: Lucio's wife, Mila, and their daughter, Dayana, appeared at the top of the ladder, gasping for air, and groping for allusive courage. They sealed the secret door closed then crept to the corner to join Lucio and the boys in a desperate embrace. Mila shielded herself, Dayana, and Dario from watching the turmoil in the piazza below, but Lucio was compelled to watch; so was Chiano.

The happy ambience cast out by the Victrola and the dancing had plunged into a vortex of fear. Merchants scurried back into their shops and locked their doors. Shoppers scattered. Happiness vaporized like doused candlelight. Two colorless German military jeeps whipped around the corner devoid of concern for pedestrians that might be in their path. People scattered and ran randomly in hopes of finding safety. Both jeeps swerved directly toward Vieri and Giuliana's family huddled in a frightened, fragile bubble around the Victrola. Marcello felt something he had never experienced when being held in his father's arms: fear.

"What do they want with us, Papa?"

"Nothing, they want only Jews."

"Why?"

"There's no good reason, Marcello."

A Nazi lieutenant rose from the second jeep. He was notably tall and appeared even taller, donning a grey Cosplay woolen German officer's cap that peaked to a rounded apex some six and a half feet above the ground. He was fair. Blond, with steely, bluish, icy eyes. A firm jaw. Anger melted through the arrogance on his face, forming his features into a caricature of hatred. He stepped directly toward Vieri, patting his leather swagger stick with deliberate, intimidating intention.

"You like Jews," the lieutenant said to Vieri, eagerly smacking his stick into his palm, a gesture signaling something bad was about to happen. Vieri said nothing. He huddled his family closer to him. Their collective terror choked back the screams they craved to expel. The lieutenant commanded his soldiers to his side. He poked Vieri in the teeth with his swagger stick. Two of the soldiers tore Vieri from his terrified family and slammed him to his knees. The Nazi lieutenant knocked the Victrola to the ground with a swipe of his stick. He drove his boot into its delicate wood, smashing its beauty into shards and splinters of rubbish. He picked it up by its horn and flung it across the piazza, into a building, crushing its horn, sending its tone arm and reproducer into broken bits of sorrow.

"No more fucking music!" The Nazi lieutenant screamed. Marcello's eyes swelled in a salty sea of tears. His ears resisted the cruelty echoing in the lieutenant's voice, and the sadness resonating from the Victrola's parts smashing and tumbling across the cobblestones. He attempted to charge the lieutenant, but his mother tightened her hold on him. The lieutenant viewed Marcello's courage as stupidity through cold eyes and an arrogant grin.

"Vieri Luciari. Jew lover," the lieutenant said with deliberate disdain. "We have information that suggests you like to hide Jews from us, Mr. Luciari. This is true?" The lieutenant poked his leather baton into Vieri's cheek then drew it back and administered a wicked and hateful blow with the baton across Vieri's face. Then another blow, slicing his face open from his cheek to the top corner of his lip. He motioned for the soldiers to restrain Vieri. One of them forced the butt of his rifle into Vieri's back, causing him to fall face first into the stone street. Another soldier pushed his family back, leaving Vieri alone at the sole of the lieutenant's boot; the soldier lifted him back to his knees for the lieutenant to drive a vicious kick into Vieri's ribs, doubling him over. The blow cut off his wind causing him to wheeze and choke for air as he felt his body collapsing. No breath. No air. Just fear. Anger. Rage.

"You Jew loving fool!" The lieutenant smashed the heel of his brutal Nazi boot into Vieri's jaw, knocking him to the ground, his tongue split open, fragments of his top front teeth flew from his bloody mouth. His bottom teeth were jammed into his gums. "Pick him up," the lieutenant commanded. The soldiers peeled Vieri from the street's dusty stone and held him up by the hair. The lieutenant rammed his boot into Vieri's nose, splitting his face open, producing an animal-like squeal and a gush of blood from Vieri.

Giuliana and her children treaded desperately in the currents of horror's tide, watching their helpless husband and father be humiliated and beaten. Marcello choked on his terror and sheer helplessness. Giuliana desperately held her children in a grip of disbelief, shock, and hatred for the man brutalizing her husband, her children's father, right there, before their eyes, in what was their joyous piazza all their lives.

"Leave him alone," Giuliana screamed. A Nazi soldier slapped her into silence with a blow that knocked her to the ground. Her children clenched into a ball around her, blanketing her in their tears, horror, and fear.

"Get up," the lieutenant demanded. "You– the mother! Get up!" He motioned to a soldier to bring Giuliana to him. The soldier shoved the three children aside, out of the lieutenant's way while another soldier grabbed Giuliana by the arm and thrust her toward the lieutenant. She stumbled. Her eyes never left her crumbling husband's broken body. The dizziness induced by the blow she took froze her ability to think. She stood numbed by disbelief, petrified by fear, enraged by anger's hot sting. She broke from the soldier's hold and charged the lieutenant and pounded his face with clenched fists, screaming.

"You filthy bastard! You filthy, rotten bastard! How could– " The lieutenant smacked her with a hard backhand across her face, knocking her back to the ground.

"Get her up!" Just as the soldier pulled Giuliana from the stone and dirt, Marcello charged the lieutenant, swinging his fists wildly. "You're willing to die for your mother and father, little man?" the lieutenant asked with a sick grin. He grabbed Marcello by the ear, roughly, and shoved him hard to the ground. Marcello shivered in silence, drowning in a blur of tears. His sisters were too terrified to move. They held onto their Uncle Salvestro's cassock like a knot hanging onto rope. Their uncle held them with fierce protection and rigid resolve.

"Lassen Sie in Ruhe. Nimm mich Sie haben dir nichts getan! Take me. Leave them alone. They did nothing to you," Father Frischetti pled in German to the lieutenant.

The lieutenant strutted over to Father Frischetti– Uncle Salvestro– in a deliberate swagger designed to evoke more fear, more terror, exert more callous power over a helpless priest and a poor man's innocent family. He poked Father Frischetti's chest with his baton as he spoke.

"I would shoot you, priest, but I might be able to use you. Or maybe you're just worthless to me," the lieutenant said before smacking his leather swagger stick across Father Frischetti's left cheek with a vicious backhand. He followed with a forehand blow to his right cheek. One of the soldiers shoved him to the ground and jammed his heel into the priest's neck, pinning him to the cobblestone street. "Shut your mouth, priest; the next collar you wear could be made of rope, you fool," the lieutenant said.

The lieutenant returned his attention to Vieri. Then Giuliana caught his eye. He strode over to her, grinning, nodding in approval and wondering in lust. He motioned to her with the waft of his hand commanding her to step toward him. One of the soldiers shoved her toward the lieutenant.

"You are the wine of temptation," the lieutenant said, still nodding. He stuck his swagger stick into Giuliana's neck and his face fell into a stern-mouthed, frozen glare. He circled her as though examining a coat on a mannequin. Admiring. Approving. Wanting. He stepped closer to her. She could smell and almost taste the rank aftermath of his consumed lunch: bratwurst with onions, mustard, and flat beer. Cognac. He looked younger than a lieutenant should look. Meaner. Colder. Hollow. Empty. He nodded in approval, imagined more, grinned more. Wanted more. Vieri was hyperventilating at the lieutenant's feet. The lieutenant stared through Giuliana's sundress then tapped at her top button and gestured with his head for her to undo it. She did not flinch nor cower, she looked him dead in the eyes and undid the button, somehow managing to demean him. Her glare was more piercing than the lieutenant's.

He pondered what to do with her– with all of them. He strummed the barrel of his pistol across her right cheek, down her neck, deliberately over her breasts. He smiled a degrading, smug grin. He slid his gun back into its holster. He stared into Giuliana's eyes for a long moment then ripped her dress open. He pulled his Wehrmacht-issued Heer Dagger from a sheaf attached to his belt and held it up to her nose. Then he forcefully sliced the shoulder straps of her dress causing it to fall to the ground. She stood before him with her breathing swelling through her bra. He stared at her as he sliced one of the straps of her bra, then, the other. She glared back without flinching, without yielding. Then, the Nazi lieutenant pressed his dagger between her breasts and sliced the front of her bra open and flicked it to the ground. Her naked breasts spilled into the glare of the bright sun, exposing her vulnerability, magnifying her defenselessness. He lustfully eyed her while deliberately strumming her nipple with the metal pommel of his dagger. He stared at her, alight with lust and drunk with power over her, over all of them. Giuliana's anger burned through her like electricity through light.

Vieri's earlier words with Giuliana ran through his mind. *Will our love and nurturing help these innocent 6-year-old boys overcome the hatred and horrors of war? The only thing we can do is to do everything we can do.*

Vieri bolted toward the lieutenant but the soldier drove him back to the ground with the butt of his rifle. Twice. Undeterred, the lieutenant lustfully eyed Giuliana, now slowly strumming his hand over her breasts. Contemplating. Smirking. Then he moved toward Marcello's twin sister Gaia and circled her as he had Giuliana. He ran his gun barrel through the part in her hair.

"She has your eyes. She's beautiful. You must love her dearly," the lieutenant said to Giuliana while contemplating how best to inflict pain and terror. He returned to Giuliana and stared into her eyes with stone-like coldness. "Does she hide Jews, too?" Giuliana said nothing. She just stared back. Her arm instinctively cradled Gaia to her side. "Does she hide Jews, too, I asked!" the lieutenant demanded. His head swung sharply to his right and down toward Gaia. "Do you like Jews?" Gaia shook her head in meek, apprehensive affirmation. "Do you hide Jews?" Gaia clutched onto her mother's side for dear life, trembling, sobbing.

"Mommy. Mommy."

"Do you hide Jews!" the lieutenant screamed, pulling her up onto her toes, with a fistful of her hair in his hand. He spattered her face with his sour spittle. He screamed, "Do you hide Jews?" He shoved her toward one of the Nazi soldiers and returned to Vieri. The lieutenant held his pistol to Vieri's temple in one hand, and with the other, he grabbed hold of Marcello's hair, ripping a shock of it from his head. He shoved Marcello nose-to-nose with his father.

"Your father is a pig. Spit in his face!" Marcello trembled in sheer horror, his face saturated in tears. The lieutenant slapped Marcello's face.

Hard. The red imprint of the lieutenant's hand was stamped on Marcello's 6-year-old cheek and his eternal memory.

"I said spit in his face!" He released Marcello and backhanded Vieri sharply across the face, then grabbed him by the shirt and tore it open, popping its buttons off. "Any Jews hiding under your shirt?" he asked mockingly. He ripped the shirt from Vieri's body and threw it into Marcello's face and grabbed his hair tighter.

"Spit, you stupid little fuck! Spit in this Jew-loving bastard's face!" Marcello stood firm. He locked tear-filled eyes with his father's eyes. They both cried, steeped in deep love for each other, swallowed by fear's dreadful ache, horrified in anticipating what was to come.

"Spit!" the lieutenant screamed.

"No!" Marcello screamed back.

The lieutenant slapped Marcello harder, drawing blood from his nose. He motioned for the soldier who was holding Gaia to release her; he shoved her forward toward the lieutenant. She stumbled in front of him. She stood before him brave and petrified at the same time. The lieutenant turned back to Marcello and commanded, "Spit!"

"No! I can't! I won't!"

"Do it!" the lieutenant commanded. "Fucking do it!"

"No!"

"Do it! Spit in his Jew-loving face!"

"No!"

The Nazi lieutenant wheeled around toward Gaia and fired a single shot into her tiny chest, killing her.

A collective shriek erupted from Marcello's family. Vieri lunged at the lieutenant again and managed to land a punishing blow to his ribs. But the Nazi lieutenant whacked him back with a sharper blow to the head with his gun and another with the heel of his boot. Giuliana and Mia screamed and sobbed, clutching Gaia's innocent, lifeless body. The Nazi lieutenant motioned to the soldier who was restraining Gaia to hold Marcello's barely conscious father up on his knees; the soldier pulled Vieri up by the hair.

The lieutenant grabbed Marcello by his ear, nearly lifting him off the ground. He shoved Marcello to Vieri's side and grabbed his little hand, forcing it under his own hand and around the trigger of his Walther P-38 pistol. He pointed the gun at Marcello's dead sister.

"Look what hiding Jews did for your family! He pulled harder on Marcello's ear. "Do you still refuse to spit on your Jew-loving father's face?"

"I won't do it," Marcello managed to mouth through the anguish of his sobs, terror, and rage. The Nazi lieutenant pulled Marcello's ear even harder, causing it to bleed, he grabbed a fist full of Marcello's hair.

"You will shoot him!" The lieutenant forced Marcello's harmless 6-year-old finger tighter onto the trigger beneath his own hand.

"Shoot him!"

"I can't! No!"

"Shoot him!"

"No!"

The Nazi lieutenant fixed Marcello's finger tighter around the trigger. He squeezed the trigger with Marcello's hand in his, and sent a bullet searing into Vieri's temple shattering his head into a mass of blood-soaked, butchered skull and exploded pieces of human brain. Vieri fell from the soldier's hold; he, too, now, was dead.

The lieutenant squatted down to Marcello's shocked, terrified face.

"Look what hiding Jews did for your family!" He twisted Marcello's ear hard and cast him to the ground. "I say spit, you fucking spit," he said then spit violently into Marcello's face. He grabbed Marcello's right hand. "Every time you use this hand for the rest of your life you will feel it pulling the trigger that killed your Jew-loving father. Little Fool!" Marcello ran after him, screaming.

"You're a bully! You're a mean bully! You can't do this! I won't let you get away with this!" Marcello screamed. He raised up and began swinging his little fists at the lieutenant's face while still yelling. "You can't hurt people!" The lieutenant plopped his hand over Marcello's forehead and shoved him to the ground, crying. In shock.

"I just did, you little fool," the lieutenant said, and continued back toward his jeep. Father Frischetti scooped Marcello into his arms.

"I've got you, Marcello. I've got you," his uncle whispered in his bleeding ear.

"Who's gonna protect us, Uncle Sal?"

"We are, Marcello. We are," Uncle Salvestro said, while glaring at the Nazi lieutenant, who was reenacting the shooting in mockery to entertain his underlings.

Marcello ran and embraced his mother, Mia, and Uncle Salvestro embraced all of them. They held each other desperately curled in a ball of agony that will last the rest of their lives.

"We'll be back for the Jews," the Nazi lieutenant shouted over his shoulder. He returned to his jeep filled with a sick satisfaction. Watching it all from behind the wall in a corner of Vieri's attic, Lucio and Mila held their children in their arms. Crying.

"Why did the Nazis hurt Marcello's Papa? And Gaia? Why are they so mean? Are they crazy, Papa?" Chiano asked, struggling through a sheet of tears.

"They are very sick, Chiano."

"What sickness do they have that makes them so mean and hurt people?" Chiano asked.

"It's called hatred, son."

"Will they kill us, Papa?" Chiano pleaded, nodding his nose toward the tragic scene in the piazza below. Lucio held his son close to him.

"They can shoot people with guns, and smash Victrolas with their boots, but they will never kill our spirit, Chiano." He hugged his son more deeply. "Our lives will not be defined by the force of guns beating people down, but by the power of achievement and compassion raising people up. I will see to that, and so will you." He kissed his son's head, holding him closer still, as loathing and tears dripped from his eyes. "This will not define us," he whispered.

"Marcello has no more father. No more sister. They even smashed the Victrola, our music," Chiano managed to say through his sobbing.

"We will spend our lives bringing music and joy and happiness to every person we ever touch, Chiano. Me and you and Mama and Dayana and Dario. We will be especially good to Marcello's family." Lucio's family cuddled together in a cocoon of love, warmth, and fear.

Lucio returned to peeking down at the piazza below where Giuliana, Marcello, and Mia snuggled into Uncle Salvestro's arms, sobbing at the side of Gaia and Vieri's lifeless bodies.

CHAPTER 2

Stained Glass

Two Wednesdays after the catastrophic murder of Vieri and Gaia Luciari, Giuliana woke Marcello and Mia early. Wednesday was the day the pope greeted crowds in Saint Peter's Square, and said prayers over the multitudes of faithful Catholics and other Christians that flock to Rome to see him. The bus trip to the Vatican was not an easy one, especially in occupied Rome, but Giuliana was not one to allow her ambition to be thwarted by obstacles, nor stifled by convention's conformity. She was committed to, and valued courage, and genuine, yet humble righteousness: they mounted a bus to see Pope Pius XII.

They arrived among the first people at Saint Peter's Square in order to get a position close to the pope's balcony. Determination reflected on Giuliana's face like blue defining a perfect sky. Marcello and Mia were still deciphering the horrible violence that they had recently experienced, and would relive thousands of times over for the rest of their lives. They obediently accompanied their mother to Saint Peter's Square, despite a notable disinterest in waiting a long time to see the pontiff. They passed the time playing tag, running around the magnificent square, peeping behind archways, statues, and vendors' tables filled with religious articles and papal souvenirs. The more crowded the square became, the closer Marcello and Mia remained close to their mother. And the more crowded the square became, the more protective Giuliana became of her position.

Finally, after nearly two hours of waiting, the double doors to the pope's balcony opened, and Pope Pius XII emerged, with raised arms. He turned quarter turns to grace the crowd with a glimpse of his face from hundreds of feet away. Much of the crowd cheered and applauded. But Giuliana was silent. The pope absorbed his adoration like a cloth absorbing color. He offered another round of quarter turns, making a sign of the cross as a blessing to each section of worshipers. When he finished, he faced forward, directly above Giuliana and her children. Saint Peter's Square fell into an obedient and expectant silence. Again, the pope paused to drink in the adoration, but it was to be short lived.

"Why don't you condemn the Nazis? Giuliana screamed out. "Why don't you do something? Say something! Coward! You are Hitler's puppet!" Her screams drew murmurs from the shocked crowd. "Say something! Do something? End your silence! End your silence, coward!" she screamed. The pope might not have heard what she was saying but it was clear that she wasn't complimenting him. The stunned pontiff turned his gaze toward the polizia rushing toward Giuliana. He looked down from his perch on the fringe of heaven with a vile sneer. She could feel his mousy eyes glare at her through his pane of shame, as he felt the rage in her own eyes burning with anger's clarity. Regret and disgrace dripped from the pontiff's face like rain turning dust into mud. In that very moment, Giuliana became to Marcello what the Victrola was to music: she empowered his vision with an awakened voice. She animated his life path with dance. She seeded the aria of his destiny with meaning and purpose.

"Do something. End your silence!" she screamed again, and continued screaming as the polizia grabbed her and forced her and her children out of the square, kicking and screaming at the pope. They dragged her to a police car parked on Via di Porta Angelica, a crowded, litter-strewn side street parallel to Saint Peter's Square. The polizia shoved her into the police car unceremoniously and put the children into the car more gently before slamming the car door shut.

"What's the matter with you, screaming like that, wanna get yourself killed?" one of the policemen shouted, as he dropped himself into the driver's seat of the tiny car.

"I am showing my children to stand up and speak out for what's right and against what is wrong," Giuliana snapped back. "The pope is the Nazi's puppet!"

"You better teach your children in private, or none of you will be here long enough to do what is right," the policeman barked back. "We all hate the Nazis as much as you do, but you can't make dangerous outbursts in public. Do what you have to do behind the scenes," he advised. "Tell me where you live, and I will take you there safely. We will pretend this never happened. It will be our secret."

"The Piazza Mattei," Giuliana said, as her anger fused with a flicker of accomplishment, and her natural composure began to return.

"Ever been in a police car?" the policeman asked, looking into the rearview mirror at Marcello and Mia.

"No," they said in synch, excited by the opportunity.

"I will give you some fun," the policeman promised. He turned on the car's siren and lights and they sped away. Marcello and Mia hugged their mother, smiling with pride, wonder, and a much-needed morsel of happiness.

With his father and twin sister murdered, and his best friend, Chiano vanished, Marcello desperately needed a father figure and a new friend. Mia and Marcello were deeply bound as loving siblings, but they both needed more; so did their mother. Giuliana quickly enlisted her brother Salvestro to comfort, engage, and somehow, inspire Marcello. She became a pillar of strength and inspiration to Marcello and Mia, and their uncle Salvestro, Father Frischetti, stepped into the critical role of surrogate father to a very fragile little boy, Marcello. As pastor of San Gregorio della Divina Pietà, Uncle Salvestro had plenty of ways to keep Marcello busy. Knowing the background and the current state of affairs in Rome, and in the world in 1943, Father Frischetti's superiors in the church were willing to accommodate the demands of caring for a child— as long as there was no cost, inconvenience, or danger posed to them, or the Church.

Marcello was beginning to find solace and even threads of occasional comfort through Uncle Salvestro's compassion, and maybe even through God's mercy. He would clutch his uncle's frock and follow him around the church like a glow following light. Uncle Salvestro's hand was nearly always on his nephew's shoulder. Marcello hummed almost unconsciously and perpetually to drown his despondency in music's relief, in search of comfort. He often swayed into calming dancing at random to soothe himself. His head was perpetually tilted sadly toward the ground but little by little, day by day, over time, Uncle Salvestro's effort and love managed to help Marcello look upward more frequently to absorb the inherent serenity and peace within the church's beautiful stained glass, sculpture, and art.

The church was empty most of the time and Uncle Salvestro and Marcello liked it that way. They ambled down the church's center aisle in what had become their daily routine; as always, Father Frischetti's arm around Marcello, and Marcello's arm around his uncle's waist.

"You will always find peace in God's house, Marcello. I promise you this." Uncle Salvestro led Marcello into a pew where they knelt together. Tapping Marcello's shoulder, he said, "You will hear the best sermons when nobody is talking … the words will be right here in your own head when you talk to God, Cello," his shorthand nickname for Marcello. "I promise you this," he vowed. "This is a gift; we have the church to ourselves, but we will never be alone. God will always be with us, Cello."

"Why can't I see God? Or hear Him?"

"No one can see Him, sweet boy. But, as I said, you will hear Him— in your very own mind. And you will feel His power and comfort in your heart," his uncle promised, gently tapping his nephew's heart. "Let's talk to God. Tell Him anything you want, tell Him how you feel, ask Him any questions you want, He will hear you, and He will answer you in His own way," Uncle Salvestro said, then clutched his rosary beads and bowed his head in prayer. *Dear God, please help me help this child. Please touch him, soothe him,* Uncle Salvestro prayed. Marcello closed his eyes, too, and began speaking to God.

> *Hello, God. This is Marcello. Uncle Salvestro says you can hear me but I don't really think so. He says I can ask you anything, and tell you anything. Is he right? I don't know what to say.*
>
> *Will I ever see my Papa again? And Chiano? I miss them both so much. And Gaia, too. Will I always feel sad like this, God? I feel really sick inside. It hurts. Will I always hurt like this inside?*
>
> *How come you didn't stop that man, God? Did you make him kill my father, and my sister? I thought you were supposed to be good but why did you let those terrible things happen?*

Marcello retreated deep into his wounded soul, wondering, doubting, and hurting. Confused and suspended from consciousness by chronic emotional pain, he knelt in the pew, numb. Tears he couldn't feel anymore ran down his cheeks, but he felt the sickness of sadness deep inside. His breathing heaved upward then dropped into the deep of his being. He had no sense of how much time had passed, unsure even of where he was, his only certainty was the vast ache consuming him from inside. He had no sense of his uncle leaving the pew, no sense of his absence. No sense of time. Marcello continued wrestling with his monstrous memory, his monumental loss, his summit of pain. The tenuous solace of the empty church fell far short of Marcello's need for comfort and peace. He took the marble Chiano had given him *that day* from his pocket, but it did not reflect the beauty and intrigue of a marble; instead, reflections of his father's face showed in Marcello's mind over and over and over. Seeking comfort, he caressed, rubbed, and stared at the marble's shiny surface, comparing its wondrous colors to the crystal clarity of the glass encompassing it. He admired its perfect shape, its strength, its beauty, its meaning, its connection to Chiano, to innocence, to being a little boy. *I miss Chiano and my Papa so much,* he thought. He held the vibrant marble up to the fused light seeping through the spangle of colors of stained glass backlit by the brilliant Roman sun. He marveled at his treasured marble, then an unexpected noise in the aisle demanded his attention.

He looked into the aisle and saw the tan-light-brown puffy sections and lace of a brand-new football rolling toward him. Looking up, he saw his Uncle Salvestro at the back of the church making a kicking motion and wearing his trademark ear-to-ear grin. His hands and arms spread wide at his sides in a silent introduction of the wondrous new football. Uncle Salvestro darted down the aisle to join Marcello thinking, *Please, help me help him, Lord. It's tearing my heart apart to see him in so much pain. Dear God, please help us.*

"A boy must have a football. When you have a football in your life you will have happiness and fun," Uncle Salvestro said. "Maybe that's where the expression, 'have a ball,' comes from, yes?" he considered. "It's yours to keep, Cello. Yours to enjoy."

"It's mine?" His uncle shook his head to affirm that the ball was Marcello's to keep. "Thank you," Marcello said, as a scarce smile slowly formed on his lips as he breathed in the fresh leather scent peeling off the ball. He examined its feel: the smooth, brand-new texture, its soft but durable sections sewn into the curves of the ball. "Can we play?"

"We'll play this afternoon. Maybe every afternoon."

"I have another kind of a ball, sort of" Marcello said and showed his uncle his blue, yellow, and greenish marble. "Look," Marcello said, handing his uncle the marble.

"It's beautiful, Cello. Beautiful. Perfect," he said. "Look, it has no beginning, no end. It's clear, but filled with color, too. Strong and perfect. You can hardly tell the inside from the outside. It is marbleous!' Marbleous is a better word than 'marvelous,' yes? Where did you get such a marbleous marble?"

"Chiano and I traded marbles ..." Marcello said, stumbling over his mixed emotions. After a painful pause, he asked, "Will I ever see Chiano again?"

"This, we don't know today, sweet boy. But," he punctuated his point with a raised index finger, "when we know, we will know, yes? In the meantime, we can hope." Kneeling down to Marcello's eye level, Uncle Salvestro said, "Do you know what hope is, Cello?"

"It's when you want something."

"True, something you want very badly. And there is some faith involved also— a feeling like you believe what you want can really happen. I know you hope to see Chiano again, so, let's continue hoping." He held Marcello's shoulders in his hands, looked deeply into his eyes, and continued. "I will hope along with you, and we will pray. But I must warn you, we must be prepared that what we hope for sometimes does not happen, OK? But we will still hope and pray, and we will still believe it can happen. Yes?"

"Yes."

"Great. You hang on to this marbleous marble, and maybe something marbleous will happen," Uncle Salvestro said, as he handed the marble back to Marcello. "Now, come, help me with a few church-keeping chores— they're like housekeeping chores but in the church." He led Marcello to the altar where he took a box of wooden matches from behind the pulpit.

"Do you know that there is a secret to this pulpit," he claimed, rubbing the pulpit. "The wood this pulpit is made from came from a pirate ship that washed ashore in Fiumicino many years ago," he said. "Every time I step into this pulpit, I hear the pirates sing."

"Real pirates?"

"Very real. Fierce pirates. But the pulpit is not just a place for me to speak from, it is an important platform we teach from, and where we learn how we must conduct our lives. I love to stand there and share God's words," Uncle Salvestro said, "but it is action– what we do, and how we treat people– that's what matters most, not just the words." He tickled Marcello's belly, then said, "Listen: I think I hear the pirates singing," undermining the credibility of his tale.

"You're silly, Uncle Salvestro," Marcello said, slowly rediscovering his smile.

"Silly is the first ingredient in a Happy Cake. Here, help me strike this match to light the candles. Do you know the reason we light candles in the church? This one that burns at all times," he said, waving toward a candle on the corner of the altar. "It reminds us that God is always present. And I will tell you this secret: I believe the candles remind us that His flame will always warm our hearts and light the way for us. Here, help me light another candle to keep this one company," he said, as he took a wooden match from the box and together, they scratched it across the flint of the box. The match crackled to life, sparks triggered a flame, and a waft of burning sulfur streamed from the match as a small flame climbed to life. They put their hands together and Uncle Salvestro moved the candle close enough for them to light. *Please bring your warmth to him, Lord. Lighten and light his path,* Uncle Salvestro prayed.

"How about that, the presence of God can be seen after all, see?" Marcello nodded his agreement. "Now, sweet boy, we must bow for a moment before this beautiful crucifix to pay honor to our Lord, Jesus Christ. For now, we will just thank Him and try to live as honorably as He did … and He will be with you everywhere you go for your entire life," Uncle Salvestro said. They genuflected before the crucifix for a moment then Marcello followed his uncle's lead to rise. Uncle Salvestro took in a deep sniffing inhale.

"Can you smell that?" he asked.

"I just smell the church," Marcello said.

"Of course. Do you know what that smell is?"

"The church?"

"Incense! Why do we use incense? To bless our church and to symbolize our prayers rising up to God," he said, emphatically raising his hands. "It's a good thing, yes?" He handed Marcello a stick of incense. "Smell this. Good, yes?"

"Will I hurt inside like this my whole life, Uncle Salvestro?" The question tripped Uncle Salvestro up. He thought for a moment before answering.

"Let's think about it this way: You know that little yellow egg timer your Mama keeps by the stove?"

"Yeah."

"Well, it's like the egg timer: In the beginning– right now– all of the sand is filling the top of the glass, like the hurt you feel now inside– in your stomach, your chest, your heart. You feel all filled up with it, yes?"

"I do."

"But, Cello, in time, every second of every day, some of that sand– some of that hurt– falls to the bottom, and before you know it, all the sand is in the bottom, it moves from the top of you to somewhere else. It can even leave you, almost completely. It goes away, maybe to the back of your mind. It's still in you, but just a little, but it's not on the top of you where you feel it so much. In time, your Cello-egg timer will run out of sand, and you will feel much better. I promise you this. Make sense?"

"I guess so," Marcello said. "I hope so."

"I know how it feels to be in this kind of pain, Cello. When I was just a little older than you, my father was killed in the war, World War I." Uncle Salvestro took Marcello's little face in his hands. "I also know exactly how you feel. But as time goes by, you will feel better. You must believe this. The Church will comfort you like balm on a wound, Cello. I will comfort you, your Mama and Mia will comfort you, and you will come out on the other end OK. I promise," he said, and kissed his nephew's forehead.

"When I go home, I'm going to turn that egg timer over," Marcello said, then he sniffed the stick of incense and said, "This smell makes me feel good." *Thank you, God,* Uncle Salvestro thought, and breathed a bit easier.

"Good. Good is a good thing. I have something else to make you feel good. Come," Uncle Salvestro urged. "I want to show you the world," he claimed. "Come." Uncle Salvestro led Marcello to the back of the church and up the creaky, narrow, worn stairs leading to the balcony. In the balcony, a handful of folding chairs were arranged in a tight semi-circle where two vertical stained-glass windows were encased in a thick wooden frame supporting a much larger stained-glass window. Collectively, the three windows presented a depiction of Joseph and Mary on bent-knee, admiring the baby Jesus. There were eight rows of pews in the balcony, but the last three rows appeared to be sawed apart recently, and the wood nowhere to be seen.

"What happened to those pews?" Marcello asked.

"The wood was used for something else," Uncle Salvestro answered quickly, while leading Marcello to the stained glass windows. The morning sun's diffused glow brushed the floor with a spangle of colorful light shining through the windows. "I would have to say that stained glass windows are my favorite part of the church," Uncle Salvestro said. "How about you? What's your favorite part?"

"To spend time with you."

"Ah, you're right. You are my favorite part of the church. Then comes the stained glass." Marcello's head sank toward the floor with his eyes focused on nothing as he slipped back into sorrow's merciless gravity.

"One of the original purposes of the glass was to tell bible stories to people who could not read," Uncle Salvestro explained. "But I have more reasons to love stained glass. Come, we will examine them up close," he said, as he led Marcello closer to the glorious colored glass canvas. "Look at how beautiful these colors are against the sun. It's pure beauty. To enjoy beauty of any kind, Cello, is one of the best parts of being a human being," he said. "There is something very magical about stained glass. Can you think of what it might be?"

"I don't know. It just feels good to look at."

"You got it! It just has a way of making you feel good. It's magical. This beautiful glass has secret powers. You are such a bright boy. Such a sweet boy," he said while rubbing Marcello's head. *Thank you, Lord, you are sending the soothing salve my sweet boy needs so badly,* Uncle Salvestro thought. "Another thing I love is this," he said, holding his hand out into the soft yellow and crimson light cast through the window, warming his palm. "Look. It brings not only light into the church, Marcello, but beautiful colors and warmth to our souls. Look at this," he said, admiring the colors gracing his palm. "And you know what, the colors remind us that God's people come in many colors– all of us in one window like brothers and sisters." He looked to Marcello in a spirit of discovery. "You know, without light, we have no color, and without color, we have no light or flavor in our lives. Yes?" Marcello looked into the brilliance of color in the ruggedly smooth pieces of glass fixed into the lead-bordered beauty before him with inspired wonder: brilliant ruby reds, vibrant icy blues, intense concentrated yellows, robust greens, and deep violets, arranged into a moving mosaic depicting the Holy Mother watching over her son, Jesus Christ.

"As you so wisely pointed out, sweet boy, the stained glass makes us feel good. It makes us feel– I will teach you an important word now– it makes us feel *reverent*. That is a new word for you: *reverent*. It means a deep respect ... maybe another new word ... *respect*. Respect means you really admire someone or something, you think they're really special, and you treat that someone or that something with honor. This is that 'good' feeling that the windows make you feel, that important feeling, that peaceful feeling. Feel it?"

"Yes."

"Let's enjoy it for a few moments." *Thank you, Lord. Thank you. Every second he is relieved of his pain. I am relieved of mine.*

Uncle Salvestro and Marcello sat basking in the stained glass' beauty and awash in its reverent peace without saying a word. The color, light, and warmth soothed Marcello and prompted a few more grains of that sandy pain to fall from the pit of his stomach, to somewhere in the background of his being. After several minutes in the calm of color, Uncle Salvestro guided Marcello to the front pew. He sat and took in the view of the church for a moment and silently prompted Marcello to do the same. Despite the temporary relief from sadness' pain, the burden of grieving's weight often returned and continued pressing its unwelcome force on Marcello and Uncle Salvestro, like dark stirring in the fury of a storm.

"Sweet boy, let me show you a view of the world. We must use our imaginations for this," he said, shuffling to get more comfortable, leaning forward on the short balcony wall. Marcello assumed the same position. "Imagine this church as the whole world created by God," Uncle Salvestro suggested, shaping a globe with his hands. "God has given us this wonderful world. See how He's watching over us, and His world," he said, motioning toward the crucifix behind the altar in the front of the church. "We can see the presence of God after all, I suppose, yes?"

"Yes."

"Now, imagine that all of the pews down there are different countries of the world. Look, there is Italy, and France, Switzerland, and Germany," he said, pointing out different pews. "And let's imagine that the middle aisle is the Atlantic Ocean. Look, over there is America, and way over there, on the other side of the other aisle, I see Japan. See it?"

"I think so."

"Yes, it's there. So, here we are, all these countries, all of God's people, in one world, all together. It can be very nice, very peaceful, yes?"

"I wish it was."

"It will be, sweet boy," he assured Marcello. "We must understand that every one of the pews— every country— has its own way of life. They all have their own language, foods, music, and art and some believe in different things. We call all these things their culture. But as you can see, even though we have different ways of life, like these pews, we are all very much alike, yes?"

"I guess so," Marcello agreed.

"The best place to start to understand people from different countries is to understand their language. So, guess what wonderful gift I am going to give to you?"

"You already gave me a football."

"I am going to give you a magnificent gift, Marcello, a gift that will last you a lifetime." Marcello's eyebrows raised in anticipation of something good. "I am going to give you an education! I am going to teach you to speak English because that is the language they speak in America, and America is the most important country in the world— after our own home in Italy, of course. By the time you are ready to become a man and go to college, I will make sure that you are able to speak excellent English," he promised. "I am going to teach you just as I teach the students at the American School. Language opens the doors to the world, Marcello." What do you say about that?" Uncle Salvestro asked.

"Will you teach Chiano to speak English too— if he ever comes back?"

"Of course. You will both be my private students. And if you like, I will also teach you all the languages that I speak: French, Spanish, and German."

"We would love to learn those languages. Can we visit America someday, Uncle Salvestro?"

"We will make it a plan, and a plan is far more meaningful than a promise," he said, affectionately rubbing Marcello's head. "We will begin our journey in language in a special school soon, Cello ... you and Mia both. But more about that later, for now, look down there, look at the pulpit: that little stage for one person is where God speaks to all the pews— to all the countries in the world through what He whispers in the priest's ear. It is a good world down there with God looking down upon us, yes?"

"Yes, I guess so."

Looking up toward the heavens, Uncle Salvestro said, "God up there, as our Father, loves us and gives us wisdom— he makes us smart. God, the Son, that you see there on the cross," he said, pointing to the crucifix, "teaches us how to live, and God as the Holy Spirit," he said, opening his arms wide, "lives everywhere, especially in our hearts," he said, tapping Marcello's heart. "He guides us, and loves us, speaks to us, teaches us. Make sense?"

"I guess."

"You will understand such things more and more as time goes on, sweet boy," Uncle Salvestro said. He held Marcello closer to him and kissed his head.

Marcello looked tenderly into his uncle's eyes and said, "I know you're not my Papa, but you are kind of like my father."

"Father. Yes, that is my title, my name, my job. And you, you are kind of like my son, and to be your father is my purpose. And it is a purpose I am honored and very happy to have. Purpose is among the most important things a man must have, sweet boy."

"I'm glad that you're kind of my father, Uncle Salvestro," Marcello said, and snuggled closer to his uncle.

"Me, too, Marcello, me, too," clutching Marcello closer to him, squeezing a tear from his eye. They sat in silence for a few minutes, looking down on the symbolic world below until Uncle Salvestro broke the silence. "Now, Cello, a very important event awaits us. Mrs. Capatello has prepared our lunch, and there are no lunches as delicious as Mrs. Capatello's lunches. Her cooking is the stained glass of lunches."

Uncle Salvestro took up his natural stance holding Marcello tucked under his arm— under his wing. They carefully navigated the treacherously steep and exceedingly narrow creaky balcony stairs and out of the church, onto the piazza outside. They walked arm-in-arm across the piazza that would become the foundation of Marcello's childhood, his manhood, and his life.

Many years of delicious, jovial Mrs. Capatello lunches, instructional, inspirational discussions with Uncle Salvestro, tender conversations, and reverent moments in the stillness and silence of that empty church, followed that day. Countless moments in silent prayer, saturated in solace, absorbing what came to be Marcello's closest friend, the Holy Spirit, strengthened him day-by-day. The tender and reverent moments with Uncle Salvestro sowed the seeds for the man that could one day blossom into brilliance under the fervor, chaos, and glory that is Rome. And grain-by-grain, the sands of pain slowly passed from the depths of Marcello's heart to burrow into the background of his mind, and the deep fissures of his soul.

CHAPTER 3

The Pulpit

The pulpit built into the altar at San Gregorio della Divina Pietà church held a greater secret and served a greater purpose than Father Salvestro Frischetti shared with Marcello: Vieri had cut through the floor of the altar in order to gain access to the crawl space below the church. Only four feet of space separated the bottom of the altar and the crawl space's dirt floor, so Vieri and Father Frischetti dug down another three feet to accommodate a hideaway for Jews. Vieri reconstructed the pulpit floor to swivel when a spring-loaded lever disguised as one of the pulpit's spindles was released. Once the pulpit swiveled open, the Jewish families Father Frischetti was hiding from the Nazis were able to safely enter the secret bunker built into the dank crawl space below.

A rough block wall was assembled to appear as housing for electrical and plumbing lines, but in practice, the pipes running into and out of the bunker brought oxygen into the tiny secret room and expelled carbon dioxide. The Prattos and other Jews that Father Frischetti aided were able to use the church's main space and a tiny bathroom in the sacristy during carefully chosen hours. Volunteers served as watch guards positioned in the church belfry. They signaled Father Frischetti with two beams from a flashlight when the coast was clear, four beams when there was danger.

Father Frischetti snuck Jews he was harboring up to the church balcony for hushed gatherings behind slightly opened windows that enabled them to fill their lungs with precious wafts of fresh air. But for almost twenty four hours a day, Jews in hiding under Father Frischetti's courageous cloak like a fluffle of innocent bunnies cuddled in their den – the secret room affectionately known to the occupants as *The Pulpit*.

There were no lights, just pillows, blankets, sparingly used candles, six old paint buckets for seats, water jugs, and on occasion, a few unexpected provisions. Bare necessities only. A thick mustiness dominated the room. The stale stench of perpetual moisture, stale air, and unbathed bodies in unwashed clothes in tight quarters created a sickening pungent musk punctuated by the rancid advance of progressive mold. Despite its wretched glum saturating *The Pulpit*, it offered a sense of security in a time of profound fear. It was about eight feet by eight feet, and just over five feet high. The dirt floor was soft from frequent flooding which made digging the room's foundation easier but breathing unpleasant, at best. Whatever dirt they removed from the hole that housed the bunker was scattered throughout the crawl space to look as though it were there for centuries. The walls were made of scrap masonry blocks, wood cut from the pews removed from the church balcony, and whatever other scrap material Vieri and Father Frischetti could find and maneuver down the 3-by-3 foot opening of the pulpit floor. The church's foundation contained a rusty grate on each of its four sides in order to enable frequent floodwaters to flow through the space before reaching the church's main floor: these grates also enabled Jews that were hiding in *The Pulpit* to escape quickly if necessary. There was an unmortared section of wall in the bunker that could be easily kicked away in the event a fast escape was required. The escapees could then squeeze through the grates in the foundation to run for their lives. Vieri carefully placed debris around the wall's base to make it appear as a natural element of the church's construction, complete with random rubble presumably swept up in the path of floods. There was little room to do little more than play cards, read by candle-light, pray, and sleep in *The Pulpit*, but despite its shortcomings and concessions, it proved to be an effective safe house of sorts for Jews fleeing Nazi murderers.

Father Frischetti brought whatever inconspicuous morsels of food he could spare and hide under his clothing to the Prattos twice each day. He became adept at hiding loaves of bread and various forms of produce under his frock. He also collected donated provisions from parishioners who knew what they were contributing to, and why, but never asked questions and never uttered a word that would jeopardize life.

Father Frischetti entered and locked the church behind him. He crossed the altar, genuflecting before the crucifix as always, and proceeded to the pulpit. He cautiously pulled the lever on the secret pulpit spindle and the latch released its hold on the faux floor below the pulpit. He pivoted the pulpit floor aside to gain access to the bunker below. He freed two burlap sacks tied with twine from under his frock and lowered them down to outstretched hands below, then climbed four steps down a rough wooden ladder made of wood milled from the pews in the balcony.

A candle lighted the room's dark walls and cast eerie shadows of the family in hopeful hiding. Father Frischetti climbed down the crude ladder and huddled together with Lucio, Mila, Dayana, Dario, and Chiano Pratto.

Up to that dreadful day, Lucio and his family were able to avoid detection by the Nazis by using counterfeit papers that Father Frischetti obtained from a friend who worked in the Vatican print shop. The friend specialized in, and prospered from creating authentic looking phony documents, mostly to shield Jewish doctors to enable them to serve patients throughout Rome, but when necessary, the friend could also be counted on to assist a broader population: Roman Jews in hiding.

Lucio quickly untied the twine from the burlap bags and emptied the contents onto a crate that served as a table. The first bag held bread, cheese, an apple, two oranges, and a handful of dates wrapped in a page torn from a book. The second burlap bag contained an assortment of clothes. Lucio returned the bags and rope to Father Frischetti and they all quickly bowed their heads in silent prayer.

"I am gathering whatever clothes I can for each of you; I'm trying to get you out of here soon, and you will have to have more clothes than what you have here." Giuliana had been sneaking into the Pratto's flat and bringing articles of their clothing to Father Frischetti to bring to them day-by-day– just enough to have a few changes of clothes without sacrificing precious space or creating suspicion.

"Now, please listen carefully. We have a very important problem to address. Last night, I heard Dario's voice protesting from down here, and this is not the first time; we can't have that, Dario. Voices could kill all of us. Dario, is this crystal clear to you?"

"I can't help it. I can't stand it down here. I can't breathe, I can't," Father Frischetti covered the boy's mouth with his hand.

"Silence! Do you understand that your complaining can get your family and yourself and me killed?" Father Frischetti scowled at the boy and then to Lucio. "Lucio, I'm counting on you, and you," he said, now looking to Mila, "to keep him quiet."

"I'll help, too," Chiano offered.

"It is a matter of life and death, Dario. Life and death– for all of us," Father Frischetti said. "All we need from you is for you to be quiet. That's it. Quiet," he repeated. "Now, nod your head if you completely understand me." Dario meekly nodded his head while embarrassment and resentment swallowed him up like sound melting into noise. Then, in a flash, Dario scampered up the ladder and out of the opening in the pulpit floor, and into the church. He ran up the side aisle toward the door with Father Frischetti, Chiano, and Lucio chasing him. Their collective footsteps echoed and reverberated in the empty church. Father Frischetti was the closest to him but Chiano was just a step behind, then he passed the panting priest and gained ground on his older brother. The footsteps grew louder as they all approached the side door at the back of the church. Dario began tugging on the large door. It was locked. He made a run for the main doors but ran smack into Father Frischetti. Dario began screaming.

"Let me go! Let me go!"

Father Frischetti had no choice but to smack Dario briskly across his face. He grabbed Dario and held his hand over the boy's mouth. He held him tight and whispered.

"It's alright. It's alright. You're going to be alright. Shhhh." Dario was crying out of fear, frustration, and the raw sting ringing from his face.

"The second to last thing I want to do is hurt you, Dario … or anyone. Ever. But the absolute last thing I want is for the Nazis to find us," Father Frischetti said, holding Dario tenderly. "Would you rather be quiet and alive in *The Pulpit* or have the Nazis find us and kill you, and kill your family? Kill all of us? These are the choices, Dario." Father Frischetti held him, rubbing his shoulders to calm him down. "Let's go up to the balcony and relax, yes?" He led Dario, who was still whimpering, up the stairs to the balcony and the rest of the Pratto family fell in line behind them. Father Frischetti took a handkerchief from his pocket and dried Dario's eyes. "You're going to be alright, Dario. We're all going to be alright, we just have to be very quiet," Father Frischetti whispered.

"I promise. If you stay quiet, we'll all be alright."

At the top of the stairs, they sat in the chairs close to the windows while Father Frischetti cautiously cracked them open. The Prattos were accustomed to limiting their movements and whispering. Father Frischetti nodded for Lucio to join him in a corner near the stairs.

"I am terribly sorry for hitting your son, but I am sure you understand; I had to," Father Frischetti whispered. "I'm sure you are upset by that. I am sorry. But I had to."

"I understand, but you should have left that to me."

"There was no time, Lucio. And when lives are on the line, I'm not leaving anything up to anyone, Lucio. I can't."

"I understand," Lucio said, biting back a thread of anger.

"Listen, we are working on a plan to move you out of here in three days' time. You must have your family ready to move on my notice immediately after Mass on Sunday. I am sure this is good news, yes?"

"Yes. Very good news. Yes. What is the plan?"

"It is still being formulated. For now, just have everyone ready to move early Sunday morning, and have everyone ready to do exactly as I say when the time comes. Bring as little as you can but bring what you need. Good?"

"Good," Lucio said, relieved, even motivated, becoming excited. "Father?"

"Yes?"

"Forgive me for being angry. But it's not easy to see someone slap your son."

"The alternative would be much worse, Lucio," Father Frischetti said, tapping Lucio on the shoulder and smiling that warm Father Frischetti smile. "Let's go tell them the good news. And Lucio ... you must control Dario."

They sat by the windows while Father Frischetti told Lucio's family the good news; they were getting out of *The Pulpit*. They hugged each other and smiled, for the first time in a long time. Father Frischetti took Dario by the arm and led him to the front of the balcony to look down on the church below, out to the altar, where a faint strand of moonlight streamed across the crucifix, lighting it with a brook of soft white, defining it with mysterious shadows.

"Look down there– at the crucifix– the cross, with Jesus on it. We celebrate life on that altar every day, Dario. Some of the prayers, we say out loud, but the ones that God hears the loudest, are the ones we pray in silence. If you promise silence, I will promise you will celebrate life for a very long time. Can we shake on that?"

Dario peered through his tear-glazed eyes, and his pout rose into a near smile. He shook his head 'yes' and shook Father Frischetti's hand.

"Deal," Dario said.

"Deal," Father Frischetti agreed. He looked to Lucio and Mila and shook his head in relief, then ushered the Pratto family back down the stairs and to the center of the altar. He put his hands on Lucio and Mila's foreheads and whispered a prayer to himself.

"I will return as soon as I can with whatever I can bring. Until then … God bless you." He made the sign of the cross and the Prattos climbed down the ladder. Before closing *The Pulpit* door, Father Frischetti poked his head down into the bunker.

"Chiano?"

"Yes," Chiano answered.

"Your best friend Marcello loves you and misses you very much. He showed me your marble. He carries it with him all the time." Chiano and his family smiled for the second time in the same hour for the first time in a long time.

"Marcello carries my marble … all the time, Papa. Look," Chiano said, "I carry his all the time, too," he said, proudly flashing his marble for all to see.

"You two will never lose your marbles," Father Frischetti said with a warm smile, and he reached down to rub Chiano's head. "Never give up hope," he whispered to Lucio's family. "Hope is the light that illuminates the path out of despair's darkness."

Before sealing *The Pulpit* closed, Father Frischetti looked down into the passage in the floor. He looked to Lucio and whispered, "You must keep Dario quiet." Lucio nodded his understanding and Father Frischetti sealed *The Pulpit* closed and genuflected in reverence and hopefulness before the crucifix.

CHAPTER 4

The Bus Ride

The day had come. The arrangements were made, the people in place. Just as the rising sun kissed the cross at the top of the San Gregorio dome, Father Frischetti slid into the empty church like a sparrow vaporizing into the thick of a tree. Once inside, his movements were hurried. He went directly to the crucifix, sank to his knees and prayed for God's intervention in this day's plan. He rose and moved quickly to the pulpit and tugged at the secret spindle to free it to slide open. He slid the faux floor aside and dumped a pile of clothing on the altar floor then climbed down the ladder.

"Is everyone ready?" he asked Lucio.

"Yes. Absolutely," he answered. The Prattos hurriedly grabbed their respective sparse belongings. Father Frischetti instinctively held his hands out to Lucio on his right side and Mila on his left. They all joined hands and prayed in silence for a few long-lasting moments.

"OK, this is it. Everyone has their papers?" Father Frischetti asked. They answered in a collective 'yes.'

"Great. Let's say goodbye to this place and get you out of here." He led them up the ladder. They stretched and yawned and stretched some more and soaked in the precious oxygen and residual incense-laden air of the church. Father Frischetti closed the pulpit floor. He double-checked that the pulpit floor was sealed and whisked them to a pew near the church's side door.

The Prattos were elated to be out of *The Pulpit* but it was too soon, too uncertain, too dangerous to celebrate. But they did rejoice internally, leaving the mildew and dank of *The Pulpit* behind. Soon, they would be breathing real air, fresh air, and they relished the thought of seeing daylight, and feeling the sun on their faces. They found standing upright a bit of a challenge but a joy after being cramped in *The Pulpit* for nearly twenty-four hours a day for six weeks. They scurried like obedient puppies, following Father Frischetti. Dayana tugged at Chiano's sleeve and showed him the most hopeful and thankful smile. Chiano expressed his happiness with an affectionate rub of her hand. Dario instinctively put his hands on both of his sibling's shoulders. Lucio wrapped an arm around Mila's shoulders and she in turn held onto Dayana. They moved forward, attached by hope, connected by fear, and bound by love. They advanced closer to escape, freedom, capture, and death simultaneously with every step. Father Frischetti motioned for them to take seats in a pew and squatted into the pew in front of them.

"Here's what's going to happen," he said, leaning over the pew. "You will go into the sacristy– behind the altar– to wash up, change clothes, and come back to this pew looking as close as you can to a Catholic family at Sunday Mass. Leave your old clothes and shoes in the empty bags that you will find in the sacristy. We'll get them to you later." The Prattos nodded their understanding. "So far so good?" Again, they nodded a collective 'yes.' "Good. You will sit here through the Mass; I will make it as short as I can. After Mass, I will station myself at that side door and greet parishioners as they leave the church. When it is safe for you to leave, I will hold up two fingers– without looking at you– and when I hold up those two fingers, the boys will come to the door and exit. Boys, go out the door, and there will be a bus at the bottom of the stairs. Get directly on the bus. Sit wherever there's a seat but do not sit together. When it's safe for Dayana to leave, I will hold up one finger, without looking at you, so, Dayana, you have to watch me closely. Dayana, you will come to the door and get on the bus and sit by yourself. When I raise two fingers again, Lucio, you and Mila will come to the door and get on the bus," he said. "Still good? The Prattos nodded 'yes' again. "Good. I will join you on the bus after the last one of you is safely on board. There can be no deviations from this plan. It will happen fast, there will be chaos and that chaos will work for us. All you have to do is get on the bus and act like you belong there," he said, checking their faces to secure a sense of assurance. "Lucio, can you drive a small bus?"

"Of course."

"Excellent. You will take the driver's seat and drive. Good?"

"Good," Lucio said.

"Good. Let's go get washed up and I'll get ready for Mass. When you come back in here, there will be people here for Mass. I'll make sure this pew is not taken." He clapped his hands and shooed them toward the sacristy. "Off we go."

Father Frischetti chose a Sunday morning for the move because it was a natural day for a lot of people to be at church for Mass, and a natural cover, and a natural day for the Nazis to be nursing hangovers from events Father Frischetti orchestrated specifically for his purpose– the escape under the camouflage of all things natural.

Just as planned, a battered, rickety bus pulled up to the side of San Gregorio della Divina Pietà at 9:45 a.m. Father Frischetti had arranged for scaffolding to be erected at each of the church's doors under the guise of maintenance being performed, thus requiring all parishioners to use the side-forward door where the bus was parked; all the congregants entering and exiting the same door would make concealing the Pratto family easier.

Father Frischetti zipped through the Mass as quickly as possible without appearing rushed. When the Mass ended, he proceeded to the side doors and opened the doors wide. He welcomed the bus driver and his wife into the church as the parishioners began pouring out that same side door and onto the street. The driver and his wife moved quickly toward the sacristy. A handful of children and their parents were gathered at the steps boarding the bus. He commanded some of the group inside the church as parishioners were exiting in an intentional haphazard chaos Father Frischetti devised to make counting them and identifying them difficult in the event they were being watched by the Nazis. He guided parents and children into and out of the church door at random, purposefully creating a sense of chaos. Yet organized, it was. As he guided two young boys into the church, he looked toward the Prattos but not directly at them and held up two fingers. On cue, Chiano and Dario got up, and walked quickly to the door. Two children entered and three exited, including Chiano and Dario. Father Frischetti shook hands with several parishioners exiting the church before he called out and waved two more young girls back into the church. He held up one finger and Dayana moved to the door. Father Frischetti patted one of the girl's shoulders then sent her back outside, with Dayana at her side.

"Get right on the bus," Father Frischetti whispered to Dayana, from behind the camouflage of a smile. Father Frischetti bobbed in and out of the side door, directing parishioners in and out of the doors. Amidst the chaos he created, the bus driver and his wife brought the Prattos bags of clothes onto the bus then melted into the throng of parishioners.

As he did with Chiano and Dario, Father Frischetti held up two fingers. Lucio and Mila got up and quickly melded into the crowd with a small group of people leaving the church. "Smile, big churchy smiles and get right on the bus. Lucio, get behind the wheel," Father Frischetti muttered. "I'll be there as soon as I can." Lucio ushered Mila down the stairs and onto the bus; Lucio got behind the wheel and Mila took the seat behind him. She looked around behind her to assure their children were safe and sound; she quickly spotted Dayana, then Chiano, but not Dario. Mila started to jolt out of her seat but froze in fear's icy hold.

"Dario's not here," she whispered in a panic sharply to Lucio.

The bus was just about one third full. Father Frischetti continued shuffling people around for a few minutes then ushered a half dozen more people onto the bus.

"We're in your good hands, driver," Father Frischetti said to Lucio, prompting him to leave– immediately.

"A quick safety check before we go," Lucio said, rising from behind the driver's seat. Father Frischetti's face turned scarlet red. Something was wrong.

"What is it?" Father Frischetti asked Lucio under his breath.

"Dario," he answered back from behind a pathetically fake disinterest. He looked up to the passengers and said, "Just a quick count before we go," he said, moving down the bus's aisle, counting passengers. Father Frischetti and Mila looked at each other, desperately hiding their trembling. Lucio proceeded down the aisle checking every seat. Mila could see and sense the tension in his shoulders as he progressed toward the back of the bus. He was near the last two seats in the bus when that weighty tension in his shoulders flattened into calm. Lucio turned back toward the front of the bus and exhaled deeply to indicate that he had found Dario; he was asleep in his seat. The angst brewing in Lucio, Mila, and

Father Frischetti collapsed into a welcome sea of relief.

Lucio got behind the wheel of the bus. Mila relaxed into the seat behind him. Sister Volpinello, a very young nun, stuffed a guitar case into the shabby shelf above her seat and sat down behind Father Frischetti. Everyone had a window seat which enabled them to fill their lungs, hearts, and minds with precious fresh air. Just minutes into the ride, Sister Volpinello passed out fruit, cheese, and rolls to the children, treats that the Pratto children devoured almost lustfully, regardless of the odd looks from other children. The Pratto family saw the sun for the first time in weeks and soaked it in like the shore soaking up the ocean. Their eyes beamed with gratitude, hope, and wonder. Once Lucio navigated the bus out of town toward the east and into the Roman countryside, and the children finished indulging in their treats, Sister Volpinello took her guitar from the shelf above her seat and led the children in singing happy songs. Very happy songs. As they entered the countryside, the scent of olive groves and flowers and life filled their lungs with energy and joy, just slightly tempered by apprehension's shade. They looked to one another and smiled and closed their eyes to pray and hope and thank God, and Father Frischetti.

Lucio guided the bus over the rolling roads east of Rome, toward the mountainous Abruzzo region of Italy. It was a long, windy climb into the mountains but a peaceful ride out in the wide-open world of North Central Italy. Much of the road was uninhabited, difficult to traverse, and of little military value to the Germans, but it was priceless to Jews running for their lives. But priceless was in their case tangible: discovery meant death. The comfort of freedom and fresh air filled the bus and the hearts and minds of the Prattos despite the omnipresent apprehension lurking in threat's fringe. A sense of ease increased with every mile from Rome they traveled, believing they would one day return to a free Rome and the peace of their own homes. But not yet.

The road stretched eastward, meandering toward safety. The din and shadows of Rome faded into the background, seemingly being swept into the thickening wilderness where truffles grow wild, and tiny villages perpetuated the simplest way of life generation after generation. The sweet lull of contentment eased the Prattos and everyone else on the bus into a peaceful bliss, a bliss they embraced and craved and needed so badly.

"What's this?" Lucio asked Father Frischetti apprehensively, as the bus approached a blockade gate across the road. Two Nazi soldiers were manning a small makeshift guard house tucked into the hillside at the gate.

"It's just a checkpoint. Just relax and do as they say; try to appear casual," Father Frischetti advised. Lucio brought the bus to a stop. Father Frischetti nodded to Sister Volpinello to play more songs on her guitar. As she strummed and sang, the children joined in, half-heartedly at first, then Father Frischetti jumped up and led them as an exaggerated conductor singing in a voice the bus could barely contain. The younger of the two soldiers crossed in front of the bus and motioned for Lucio to open the bus door; he complied, and the young soldier mounted the bus carrying a menacing looking MK42 assault rifle. Father Frischetti continued conducting, singing, and stirring the children into laughter and raucous singing. He acknowledged the German soldier climbing onto the tattered bus with a friendly wink while prompting the children to sing louder and with more spirit.

"Silence!" the young Nazi soldier shouted. "Get up," the soldier demanded. Sister Volpinello stopped playing and the children stopped singing.

Father Frischetti instructed everyone from the front of the bus. "Cooperate and we will be on our way quickly." Lucio took a deep breath and made eye contact with each of his children in the rearview mirror. Father Frischetti leaned close to the young soldier's ear and whispered to him– in German:

"Sie sind geistig behinderte Kinder - nicht so glücklich wie Sie und ich– They are mentally impaired kids– not as lucky as you and me," he suggested, hoping the soldier would buy his tale and allow them to pass without incident. "We're taking them to Saint Lucia's, a special school for children like them. Good kids, but as I say, not as blessed as you and me."

The soldier raised his weapon and pulled its trigger. He riddled the length of the bus's ceiling with gunfire, blowing holes through its thin metal and terrifying the children into a startled silence. He checked the area around Father Frischetti's seat, then, finding nothing out of order, he jammed the priest down into his seat.

Father Frischetti pleaded in German, hoping to establish an evasive rapport with the soldier. "Sie sind keine guten Kinder und wir– They're not well children and we– "

"Shut up!" the Nazi soldier screamed, cutting Father Frischetti off. A morsel of food tripped off his lips and onto Father Frischetti's shoulder; he knew better than to acknowledge it. The soldier looked around the bus to pick a child to confront. His eyes locked onto Chiano.

"You, in the aisle," he shouted, just inches from Chiano's face. Ready to pounce, Lucio edged up in his chair and gripped a long screwdriver he found under his seat.

"Yes, Sir," Chiano said, stepping into the aisle with poise and a confidence that surprised and relieved Lucio and Mila. They were relieved, too, that the soldier had not selected Dario to question. The soldier examined the area below Chiano's seat, then the rack above, then, finding nothing of concern, he shoved Chiano into his seat. He moved toward the back of the bus and repeated the process with four more children, then returned to the front of the bus. He nodded at Mia and Sister Volpinello.

"Off," the soldier ordered, while pointing to the bus door with his weapon. They obeyed; they stepped down the bus's rusty stairs and off the bus. The other, older soldier on guard duty met them in front of the bus.

"Look what we have here," the younger soldier said to his comrade, smiling a degrading smile.

"A singing nun, and what are you?" he asked Mila.

"A teacher," Mila said.

"Can you teach me to sing?" the soldier asked Sister Volpinello sarcastically?

"If you would like," Sister Volpinello offered.

"I would like this one to teach me," the soldier said. "You want the other one?" he asked his senior soldier.

"Let it go," the senior soldier said.

"I'll tell you what," the younger soldier said to Mila, "you will pleasure me, then," he said looking at Sister Volpinello, "it will be your turn. And if you refuse, if you refuse, I will kill every kid on your bus," he said, while stroking Mila's dark hair.

"I will protect the children," Mila said. "But I must warn you, I have been ill for several days."

Lucio hobbled out of the bus with his screwdriver hidden in his pants leg.

"Back on the bus!" the younger soldier directed him.

Lucio ignored him, and scurried right toward the man, motioning him to the side as if they were pals. The soldier took the bait and stepped aside to meet him.

"I have to piss like a horse; can I go behind the shed?" he asked, nodding toward the guard house.

"Back on the bus!" the soldier snapped. Lucio complied, never taking his eyes off Mila as the young soldier led her and Sister Volpinello toward the guard house.

Father Frischetti stirred the children into another song and directed them off the bus singing and formed them into a circle singing and dancing fanatically. The young soldier stopped and turned toward the children. He sprayed a hail of bullets into the ground dangerously close to them. They froze. Screamed, terrified. Several instinctively dove to the ground. "Dance!" He shot more. "Dance you little guineas!"

"Bastard!" Lucio screamed from the bus!

"Enough," the older soldier shouted to his junior comrade.

Father Frischetti kept singing– louder and louder and the children joined in apprehensively following his lead.

The younger soldier grabbed Mila and Sister Volpinello by their arms and shoved them toward the back of the shed. Father Frischetti looked to the older soldier, his face pleading for help.

"Put them back on the bus," the older soldier ordered. Father Frischetti guided the children back onto the bus and turned to the soldier.

"Please let us go, we are no threat, we are just trying to help innocent children. Do you have children?"

Behind the shed, the younger officer leaned back into the wall and undid his belt and lowered his pants to his knees.

"You know what to do," he said to Mila. "And you, come close and watch … then you take turns," he said to Sister Volpinello. Mila bent forward toward the soldier then looked up at Sister Volpinello, then she turned her head away from the soldier and shoved two fingers deep down her throat, desperate to induce vomiting, desperate to derail the young Nazi's plans by making herself distinctly undesirable to him, disgusting to him. She began to gag immediately then gagged more intensely. More deeply. She began to choke. Then a geyser of vomit spewed from her mouth. She looked up at the young soldier with the cookies and juice she had just ingested, oozing gobs of vomit from her chin. He drew his hand back, poised to strike Mila across the face. A single shot rang out.

A bullet ricocheted off the corner of the guardhouse. They all snapped around in the direction of the gunshot and saw the older soldier holding a pistol in the air.

"I said to let it go," the older soldier said to his junior. The younger soldier glared back at him then at the women. "My brother has a child like them. And my sister, my sister is a nun," the older soldier said. "Let it go." The younger soldier pulled his pants up in disgust, disappointment, and anger.

"Get away from me!" the young soldier grunted. Mila and Sister Volpinello rushed to the bus and climbed on board. Lucio started the engine. The older soldier lifted the gate and with a deep collective sigh of relief, they drove off. Father Frischetti gave Mila a towel to clean her face and a silent blessing to soothe her soul following this traumatic incident. She rinsed her mouth with several swigs of water, wiped her face, and wept. Lucio reached over his shoulder to touch her hand, soothe her, and express his love for her.

"Thank God it wasn't any worse," Father Frischetti said to Mila, then he and Sister Volpinello moved down the aisle, moving from child-to-child to comfort them after the harrowing experience. Dario was on his seat curled up in a fetal ball. Mila sank into the seat and hugged him, blanketing him with love and scarce security.

"Can I cuddle too, Mama?" Chiano asked.

"Me, too?" Dayana asked.

"Of course. Come here, snuggle in with us," Mila said. Chiano and Dayana crawled up next to their brother and their mother, and her love spread over them like a warm blanket over a cold bed.

They drove deep into the unceasing winding mountain roads, holding their breath around sharp turns that were unprotected by guard rails that might save an out-of-control vehicle from running off the road. The bus's bald tires were often just inches from a tragic fall off steep cliffs that dropped deep into the vast, rugged valleys of forest below. They drove the treacherous climb into Abruzzo's mountains for the better part of the day. The songs on the bus faded into quiet rest, like day slips into the slippers of dusk. The children slept. Lucio breathed a bit easier. Mila melted into a deep slumber. Dayana cozied up in a ball next to her mother by the open window, Dario slept deeply in the discomfort of a bus seat yet immersed in the lasting comfort of his mother's loving warmth.

And Chiano sat up and stared out the window in wonder and awe. He almost felt free. Liberated. Alive. Filled with purpose. Filled with hope.

CHAPTER 5

Trout

Schools, as it was called, was nestled into a natural phenomenon, deep in the beautiful Bosco Sant'Antonio mountains in the Abruzzo region of Italy. Natural beauty and bewildering bounty arose from every step of the mountains. The Franciscan monks who owned and operated *Schools* managed to ingeniously harness the mountains' runoff waters and raise blue ribbon trout, as well as a small but abundant crop of vegetables, olives and other fruits in these rugged mountains. A few dairy cows, sheep and chicken provided milk, cheese, butter and eggs. The property was a hidden holding of the Catholic Jesuit order that Father Frischetti belonged to. As the Jesuit order reveres education and practical values that drive social action and service to their communities, *Schools* reflected the Franciscan ideal like branches shape a tree. *Schools* was used as a seminary within the order, and was more than well suited to hide Jews, as well as teach children. *Schools* was named by American and British Franciscan monks as a reference to its double entendre defining its dual function as a school and an active trout farm teeming with schools of fish.

Lucio maneuvered the bus into the long, narrow dirt road leading to *Schools*. Its bumpy passage jostled the children awake, and its surprising beauty moved them to a state of absolute marvel. The bus choked to a stop and Lucio opened its squeaky, rusted door. Father Frischetti led everyone out of the bus. One-by-one, the sleepy children ambled off the bus, and one-by-one, they came alive and aroused by the serene tranquility around them. This unexpected parcel of paradise tucked into these hidden mountains housed six stone buildings the size of large houses. The bombed ruins of Rome and the horrible threat of murderous Nazis seemed a lifetime away. For the first time in months, the children, the adults, and as far as they knew, the world, seemed safe, even peaceful, despite the revulsion of a madman and his war ravaging the human race.

A short, chubby Jesuit priest popped down the stairs of the brick building closest to the bus. His face was round and red, defined by warm, gentle blue eyes and an easy smile. He was mostly bald, what white hair he had left, was cropped close to his head. He instinctively reached out to greet Father Frischetti.

"Monsignor Buongiorici," Father Frischetti said, with arms open to hug the huggable, chubby man. "So good to see you."

"Welcome, Father, a pleasure to see you again," he bellowed in a voice unexpectedly deep and robust for a man his size. He turned quickly and happily to Sister Volpinello and hugged her. When he turned to his right, he exposed part of the price he had paid for being a Catholic clergyman voicing criticism of oppression amidst Hitler's mayhem: most of his left ear had been cut off. As the story is told, just months ago in a church in Compa di Giovi, a Nazi officer and four soldiers interrupted the monsignor's Mass by shooting out all the stained glass windows and blasting statues of saints with hails of hatred's bullets. The officer approached the altar and Monsignor Buongiorici met him nose-to-nose and ordered him to leave the church. The monsignor told the officer that the officer had the power to kill like a coward, but the monsignor had the power to help people live in eternity. He told the Nazis officer not to dare disrupt his Mass. The Nazi officer told the Monsignor Buongiorici to shut up and grabbed him by the ear. He pulled it hard, then sliced it off with his knife. He told the monsignor and the parishioners that 'this will remind all of you to be more careful when choosing an ear of arrogance,'" he said, making a sick play on words before tossing Monsignor Buongiorici's severed ear onto the altar.

"Sister V., so good to see your beautiful radiant soul," Monsignor Buongiorici said, as he hugged Sister Volpinello with robust yet tender affection. Then he turned to Lucio and Mila. "Welcome to *Schools* and our farm. I'm Monsignor Buongiorici. Call me Monsignor B. Welcome. Come, come," he said, while shaking their hands. Then he addressed the children with arms raised wide and high. "Welcome everybody!" Waving to the beautiful surroundings, he called out, "This is your new school! We call it *Schools*. This is your new home for a time! Welcome! Come. Let us show you around. Come." Two brothers, and a nun exited the same building Monsignor B. came from and waved the group toward them. They all moved toward the building, sorting through the joy, apprehension, uncertainty, gratitude and hope spinning through their minds.

They followed Monsignor B., the two brothers, and the nun while soaking in the picturesque charm of the brisk, churning streams and placid ponds as they walked. They chatted in happy wonder as they were led to a small fishing dock that jutted into an outlet feeding into a pond. An elaborate system of shallow canals and streams were chock full of prize rainbow and brook trout that reflected dazzling showers of color and grace gliding through the crystal, clear waters. Crops raised with abundant vigor and the animals that sustained all those blessed to be living at *Schools* grazed in subdued glorious bliss. It was hard to imagine a war and inhumane carnage raging just hours away from this secret placid retreat.

The brief tour was followed by a wholesome meal arranged especially for these new arrivals. They enjoyed fresh trout and vegetables raised on the property. The sense of gratitude everyone on the bus felt reached far deeper and broader than the genuine 'thank yous' uttered over and over. Not long after night wrapped *Schools* in its cozy warmth, everyone was shown to their bunks. The accommodations were humble, but a drastic improvement from the dank of The Pulpit. The Jesuits had accumulated small cots, relatively comfortable mattresses, and a supply of pillows, sheets and blankets from a French hospital sympathetic to the Franciscan cause. The sleeping assignments appointed three, four or sometimes five, sometimes six, sometimes more to a room. Lucio and Mila Pratto were given a room of their own. Dayana was assigned to a room with three other girls. Everyone had their own cot, a shelf, and a trunk for their belongings. Chiano was to share a small dormitory style room with Dario and one other boy that was already established at *Schools* but was not in the dorm room at the moment. Chiano nestled into his bed, hugging the first real mattress he had laid upon in weeks. This was the softest, coziest mattress he had ever known. There was a lamp on a small night table next to his bed and a book of short stories. Dario and Chiano looked at each other in elated disbelief.

"This sure beats *The Pulpit*," Chiano suggested.

"Sure does. I'm loving this," Dario said. "Look," he said, looking out the window where a nun was carrying a wire basket full of eggs.

"You think they're for us for breakfast tomorrow?" Chiano asked.

"I hope so, maybe we–" his sentence was cut short by Father Frischetti entering the room while still knocking.

"Beats *The Pulpit*, right?" he said, tapping Chiano's bed as he sat on it.

"Sure does. We were just saying that, Father," Chiano said.

"Yup, it sure does," Father Frischetti agreed, then after a pause, he said. "I have to talk to you, Chiano."

"What is it?" Chiano asked.

"I need your help. I think you can help me and another little boy out. There's a little guy here that has had some really sad things happen to him. He's OK, but he's quite sad and could use some cheering up. I was thinking, if I were to show him your marble, even let him play with it, just a little bit, it just might make him a little happier."

"But it's really Marcello's marble. What if he loses it?"

"I promise, Chiano, I'll be right there with him the whole time, and I promise you that I'll bring it right back. In fact, I'll bring him back with me. I promise I will bring it back to you faster than you can say 'where's my marble.'"

Reluctantly but trustingly, Chiano pulled his special marble from his pocket, and handed it to Father Frischetti.

"It's very special and important to me, Father. Please promise to take good care of it, and to bring it back."

"You're a good guy for doing this, Chiano. I sincerely promise, I'll bring it right back." He patted Chiano's head and left the room holding the marble and a tiny piece of Chiano's heart. The door clicked shut and Chiano returned to indulging in his mattress a little less enthused than a moment ago, a little more apprehensive, maybe even a little sad. Again. He stretched out on his newly assigned bed wondering what was to come. What had become of Marcello and his family? What would happen to his own father, sister, mother and brother if they were caught? Would the Nazis find *Schools*? Would they find him? Hurt him? Kill him like they killed Marcello's father and Gaia? He looked around the room and fixed his eyes on a small crucifix on the wall and wondered why Catholics put reminders of Jesus Christ being killed almost everywhere they went, even around their necks. Living in Rome, he had become familiar with many Catholic icons and practices, but he never understood the apparent compulsion to display the crucified son of their God. *Must be something to it,* he thought. He wondered if he had made a mistake by lending his marble to Father Frischetti. He recalled hearing Father Frischetti's voice once saying, *You two will never lose your marbles.* And that made him happy, scared, and sad all at the same time.

After a bit more daydreaming, wondering, thinking and just laying still, Chiano heard footsteps approaching his room, it sounded like more than one person. His instinct was fear; was it the Nazis? Did they find him? But the footsteps didn't sound mean or urgent like Nazi footsteps. There was a tapping on the door and to Chiano's relief, Father Frischetti entered the room, again, while still knocking.

"Do you have my marble?" Chiano asked while sitting up.

"Yes, I have your marble." Father Frischetti opened his hand and Chiano's eyes opened up like a flower blooming in a time-lapse photograph as he focused on the marble – it was the marble he traded with Marcello. And at that very moment, Father Frischetti waved his arm near the door, and Marcello burst into the room screaming.

"Chiano!"

"Marcello!"

The two inseparable pals hugged and danced and jumped and cried and laughed and hugged some more, and more and more.

CHAPTER 6

Schools

It was far from an ordinary school. Its curriculum included the traditional fundamentals, but Monsignor B. and Father Frischetti added much from their own perspectives: music, foreign languages, dance, what Monsignor B. called *enlightenment*, which amounted to light-hearted, philosophical pondering, formal daydreaming, brotherhood, and chores. The children attended classes, trained as apprentices in adulthood in 1940s Rome, and took Father Frischetti's English classes. There was great hope that by joining forces with the Allies that Italy would emerge from the war far better off, but the end of war was not yet imminent. There was, however, an air of optimism and hope that the Jews hiding at *Schools* embraced with vigor. But for Marcello and Chiano, *Schools* was about reunion, continuing their special friendship, and doing their best to be little boys within the trappings of war.

They woke every morning before the sun and looked across their beds and smiled at one another with gratitude and a knowing maturity, tempered by innate innocence. They tossed a rolled-up sock back and forth before Dario awoke. They waited in content silence until it was time to wash up and dress. When the breakfast bell rang, they sprinted to the makeshift dining room in the rear of a barn. These two indivisible friends lived in a bubble all their own. They attended classes and interacted with the other children but never left each other's side, or lost sight of the other throughout the day. They looked after each other like a happy old couple, and despite the misery brewing in the world around Abruzzo, they wore perpetual smiles, and a renewed brilliance in their eyes.

Marcello was blessed with his mother's athletic grace, and Chiano was cursed with his father's physical gaucherie. Giuliana was at *Schools*, too. So was Mia. Monsignor B. miraculously managed to have an old piano donated to *Schools*. He also inexplicably got someone to deliver the piano up the narrow mountain roads, and hall it into a chapel nestled into a hill on the grounds at *Schools*. Knowing that the human mind and spirit need a variety of activities, and that the body served the mind, Monsignor B. turned Marcelloel into a gymnasium and dance hall for physical activity every afternoon. This provided a physical and psychological lift, and a productive departure from traditional studies. Giuliana taught dance, and everyone was required to participate; none of the eighteen children housed at *Schools* objected, and all enjoyed it. The school day always began and ended with journaling as a means of clearing and stimulating the mind in the morning and exploring it at night. Monsignor B. believed deeply in the power of words in any and every form. He incorporated oral presentations and encouraged and nurtured even the youngest of students' appreciation for, and skills in, expressing themselves.

"You cannot share yourself unless you can express yourself, yes?" Monsignor B. said. "You must be able to express what is on your mind and in your heart with your voice, and with your pen," he declared with passion and vigor, waving a stout, stylish chrome pen. "Whether we are seven or ninety, we must have a firm command of words. Words are the food that feed the mind, and the mind feeds the heart," he concluded. "Embrace words like light embraces day," he urged. "The only way for me to touch your heart is to do good things and to share my love for you with words and more importantly, deeds. Yes?" He paused, then added, "Of course, yes." Everyone wanted to hug Monsignor B. every time they saw him. Most did. He lived for *Schools* and risked his life to assure its welfare. "Learn the power of your voices and be sure that your words will always be heard," he concluded.

Marcello and Chiano formed a deeper bond and forged the cornerstone of their lives in their months at *Schools*. Chiano attended all the Catholic rituals and learned all the Catholic prayers and practices that Marcello followed, and Marcello joined Chiano in all his Reformed Jewish education and observations that a rabbi named Rabbi Yair taught and conducted. Rabbi Yair, which means 'he will enlighten,' taught Judaism at *Schools* at Monsignor B.'s insistence as a means of helping Catholics and Jews understand and appreciate one another. All children attended all the Catholic and all the Reformed Jewish classes. Marcello and Chiano embraced the similarities and appreciated the differences in the two religions by looking through the same lenses that their families viewed the world through: compassion, honor, and unity.

It wasn't the math, reading, writing, and traditional subjects that were most valuable to Marcello and Chiano at *Schools*, it was the time spent listening to Monsignor B., Father Frischetti, and Rabbi Yair during their free-form *enlightenment* sessions. These daily sessions took place at picnic tables next to a gurgling brook in the late afternoons. Marcello was enthralled by the stout, chrome-plated pen Monsignor B. always used to write notes.

"Can I try your pen, Monsignor?" Marcello asked.

"Sure. Give it a spin," he said, handing Marcello the pen, and his notepad. Marcello scribbled a few lines and a few letters, then said, "Thank you. It's a really neat pen."

"You have a good eye, Marcello. This is a very special pen," Monsignor B. said. "My parents had very little money, but they wanted to give me something meaningful, something special when I was ordained as a priest. They found this pen in a pawnshop in Verona," he explained. "Years later, my mother told me that my father traded his fedora and his only sweater to get this pen for me. Special, right?"

"Sure is."

"You know, a pen is not to be taken for granted. In addition to enabling you to write, a pen should help you think more clearly, more deeply. If your pen doesn't do that for you, you have to change pens– immediately," Monsignor B. said, with good-natured wisdom and conviction, then he turned his attention to a chalice he had brought to this session. He held up the chalice and examined it from every angle. He asked, "What is this?" holding the chalice up for all to see.

"A chalice," one girl volunteered.

"You're right. But could it be more?" he asked, then paused. "What if you think of it as a vessel?" Rabbi Yair began passing out candies, one per child. "Rabbi Yair has candy. He's going to give you one each. I want each of you to decide that your candy stands for something good, like fun, happiness, strength– things like that. Then," he continued, "I want you to tell us what your candy stands for. Then put it in the vessel." Rabbi Yair finished passing out the candy to each of the giggly kids. "OK, Mia, you go first. What does your candy stand for?" Monsignor B. asked, holding the chalice before Mia. "Happiness," she said, and put the candy in the chalice.

"Marcello, what about you?"

"Family." Marcello added his candy to the chalice.

"Perfect. Who's next?" Monsignor B. passed the chalice around and collected candy as the kids assigned meaning to their respective pieces of candy. They suggested freedom, peace, courage, laughter, intelligence, trust, and an assortment of additional thoughtful values.

"Now, if you were this vessel, and you had all these good things inside you, is it better to keep them all to yourself?" Monsignor B. asked. "What would you do with all this goodness?" Monsignor B. asked. "You would be chubbier than me," he said, drawing laughs.

"Pass them out," Chiano suggested, with an appetite for candy, along with insight in his answer.

"Perfect. What's another word for 'passing them out'?" the monsignor asked. After a few moments, Marcello offered a guess.

"Sharing?"

"Bravo, Marcello," Monsignor B. praised. "All these wonderful things are best when shared, yes? They make two people, even more, feel better," he said. "Now, we will do something you will always remember," Monsignor B. said. "Come, we must all take our shoes off. And socks if you have socks, take them off, too. And roll your knickers up to your knees. We're going to have some fun," he promised, as he removed his shoes and socks and rolled up his pants. "I can barely get my pants to roll over my perfectly chubby legs," he said, adding his trademark giggle and smile. The children giggled, too. They smiled, too, as they always did around Monsignor B.

"Are we gonna get our feet wet?" Marcello asked.

"Of course," Monsignor B. answered. "Wet and happy. Come," he said, leading the children into a running brook, with no sense of transition from dry land to the cool streaming water. Rabbi Yair and the children followed without hesitation, except for one boy and one girl who tiptoed into the brook sheepishly, curling their spines backward at the first touch of the cool water.

"I think I misjudged. I am sorry that the water is much higher than our knees; let's consider this a blessing, yes?" He moved to the center of the brook, ignoring the water bubbling up his pant legs. Rabbi Yair joined him and they took hold of each other's hands. "Ok. Let's all put our hands together and form a circle. Be careful of the stones. Don't let the fish worry you, they are peaceful," Monsignor B. promised. "Now, let's close our eyes and just listen to the peaceful sound of this brook … and feel the warm sun on our faces … the warm friendship we hold in our hands." He patiently waited, enabling the serenity of the moment to take hold. "I am about to speak for a few moments to help us soak in the privilege of this moment, forgive my little joke about soaking," he said, causing a collective giggle. "This will be a moment we will always remember very fondly. You won't know what all these words mean, we will talk about them later, but for now, just enjoy these moments." He hesitated again, methodically inviting peace into their hearts, and ushering calm into their minds. Then he began:

> "This pure, running water symbolizes the purity that
> runs through our hearts and our minds with kindness.
> The cool temperature reminds us, that even when the
> world around us is cold, our hearts must
> remain warm. The clarity and beauty of this brook
> reminds us to act with clear, unquestionable honesty.
> The soft soil and hard stones in this glorious brook
> symbolize the softness in our hearts, and the solid
> strength and courage we find in our faiths, our values,
> and in each other. Rabbi Yair, your turn."

Rabbi Yair spoke on cue.

> "The magnificent colors of the beautiful trout in
> this brook remind us how each one of us, of all
> colors, religions, and nationalities, are so very
> beautiful on our own. We are even more beautiful
> when we swim together, in harmony.
> The reflection of our beautiful faces on the
> surface of this beautiful water that surrounds us

reminds us that we are all reflections of God.
He is all around us at all times, seeing, watching,
and guiding us. Our lives are most enjoyable and most
fruitful when our actions reflect what God has taught us.
Standing in this wonderful brook reminds us that
we are all planted on this earth to perfect God's
world, just as this water is the perfect form of life."

After soaking in the moment, the words, and the experience, Monsignor B. spoke again.

"Let's step out of this brook in silence, thinking about the words and images and the experience we just had, a *Schools Experience*. And let us remain silent for the rest of the day in order to reflect on this soulful and soleful experience," he said while showing the sole of his chilly foot. He and Rabbi Yair led the children back onto the shore in a reverent silence that became an energy of its own. They sat quietly, put their shoes and socks back on, and sat, wondering and thinking. Monsignor B. and Rabbi Yair sat quietly, too. They all thought about what they had just heard in their own terms at their own levels, within their own respective capacities and abilities. No doubt, the *Schools Experience* would become an experience they would all remember for the rest of their lives. Fondly.

Four months at *Schools* were sweeter than candy and more rejuvenating than its brooks and streams. Marcello and Chiano were reunited after suffering a horrible separation and the indignation, emotional and physical misery that the Nazis inflicted on Roman citizens. *Schools* shed light on hope and the promise of happiness for every child and adult welcomed into their open doors and open hearts. Marcello and Chiano found joy and bliss through being together, learning together, listening, and engaging with Monsignor B. and Rabbi Yair in pleasant afternoons by trout-filled brooks. They frolicked through breezy happiness, rousing swing and big band dances that Giuliana taught day in and day out. Marcello was learning to dodge sorrow's imposition, and Chiano evolved his gaucherie into a command over how to move his body in accord with music– how to dance.

Twice each day, every child in *Schools* put a new word in their journal that represented a value or a source of inspiration. The words were accompanied by a sample sentence illustrating the word, and they were assigned to write their own sentence using the word, no matter how simple, no matter how raw. No matter how young, or old, each day, each child put an important value into the vessels of their character. These values would become valuable one day, when converted into socially beneficial actions. Every day, the children at *Schools* were being taught to use their lives to share the bounty of their blessings in the chalice of their souls. They were also being taught how to survive during the turmoil of war.

Every day, everyone at *Schools* participated in emergency drills in order to be prepared to hide in the event the Nazis discovered *Schools*. The *Schools* property housed four secret tunnels leading to small underground bunkers. Each entrance had a natural-looking faux door for an entrance: three were faux tree stumps, and one a faux chicken coop. The procedure called for everyone to run to the nearest tunnel at the sound of Marcelloel bell ringing. If they were all in one location, they ran to their pre-assigned tunnels. The staff was assigned to run to Marcelloel to feign a ceremonial Mass. A lookout person equipped with a walkie-talkie was posted in a tree at the entrance to *Schools*. His role was to alert staff members who were manning a radio hidden in the chapel that there was danger on the grounds. In turn, those staff members would ring the *Schools* warning bell. The Jesuit staff member assigned to Marcelloel was assigned to ring the bell with urgent intention when the lookout man signaled danger. Each day, at an unannounced time, occasionally in the middle of the night, the staff at *Schools* conducted emergency drills that everyone participated in.

As Monsignor B. and Father Frischetti were picking tomatoes and peppers in the garden, and the children were in Giuliana's dance class, Marcelloel bell rang out with a louder clang than usual. Everyone sensed its clear ring of urgency, a distinctly different resonance from the ring of the drill bells. Everyone scattered to their assigned tunnels. The staff and a handful of volunteers took their respective positions: celebrating Mass in Marcelloel, digging trenches for trout canals, pretending to repair fences, tending the trout, and raking the grounds. Every one of them was armed.

A Nazi jeep, occupied only by its driver, bounced recklessly up the rocky, dirt road. The driver took a long swig from a bottle of whisky as he lurched and jerked his German Army jeep over the boulders and into gullies on the dirt road leading to *Schools*. The facility held the strategic advantage of being almost a quarter of a mile off the road, which gave everyone time to hide and get into place when necessary. The Nazi driving the jeep took another long swig of booze. Then another. He was near the end of the bottle as he neared the entrance leading to the *Schools* buildings. He drove dangerously close to one of the brothers who was pretending to be repairing a fence next to the building where Lucio was digging a drainage trench. The Nazi stumbled out of the jeep, clutching his bottle.

"What goes on here," he shouted in slurred words to the brother.

"It's a seminary," the brother said.

"I'll see about that." The soldier advanced, coming inches from falling into Lucio. He stumbled, then stopped. He stared at Lucio, who looked toward the ground in silence. "Look at me," the soldier demanded. Lucio looked up slowly. He immediately recognized this man as the young Nazi soldier that shot up the ceiling of the bus and tried to force Mila to pleasure him. The soldier stared at Lucio more closely, squinting, stooping close to his face to see more clearly through whiskey's cloud. Lucio turned away at the stench of liquor defining the soldier's breath, hoping to avoid trouble.

"You. I recognize you. You're the, you're that bus driver," the young soldier said. A dirty laugh tripped from his slurring mouth. "If you … if you're … you're here … she … she's here," the soldier spluttered out. "Bring her to me." He raised his hand, giving Lucio an order. "Go … get her. Both of them ladies you had … on the bus," he said. "Bring 'em here. Now!"

"There are no women here," Lucio said, clutching his shovel and shifting his weight to strengthen his balance.

"I'll see for myself." The soldier pushed Lucio aside and tripped up the stairs, into the building housing the room Lucio and Mila slept in. Lucio stayed right on the soldier's heels, shovel in his hand, anger in his heart. The soldier burst into the dorm-like room and took another healthy swig of booze while surveying the room. He moved to the dresser. "What's this," he said, ripping a drawer clear out of the small dresser. He lifted the drawer overhead and emptied its contents onto the bed. A small pile of women's underwear fell into a heap. The Nazi soldier swayed in place, wavering in the stupor of drunkenness, his eyes bulging open with delight in his discovery. He swigged the last of his booze and wiped his mouth with a pair of Mila's underwear. He looked through his squinting, drunken eyes at Lucio. "No women, hey? Are these yours?" he asked, through a clumsy laugh, and rubbed the panties in Lucio's face. "Put them on, fool. Put them over your ugly face." He shoved the panties toward Lucio's face again, but Lucio blocked the Nazi's arm and cast it sharply aside. He knew instantly that he'd made a mistake. The Nazi's eyes bulged with rage. He instinctively raised the liquor bottle and smashed it over Lucio's head, dropping him down on one knee. Blood seeped out of a long cut carved into Lucio's head between his temple and left eye. In a flash of raw instinct, Lucio jammed the blade of the shovel into the bridge of the soldier's nose. The blow split the Nazi soldier's face open and knocked him back. He reached for his pistol but in that very millisecond, Lucio raised the shovel and blasted it down across the soldier's head before he could fire a shot. The shovel struck the soldier hard on the side of the head making a dull short thud and an oddly victorious ring. The soldier fell to the floor. Lucio raised the shovel again and struck him again, harder. Fire burned in his eyes; adrenaline burned in his belly. The Nazi laid on the floor lifeless. He tried to speak but could only manage to spew a gurgle of bile, liquor, and blood. Propelled by blind rage and adrenaline's intensity, Lucio struck the revolting soldier again. And again. And again. And again. The soldier went unconscious. He went dead. The brother who was stationed by the fence rushed into the room.

"Oh my God! Oh my God!" The brother stood in shock looking at the lifeless Nazi soldier on the floor. He looked to Lucio in shock then back at the soldier heaped on the floor, bleeding. "We have to get him out of here– fast," the brother said. "Help me get him in that jeep. Fast." Lucio grabbed the soldier under his arms and the brother picked him up by his feet. They carried the dead soldier down the stairs and dropped him into the back seat of his jeep. His body slumped into a curl of human ruin. "We have to get him off this property."

"I'll drive the jeep. Can you drive the bus?" Lucio asked the brother. "Yes."

"Follow me. Keep my tail lights in sight but don't stay too close. I'll look for a place to … just keep me in sight …" Lucio started the jeep's engine and the brother started the bus's and waited as Lucio bounced down the dirt road toward the no-man's-land of the mountain roads below. The sooty road rolled clouds of dust from the two vehicles into the late afternoon setting sun. When they reached the road, the jeep turned to the east, and the brother chugged behind in the bus. They drove fast, trying to put as much distance between the jeep and *Schools* as quickly as possible. The approaching nightfall worked in their favor. Lucio drove in an adrenal stupor, unaware of time, space, or distance, trying to keep pace with his racing mind. He drove for nearly forty-five minutes constantly checking for the bus's headlights in the jeep's rear-view mirror. Frightened. Terrified. Regretful.

The cover of night was a minor comfort. The mountains held little reason for anyone to be driving through its treacherous roads at this hour. Lucio drove a section of curvy road down a steep descent. There were no guardrails, no means of catching an out-of-control vehicle failing to navigate a sharp, near hairpin turn. The perfect spot for a drunk driver to lose control of a vehicle and plunge over the cliff. Lucio's mind became sharp and alert. He slowed the jeep to a near stop and checked again for the bus's lights and saw their dull glow at a safe, comforting distance. He stopped the jeep at the top of a sharp descent in the road about a hundred feet from an exposed cliff. He set the jeep into neutral and pulled its emergency brake up into a reassuring locked click. He left the engine running. Adrenaline came to his aid again. He maneuvered the soldier from the back of the jeep into the driver's seat. There was another bottle of liquor in a sack in the back of the jeep. Lucio forced much of it down the soldier's throat and set the bottle between the Nazi's limp legs. He wrapped his arms around the soldier's jaw and head, and in a single moment of fury, fear, and desperation, he twisted the soldier's head hard and sharp and a sick-sounding crack gave Lucio the sad, sickening assurance he needed. The soldier remained slumped in a lifeless heap. Dead. Lucio propped the soldier's hands on the steering wheel and released the jeep's brake. He grabbed hold of the side of the jeep and pushed forward. The jeep inched toward the cliff's edge. Gravity sucked the jeep toward the cliff. As the jeep inched down the descent, closer and closer to the cliff's edge, it became easier to push. With one hand on the steering wheel and one on the side of the jeep, Lucio steered straight toward the cliff, steering as a drunk driver in a sensory stupor bordering on black-out would steer. He pushed and steered. The jeep picked up speed. Lucio was in a near run now to keep up with the jeep's increasing speed. Closer and closer to the cliff's edge. Closer. Closer. Closer. Faster and faster. The jeep reached a robust, full roll. Lucio let go of the jeep as he was just a few feet from the cliff's edge. The jeep had the momentum needed to drop off the cliff into Abruzzo's rocky, mountainous forestland. The drop was several hundred feet straight down. Lucio heard nothing for several seconds that seemed like hours. Then it happened. The jeep crashed into the treacherous rocky terrain below. Glass and metal crunched, the thud of the crash was muffled by the countless trees and the raw distance the jeep fell. Lucio felt comfort in knowing that the sharp bend was a plausible spot for a drunk driver to sail off the road, several hundred feet down into the rugged mountainside. And certain death.

The bus's dim lights cast a yellow halo on Lucio standing on the side of the road. The brother driving the bus pulled toward the side of the road and stopped. He opened its squeaky door. Lucio popped up the stairs into the bus and dropped into its front seat.

"Turn us around and get us back as fast as you can," Lucio said. "We have to camouflage the driveway the moment we get back," he said. Those were the only words spoken on the ride back to *Schools*, and the only words Lucio and the brother ever uttered about the drunk soldier and his jeep.

CHAPTER 7

Syndrome K

Salmon-colored walls marinated in soft light cast by shaded sconces dimmed the room to seduction's edge. A piano player plinked out romantic standards in a shadowy corner of the room. A female singer crooned in German and swayed with a microphone stand as though it were her dance partner. Senior German officers sat in tables of twos, threes, and fours sipping cognac, mouthing thick cigars, and vacuuming the fire out of cigarettes and into their lungs. An air of subdued brawniness mingled through the smoke, dirty laughs, music, and singing. Four women dressed in scant offers of skin's suggestion served drinks, skillfully flirted with the officers, and assured the perception of a good time. Around 10:00 p.m. each night, a show featuring a bawdy troop of strippers took place on the room's small stage. The shows were alluring and on occasion, stretched to the edge of an eroticism that penetrated the macho beasts of war's armor with powerfully disarming weapons: feathers of femininity, and sexual arousal.

This room is a private, unmarked, secret exclusive club called *Der Rat von Rhodium* which translates to *The Rhodium Club*. The club was named *The Rhodium Club* to associate its members, who had earned the German military's most precious metals, with the world's most precious metal: rhodium. *Der Rat von Rhodium* became affectionately referred to as *Der Rhodium– The Rhodium*. This association emerged from a U.S. and British intelligence strategy to exploit the one commodity these German officers viewed as most precious: their sensitive and voracious egos.

The Rhodium Club name itself served as a deliberate invisible offensive.

U.S. and British intelligent agents converted this once forgotten Roman restaurant into a hub for gathering information from unsuspecting high-ranking German officers. Admission was by secret invitation only, determined by Ally intelligence sources and objectives. The invitations were issued through sophisticated channels and included elaborate membership materials: fancy membership cards, password codes, profile questionnaires to define meal, drink, tobacco penchants, and the most desirable traits in social companions,' aka sexual preferences.. The most significant membership article was a lapel pin in the shape of an imitation rhodium "R" mounted on a round gold pendant. It was to be worn to gain entrance to the club and only in the club.

The officers admitted were more targets than honorees. The intelligence agencies planted spying equipment throughout *Der Rhodium*. Lantern-style lamps and bud vases on each table housed listening devices ingeniously networked into recording equipment in a basement next door to the *Der Rhodium*. The women operating as strippers and flirtatious waitresses were actually well-trained, undercover intelligence officers, and the free-flowing booze they served was laced with concoctions of dizzying imperceptible drugs designed to loosen the Nazi officers' drunken lips and numb their memories. Giuliana Luciari was one of the women volunteering alongside the trained intelligent agency women as a proactive means of avenging the horrible pain that Nazis inflicted on her family and so many others. She converted her hatred and anger into productive action in the name of the greater good.

Giuliana's role at *Der Rhodium* was to serve spiked drinks to Nazi officers and dance them into an unguarded trance of vulnerability. She wooed them into a blissful calm of self-confidence that enabled her German-speaking colleagues to tickle secrets out of their liquor-coaxed, swelled egos. As the officers unconsciously lowered their guard and slipped into a vortex of stupor's bliss, the undercover waitresses and dancers moved in. They learned how the Germans thought, what they feared, craved, what they aspired to, and every now and then, what they planned. In addition to dribbling valuable information from whiskey-saturated lips, these egocentric, influential officers served as fruitful ground in which to plant and fertilize the seeds of misinformation's bounty.

Bits of information passed through listening devices embedded in

Giuliana and the other waitresses' wrist watches, pins, hair ornaments, and earrings. Giuliana danced on a few occasions with the Commander of the SS, Heinrich Himmler, one of Hitler's most influential officers. They danced in silence since Giuliana did not speak German and Himmler did not speak Italian. But they both understood the universal language of dance. Giuliana hid her gritted teeth, anger, and utter disdain for the Nazis by locking on to her mission like sound on noise. Her task? Lull the German officers into confidence and comfort by amplifying their egos with an elixir of a dancer's charm and drenching their brains with doctored liquor.

Dancing to a slow romantic ballad with Himmler, Giuliana gripped his robust girth with cold, unfeeling arms. She had been feeding him concoctions of whiskey, 3-quinuclidinyl benzilate and sodium thiopental that trapped him in a surreal daze. She ignored the repulsive reflections of lust oozing from his belly-like eyes. As Himmler's eyes oozed want, Giuliana's eyes began to tear with rage and swell with vindication. She succumbed to an open cry, a genuine cry. Himmler stepped back from her and stopped dancing, and Giuliana scurried off the tiny dance floor and slumped into a booth. Himmler stood alone, embarrassed and confused. Dazed. His hands raised upward, his indignant eyes demanded an explanation. One of the waitresses rushed to Giuliana to console her and advanced their preplanned scheme. She soothed Giuliana for a few minutes conversing in Italian. Himmler made his way to the booth where Giuliana remained slumped over the table. Speaking in German, Himmler asked her co-worker– an undercover intelligence officer– what was wrong.

"She is still grieving, she's very distraught," the waitress said in German while she waved to another undercover officer posing as a waitress to come to Giuliana's aid. The waitress guided Giuliana behind the stage as her colleague took Himmler by the arm and pulled him into a seat in the booth Giuliana had vacated.

"She lost her husband and her daughter to *Syndrome K,*" she said. Himmler made a face and shrugged his shoulders, kinetically asking, *What the hell is Syndrome K.* "It's a very contagious, very deadly neurological disease," she said. "Her husband and daughter were working in the kitchen at the Fatebenefratelli Hospital and were exposed to *Syndrome K.* By the end of their shift, they came down with full-blown cases of

Syndrome K. She never saw her husband or daughter again. It's a horrible disease. Awful," the waitress said, then lit the cigarette Himmler was struggling to secure between his fumbling lips.

"*Syndrome K?*" he asked, in a cloud of pondering wonder and cigarette smoke.

"Yes. So many are dying. Convulsions. Paralysis. And after long, horrible, painful suffering," she said, stretching the air with her fingers, "they die." She pulled the cigarette from Himmler's mouth and took a drag. "And there's no treatment, no cure. The doctors are puzzled. All they know is that it's deadly." She exhaled the smoke, waved her hands, and placed the cigarette back in Himmler's mouth.

Himmler took the bait. His fat face twisted into wrinkles of confusion. He returned to his table and hunched over the collection of cocktail glasses to confer with his colleagues.

"Look into a disease ... it's, it's ... it's called *Syndrome K* at Fatebenefratelli Hospital. They say it's a deadly disease spreading there," Himmler slurred, just before passing out in a drunken thud, face first on the table.

Syndrome K originated in the 450-year-old Fatebenefratelli Hospital perched on a 270-meter-long island in the middle of Rome's Tiber River. Fatebenefratelli had a reputation of being a safe haven for Jews. Using a secret and illegal radio transmitter and receiver hidden in the hospital basement, its director, Professor Giovanni Borromeo communicated with local Jewish sympathizers and systematically recruited Jewish doctors and supplied them with false papers that enabled them to work safely, and undetected at the hospital. On the day the Nazis raided the Jewish ghetto, Professor Borromeo opened the hospital doors to all Jews seeking shelter. Knowing the Nazis would comb the hospital in search of Jews, two young Jewish doctors, Vittorio Sacerdoti, and Adriano Ossicini created an ingenious yet simple plan in the form of a very clever scam: they declared that any Jew seeking safety at the hospital would be admitted as a new patient suffering from a highly contagious and deadly neurological disease known as *Il Morbo di K– Syndrome K*.

Syndrome K was claimed to cause paralysis, disfiguration, convulsions, and certain, painful death. Its most potent indications were the fear it awakened among Nazis, and the safety it provided Jews hiding in Fatebenefratelli under an inventive fictitious fabrication named, *Syndrome K*. The name *Syndrome K* was sardonically chosen to mock two notorious Nazi officers: Albert Kesserling, the German commander in charge of the Nazi troops in Rome, and the city's SS Chief of Police, Herbert Kappler, one of the men responsible for the Ardeatine Massacre, a retaliation killing of 335 Italian civilians. To aid in the deception, designated rooms were set up to house Jews in hiding in order to distinguish them from actual patients. The Jewish patients were instructed to cough violently in the event any Nazis approached to search the hospital.

Two days after Giuliana's tearful dance, a small squad of Nazi soldiers jeeped across a narrow bridge crossing the Tiber to Fatebenefratelli Hospital. Their arrival was tipped off in a conversation secured from listening devices planted in a sconce above a table at *Der Rat von Rhodium*. In preparation for the Nazis anticipated arrival, several doctors and staff members at the hospital filled some thirty-plus body bags with pillows, unlaundered sheets, pillowcases, blankets, garbage, and whatever else they could find and use to simulate dead bodies. They arranged the stuffed body bags at the hospital entrance early the morning the day before the expected Nazi search, in order to attract flies and enable the offensive hospital odors to ferment.

The Nazis approached. Slowly. Upon seeing the grotesque pile of fly-laden body bags, presumably filled with decaying bodies, and inhaling thick wafts of human waste, medical waste, the reek of disgust's disgust, the driver jerked the jeep to a jarring stop. Its driver jammed the jeep into reverse, and they bolted back over the bridge– in reverse– fearing for their lives.

Back in the hopeful comfort and presumed safety of her sleeping quarters at *Schools*, Giuliana cradled Marcello and Mia like the sepal of a plant cradles its flowers in a protective cuddle.

CHAPTER 8

Seeds

The war had finally ended, and five years of recovery had been accomplished, yet there was much to address, and achieve. Rome was slowly reemerging as Rome. A new decade had taken root in the arrival of the happy-go-lucky '50s. Marcello and Chiano were both fourteen now and were sowing the seeds deeper into the soil of their destinies. Their days were occupied by school, football, helping at church, home, and synagogue, and serving as Giuliana's assistants at her dance school in the Trastevere section of Rome. Father Frischetti had been reassigned to the beautiful Santa Maria church, also in Trastevere, a miraculous departure from the rustic ruins in the Roman Ghetto, a profoundly welcome change for Father Frischetti– and Marcello. Masses swelled with people who actively supported the church. Some of the most beautiful frescoes and mosaics in the history of the world adorned the walls of Santa Maria. Father Frischetti did manage to swap out one window of stained glass that he was sentimentally attached to from San Gregorio, a small window depicting Christ on the Cross. As the new pastor of a much larger, much more active, and much more visible parish, Father Frischetti's role and life became more administrative, but he vowed and worked to assure that his spirituality and sense of social service was never compromised. He committed to avoiding the trap of being sucked into the organizational vortex of the Church. He also vowed to retain the values and vigor that drove him as an active resistor to Nazism. All in all, life was on an enjoyable trajectory now, and history was granting the world a hard-earned, well-deserved reprise from war's indiscriminate suffering.

The brand-new football that Father Frischetti rolled down the aisle to Marcello at San Gregorio eight years ago was well worn now. Marcello and Chiano passed it back and forth on their way home from playing football in a bombed building that was configured in a rectangle, perfectly suited for a shortened football field.

"Cello, who do you think the prettiest girl in school is?" Chiano asked.

"I don't know."

"When you dance with Sandriana in your mom's school, do you get nervous?"

"Why would I get nervous dancing with Sandriana?"

"Cuz she's so pretty. I guess I don't want her to think I'm a jerk or something because I'm younger than she is," Chiano explained.

"I'm sure she can find a lot of other reasons," Marcello said as he playfully jabbed Chiano's shoulder.

"I don't really get nervous. I like dancing with her. She's smooth, and I like how she smiles all the time. You get nervous?"

"I do. My hands sweat. I wipe 'em on my pants when she's not looking."

"That's funny."

"Hey, is that Army guy coming to see your uncle today?" Chiano asked.

"Marcellolain, yeah. He's gonna stay at my uncle's parish for a few weeks. I'm gonna meet him tonight. You wanna come meet 'im?"

"Course, I wanna meet him, but I have to help my father. Can I come tomorrow?" Chiano passed the football to Marcello one last time before they performed their special handshake and went their separate ways. Marcello headed for Santa Maria Church, and Chiano headed home.

The beauty and intrigue of Rome was reappearing and Trastevere was very much in the heart of it. When Marcello arrived at the church, he found his Uncle Salvestro in the sacristy.

"Marcello, sweet boy, come give me a hug," his uncle said. "Come, I have something exciting to show you." He hugged Marcello with gusto and then opened his clenched hand. "Look," he said, showing several tiny flower seeds in his palm.

"Seeds?"

"Yes, geranium seeds. We're going to grow flowers from these little seeds. Bloom after bloom after beautiful bloom ... they will last a long time. Here, hold your hand out for me." Uncle Salvestro plucked several seeds from a small packet and put them into Marcello's hand. "Look, they look like little brown oats ... with a little slit in them ... Four– five wonderful things happen when you plant seeds, Cello. First, they grow into beautiful flowers. Second, they make you happy– every day. Third," he continued, "they make you proud– everyday, fourth, they make the world a little more beautiful, and fifth, they smell so good."

"Why geraniums?" Marcello asked.

"Because they're strong, they're beautiful, and they're fragrant. I love them. They're vibrant, colorful, always reaching for the sun, and spreading happiness all the time. They're just wonderful flowers," Uncle Salvestro proclaimed. Marcello followed his uncle's lead, laying the seeds on a damp cloth. They positioned four similar cloths of snuggling seeds in the warmth of a southern exposed window of the sacristy. "They'll germinate in just one day's time, then, we will put them in soil, and feed them once a week. You'll be quite impressed, Marcello," Uncle Salvestro promised. "They will grow into beautiful flowers like this one," he said, holding up a perfect, robust geranium in a clay pot.

Marcello was also to be quite impressed by the church itself. Santa Maria is a titular church– a church assigned to a cardinal, Cardinal Antonio Lupinieri. Cardinal Lupinieri personally requested Father Frischetti to be assigned to Santa Maria after they secretly worked together to aid the Resistance during the Nazi occupation of Rome. Cardinal Lupinieri was also courageously critical of Pope Pius XII's silence during the Holocaust. He and Father Frischetti had many conversations about how to move the Church toward a more noble, more honorable course, and live by the word they preached. Many of their conversations and spiritual fervor seeped into the ears and mind of a bright 14-year-old, Marcello Luciari, and unconsciously sewed virtue's seeds into his character.

Santa Maria claims to have been the first church built in Rome, and the first dedicated to Mary, the mother of Jesus. The church served as a constant reminder to Marcello to honor his own mother, and all mothers. Its twelfth and thirteenth century mosaics depicting the Virgin Mary and magnificent works from such masters as Raphael and Bellini adorned the church. Marcello marveled at the beauty and audacious splendor of the church, not for its opulence or scope, but for its profound and inspirational reverence to God through its architecture and art. It was rare for Santa Maria to be empty, but Marcello made the effort to spend time in its silence in the early hours before school, and in the quiet hush of early evenings. He found an empty church to be his second-best friend, second to Chiano, through its abundance of steadfast solace and soulful clarity. He knelt and prayed and sat and contemplated or immersed himself in the holiness that saturated the church with hope and inspired purpose. He walked its main aisle, looking up to the glorious mosaic behind the altar, depicting Christ surrounded by innocent and loyal sheep. Marcello often imagined himself in that scene, amidst angels and saints, and he wondered which sheep he might be, and what God was calling on him to do. To be. He often stood in the pulpit and imagined what he might say. He breathed in the deep, musky smoke of incense, closed his eyes, and waited for the scent to move him with the calm he so deeply sought and needed. Flashes of his mother, Mia, his father, Gaia, and Chiano would speed through his mind. Happy flashes of his Uncle Salvestro and himself were contaminated by flashes of that Nazi lieutenant. Flashes of God confronting that Nazi lieutenant appeared. Reliving that Nazi lieutenant violating his mother's dignity and the vision of his sister and his father being shot and dying flashed through his mind. Flashes of rainbow trout wriggling around his legs and crystal, clear water rolling over stones ran through his mind. Flashes of full-grown geraniums prompted him to smile and breathe easier. Sometimes, he would don his altar boy vestments and stand behind the altar and imagine himself as a priest blessing the hosts and wine that symbolize the body and blood of Christ, and he would whisper the words he heard his uncle utter as a blessing almost daily for much of his life:

> *Behold the Lamb of God, behold him who*
> *takes away the sins of the world. Blessed*
> *are those called to this supper of the Lamb.*
> *I am not worthy to receive you, but only*
> *say the word and I shall be healed.*

Marcello was most comfortable, most himself, and most alive when he was alone in church. He relished the presence of the Holy Spirit seeping into his soul day-by-day. He reveled in the peaceful energy saturating his soul. He would run his hands over the smooth, worn edges of the back of pews, and feel soothed. He would watch the sunrise burn through the stained glass in the east in the morning and the sunset's soft hue snuggle the day's fade in the west in the afternoon. He marveled at the soft reds, vibrant yellows, regal purples, and pure greens in the spectacular stained glass. He wafted the heat of scentless candles into his nose, savoring the neutrality of the hot wax, and he sniffed the residue of incense coating the thurible, the ornate metal vessel used to burn incense during Masses. He would walk down the aisle with intention, just to hear his footsteps click and echo off the glorious, ancient marble floor. Then he would return to the rear of the church and more deliberately approach the altar, practicing blessing parishioners himself one day. Church filled Marcello Luciari's emptiness like water fills an ocean. It freed his mind and soul like a key in a lock, and he was eager to turn its tumblers and open the door leading into the living chapel that would become the mosaic of his life. He was soon to take an important step leading toward his life's sacred door– the sacrament of Confirmation.

For most Catholics, Confirmation is viewed as an obligatory ritual required in order to be an official member of the Church, an obligation many Catholic parents force on their children as a means of self-affirmed piety. The war had forced the postponement of Marcello's Confirmation, which in the end, worked to his benefit in that he was more mature, more open, and more intellectually and spiritually prepared.

Marcello was kneeling before the crucifix immersed in fantasizing about being a priest when Uncle Salvestro entered– unnoticed. He knelt next to Marcello and prayed in silence. After a few minutes, they rose to and instinctively draped their arms around one another.

"So, sweet boy, you are soon to participate in Confirmation– to receive the gifts and blessing of the Holy Spirit ... this is intended to bring you deeper into the Church. This agrees with you?" Uncle Salvestro asked.

"Honestly, Uncle Sal, I feel like I'm already deep into the church. It's like I just have to go through the motions of Confirmation now," Marcello responded.

"I see ... well, I think you're right. Your grasp of the Holy Spirit is firm, despite the Spirit's vaporosity," Uncle Salvestro said. "A new word for you, 'vaporosity.' You have done well to grip the vapors of faith, sweet boy. So, we will go through with the ritual, and we will make your mother and your sister, and your loving Uncle Salvestro very happy and proud … and Marcello, in the end, this is a most important aspect of your Confirmation … we will have cake!"

"Perfect," Marcello said. "Count me in."

"Of course, you are in, without you, there is no cake!"

But Confirmation meant far more than cake to Marcello. It did in fact mean accepting and embracing the gifts of the Holy Spirit, but more importantly, it meant *seeking* the gifts and blessing of the Holy Spirit. The distinction between accepting and seeking was an astute distinction Marcello made early on. He understood that learning was a proactive, two-sided coin: the student must actively seek to learn and seek out the best teachers from whom to do their learning, not merely expect to be taught. Marcello deemed Jesus Christ to be the best choice as a teacher, so he began immersing himself in reading the New Testament.

While Marcello was engrossed in preparing to make his Confirmation, Chiano was actively engaged in preparing to become a Bar Mitzvah. Marcello found as much, if not more meaning in Chiano's Bar Mitzvah than in his own Confirmation. He found the Bar Mitzvah ritual more relevant and practical, and more meaningful overall, especially the notion of accepting responsibility for one's actions – for one's life.. When not immersed in helping his uncle with church duties, or at school, or playing football, Marcello was in Chiano's grandfather's small grocery store earning a small wage, more as a gesture of kindness from Chiano's grandfather than an actual job. But a job is a job.

He and Chiano leisurely chatted as they unpacked crates of local produce, and an assortment of provisions.

"I really like the Bar Mitzvah idea. I like that you're thought of as an adult, kind of, and that you do a real project– the mitzvah– to do something good," Marcello said.

"Some of the adult and responsibility stuff can be a bit overrated," Chiano quipped. "Like working in my grandfather's shop," he said. "But at least that gives us a job, right?"

"Right. It's great that we have jobs here," Marcello said, as he placed jars of sardines packed in olive oil on a shelf. The shelves in the tiny grocery store were filled with anything and everything from avocados to zucchini. Chiano's cheerful grandmother measured out dry goods and cut fresh cold cuts for adults and counted out pieces of gum and candy for kids. Marcello and Chiano stocked the store's shelves, made light deliveries, and unpacked goods when new supplies arrived. Their wages were miniscule, but the experience was a priceless joy. They learned to plan for what was needed and to present what was to be sold. They learned to care for customers and to serve a boss. Most of all, they had fun just being together daydreaming about the future while savoring the moment.

"So, I decided on my Bar Mitzvah project," Chiano declared. Marcello stopped stocking the shelves for a moment to hear Chiano's news. "Remember how Monsignor B. used to read to us at night at *Schools*, and how we loved it so much? Well, there's an orphanage ... I'm going to read stories to these kids a couple nights a week," Chiano said, enthused and proud. "I already arranged it with the woman that runs the orphanage," he said.

"I'll do it too– if that's alright?" Marcello asked?

"Alright? You kiddin' me? They'd love that, and so would I. And so will you," Chiano said, now even more enthused. More validated. Marcello reached out and hugged his pal and Chiano welcomed him with open, grateful arms.

"I'm eager for you to tell my uncle, can you tell him today?" Marcello asked, eagerly.

When the two comrades arrived at Santa Maria, it was near dinner hour. There was a light on in Uncle Salvestro's office, an office of his own in a building adjacent to the church entrance, one of the luxuries in his new assignment. The boys ran up the steps and into the building and toward the lighted office. When they saw that Father Frischetti had a visitor, they stopped in their tracks at his door.

"Come in, come in, boys, meet my friend, United States Army Chaplain, Father Francis Finlay. I have been telling the boys all about you, Father." Father Finlay stood up, standing just barely taller than the boys. His small frame supported a broad smile and a hardy handshake. They expected a more rugged man as an Army Chaplain, but inner strength doesn't always reflect in one's appearance.

"This is my nephew Marcello and my adopted nephew, Chiano, two of my favorite people in the world," Uncle Salvestro happily claimed. "Boys, Father Finlay is a dear old friend."

"Pleasure to meet you boys. I'm Father Francis– Frank Finlay."

"We're catching up on old times. What can I do for you guys?" Uncle Salvestro asked.

"We just came to tell you some news," Marcello said. "Go 'head, tell 'em, Iano," Marcello said, using his nickname for Chiano.

"I decided on my Bar Mitzvah project," Chiano said. "I'm Jewish … I'm becoming a Bar Mitzvah this year," he said, addressing Father Finlay. "So, for my Bar Mitzvah project, I'm going to read stories to kids in the orphanage by the Ghetto … every week. Marcello's gonna do it, too." He took a healthy breath and dipped his toes in a pool of pride.

"Bravo, Chiano. Bravo. Good for you, both of you. And good for those kids, they will love to have you read to them," Uncle Salvestro affirmed.

"Very commendable, Chiano. I don't even know you guys yet, but I am proud of you already," Father Finlay said.

"You should come to Mass with Marcello tomorrow, Chiano. Father Finlay will be serving Mass, you can hear him speak. He is a wonderful speaker, a wonderful priest … and a great guy all around," Uncle Salvestro said.

"I need a topic for my sermon, maybe you fellas can help me find one," Father Finlay said. Looking over Uncle Salvestro's shoulder to the geranium plant, Marcello blurted out a suggestion:

"Seeds! What if the topic is seeds– like the ones Uncle Salvestro and I planted the other day? How 'bout that?" Marcello asked.

"Seeds? I'll consider that," Father Finlay said.

The next morning, Santa Maria's nine o'clock Mass was a little more full than usual. Catholics in Rome did not view attending Mass as an obligation, but as a tradition and privilege. It was their indulgence in hope, piety, and a plea for absolution for weaknesses, indiscretions, indulgences, and for some, forgiveness for outright crimes. But at least for an hour and fifteen minutes or so each Sunday morning, all were dressed in a gown of honor's hope, at peace, and respectful in their genuine reverence for Jesus Christ.

Father Frischetti entered the church in a procession made grand by his smile and gleaming brown eyes, made memorable by his jubilant swinging of the thurible, wafting fragrant, gray-white clouds of incense throughout the church. He was preceded by Marcello and another altar boy in full altar boy regalia, and Father Finlay, donned in full vestments. The ancient church organ belted out an entrance hymn and the congregation stood in collective reverence, respectful anticipation, and rote habit. As the stirring organ subsided to silence, Father Frischetti took his position at the center of the altar. Making the sign of the cross with purpose and sacred attachment, he began the Mass.

"In the name of the Father, the Son, and the Holy Spirit, Amen." He paused to prompt a collective, "Amen," from the congregation, followed by a "Good morning, everyone." They responded with a rigorous "good morning" in return.

"We have a special guest today. Father Finlay from America will be delivering our homily this morning. Father Finlay is not only from the United States, but that United States Army that liberated Rome, and ended the war. Father Finlay was a chaplain in the army. Please welcome my friend, colleague, and spiritual confidant, Father Francis Finlay." The congregation offered a polite and respectful round of applause and Father Frischetti began the Mass. The order of the Catholic Mass leaves little or no room for deviation, but the homily— the sermon— however, yields the celebrant some leeway, within guidelines, restricted only by his proficiency. That task of delivering the homily for this Mass was passed on to Father Finlay, a task he embraced with insight and earnest devotion. He spun his homily from Marcello's suggestion.

"Yesterday, I met two very impressive boys in Father Frischetti's office. I asked them what the topic of my homily should be, and Father Frischetti's great nephew Marcello gave me an idea," he said, waving a hand toward Marcello. "When I asked for a suggestion for my homily, Marcello looked over his uncle's shoulder and saw a tray of Geranium seedlings that he had planted with his uncle, and he said 'Seeds.' So today, I want to thank Marcello for planting that seed in my mind.

"The seeds we blossom from as people are defined by our choices, and our actions— how we treat one another, not merely how we embrace the word of God." Father Finlay bowed his head and paused, enabling the seeds of his thought to take root. Lifting his head back to the congregation, he continued. "As we go forward into our lives, let us carefully consider how the seeds of God's words and actions become the seeds that we sew as the bounty of our lives. Yes, we will reap what we sow, what then, will we sew?"

The congregation sat in silence, digesting the surprise of Father Finlay's brevity, and the fruits of his word– his sowing the seeds of wisdom in faith's soil. Father Frischetti presented Father Finlay with the brilliant red geranium that he had shown Marcello two days before. Father Finlay respectfully placed the plant on the altar.

After the Mass, Father Frischetti and Father Finlay greeted parishioners outside the church steps, then retreated to the sacristy to change out of their vestments. Marcello and Chiano joined them and helped them out of their lengthy cassocks.

"I liked what you said about seeds, Father, it made me think." Marcello said. Father Frischetti considered what psychological and emotional seeds might have been sewn into Marcello's psyche the day the Nazi lieutenant forced his hand to pull the trigger that sent a bullet into his father's head and a never-ending charge of sorrow into Marcello's heart. He blinked back to the present moment as quick as his conscious mind enabled him to return to hanging up his vestments.

"I liked it, too. Makes me want to grow something," Chiano added.

"I'm glad you got something out of it," Father Finlay said. "Speaking of seeds, I have something else for both of you to think about." Father Finlay reached inside his jacket that was hanging in a narrow cubby and removed something from its pocket. "I thought you fellas might like to have these," he said, handing them each an olive drab, Army green patch with black lettering that read 'Pro Deo Et Patria,' Latin for 'God and Country.' An eagle holding an open book– presumably a bible– and an olive branch in its beak was embroidered in lighter green thread. "These are United States Army Chaplain patches. The same one I wore throughout the war."

"Wow. Thank you," Marcello said. His eyes devoured the patch as his mind devoured Father Finlay's spirit. Part of him reveled in fantasies of heroic military illusions while a conflicting part of him shriveled into a helpless child, melting like ice under hot water. He struggled to change the channel that was involuntarily projecting uninvited and unwelcome reruns of *that day* on the screen of his mind.

"We can keep them? Wow. Thank you, Father Finlay," Chiano added. "Look how cool the eagle is. I'm gonna ask my mother to sew this on my jacket," he said.

"Maybe that's some sort of seed for you guys," Uncle Salvestro said. "Come over to the rectory and have some pastry with us."

Father Finlay stayed with Father Frischetti for the next two weeks, visiting Rome, serving Mass, and chatting with Marcello and Chiano after dinner each night. He shared some inspiring military stories yet protected them from the grim memories of wartime experiences that haunted him. The depth of human service and the valuable comfort and inspiration he provided soldiers in their most needy hour became clear, even though an opaque shroud covered his unspoken thoughts. He obscured the horrors of war with compassionate tales of peace. He alluded to helping the wounded, understating the dangers, horror, and terror he felt when dragging dying soldiers from bombed-out rubble, or holding men's limbs together with his bare hands. He squelched the memory of lying in trenches filled with mud made from soldiers' blood and dirt. He didn't tell them how it felt to be running while under fire to give Last Rights to a soldier pinned to a tree under machine gun fire that ripped the soldier's body into shreds, or how he threw his guts up for days after witnessing Nazi soldiers set fire to captives and forcing them to race for sport. The smell of their burnt flesh and burning hair still chokes him every time he is near a flame. The vision of their naked, inflamed bodies running chaotically, desperately, and their inhuman cries still startle him awake many nights. Memories of Nazis being shot dead by Americans satisfies him yet disturbs him with a torment forged by the conflict between the forgiveness he preaches and the anger he harbors. But all this remained behind Father Finlay's gentle eyes, eyes that conceal and camouflage the anguish and shock inflicted by war. Tapping the patch, he said:

"Compassion was the seed; comfort was the flower we grew, boys." Father Finlay reached into his pocket once more and retrieved two slim brochures. He flashed them to the boys before handing them over; the cover read, 'Discover Catholic University.' "Another seed," Father Finlay said. "Have you boys heard of Catholic University? It's in the capital of

the United States– Washington, D.C. I'm the Dean of Admissions there–
when I'm not vacationing in Rome here with your uncle. I'd be more
than happy to help both of you find your way into Catholic University,"
Father Finlay said. Marcello's eyes nearly popped out of his head. He
looked from the brochure to Father Finlay and back again, and again,
sensing the importance of this moment. He made the inspiring connection between what he held in his hand, with what he hoped for in his
heart.

"Wow," was the only word Marcello could muster. He and Chiano
looked at each other a bit puzzled yet knowing something good had just
happened.

Chiano said, almost sadly, fearing a golden opportunity might be
escaping his grasp. "But I'm Jewish, Father."

"We're all Jewish, Chiano. Most of us just don't know it," Father
Finlay said, with a good-natured grin. "You'll be more than welcome
and more than comfortable at our university. I'll see to it," he said, as he
patted Chiano's shoulder.

CHAPTER 9

Uncle Jewels

His legal name was Lorenzo Pratto. Lorenzo was Lucio's brother and Chiano's uncle. He was the loveable black sheep of the family, only because he was unconventional. Lorenzo was clever and kind, under-educated, but incisively wise. Most of all, he was a brilliantly talented jewelry designer, and a caring man who had a knack for knowing things before everyone else, and the will to do what success demanded in any endeavor. Eight weeks before the Nazis occupied and terrorized Rome, Lorenzo had the foresight to know something terrible was brewing, so he boarded up his shop and pasted an 'Out of Business' sign on its doors. He moved most of his clothes and all his jewelry inventory to a small apartment he and his wife, Tessera, rented on the coast of Puglia. Unbeknown to anyone else in his family, Lorenzo also had a stake in a small, but very lucrative vineyard in Puglia, as well as owning three additional apartments on its gorgeous beach-lined coast. Uncle Lorenzo and Tessera were unable to conceive so Lorenzo practically adopted Chiano and his siblings as their surrogate children. He earned the affectionate nickname Uncle Jewels because he was a gifted jeweler as his profession, and a jewel as a man, and as an uncle.

Uncle Jewels quietly developed a lucrative business. His jewelry business thrived under the radar and scrutiny of taxation, which he was very adept at dodging. He operated with a low profile, yet he exclusively depended upon referrals and repeat business. The quality of his jewelry and commitment to his customers were second to none. When Uncle

Jewels returned to Rome after the war had ended, he reopened Pratto Gioiellieri, and Father Frischetti introduced him to a friend in search of a custom-made ring for a friend named Cardinal Puselli. Lorenzo designed and crafted a stunning ring for the cardinal, and in turn, Cardinal Puselli introduced Lorenzo to Cardinal Assiano. Lorenzo designed an equally beautiful ring for Cardinal Assiano, who in turn, introduced Lorenzo to Cardinal Klecko, who introduced him to Cardinal Viejo, who introduced him to Cardinal Zachirelli, who introduced him to Carmino De Luvorro, an influential underworld boss. Carmino introduced Lorenzo to starlets, and movie producers, who all collectively introduced Lorenzo to an affluence that he kept well-guarded. When someone suggested a design of their own that Lorenzo objected to artistically, rather than turn down the sale, he accommodated such clients in a special way:

"Your exceptional, distinctive, irreplaceable, exclusive, inimitable design is sure to attract notable attention," he would say. "But, despite how important referrals are to me, attention can sometimes not be a jeweler's best friend; I'm sure you understand," he would coax, assured the client had no idea what he meant. "For your protection, and mine, I must ask you, as partners in this artistic venture, I must ask you that you describe this work exclusively as your personal design– not mine. And I am to be referred to only as 'the jeweler' who you commissioned to bring your magnificent design to life," he would say. "And as a courtesy to you, I am happy to take equal superior care of any of your friends that you would like to refer to me, but my name must never be associated with designs other than my own. Is this agreeable to you?" To a person, each taste-challenged client agreed to Lorenzo's request for discretion, and each one of them left Pratto Gioiellieri feeling proud, smart, and privileged– and carrying a notably lighter wallet.

When taste-challenged clients asked Lorenzo to bring their aesthetically displeasing designs from their convoluted and abstract concepts to physical reality, he would engage in an unorthodox but effective process aimed at pleasing his clients. Uncle Jewels would retreat to his studio and begin working on the repugnant designs by sitting behind two full bottles of Grappa, a bottle of Limoncello, and a bottle of San Pellegrino Sparkling Mineral Water. He would mix four parts Grappa, three parts Limoncello with two parts San Pellegrino. He would drink his potent cocktail until he deemed himself definitively drunk, and/or sufficiently incapable of most motor skills, and at the point at which his judgment was impaired enough to find the deplorable designs acceptable, he would begin work on the awful, incoherent, impossibly dreadful designs that he considered 'competing fusions between the absurd and the hideous.' When he finished the distasteful work, he would present the horrid designs with a passionate assertion that they were the only one of their kind on the face of the earth and could never possibly be duplicated– or even imagined. He would tack on an additional thirty to forty percent onto his normal price as a means of inferring the highest perceived value. And before turning over the ghastly design, he would insist that clients sign a 'DiGiulianazione di Riservatezza,' a Declaration of Confidentiality. He would certify such pieces with an official-looking 'Certificato di Autenticità,' a Certificate of Authenticity– bearing only the client's name, never his own.

Uncle Jewels happily and eagerly shared his prosperity with Chiano and his family. He gave Chiano and Marcello simple jobs in the jewelry store to supplement their earnings when they were not working in Chiano's grandfather's grocery store. They would clean and polish the windows and display cases, make deliveries of lower-priced items, help distribute sales letters to exclusive customers, and do whatever else Uncle Jewels asked. Their jobs were created more by Uncle Jewels' desire to help the boys than out of business necessity.

Working for Uncle Jewels gave Marcello some money to turn in to help his mother and on occasion, splurge for gelato, or even a movie. The earnings gave Chiano a taste of a new treat called fun. The boys were eighteen now and in the final year of high school and morphing from adolescence into young adulthood. Chiano's hand no longer sweat when he danced with Sandriana, or any other young lady. He became most proficient at leading young ladies around the dance floor of Giuliana's classes, at school dances, and even at an occasional nightclub. It was 1956. Rome was enjoying an economic and cultural boom and riding its tide with style and grace. And Chiano embraced that wave like a breeze on the wind. He had discovered fun, laughter, and life. And girls.

One summer afternoon, Chiano returned from an errand to Pratto Gioiellieri bursting with excitement. His face was flush, his breathing short and choppy. Marcello was in the back room unpacking watches when Chiano rushed in.

"Cello," he said, quickly. "Com 'ere quick, close the door. I gotta tell you something … something amazing just happened." He launched into his story without pausing to take a breath. "You know Uncle Jewels sent me on an errand, right? Well on my way back, I was walking by the Spanish Steps, and you know how there's always a ton of people sitting there? Well, this one lady, really, really pretty lady, I would say she was American, she had on a dress the wind kept blowing up, and it blew her dress way up and I could see her underpants! Can you believe that? And she was kissing the guy she was with, and she didn't know it, but her underpants were showing, and she had really, really– I mean really, really nice legs and I couldn't stop looking. So, I made believe I was tying my shoelace– I did both shoes– and I kept sneaking peeks at her. Cel, her underpants were really small and thin … I could see right through them! Can you believe that? And she kept sitting like that, and the wind kept blowin' her dress up. Then, get this, she opened her legs a little while they were kissin' and, oh my God, Cel, I could see the bottom of her butt! And her underpants almost disappeared into her butt! I kept looking and hoping she didn't see me. I was wishing I had four feet so I had more shoes to tie. It got to the point where I could see more skin than underpants. It was unbelievable, Cello. Unbelievable!" Marcello absorbed all this with curious uncertainty, and maybe a portion of envy. "I don't know what it is, Cel, I feel this buzzing fluttering around my stomach every time I'm around a pretty girl. Even ladies. Even if they're only in magazines, not just when they're real, even if they're just in movies or magazines," he said. "Do you get that feeling?"

"I did … a few times. Sure."

"I get it all the time. Sometimes, I can't stop staring at girls … or ladies. It's like something takes over in me and all I can do is stare, and I imagine what they would look like naked. And it feels really good, like the whole world is stirring inside me, like I'm full of bubbles inside," Chiano explained.

"What do you do when it happens?"

"I enjoy it!" he exclaimed with a grateful laugh. "I don't know what to do. I just want more of it. When I see these girls, or ladies, I just want to see them naked. You think something's wrong with me?"

"Na, I think it's just our age."

"I get crazed over these girls– and ladies, too. Do you?"

"A little, maybe, not enough to tie-my-shoes-for-twenty-minutes-crazy, but a little, sure."

"Like last weekend, Uncle Jewels took me to the movies, and we saw "*La Fortuna di Essere una Donna,*" *The Luck of Being a Woman*, "with Sophia Loren. Oh my God, Cel! Oh my God! There's this one scene, and she's doing a photo shoot for this magazine, and she's in a bathing suit, and the photographer gets this bright idea to make it look like she's naked underneath her towel. So, she takes her bathing suit straps off her shoulders and– Holy cow, Cel! Oh my God. She's the most beautiful woman ever born! She lays back on this couch and you could see those gorgeous, shiny tan legs and her crazy beautiful face. She has these lips, Cel, these amazing lips, and huge eyes that feel like they're looking right through you. Then a few times, she bends or turns, and you can see part of her jugs! You can see where they form ... and oh my God, I was starting to get aroused– right there in the movie theater. Can you believe that? This weekend, we gotta go see it– you gotta see her."

Yes, Chiano had discovered girls alright, and much of himself in the process. He was also busy discovering an interest in literature and drama, especially the brilliance of the psychological insight threaded into all of Shakespeare's plays. Chiano was becoming fascinated by the human psyche and the collective social psyche inherent in and perpetuated by different cultures. He was beginning to think about global events and universal themes such as forms of government, immortality, mortality, greed, compassion, human service, social service, even medicine. His parents and Uncle Jewels were forceful, beyond encouragement, to insist on urging and preparing Chiano for a college education. And beyond. Uncle Jewels would also often offer advice and direction to Chiano and Marcello when they spent time in the store cleaning jewelry and polishing showcases.

"Even though you are very young, you must understand that life is very short, and very wonderful– if you are smart enough to be smart enough."

"Not to be disrespectful, Uncle Jewels, but what the heck does that mean?"

"To be smart requires that you are dumb enough to know that you know very little, and smart enough to know that you can change that– by learning what you want and what you need to know. The more you learn," he advised, "the more you will understand that you know less than you think. So, if you are smart enough to know that there is more to learn than you can ever know, you will always be getting smarter." He paused then raised his bushy black and grey eyebrows and jabbed the air with his chubby index finger as he spoke. "But the smarter you become, the dumber you are." Make sense?" Uncle Jewels asked.

"Not even a little," Chiano said.

"It will, one day. The most important thing to learn is that life is very short, so you must squeeze every drop of life from life itself– every single day," he said, underscoring his point by poking a glass showcase with his finger. "Never take your life for granted. Never. The more you learn, the more there will be to enjoy– if you are smart enough to be smart enough," he finished, and patted them both on the head. "How appropriate that we are having this talk while you are unpacking the gift of time," he said. "To learn boys, is to earn– you earn freedom, independence, options, spending power, peace, and wonderful experiences. But only education will enable you to have all these wonderful things. And then, my handsome boys, you will be in the position to do good things for the people who need good things done for them. You will be able to make the world better by what you do while you're here."

He took one of the watches from its case and judiciously examined it, propping it up in his chunky fingers and slowly rotating it, raising it higher, tilting it up then down. He admired the shimmer of energy and light flickering over its polished crystal, like moonlight dancing on the ocean's eyes. He revered the seamless merging of art and design in engineering emitted in the watch's overall impression that created a life of its own. With his head bent backward and his eyes peering through the lenses of tiny reading glasses past the swell of his round cheeks, he shook his head in appreciation and reverently returned the watch to its case.

"Did you ever carve your initials into a tree? Or write your name on the rocks in a cave? Your actions on this earth will be what you leave behind– what you carve in your life's tree." And you only get one chance– one time to do it right?" Uncle Jewels led them to the front of the store with one arm around each of them. "We are mere seconds in the hours of a day, boys," he suggested. "Better enjoy ourselves," he said. "Come on, we will close early today. We will use the rest of the day to enjoy ourselves by indulging in pizza and gelato." He locked the door, smiling in response to the little jingle from the little bell on the top of the door.

"That little bell brings big happiness," he said. He looked up at that bell and smiled every time it jingled since the day he opened the store. He turned the dead bolt with his key, and its cylinders locked into place, securing the door shut with a reassuring clunk.

"Before we know it, you boys will be packing your bags for college life and pondering the wonders of the world. And I will be smelling the dough from the bakery next door and hearing the music from the accordion player on the corner and feeling the rounded bumps of these cobblestones pressing into the soles of my shoes. And you know what I will be thinking? I will be thinking of you boys, and how much I love you." He ended his sentence with a grateful chuckle that left a lingering smile on his chubby, red cheeks. He tugged his ivory-colored fedora lower over his forehead and smiled a broad smile, sending the pencil thin moustache outlining the contour of his upper lip into a perky line of stubbles. He snapped the lapels of his white linen suit twice to tighten the fit and moved down the street with pride and purpose. Uncle Jewels was also thinking of how badly he would miss these boys being with him. He was thinking how badly he would love to have had sons of his own. But he quickly hosed away the voids in his life with the cleansing waters of gratitude and the knowing power that he could change nearly anything in his life he wanted to change.

"I will blink my eyes and you two will be off to college."

"If we are smart enough to be smart enough," Marcello said.

CHAPTER 10

Stars

At the top of the glorious Spanish Steps overlooking the bustle of the Piazza Tinte de Monte, the largest park in the city of Rome, Villa Borghese embraces its guests and shrouds them in an invisible peaceful shawl. Its gardens burst with humble beauty, its trails invite private contemplation, and somehow seem to provide fulfillment for whatever its visitors seek. The park's watchful monuments honor their positions with a silent, regal salute to solitude's honor. Villa Borghese belongs to everyone and no one. It is where lovers discover and express their love, where the hopeful court the hoping, and where the conflicted affirm their being as one, and reconcile their differences as two. It is where the lonely find solace and the gregarious celebrate. It is where nature smiles on the Eternal City below, while scratching the insistent itch demanding attention in the vast and mysterious sky above. It is where Marcello and Chiano laid in the grass, their heads side-by-side, underscoring their similarities. Their feet point in opposite directions, symbolically punctuating their differences, and the inevitable parting of their respective directions along life's path.

They laid content on the soft grass in a private corner of the park staring deep into the unending, star-filled sky, searching for clues to their tomorrow in a vivid mosaic of reflections of yesterday.

"Are we so different?" Chiano asked.

"You and me, or you and me compared to everybody else?"

"Jews … are we that different from the rest of the world."

"Some of the things you do and believe are different, but as people, no, you're no different than anybody else. Well, some of the things you eat are a little questionable," he said with a grin. "And I'd have to say, some of the extreme Jewish sects are a little ... peculiar. I mean the really extreme ones," Marcello said.

"We call them super Jews, but honestly, they're more a cult than Jews," Chiano said. "Why do you think the Nazis hate us so much?"

"There's no answer to that, Chiano. They hate everybody but themselves."

"It's like they trained people in the art of hatred. And it gets handed down generation-to-generation. It means so much that your family never hated us," Chiano said. "You loved us." They laid staring at the stars with their heads nearly touching, searching to understand the whys of the world for several minutes in silence. They cherished this moment in peaceful contemplation, considering the future, the past, the world, the fireflies softly sparking sporadically like pleasant thoughts drifting into the mind with welcome ease.

"I asked my Uncle Salvestro that question, not long ago; he said it's part envy, part jealousy, part fear ... and ignorance."

"Could be. Anyway, it came up when my parents and I and Uncle Jewels were talking about what colleges I should apply to; they think it's important that I go to a college that welcomes Jews."

"That makes sense," Marcello said. "There's a lot to consider ... if we're smart enough to be smart enough," he added.

"What's top on your list for 'must haves' in a college?" Chiano asked.

"Scholarship. If I don't get scholarships, I can't go. Simple as that. After that, I would say the courses ... the majors they offer." Marcello said. "I want to major in Religious Studies, so schools that excel in that are at the top of my list. My mother and Uncle Salvestro, especially my Uncle Salvestro, have been helping think through all this college stuff," Marcello said.

"I'm pretty lucky in that way; my Uncle Jewels said he would help me when the time comes. But I don't really know exactly what 'help me' means," Chiano said.

"We've been talking about it too– a lot lately," Chiano said. "Lots of things are really important: faculty, real training, what kind of extra help and programs they offer, practical stuff ... thinking about what they can really prepare me to be, or do," he said.

"Remember Father Finlay, the Army Chaplain that was the Dean of Admissions at Catholic University? We wrote to him to ask if he can help us. I sent him a letter and all my school records, but it's been a long time since we sent that letter to him," Marcello said.

"Would you really go to college in America if you could?"

"I would love to, but I would love to stay here, too. I would be worried about my mother and my sister. And I would be kind of lost without my Uncle Salvestro if I were to go to college in America. And you, I'd really miss you," he said. "My uncle said he's been preparing me to fly from the nest one day. So, I guess someday is pretty close. I'm kind of nervous but excited, too."

"Wow, that's a big step, Cel."

"We're both about to take big steps," Marcello said. They soaked in the serenity of the night in silence for several minutes, each imagining themselves in a new world, imagining what a new world would be, and where, what life would be like without one another.

"What about those Pontifical Universities ... you looking into those for Religious Studies?" Chiano asked.

"Uncle Salvestro advised against them. He said that they're too focused on the organization and bureaucracy of the Church, not enough on the spiritual and social needs. He thinks it's better if I get a broader view of what he calls the 'social fabric' of the world, not just what he calls, 'the processes and politics of dilatants.'"

"What kind of priest is a dilatant?" Chiano asked.

"It's not a priest, it means someone who has a superficial interest in something ... kind of like a wannabe, or a faker," Marcello said.

"Oh ... Uncle Jewels calls guys like those bullshitters," Chiano said.

The two lifelong friends laid in silence for some time, appreciating the stars. The clouds seemed closer and softer this night. The sky, deeper. The stars, brighter. The world, more accessible, more sizzling with fervor's flavor, more within reach. Smaller. The comfort of solace embraced them as a soft Roman breeze whispered encouragement into their ears, into their hearts. The thought of being apart for the first time since they were born, just days apart from one another lurked in the deepest dark of the incalculable sky. Mercifully, the brilliance and comfort of being together– in this moment– beneath the stars twinkling their reflective assurance, tempered the sting of separation's unspoken anxiety. After a very long and enjoyable silence, Marcello spoke.

"This will be the first time we'll ever be apart since *The Pulpit*, Iano."

"I know." They said nothing more for some time. But they thought a lot about what being apart from each other would not merely be like but feel like. They deepened their comfortable posture with their heads imprinted into the soft grass.

"It's gonna be weird not seeing you every day," Chiano said.

"I know," Marcello said. "I'm not gonna like that." And that was all they said for another long time. Their armor of silence and avoidance camouflaged the froth of sadness pooling in their stomachs. They suspended their minds in the calming elixir and the comforting nectar floating in the buoyancy of the sky's solace. Their alluring glow of opportunity's rewards sparred with the pangs of separation's pain; an inner conflict as present as the prominent flickering stars persisting ever so brightly in the summer night. After pausing in a quiet contentment for several more moments, Marcello spoke:

"Iano?"

"Yeah?"

"Will you write to me?"

"Of course."

PART II

CHAPTER 11

Letters

21 Sep 58
Dear Iano:

It's been two weeks already and I am just now getting a minute to write to you. I have to tell you, you would absolutely love Washington, D.C. It is the Rome of America. Of course, New York is a fabulous city, too, but I can't imagine it can compete with the pageantry and reverence for these monuments here. They aren't as glorious, or as artful, or ornate as the Roman monuments, but they sure are impressive. When you walk the streets here, you can feel the power of the entire country. I understand even better now how and why the world looks up to America. At some point, I will have to serve America as a means of paying back the debt for the scholarship Father Finlay arranged for me through the ROTC program. I don't know exactly how I will have to pay back that debt, it's kind of sketchy at the moment. I'll be happy no matter what it is I have to do to pay for this amazing opportunity.

Now, about my classes. They're tough! I thought my English was pretty good, until I got here. They *speak in metaphors sometimes, and sometimes in riddles! And they often pronounce in a sort of shorthand that I am finding hard to follow, but I'm getting by. Father Finlay was able to help me get a job. I work in the college bookstore about ten or twelve hours a week, which gives me a little spending money but mostly, I try to save it to send it to my mother. Which reminds me: I got a mysterious letter from Rome. It had no name on it, just a note that said, Dear Marcello, this is for you to enjoy yourself! That's it! And there was money in it— five American dollars! Can you believe that? Five dollars out of the blue! I don't have any idea who sent it but it was addressed to me. Go figure.*

I am very eager to hear about how you are doing in Tel Aviv. It is so exciting to think about you in that huge university making your mark and immersing in the wonders of learning. I know you're very busy, but I sure would love to hear from you soon. All the best, my friend, my very best life-long friend,

Love, Marcello

24 Sep 58
Dear Marcello:

I am sorry I have not written yet. It has been a big whirlwind of activity and adjustment. Tel Aviv's amazing! The beach is only a ten-minute bike ride, so I am now a beach bum! Whenever I'm not in class, I'm at the beach reading and studying and loving it. I sure wish you were here with me. My roommate is a nice guy and we get along, but a roommate is not a best friend. You are.

It's interesting being at a brand-new college like Tel Aviv University. It's almost brand new, just get-

ting started so the classes are small. Now I know why my family pushed me into attending here. It's fantastic, Cello. You would love it. Its history is interesting. It is sort of an attachment to the movement to build Israel as a nation so there's a national and international sort of energy here that you can feel despite it being so small. There are only a few hundred kids here. The mission here is to "pursue the unknown." They value innovation which depends on education, and tradition, which relies on, well, tradition. I guess we are looking forward as we peek into the rear-view . mirror expecting to find the future in the past. The Americans and a few European countries have been providing financial and academic support to Tel Aviv and it's really helping. I really feel at home here being Italian and Jewish, the best of two worlds for me. I'm learning to speak Hebrew and most of the professors speak English. There's a special track I'm on called Jewish Studies for International Students that's taught in English, Italian, and Hebrew. The more we get into it, the more Hebrew I'll be learning. It's challenging but inspiring to be around such smart people.

I am taking a lot of required courses but we have a great class that is designed to help you find your interests and strengths, so I am hoping that by the end of the semester I will have a better sense of what I want to major in. I am trying not to put pressure on myself to decide, but I would sure like to know what I am going to be!

I hope Washington, D.C. is all you hoped it would be. I really don't know anything about it other than that you are there and it's the capital of the United States. So that makes it good, I guess. I hope the food is good there. It's ok here. We Italians are spoiled when it comes to food.

I better sign off now, it's late and I have an early math class tomorrow. I am looking forward to the weekend. There aren't too many kids here, but there are a few activities and some pretty girls! There's one in my World History class that looks like the lady I told you about on the Spanish Steps! How about that! (Better untie my shoes, right?) Our letters will probably cross paths somewhere over the ocean! Until next time, enjoy! I love you, pal!

Love, Chiano

26 Sep 58
Dear Iano:

I went to the Smithsonian Museum here in Washington, D.C. twice this weekend! It would take a lifetime to see that entire museum! You would love it. I know how you love sculpture and all things beautiful and man o man, is there beauty and everything amazing known to man there. I might be able to get a job there on the weekends— if I can manage studying and my other job at the bookstore. I had to tell you about the Smithsonian as soon as I could. Iano, there's EVERYTHING here! I am beside myself, I don't think I have ever been so excited in my life! Never! Imagine the best achievement in every subject in the world and you will find it on display here. My roommate and a few classmates went twice, and just loved it.

I haven't told you about my roommate yet. He is a very nice guy from California, up around San Francisco. His name is Alex. Really nice guy. I told him what a great guy you are. He speaks slower than a lot of people, so it's easy to understand him and he's helpful with my English, which is getting better all the time. I knew classes taught in English would be a challenge for me but luckily, Uncle Salvestro started teaching us English when we were young.

We have Masses in the most beautiful cathedrals and chapels. We have some beautiful stained glass in Marcelloels but there are no churches like the ones in Rome. My classes are not overwhelming, but they are demanding, I can't fall behind. I have very little downtime for socializing. I haven't made many friends yet, but I'm getting comfortable here and still getting my routine down. The washing machines here are a lot bigger than my mother's washbasin at home. They're great.

I'm sure that you haven't received my letter from the other day yet, but I had to write you and tell you about the Smithsonian. I would love to show it to you someday. How terrific it would be for us to visit each other's colleges! I forgot to tell you. There are some great television shows here! And American football. Man o man, do I love to go to the football games here. I'll tell you all about it soon. I'm so excited to be here, Iano, but I sure miss you. Hope you are well!

Love, Marcello

30 Sep 58
Dear Marcello:

Settling in here in Tel Aviv— kind of. Our campus, if you can call it that, is in the Jaffa section of Tel Aviv, an area called Abu Kabir. I like it. There are a lot of really interesting buildings, old shops, and little nooks and crannies to explore. And it's on the Mediterranean Sea and I love the beach. It's been a big adjustment trying to juggle my classes and get my work done. I'm starting to feel like my empty head is filling up faster than I can process it all. It feels pretty amazing to be in college, even this new, small one, and to be on my own for the most part. Part of me feels like a little kid and part of me feels like a grown-up, well, almost a grown-up. For the first time, I am starting to think about what I think just might be important someday. I think it's this immersion in education. It's making me want to be smarter. I never considered myself a smart kid, but smart enough to know I'm not dumb. Anyway, TAU seems right up my alley and I'm really eager to dive in.

Hey, the girl I told you about in my World History class has a boyfriend already. That'll teach me to hesitate, right? How are real life American girls compared to Italian girls? It's really nice to be in a city where everyone is on my side! No one wants to kill me just for being a Jew! Hebrew is spoken as the primary language here. Despite speaking only what I learned in temple and Hebrew school, and what my family taught me, I find hearing it comforting. The TAU campus is small, like I said, it's just getting started. The buildings in Tel Aviv are night-and-day different from Rome. They're modern. It almost looks like they're trying really hard to seem contemporary. I guess they're trying to push our thinking forward with this look. I'll have to look into Israeli architecture someday. Our campus is just beginning to shape up. There are always some kids roaming around coming to and from class, kind of like watching confusion bumping into wisdom!

There is so much to explore in Tel Aviv. It is very much like Rome in a lot of ways but nothing like it in many other ways. That's my profound thought for the day! I really like being on my own and I am figuring out how to do the little life things that we need to do, like laundry, prioritizing my studying time, and being places on time. My father always drummed into my head to 'take care of things immediately,' advice that is serving me well; if I procrastinate, I get really behind, really fast. It doesn't take as long to get behind as it does to procrastinate, right?

I am still enjoying the beach but spending more and more time in our little library. That's it for now, my friend. I miss you and think of you all the time. Every time I see or experience something, I wonder what Marcello would think of that. Ciao for now. I love you, pal.

Love, Chiano

4 Oct 58
Dear Chiano:

I just got your letter! Thanks for writing, pal, it's great to hear from you. Sounds like you are off to a good start. I'm jealous that you have a beach nearby! I would love to see Tel Aviv someday. Maybe Jerusalem, too! You probably got my letter or both by now and our contact is established. It's so good to hear from you. Your handwriting made me feel at home. I remember you used to write notes to Giana Santorelli, and I used to deliver them for you. (I promise, I never read them. I loved the way you wrote, "To Giana" and you always drew a curvy line on the cover with two slashes through it.) Funny what we remember.

Hope you are well and taking in all Tel Aviv and college life has to offer. I am finding my way around campus and Washington, D.C.– and my own mind– little by little, and it is a really exciting time. I have to write a lot in one of my classes, "Exploring Spiritual Metaphors." It's really a stimulating class. Every class ends with a philosophical metaphor or thought to consider. It reminds me of our sessions in the brook with Monsignor B. You might enjoy thinking about a few of these things when you're not on the beach! This week's thought is, "God is easy to please, but difficult to satisfy." Let me know what you think of that.

I got a few tests and papers back and I'm doing

pretty well so far. Americans seem to be focused on their grades more than learning the subject matter. I feel like if I make sure I have a command on the material, I'll get good grades, but more importantly, I'll have a command on the material. I am beginning to feel like I have something important to say but I have no idea what that is yet. I guess that's why I'm here, right? It is an interesting cultural experience overall. It is fun-loving in a different way than the Roman fun-loving spirit, but fun is fun, right? Speaking of fun, I got another one of those envelopes with money in it! This time, the note said, "You must promise to use this money on yourself. Have fun!" What do you make of these letters and this money? Another five American dollars! (I kept half and sent half to my mother.)

So great to hear from you, my friend. I miss being together very much, but I'm happy you're happy. I love you, pal!

Love, Marcello

6 Oct 58
Dear Marcello:

I just got your letter from 21 Sep. It is GREAT to hear from you! I would love to be bouncing around Washington, D.C. with you, seeing those monuments, and seeing what America looks like. And American girls! I was telling my friends about your ROTC scholarship and they all think it's terrific. I can picture you in the military leading the way with that quiet strength of yours, a strength that everyone somehow knows not to test!

Hey, I owe your mother a big thank you! I'm a hit with some of the girls because I know all those dances she taught us. I'm still not the most graceful guy, but at least I know the steps and movements, right? Especially Swing! It was always so much fun to have your mother teach us all those dances, now I am putting all the lessons to good use.

I can't imagine how it feels to be in America, one of these years you will have to show me around. I'm sure you will do well in school. Just a few months ago we were looking up at the stars at Villa Borghese; now, you are in college— in America! That's amazing, pal. It's really impressive that you're taking a class in a foreign language. I gotta say, I really admire your courage and I know you can do it, Marcello. I know you can. I have always admired how you just plug along and do whatever you have to do. No fuss, no complaints, you just quietly trudge ahead— like the steam rollers I see here paving roads.

Hey, that's pretty interesting about the money you received. I forgot to tell you, I've been getting the same envelopes, too! Guess we should just count our lucky stars and spend it! I'll write real soon. Thinking about you! Till next time. I love you, pal!

Love, Chiano

9 Oct 58
Dear Chiano:

I just got the news that Pope Pius died. I am surprised that I feel sad. I seem to be breathing in sorrow, and breathing out anger, or breathing in anger and breathing out sorrow, I'm not sure which. I am trying very hard to be open-minded and fair but in the end, my anger seems to be winning out. Honestly, I view him as a coward. I don't see how some people make him out to be a saint. I see him more as a traitor *than a countryman born in our very own Rome. I see him more as Hitler's pawn than the Catholic leader. Because of the time difference, you probably got this news long before me. I was in the hallway of my dorm, headed for the dining hall when the announcement came over the loudspeaker. I will probably hear that announcement for the rest of my life: "Pope Pius XII was pronounced dead at 3:52 this morning at Casto Gandolfo, the Papal Summer Residence." First, I felt absolutely nothing, Iano. Nothing. Then anger kicked in, then, I felt a little bit of sadness.*

What do you think of the pope? I know as a Jewish kid you likely don't think of him at all but living in Rome in the time that we did, he was a central figure— spiritually and politically. Now, attending Catholic University, a papal university, he's still thought about and talked about a lot, whether I am breathing anger or sorrow. Maybe he was a mix of both, anger and sorrow, good and bad, coward and hero, Hitler's puppet and Judaic savior and monster, all at the same time. Is that possible? It's like swallowing a bite of what appears to be a delicious fish and choking on the bone. I feel kind of empty, Iano. Really empty.

Had to get that off my chest and you are the person I feel most comfortable with when it comes to getting things off my chest. Hope I didn't drag you down. By the time you get this letter, the puppet will be buried— but the coward will live on, and never be forgotten. We will likely never know the truth behind Pope Pius XII's papacy, but we do know his actions; he chose silence when the world needed him to scream. Neutrality when we needed commitment, indifference when we needed conviction. I'm struggling between condemning his actions and judging his character, and I'm finding that the dividing line is as clear as a sunset in the rain. (Part of this letter comes from a paper I wrote for my 'Exploring Spiritual Metaphors' class. Hope I didn't get carried away.)

On the bright side, I got another envelope with another five dollars in it. It came at the perfect time. I used part of the money I saved for a sweater, (the first sweater I ever bought!) and part to go to a movie named 'Damn Yankees.' It was a terrific adoption of a Broadway play. (They say that the best theaters in the world are in London and on Broadway (New York). It's a musical about a guy who sells his soul to the devil in order for his favorite baseball team (the Washington Senators) to beat the New York Yankees, the most successful team in sports here in America. Kind of like Pope Pius XII selling his soul to Hitler to preserve Fascism, right? (Baseball is a HUGE, HUGE, HUGE thing here. They call it "the National Pastime.") Love you, pal.

Love, Marcello

11 Oct 58
Dear Marcello:

Wow, I want to go to the Smithsonian! Sounds amazing. What's interesting is that the whole world seems to be included, not just Rome like we're accustomed to. We tend to be very "myopic" in Rome. I just had a lecture in a Philosophy class on the subject of "Myopia," so that word and concept is at the top of my mind. The lecture was sort of a warning about the dangers of myopic thinking as it automatically limits your thinking and worse than that, it limits your thinking to just yourself, like babies and greedy people. I am going to look up the Smithsonian when I go to the library tonight. I have been spending more time there than the beach lately. Better reference section, lousy view!

I'm glad you have a good roommate. My roommate is a decent guy, but kind of, shall we say, "myopic?" But he's ok, and I'm making some good friends through my classes. I'm out and about all the time. It's fun to walk around Tel Aviv. It's such a buzzing, modern city. Classes are getting into the real nitty gritty and I am finding I really have to stay on top of things, especially the reading, or I will be in deep trouble, fast.

Hey, guess what? I have a date this weekend with a girl I met in my Math class. Well not a real date, we're gonna study together. That counts as a date, right? Or do I have to take her somewhere real for it to count? Glad you're doing well in America. I love you, pal, and I miss ya!

Love, Chiano

15 Oct 58
Dear Chiano:

I love getting your letters, pal! Absolutely love them. I am feeling like you do; one minute I feel confident and grown up and the next minute I am asking myself, "What am I doing in America? In college!" It is an amazing feeling to be so free yet knowing you have to be self-reliant, as you say … doing laundry, being on time, having work done on time. I had some good advice from one of my professors the other day: he said, kind of off-the-cuff, as they say here, "If there is one thing you take away from this class, practice initiative." It really stuck with me and I keep it at the top of my mind all the time now, to be progressive and take the initiative in everything I do.

Really good advice.

The modern campus sounds very different. I am more of a fan of traditional things, but I'd love to see those buildings. I went to a few football games here and had a blast. The players are huge guys and bash each other like crazy. They pass the ball, run with it, kick it, and block and tackle each other, it's all very exciting. I find myself smiling the whole game even though I really don't know what's going on, but I find it to be a lot of fun and it seems like the whole school turns out for the games. It's a great atmosphere and some of my friends and I have milkshakes after the game. And hamburgers! Americans love hamburgers. I like them with melted cheese on them. Really good! They serve it with french fries. They're really good, too. They have ice cream instead of gelato here. It's not as tasty, kind of sweet but still good, especially in a milk-shake, that's ice cream with milk and some flavored syrup such as chocolate, and it's all mixed together in a blender. They're really good— like our Frappès.

Anyway, I would love to visit you at TAU one day and would love for you to come here. I know Alex would like you, and I would like you to meet him, and my other friends. Still no clear answers on my ROTC obligation but whatever it is, I'm game; if it wasn't for Father Finlay and the ROTC pro-gram, I would be dusting pews and snuffing candles in Trastevere!

I keep getting those envelopes with five American dollars! Any idea who would be sending them?

Love, Marcello

###

21 Oct. 58
Dear Uncle Salvestro:

I hope you're well. I sure miss you. I have been enjoying some terrific TV shows in America. Many of them make me think of you, so fondly. Some of my favorites are Leave it to Beaver, Father Knows Best, I Love Lucy, The Danny Thomas Show, and The Jack Benny Program. And believe it or not, Superman. I love Superman.

I have to say, it's a little bittersweet for me. The bitterness is that many of these shows have these wonderful father figures, and they make me sad. I missed my dad terribly my entire life. But the sweet part of these shows for me is that they make me think of you, Uncle S. I am so grateful, lucky, and happy that you stepped in and you were every bit my father. I love you so very much, and I look up to you with the deepest admiration and respect. I could not have asked for a better father than you have been to me, Uncle S., and I wanted to make sure to tell you how much I love you and how deeply I thank you every single day. I guess there is in fact a real Superman. You! And Father does know best— Father Frischetti!

I love you very much, and I thank you with every fiber of my soul.

Love, Marcello

24 Oct. 58
Dear Marcello:

Your passionate letter about Pius' death was very moving. I can only react to what I saw, what I know. And I see him more as a coward than a hero, like you do. Hitler might not have listened to pleas for mercy on behalf of Jews, in fact, he might have even punished or killed Pope Pius, we will never know. Pius might have helped a lot of Jews escape, but like I said, I only know what I know, and what I saw, and what I saw was nothing. He hid behind the fa-cade of diplomacy, but I think it was a smokescreen to shield the truth: I think he hated Jews. He might not have supported Hitler in total, or openly, who could? But his silence was a very loud statement for his lack of support for Jews. What a paradox (another new word for me to explore). Jews, as individuals, try desperately to forget the horrors of the Holocaust, yet we're taught that we should never let the world forget. Contradiction is such a Jewish thing! It fuels our love of a good argument. Ha! Christ was a Jew, even a rabbi, wasn't he?

Well, I had my "date," studying and several more since. Her name is Batia. She's very cute. She's small with pretty, brown eyes and shiny, black, wavy hair. She always dresses up without dressing up. Always looks great. She wears great lipstick and has a great smile. We have been studying together a lot and I can feel a good tingling feeling inside when I'm with her and when I think about her. She's from Haifa, a city about ninety-five kilometers north of Tel Aviv. We are going to a dance club together next week. I hav-en't told her that your mom taught us so many great dances so I am hoping to knock her off her feet with surprise when I break out all my steps; thanks again to your mom!

The books are staring at me, my friend, so I bet-ter open them up. They remind me of another "par-adox:" the more I learn, the more I realize I don't know! Just like Uncle Jewels said. Hope one day to be smart enough to be smart enough. I still don't have any idea what that means. I love you, pal.

Love, Chiano

###

15 Nov 58

Dear Chiano:

I would classify the studying together as a practice date, but the dance, the dance, my friend, is an official date! Bravo! I hope it turns out to be all you hope for. Batia sounds terrific. I like your two new words, "myopic," and "paradox." Good ideas to consider. I have an idea for you to think about. It's from my 'Exploring Spiritual Metaphors' class: "Prophet or Prophesizer?" It's kind of a call to action and a means of distinguishing between someone who is a doer or someone who just talks a good game, a dilatant as my Uncle Salvestro would say, or a bullshitter as Uncle Jewels would say. Boy do I miss those two.

We have a long weekend break for the American holiday called Thanksgiving at the end of the month. All the American students are very excited about it. They get to go home and apparently have a belly-gorging feast as a means of expressing gratitude. Seems kind of funny to me to express your gratitude in a grand act of gluttony but as I have discovered, Americans seem to be obsessed with excess. The only means of identifying "enough" is "more." It's kind of funny and disappointing at the same time. But at any rate it gives me some down time and the OFSA (Office of Foreign Student Affairs) is offering foreign students a "Taste of America" that day, so we will get to experience an American Thanksgiving turkey dinner. I'm game. (No pun intended!)

All this holiday talk has me a little homesick to be honest because it will be the first Christmas that I will not be home. The airfare is just too much. The OFSA will probably rub its salve on the wounds of those of us left behind at Christmas. Hey, pal, I have big news: A guy named Harry Winston, a jeweler– like

Uncle Jewels— donated the famous Hope Diamond to the Smithsonian! It's the largest-known rare, dark-greyish-blue-colored diamond in the world. Wait'll you hear this: he shipped it in a plain brown package by registered mail— he insured it for a million dollars! A million dollars! I'm hoping that I can get to see it over this Thanksgiving break. I saw pictures of it and it looks amazing. A million-dollar diamond! Being in Uncle Jewels store has given me a real appreciation for how beautiful jewelry is, especially diamonds!

There is a game called "bowling" here. They set up these wooden things shaped like big bottles, that they call pins for some reason, and you roll a heavy black ball at them to try to knock them down from about twenty meters away. Whoever knocks down the most pins, wins. Tonight, Alex and a few guys and I are going to play bowling in a place they call bowling alleys. Thank God for those five-dollar envelopes! Hope I win. I love you, pal!

Love, Marcello

15 Nov 58
Dear Chiano:

You are not going to believe this! You know that person who has been sending me money! Oh my God, guess what he sent? (I assume it's a man.) He sent me an airline certificate to come home for Christmas! I'm coming home for Christmas, pal! Your winter break should coincide so we should be able to see each other! Can you believe that! I hope I can see you! I love you, pal. I'm coming home for Christmas!

Love, Marcello

CHAPTER 12

Home Sweet Rome

Home. Sweet Rome. It was a journey to say the least, but Marcello eventually lugged the tattered suitcase his Uncle Salvestro lent him up the stairs to the flat he grew up in, on the second floor overlooking a small piazza. Everything seemed a little smaller to Marcello, everything but his dreams and his gratitude for being home. Who on earth sent him the generous gift of an airline certificate and the envelopes with five American dollars like clockwork every month? The scent of earthy stone and solid wood in his building eased his mind and tempered the tiring demands of travel. The scent of delicious meals permeated from every door and every window surrounding the piazza. Vapors of delectable culinary secrets perfected and preserved over the ages filled his soul with warmth, and his belly with hunger. Bread baking. Sauces simmering. Stews braising and stewing. The click of windows being shut, as others squealed open. The cluck, cluck, cluck of a donkey pulling a wobbly-wheeled produce cart over the cobblestones echoed off the buildings forming the piazza. The sun kissed the red clay rooftops of Rome and stirred their warm, orangey-copper radiance into a colorful glow. He climbed the stairs he and Chiano had climbed almost every day of their lives. Like everything else, they, too, seemed smaller. Marcello opened the door. He was home.

"Marcello! Oh my God, Marcello! Look at you. So tall and handsome," Giuliana beamed. "Mama! Mama, I'm so happy to see you," he said as he hugged his mother dearly. "And Mia ... how about you ... Mama– Mia! The two most beautiful women on the earth! I am so happy to see you," Marcello said, spilling a tear of happiness and a tear of warmth as he hugged his mother and his sister.

"Let me look at my boy. Oh, I'm so happy you're here, Cello," Giuliana said.

"You look a little older. I like it," Mia added. "Come give me another big hug, my big college man brother" Mia opened her arms to welcome Marcello again.

"My God, look at you, Mia. You look like a woman! A beautiful, young woman. The wolves will be howling in the piazza. Mia! Mia! Mia!" he howled. "I am so happy to be home, Mama, so happy."

"So are we, Marcello. Come, sit."

"When do I get to see Uncle Salvestro?"

"I'm surprised he is not here already, he– "

"Do I see a college boy's luggage in the hallway?" Uncle Salvestro sang out while climbing the stairs. "Is this Marcello's luggage, I see?" He sprang the door open with his smile wider than the opening of the door, his eyes brighter than the Roman sun. He and Marcello hugged in a deep embrace.

"Marcello," was the only word Uncle Salvestro could manage.

"Uncle," he whispered as they held their embrace out of affection, and to hide the tears rolling down each of their cheeks.

"Let me see this college man. Look at you, you look like you should be on the cover of the Catholic University brochure," Uncle Salvestro suggested. "You must tell us all about America, the college, Washington, D. C. Everything." They all instinctively pulled up chairs around the small table and Giuliana instinctively served espresso and homemade biscotti and began preparing breakfast.

"It's amazing Uncle Sal, it's so impressive in so many ways. The monuments leave you in awe," he said. "The size, the scale, and the power they evoke … It's unbelievable. My English has gotten a lot better, but I have a long way to go. I got a job at the Smithsonian Museum. Twice a week, I take tickets and give visitors directions. It's only four hours twice a week but I spend much of the time there studying, and the best part is that I get free admission to the museums, which are absolutely amazing."

"Sounds fantastic. What about your classes, and the professors?"

"I love my classes, especially one, called *Exploring Spiritual Metaphors.*"

"What's the campus like?" Mia asked.

"Beautiful. It's big– expansive. It's right in the middle of Washington, D.C. The cathedral is beautiful, lots of marble, gorgeous stained glass, Uncle Sal. It's a different kind of beautiful than we know here, newer, but still beautiful. It's really magnificent. The campus has a lot of open area where you can study outside when it's warm out, or just hang out there." He sipped his espresso, nodding a 'thank you' to his mother. "It's relaxing and energizing at the same time. And oh, man, you should see the football games! People go nuts for football. It's American football, not like football we play here. It's so much fun to go to the games with my friends."

"And how are the Americans?" Giuliana asked, while scrambling a bowl full of eggs and eyeballing several links of sausage that were just beginning to sizzle and pop in a deep cast iron skillet. The scent of those sausages began permeating through the kitchen, making Marcello all-the-more grateful to be home.

"They're interesting, Mama. Most are very nice to me and nice in general. Some are resentful of Italians … hard feelings over the war, I guess. They're kind of casual … They love music and dancing, Mama. They would love you … and you, Mia … the boys would love you. Mama Mia!" Mia raised her dark eyebrows and flashed her brother an alluring smile. At sixteen now, she looked more like a young woman than the little girl Marcello remembered her being just months ago. She was growing nicely into the physique of a blessed woman, so much so that Marcello had to continually double check his double takes, looking at her part in admiration, part in disbelief, and part disappointed that she had grown so quickly, yet grateful and proud of how she was blossoming. "I have to say, the Americans don't treat the negro people very nicely, which is very bothersome to me. It's sad."

"I've heard that before. Very sad. A shame. So terrible for people to be mean to each other after what this world's been through. You think we'd want to be united. What about the food? Are you getting enough to eat, is it good food?" Giuliana asked, expecting a compliment in Marcello's answer.

"Not bad, actually. But it's a far cry from your cooking, Mama. A far cry." She smiled, assured, and satisfied.

"Give us your top of the head impression of being in college in

America," Uncle Salvestro said.

"Terrific, Uncle Sal, it really is. I feel like I'm on top of the world, but still looking up. I'm energized and overwhelmed a bit, but mostly, it's really, really exciting and inspiring. But it's so great to be back here with all of you. I missed you all terribly." They all instinctively rose and embraced each other in a heartfelt and lasting family hug.

"Welcome home, Marcello," Giuliana mouthed silently with her eyes fixed on a picture of her family hanging on the wall behind Marcello, a picture capturing their happiness when all five of them were together, when all five of them were alive.

Marcello had a four-week break before having to return to America and college. He knew very well, even at this young age, that time has a way of slipping away unnoticed, unchecked. Chiano was not home yet so Marcello naturally spent most of his time with Uncle Salvestro in the church. Shortly after breakfast, he and Uncle Salvestro went down to the piazza to catch up with each other.

"I am so grateful for you introducing me to Father Finlay, Uncle Sal. He's done an amazing thing for me," Marcello said as he and Uncle Salvestro sat on the edge of a fountain in the piazza. "And I can't thank you enough for teaching me English. My God, I'd die without it."

"Father Finlay's a great guy. I remember the day we met at the seminary. I was peddling a rickety old bike between our library and our chapel. Father Finlay was walking toward me and just as I moved off the walkway to let him have plenty of room to pass, the chain on the bike popped off the sprocket. My immediate reaction was to curse. I felt ashamed the moment I said the curse word, I was embarrassed. I knew he heard me. I got off the bike and said, 'I'm sorry.' He reached out to shake my hand. He said, 'I'm sure at one point or another, Jesus had a sandal strap break, and I'd bet he said the same thing you did. Wouldn't that be something to hear? I'm Frank Finlay. Come on, I'm friends with one of the custodians who can fix anything but a bad attitude. He'll have you back on the road in a snap.' From that moment on, we have been the closest of friends. We've stayed in touch all these years. I miss being around him every day. Do you see him much?"

"I do, I see him a few times a week. He checks in on me, and I check in on him."

"Good. Be good to the good and you'll never know the bad, right?"

"I guess."

"How's the ROTC program working out?"

"Honestly, I don't know, Uncle Sal. Father Finlay keeps telling me not to worry about it."

"Most times, when someone tells me not to worry, I worry twice as much, but if Father Finlay said not to worry, you can take that to the bank," Uncle Salvestro said.

"Uncle Sal … someone has been sending me money. Five American dollars every month. I have no idea who, but the postage marks are from Rome. And the same person sent me the airline voucher to come home. Any idea who it is?"

"No. They send a note with the money?"

"The notes just say

"Enjoy yourself.'"

Uncle Salvestro bobbed his head gently and pursed his lips while considering possibilities for a moment and came to a quick conclusion.

"I would take that advice. Thank God for the blessings and enjoy yourself."

"That's what I'm thinking but I would sure like to thank whoever's sending it– and someday, pay them back." Uncle Salvestro winked and said,

"Enjoy yourself. You are only eighteen for 365 days of your life. Enjoy every one of them. Then do the same thing for the next 365 days, and do that forever. Have fun, Cello. Have fun."

One guarantee for having fun was to visit Uncle Jewels. Marcello thought that maybe he could even earn some money while home for the holiday, or at least, lend Uncle Jewels a hand at Pratto Gioiellieri. Uncle Jewels was displaying one-of-a-kind watches in his window when Marcello's shadow cast over the display. He stood between the sun and Uncle Jewels' window smiling, watching as Uncle Jewels' pudgy hands carefully, even artfully, positioned the watches on the other side of the glass. The moment Uncle Jewels looked up and saw that the shadow dulling the sparkle on his watches was cast by Marcello, his eyes beamed, and a smile raced across his face. Marcello could see Uncle Jewels mouth out his name as he smiled wider and opened the door to the store, and the arms to his heart. The happy little bell on the door jingled and Uncle Jewels looked up with joy.

"Marcello, Marcello, Marcello. Come in, come in. How exciting to see you." He hugged Marcello with robust vigor and affection. "I am so happy to see you, come in, come in, boy … sit … we will talk and laugh. Soon, Chiano will be home, too, and we will be *rascaling* together, yes?"

"So good to see you, Uncle Jewels. I missed you."

"Missing each other is over now, yes?" Ever enthused about his jewelry, Uncle Jewels said. "This is a wonderful omen that you arrived home as I am introducing these new pieces today. Look here what I have to show you." Uncle Jewels lifted a very unique necklace off of his chest. The design featured a highly polished, hand-fashioned silver rectangle, about two inches high and an inch wide. It's rough, uneven edges were feathered into soft, tiny scroll-shapes. There was a gold Star of David embedded seamlessly into the silver rectangle. It was a beautiful finish of a beautiful design.

"Look, the Star of David– the reminder to be the living star of David, the reminder to live as a Jew. This is a very simple but very busy symbol, Marcello," he said, holding the pendant closer to Marcello's eyes. "These seven empty spaces inside the star represent seven building blocks that God used to create the world." He pointed out each of the seven empty areas created within the two intersecting triangles that comprise the Star of David as he spoke. "It's so good to see you," he said, interrupting himself, and pinching Marcello's cheek. "So, let me explain. Each of the empty spaces inside the star symbolize a value," he said, pointing to the areas on the medallion. "Kindness, severity, harmony, perseverance, splendor, foundation, and loyalty." He paused to enable Marcello to absorb what he had said before continuing. "And the two triangles themselves symbolize the connection between the inner connection and the external connection." Marcello was enjoying seeing Uncle Jewels being the ever-enthused Uncle Jewels. "Some say the upward pointing triangle symbolizes the good works we do that arrive at God's door. And the downward pointing triangle represents the blessings God has bestowed upon us. But this all depends upon which Jew you ask," Uncle Jewels claimed from behind his robust, patent laugh. "Some say it stands for heroism, some say martyrdom, some say whatever makes them feel good, and smart, and important," Uncle Jewels concluded. "Why triangles? The three points symbolize the connection between three important cornerstones in the Jewish faith: God, The Torah, and Israel." He held the distinctive necklace closer for Marcello to inspect. "There's even more going on in this not so simple Star of David, but enough for now. I have another one to show you, it's for Catholic customers." He took an identical necklace from the display case but this one was finished with a gold crucifix embedded into it instead of the Star of David.

"This will be more up your alley, I think," he said, again, accompanied by his Uncle Jewels chuckle. "The Crucifix! The symbol embraced by all Catholics, yes? You can teach me all about this symbol someday." Holding the Star of David pendant, Uncle Jewels said, "On this one, we have the Torah, the first five books of The Old Testament; it tells how to live through the words ..." Holding up the Crucifix pendant in his other hand, he continued, "And on this one, we have The New Testament, which shows you how to live through the example Jesus Christ set." He handed the pendant to Marcello to inspect. "I embrace both these beautiful faiths– and their beautiful customers. It's good for business," he said with a grin. I show one to the Jews, the other one to the Catholics. See, we can pick our faith, so there's something we can control, even in this miserable economy we find ourselves in, right? But you know what, as long as we are not starving, and we have freedom, and we're safe, and we have good shelter, we are very rich."

"You're a prince, Uncle Jewels. I love the pendants. They're beautiful, and I love their symbolism," Marcello said, admiring the medallion closer. "Look, I have something to show you, too." He handed the pendant back to Uncle Jewels and took a brochure from his pocket and handed it to Uncle Jewels.

"Ohhhh ... the Hope Diamond ... at the Smithsonian Institute ... in Washington, D.C. Did you see this beautiful creation, Cello?"

"I did. A few times. It's amazing. It made me think of you."

"Which made you think of me, the 'amazing' part, or the 'beauty' part of the diamond," Uncle Jewels joked. "What a treat to see such a marvel. It is over 400 years old, Marcello," he said while browsing the smooth, shiny brochure with a large picture of the Hope Diamond on its cover. The Hope family was one of the wealthiest in England. "The Diamond comes with a dark history as I am sure you know, since you have been to such a prestigious museum to see it," Uncle Jewels said. "Do you know what the most valuable aspect of this diamond is? Of course, you don't know because I haven't told you yet," he said, wrapping his words in the comforter of his chuckle. "A powerful and valuable aspect of this diamond is in its beauty, of course– but beauty as you know is only on the surface. What is most valuable about it is the power of its name: Hope. Hope has more strength, beauty, and longevity than even the strongest, most beautiful, oldest diamond on earth," Uncle Jewels professed. "How fortunate; you come in here and show me a brochure and I turn it into a life lesson," he said, again, speaking through the window of his chuckle. "I am not a wise man, but I aspire to be, so, I try to imagine what a wise man would say in any situation. Sometimes it gets me into trouble … and sometimes it gets me out … most of the time, it helps me sell jewelry to the clandestine wealthy in Rome," he said, and followed with a belly laugh. Tapping gingerly on a display case gleaming with diamond rings and necklaces under concealed showcase lights, he continued.

"I will tell you an example. The other day a man and a woman were standing right where you are admiring a necklace, similar to this one," he said, pointing to a stunning emerald-cut diamond. The stone was mounted in silver and shaped into a net-like weave pattern that was covered by a blanket of tiny diamonds. "The couple hesitated, protecting the Lira in their pockets like a cork protects its wine. So, *what would a wise man say at this moment of truth?* I asked myself … better yet, what would a wise man do?"

"And what did the wise man named Uncle Jewels do?" Marcello asked.

"I took a wad of Lira out of my pocket and said, 'Look, what good is this dirty wad of paper with blotches of ink stuffed in my pocket?' Then I walked behind the woman and held the necklace over her neck and I asked them, 'What is more valuable and beautiful, a wad of dirty money stuffed in your pocket, or this beautiful masterpiece adorning this beautiful woman's neck?' I clipped the necklace closed on her neck and it looked stunning– she looked stunning. Then, the little wise man who lives up there in Uncle Jewels' head whispered in my ear, *'Now it is time to keep your mouth shut, Lorenzo.'* So, I shut my mouth."

"And did they buy it?"

"What do you think? Of course, they bought it," he said, this time his chuckle had evolved to a full throat laugh. "Tell me now, I can see from the look in your eyes, you are not interested in pendants and my tales of selling necklaces to wealthy cheapskates. Something is on your mind; what is it?" After an uncomfortable silence Marcello answered.

"I don't know when I can pay you back," Marcello said.

"Pay me back? For what? You owe me nothing."

"The airline tickets and the money you've been sending me ... at college. The five– "

"What airline ticket? Money? I have less than the cloudiest notion of what you are talking about. Explain to me." Uncle Jewels said.

"Someone– and I think it's you– has been sending me five American dollars every month, and the same person sent me an airline voucher so I can come home for Christmas. I think you are that someone."

"Bags of money! Airline tickets! If I had bags of money to toss around and airline tickets to pass out like advertising flyers, I would close the shop and sleep all day," Uncle Jewels proclaimed. "Did you happen to bring me a sack of five American dollar bills by chance?" he asked, laughing again.

"I'm smart enough to be smart enough to be very, very grateful."

"You know, I might be a Jewel, but you, Marcello, are a gem."

Marcello hugged Uncle Jewels and left Pratto Gioiellieri lighter, happier, but still uncertain where the money and airline ticket came from, but one thing he was certain of: he was very happy to have seen Uncle Jewels. He headed home lighthearted and happy knowing Chiano would be visiting him soon.

Back home, Marcello paced back and forth before his kitchen window hoping to speed up Chiano's arrival. Then he heard footsteps, happy footsteps running up the stairs.

"Chiano!" Marcello ran to the door. "Chiano!"

"Cello!" Chiano yelled as Marcello opened the door and met his best friend with a hardy hug. They hugged and pushed each other away to survey one another. It wasn't long ago while lying on the grass under the stars at Villa Borghese that they wondered what their lives were to become. They hugged again, pushing their wondering to the back of their minds.

"You look great! I'm so happy to see you, and you, my second mother. So good to see you, Mrs. Luciari," Chiano said, moving to hug Giuliana. "Oh my God, look at you, Mia, a movie star in the making!" They settled into the kitchen where they had spent so much of their youth, and instinctively took their usual seats at the worn wooden table in their worn wooden chairs with worn thin cushions on the seats. The familiar scrape of the legs of the chairs pulled across the aged tile floor brought the two friends right back to Home Sweet Rome.

"We're talking but as I look at you, I can't help but be distracted at how happy I am to be back together with you," Marcello said. "We have so much to catch up on. Let's take a walk and get caught up," he suggested. They both kissed Giuliana and Mia goodbye and hopped down the stairs into the Roman bliss, with their arms on each other's shoulders. They instinctively meandered into the web of tiny alleys surrounding the piazza they had grown up in.

"So, my friend, let's hear it," Chiano said.

"Where do I start? God, it's good to see you."

"You, too, pal. Feels great."

"I gotta tell you, college life is absolutely great. It's a big adjustment but it's really fun. It feels like the world got a lot bigger, and I feel like I'm more a part of it. We're exposed to these great professors, and all these great ideas. I'm really lit on fire, Iano. I really am."

"Same here. I'm loving being in a big city, a young city, and it's really comfortable to be among all Jews. It feels safe and free and really comfortable. I like my classes and professors … and then there's Batia." Chiano's voice softened when he mentioned her name. He reached into the back pocket of his pants and pulled out his wallet with humble pride.

"She gave me a picture of her," Chiano said, handing the photo of Batia over to Marcello with gentle care. Marcello took the photo gently into his hands and studied it. A smile creased his face and his eyes drifted from the picture to Chiano.

"She's pretty great, Iano. I love her smile, and those soft eyes … kind of bold, but soft in a really pretty way. She looks like she's comfortable to be with."

"She is, Cel. She's really great. Smart, funny, and she's really affectionate. I had to tell you, she makes me feel amazing about myself. I feel like I have a purpose and value when I'm around her. She gives me that smile every time I see her and she's getting more and more, well, let's just leave it at that." Chiano was silent for a few moments as they passed by the familiar shops nodding and waving to familiar shopkeepers as they passed by tiny storefronts. Then Chiano stopped suddenly and turned to Marcello and took hold of his arms. He looked deep into Marcello's eyes.

"Cel, we have been doing things … things a guy does with a girl."

"Wow. That's big. What things? You don't have to tell me."

"No, no, it's alright. I have been dying to talk to you about this for weeks, I just couldn't do it in a letter," Chiano said, then they started walking again, slowly. "We started with these innocent little touches that we both believed were unintentional. You know, you brush hands or hold hands and her hand would brush my leg or mine would brush her leg. Or I would have my arm around her shoulder, and her arm around mine, and we'd let them fall, and one of us would brush the top of the other one's butt, and not say a word, but we'd file the reaction or non-reaction into memory. Or we would be in a line for ice cream or something, and we'd press against one another and hold ourselves there, kind of signaling that we both knew it– and liked it, but we were both afraid to say any-thing because if we called attention to it but we were reading it wrong, it would be really embarrassing, and could ruin everything. And we'd feel really stupid. At least that's how I look at it. Know what I mean?"

"I think so."

"Well, those little touches got to be more frequent, and more lasting, and more intense without really being intense. It escalates, you know? We both knew exactly what was going on," Chiano said, feeling relieved by getting this off his chest and his mind, and his heart.

"That all sounds pretty good."

"I'm telling you, it's great. She makes me feel like I never felt before," he said as he rounded a corner without looking at anything but the cob-blestones before his feet. "So, it gets better. We finally kissed one night on the way home from the beach. We were at a corner waiting to cross, and we happened to look at one another, and I'm telling you, Cel, the world stopped. Her eyes were like a view into the world as it's supposed to be. She had a serious look on her face, and she looked me more directly into my eyes than anyone ever has in my entire life, and I swear, I was about to fall. I felt like my knees turned to pudding. I instinctively looked back at her and without thinking a thought, but feeling everything I ever wanted. I kissed her, Cel, and she kissed me, and inside, I swear, my body quivered like an eel. I was never more alive than I was at that moment. The world seemed to shrink into the bubble we were in. It was life chang-ing, Cel. I swear to God, it was life changing."

"Wow. I don't know what to say … except, lucky you," Marcello offered.

"Well, there's more," Chiano said, twitching in a moment of discomfort. "That night, we went back to her dorm and her roommate was out with her friends at a play or something. So, I told her how that kiss made me feel, and she said pretty much the same thing. And we kissed again, a lot, and for a long time. I was afraid it could be a little awkward because I hadn't had much practice– well, no practice, and here I was in sort of the championship game of kissing … at least for me. So, the more we kissed, the more we got lost in it."

"Wow. I guess my story about the Hope Diamond isn't going to exactly light your fire," Marcello said.

"Cel, I know you are thinking about becoming a priest. But I have to tell you, before you commit to anything permanent, you have to … you absolutely have to give some thought to girls. You have to," Chiano commanded. Locked in like time on a watch, Marcello put his arm around Chiano's shoulder and Chiano put his arm around Marcello's.

The Christmas break streaked through time like pages of an open book blown by the wind. It was time for Marcello to return to America, and for Chiano to return to Tel Aviv– and Batia. As he was packing his uncle's borrowed suitcase to head back to America, Giuliana knocked on the door and entered the oversize closet that passed for Marcello's bedroom. She was holding a small parcel.

"Marcello, this package came for you today, the postino personally brought it upstairs for you." She handed him a small, rectangular shaped package wrapped neatly in plain brown paper, like a custom-made paper bag tied with coarse twine.

"I never got a package before," he said, looking to Giuliana in amusement. He examined it with his hands and eyes. There was no label, just Marcello's address written neatly on the paper. He loosened the twine and unwrapped the paper with a curious admiration. There was a small box inside, and a note, which fell onto his bed. He opened the note and read it to his mother.

> *"Dear Marcello:*
> *I remember you admiring this pen when you were visiting*
> *Schools. I also remember you being a very bright and polite*
> *young man. I understand you are now studying in Amer-*
> *ica, and considering the priesthood. I congratulate you,*

Marcello. I want you to have the pen you admired. As you might recall, it was given to me by my father when I was ordained. I hope that you will use it to write something warm every day, and something important, one day. Best of luck, and God bless you.

Yours in Christ,
Monsignor Buongiorici"

Marcello was in awe at the gesture. He opened the box and found the stout, chrome-plated pen he so admired at the trout farm nestled in black cloth. He looked to his mother, his eyes saturated in thanks. He whispered:

"I will write something warm every day and something important one day, Monsignor. I will."

CHAPTER 13

Buttons

Marcello became an admirer of American President Dwight D. Eisenhower– aka: Ike. He was fond of reading Ike's quotations and speeches, respected his character, his demeanor, and his leadership by example. He was moved by Ike's allegiance to being an American and America's president who was reelected as a reward for doing a good job, and a plea to be led. Marcello admired Ike's commitment to the task at hand for the good of all, as opposed to focusing on an agenda of a greedy few. He read a sense of honor in Ike's persona, an honor that reminded him of his beloved Uncle Salvestro. Ike aroused optimism in America through a humble heroic military leadership rooted in integrity and defined by service. President Eisenhower warned sternly to steer clear of greed's allure which sucked men's moral integrity into an ocean of deceit like a rip tide pulling unsuspecting swimmers into a helpless trap. Day-by-day, Marcello was falling in love with 1959 America.

Visiting the monuments that define Washington, D.C. became one of Marcello's most inspiring pastimes. His favorite monument was whichever one he was visiting at-the-moment, but the Lincoln Memorial drew him back more often than others, and with more veneration. Marcello described his visits to the monuments in letters to Chiano as a *passive vigor*: he depended on the monuments themselves to do all the work in his homage to inspiration. He loved the Lincoln Memorial for its stunning portrait of Lincoln precisely etched into marble in a remarkably accurate reflection of the great man. Marcello viewed the Lincoln Memorial as an inspirational testimony to his larger-than-life metaphorical stature. And he was very proud of the statue having been carved by the Piccirilli brothers, Italians from New York. Sculpted from Georgia White Marble, the Lincoln Memorial sits– rather than stands– nineteen feet high. It is surrounded by thirty-six columns made of Colorado marble, one to represent each state in the Union at the time of Lincoln's death in 1865; each column stands at an imposing and impressive forty-four feet high. The Lincoln Memorial impressed Marcello with its raw size and inspired him by celebrating Lincoln's staunch valor and unyielding leadership, despite the vigorous head winds of opposition's force. Marcello most enjoyed facing the statue of Lincoln from many different angles and distances to try to gain a deeper insight and understanding into the hero before his eyes. He often imagined Lincoln's voice reading the crisp and inspiring language of his Gettysburg Address. Marcello was unknowingly beginning to think of himself as a leader that aspired to be a priest and a priest that aspired to be a leader.

Classes were inspiring, too, sometimes from surprising origins. One day, in particular, in a class called *Christian Moral Life*, a professor ignited a passionate reaction from Marcello that he, his professor, and his classmates would never forget. Father Frederic Hofer was an Austrian priest with a doctorate in Canon Law, a Masters in Philosophy, and a PhD in arrogance. The discussion that riled Marcello into an aggressive frenzy stemmed from a lecture on 'Right and Wrong.' Father Hofer unknowingly chose a topic close to Marcello's heart to illustrate his point.

The classroom was on the second floor of Catholic University's majestic and revered Divinity Hall. Classes in the School of Canon Law, and the School of Theology and Religious Studies were also held in Divinity Hall. So was The Office of the Dean of Students, Father Frank Finlay, in his new assignment. The classroom Marcello sat in this late January morning fused seamlessly with the building's exterior splendor. Thin panels of walnut stained wainscoting capped with "L"-shaped molding four feet from the floor met a blanket of crisp white paint. Faint traces of the paint's odor wafted from grates covering the long coil of radiator tucked under the windows. The oversize windows were half shaded by Venetian blinds. The original incandescent globe lights that were installed in 1888 highlighted the chalk dust which tickled students' noses into the fringes of sneezing. The pungent scent of stubborn residue from varnish applied over the wainscoting during winter break emphasized the grain in the wood trim surrounding the windows as its chemistry persistently hung onto invisible molecules in the air. There were just thirty or so students in the class listening to Father Hofer's meandering lecture on 'Right and Wrong' as he framed his opinion as a universal truth.

"Pope Pius XII chose silence, neutrality, and diplomacy as a strategy against Nazi aggression; his strategy proved successful. Some will argue that Pius should have been more vocal, but his strategy of silence proved prudent," Marcello raised his hand to voice opposition. Father Hofer begrudgingly acknowledged Marcello's raised hand with an indifferent nod.

"With all due respect, Father, I don't see how you can call Pope Pius' strategy successful or prudent. Six thousand Roman Jews were forced out of their homes and into concentration camps and murdered while Pope Pius remained silent. Again, with all due respect, Father, how can you say that's a prudent success?" Marcello asked.

"Stand up, mister," Father Hofer ordered. Marcello rose out of his chair and stood next to his seat feeling very much alone, feeling like every eye on the Catholic University campus was fixed on him in judgement.

"Name," Father Hofer demanded.

"Marcello ... Luciari," Marcello answered.

"Italian, I should have known," Father Hofer snickered, which encouraged a few students to follow suit, but most remained in silent discomfort. Marcello stood tall, unyielding, but respectful– for the moment.

"You should have known what, Father?" Marcello asked.

"Excuse me?" Father Hofer questioned, with confrontation rising in his voice.

"You said, 'Italian, I should have known.' Based on my being Italian, what should you have known?"

"I should have known that you would have chosen the losing side of the argument, Mister– what did you say the name was, Luseri?"

"My name is Luciari. Marcello Luciari," he said, instinctively beginning to defend himself. "Why would my being Italian put me on the losing side of the argument that you have predetermined is wrong?" Marcello asked, his voice reflected his rising blood pressure as the stab of anger permeated over his face as a red mask.

"The Italians chose the wrong side in the war, Mr. Luciari, and when they smelled defeat, they– "

"That's not exactly true. And it sounds like the argument you're making is based on bias, even a dislike for Italians. I'm sure I'm not the only student of Italian descent in this class; you just insulted all– "

"Shut up, boy!" Father Hofer screamed, slamming his desk with his fist. He stared at Marcello with rage bulging from the disdain swelling in his eyes. He slammed the desk again, this time with an open hand. "I will not tolerate disrespect from some teenage Italian dissonant who has no idea what he's talking about!" he shouted, his words popping spittle onto the students seated in the front row of desks. He spoke in sharp, measured anger. "Who do you think you are, judging and insulting the pope?" Father Hofer said, raising his voice even more. "You have no idea– "

"Yes, Father, I do!" Marcello shouted back. "I was there. I lived through the Nazi occupation of Rome. I saw it! I lived it! All of it! I saw it first-hand. Did you?" Marcello's demeanor escalated from an objection, to an argument, to a challenge.

"Come up here! Get up here now!" Father Hofer pounded on the desk again as he stormed toward Marcello who was approaching the front of the class, determined, apprehensive, angry, uncertain, and confident all at once. Father Hofer met him a few rows deep into the class. He grabbed Marcello by his shirt roughly and lifted him nearly off the floor. Several buttons popped off Marcello's shirt and onto the floor. Marcello's face erupted into rage. He grabbed the priest by his frock and shoved him backward hard.

"How dare you lay hands on a priest! How dare you question and disrespect our pope! Pope Pius XII was a hero!" Father Hofer screamed, repositioning himself just inches from Marcello's face, spraying his face with vapors of stale coffee, residual breakfast gases, and rage. He grabbed Marcello's shirt again, tearing the rest of its buttons off. The sound of his buttons bouncing and rolling over the floor sent Marcello into a fuming anger.

"Pope Pius was a coward! I was there!" Marcello screamed louder. His eyes inflamed with anger's ferocity, his face, a sheet of crimson ire. Father Hofer shook Marcello violently with pronounced hatred searing through his eyes, then he shoved Marcello away, viciously.

"Out of my classroom! Out! Expect charges against you! Expect to be expelled!"

Marcello didn't say a word. He knelt down and gathered up the buttons that had been torn off his shirt. He placed the buttons carefully in his pocket and looked Father Hofer dead in the eye.

"He was a coward, and so was every priest that supported him."

"Get out!"

Marcello left. The click of the closing door behind him underscored the piercing silence saturating the classroom. Father Hofer returned to his desk with his back to the class and waved a disgusted gesture toward the door.

"Get out of here, all of you. Read chapter six."

CHAPTER 14

Cello! Cello! Cello!

Marcello walked out of Divinity Hall confused. He felt several emotions colliding in his heart and echoing off the canyons of his mind, where an unimaginable number of thoughts were spinning into one another like January's chill biting through the currents of the wind. He walked through the caverns of the campus in a daze, not knowing what to think or do. He didn't feel disrespectful, but he did not feel proud either. He felt right, and he felt honest because he had done what he believed in, and what he knew to be true. He also felt sick. Once he latched on to those two pillars of character– right, and true– he began to feel relieved. And if his convictions led to consequences that resulted in being expelled from the Catholic University, then he decided that he would prefer not to be associated with such a university. But he earnestly hoped he would not have to face that possibility. This certainly qualified as a time for comfort and a time for counsel. So, Marcello sought these consoling and inspirational entities from the two sources he knew he could depend on: Marcelloel, and Father Finlay.

Marcello was in luck; Marcelloel was empty, yet filled with spirit, grace, direction, solace, and the strength he sought– and needed. Marcelloel was ornate in an understated way. Its soft white walls and thick pillars connected by graceful arches soothed the soul while awakening it. The rounded wall curving behind the altar felt like God's open arms offering calm, warmth, and love. Unconditional love. Majestically understated lanterns hung from dutiful chains hanging from the center of sturdy wooden arches. The lantern-like fixtures cast a soft light that reflected from the varnish finish of the polished pews below. Vibrant stained glass behind a glorious gold crucifix framed the altar with warmth and gentle reassurance. Marcello slid into the pew he always chose, three rows back on the right side, facing God. Three rows back to signify his recognition of the Blessed Trinity– the Father, the Son, and the Holy Spirit. His many, many, many hours in the third row of his uncle's churches in Rome conditioned Marcello to be at his most comfortable and his most thoughtful when praying– when conversing with God. He eased down onto his knees, squeezed his eyes tightly shut, and held his torn-off buttons firmly clenched in his hand. He prayed.

> *"Dear, Father: Please forgive me if I have offended you in any way. I meant no disrespect to you, Father, nor even toward Father Hofer, though I do not– I cannot respect him. You know how deeply I adore you, Father, and how devoutly I try to follow your path, and live your way, as you hope for us to live. I have no regret for what I said in class this morning, nor do I regret, nor apologize for my words and feelings about Pope Pius. I hope this does not disappoint you, Father, and if it does, I ask your mercy and forgiveness. I confess to you that I do not like Father Hofer, and I might even hate him right now. And I confess that I have similar hatred for Pope Pius, Father. And I am so sorry if that offends you, but I trust deceiving you would be a greater offense … if I am not honest with you and myself, then I am not honest at all. I confess, too, that I contemplated striking Father Hofer for humiliating me and offending my heritage. And for tearing these buttons from my shirt. I thank you so much for this fantastic opportunity*

to study at this magnificent university, Father, and I ask that you help me remain enrolled here. Please, Dear God, help me to remain enrolled here. And please protect and bless my sweet mother, my loving sister, Mia, who I love more all the time, my wonderful Uncle Salvestro, my best and dear friend Chiano, and all of his family, and please, Lord, please bless me with your strength, clarity, and understanding. Please bless me, Dear God. In the name of the Father, the Son, and the Holy Spirit. Amen."

After several minutes steeped in blurry confusion, Marcello rose from the pew relieved, more at ease, and more content than when he stepped into this wonderfully peaceful and deeply comforting chapel. He was ever so thankful to be able to immerse himself in its healing warmth. As he neared the door at the back of Marcelloel, he turned to soak it in, saturating his soul with its calming yet energizing force, for he feared this might be the very last time he would see it. Feel it.

Once he absorbed his solace in Marcelloel, he sought counsel from Father Finlay– and from Abraham Lincoln. Braving the sharp blade of January's frigid knife, Marcello and Father Finlay, sat on the steps of the Lincoln Memorial– the very step where Lincoln rests his feet. The amber timber of overhead floodlights graced the memorial's marble walls in a curtain of warm, orangey-yellow light that appeared as cascading melon-colored veils of valor.

"Well, I won't mislead you, Marcello, if your hearing tomorrow is with Monsignor Garrity, it's a big deal. His official title is Dean of University Affairs, but his practical role is to serve as the provost's– Monsignor Allen's– right-hand man."

"Father, I feel so awful for disappointing you. I'm making you look bad," Marcello said.

"Woooo– I am not disappointed in you in the least," he said. He took Marcello's chin in his hand and turned his face to face his own. "Look at me, Marcello. Look into my eyes. The only thing I want you to see and know is that the man you are looking at is proud of you, and the young man I am looking at should be proud of himself. Period. You might have to take your lumps for this, and I don't know what that amounts to, but know this," he said, still holding Marcello's chin in his hand. "No matter what happens, you will walk into that hearing tomorrow with your head held high, and your conviction cemented to your honor, and the truth. Understand? You walk in there prepared to accept whatever the outcome is, and in the end, you will be the bigger man, no matter what, because what you did and said was right in God's eyes, and His are the eyes that matter most," Father Finlay said. "I can't be in there with you, but I know that the truth will be in there with you, God will be in there with you, and you know what, Marcello, your future will be in there with you, and I suggest you look Monsignor Garrity straight in the eye, and you tell him exactly what you think you would tell your congregation if you were a priest. You tell him what you think Jesus Christ would tell him in answer to whatever they ask you about the university, the Church, that jackass Father Hofer, who grossly mistakes being pompous with being pious ... and tell him what you think of Pope Pius. You lay out your truth– in a respectful way, you have to be respectful– and you will be fine– no matter what. And you can be respectful while being angry. Just try to stay composed within that anger. Let the truth lead the way like the guy sitting behind us let honor light his way." Father Finlay patted Marcello on the cheek and tapped the icy cold step they were sitting on. "This is the perfect spot to talk about what's right and wrong. We should o' brought Hofer with us," Father Finlay quipped. Rising to his feet and tapping Marcello on the shoulder he said, "Come on, cheeseburgers and milkshakes are on me."

They stepped into the freezing clarity of a Washington, D.C. January night, unsure of Marcello's fate. But they walked away from Abraham Lincoln certain of an encouraging destiny entrenched in the comfort and confidence one feels when embedded in the power of the truth and possessing an accurate distinction between right and wrong.

The hearing was set for 9:15 a.m. Marcello awoke at 7:00 to review class notes for an 11:00 Philosophy test, so as to be prepared for class in the event he would not be expelled. He wrote in his journal about his intentions for his hearing with Monsignor Garrity. He showered and dressed, enjoyed a hearty breakfast of a bacon, egg, and cheese sandwich on a hard roll, chocolate milk, and an apple. He arrived at Monsignor Garrity's office just before nine and was directed to a seat outside his office. The oak door separating Monsignor Garrity from the outside world was made from beautiful oak with grains that almost spoke to you. Marcello could hear Monsignor Garrity's deep, resonant voice from behind the door, but couldn't make out what he was saying. Many would have cowered if seated in Marcello's position in that waiting area, but Marcello felt only the rich assurance of confidence's calm. But occasional threads of fear wiggled through his stomach like a school of fish squirming through reeds sprouting from the ocean floor. He hoped that he would not have to sit in the waiting area with Father Hofer. He also hoped that Father Hofer wasn't already in the office with Monsignor Garrity, getting a jump on the hearing. The answer to that question materialized quickly as Monsignor Garrity swung his door open at the precise moment Father Hofer arrived.

"Mr. Luciari, I presume," Monsignor Garrity said in his booming voice.

"Yes sir, Marcello Luciari, Monsignor," Marcello said while rising and shaking Monsignor Garrity's notably cold hand firmly. He heard his Uncle Salvestro's voice saying, *when you shake a man's hand, you have to let him know somebody worthy is attached to that hand. Give a good firm handshake, let them know you're alive and you're strong.*

"Come in." He led Marcello and Father Hofer into his office. Marcello heard Father Finley's voice now. *You look Monsignor Garrity straight in the eye and you tell him exactly what you think you would tell your congregation if you were a priest.*

Monsignor Garrity took a seat behind a huge desk with a pile of folders on each side. An open file folder laid at the center of the big blotter on the center of the desk: Marcello's file. Monsignor Garrity scanned the top page in the report, the complaint– the charges against Marcello. He left the folder open. He had a blank pad next to the folder, and a pen in his hand. He looked to Father Hofer and the hearing began.

"Well, let's hear it."

"Of course.," Father Hofer said while choking down a lump of phlegm in his throat. "Mr. Luciari disrupted my class with an outburst of– "

"Excuse me, Monsignor. Father, it wasn't an outburst. An outburst implies– "

"You'll have your turn, Mr. Luciari. Until then …" Monsignor Garrity said, holding up a hand to silence Marcello.

"As I was saying, Mr. Luciano– Mr. Luciari– disrupted my class with an outburst that insulted and disrespected me, his classmates, this university, the Church itself, and the good soul of Pope Pius XII. He contended that the strategy that our Holy Father employed during the German effort in Rome during the war was an act of what Mr. Luciari called cowardice. In fact, Monsignor, he called our Holy Father himself a coward. I do not think a student that exhibits this type of behavior, attitude, belief, or conduct is worthy of this university, the priesthood, or the Church. His behavior is far from that of what is worthy of our priesthood. This said and documented, Monsignor, I move that you expel this student so he will be free to take his warped beliefs where such beliefs are tolerated."

Father Hofer took a deep sniff of self-admiration, filling himself with himself.

"Anything to add, Father Hofer?" Monsignor Garrity asked, tapping his pen on his pad.

"No, Monsignor. My statement and the report I filed are quite clear and complete," Father Hofer said.

"Mr. Luciari," Monsignor Garrity said, swiveling in his chair and nodding to Marcello. "You're up."

"Yes, Monsignor," Marcello said. "May I remove my jacket?" Marcello asked. Monsignor gestured his approval with a nod and Marcello removed his jacket, revealing his shirt with the buttons missing. Monsignor waved his sturdy mitt of a hand toward Marcello's open, buttonless shirt.

"What's this?"

"It is the shirt that I was wearing the other day when Father Hofer called me to the front of the classroom and humiliated me. It's the shirt that I was wearing when he grabbed me and shook me so violently that he ripped the buttons off of it," Marcello said. He heard Father Finlay's voice again, *you can be respectful while being angry. Just try to stay composed within that anger.* Marcello rubbed the shirt with his fingers tenderly, as his anger merged with sadness.

"This was my father's shirt, Monsignor. The shirt he was wearing the day that a Nazi lieutenant tortured him and forced my family to watch, because we were protecting innocent Jews. My father was wearing this shirt when they shoved him to his knees and ripped it from his body, sending its buttons flying. That officer made us watch him shoot my sister dead. This is the shirt my father was wearing the day that lieutenant forced my hand into his and onto the trigger of his gun and forced my finger to pull that trigger, sending a bullet into my father's temple, killing him. It was the shirt my father wore as Pope Pius remained silent while six thousand Roman Jews were killed, Monsignor," Marcello said. "My mother sewed the buttons back onto this shirt and saved it. She gave it to me to bring to college. She said 'to wear his shirt was to feel his heart and love, and to wear his honor,' Monsignor," Marcello said. The grief pouring from Marcello's recollection flooded the room in an empathetic biting chill impossible to ignore.

"I was not disrespectful in Father Hofer's class, Monsignor. Father Hofer said that Pope Pius' strategy of silence was a success and prudent; I simply asked how he could refer to an act that contributed to the death of over six thousand Jews– and dozens of Roman Catholic priests, as successful and prudent. Yes, I did call Pope Pius XII a coward because I believe that he turned his back on the people when we needed him the most," Marcello insisted. "I believe Jesus Christ would have spoken out rather than turn a deaf ear to people's suffering. I believe Pope Pius harbored an anti-Semitic bigotry behind the camouflage of diplomacy, Monsignor," Marcello declared. "I believe he was Hitler's puppet, and to a large degree, he has the blood of 6,000 Jews on his hands. I don't believe I was being disrespectful to state what I have seen, and lived through during the Nazi occupation of Rome, Monsignor." Marcello paused before continuing. "Did I shove Father Hofer? Yes, Sir, I did. And I," Marcello paused again. "And I do not apologize for that. I was protecting myself from him after he violently shoved me. I believe that Father Hofer was being disrespectful when he mocked me, and mocked my heritage and all Italians, and he ripped the buttons off of my shirt– my father's shirt." Monsignor looked to Father Hofer for an explanation.

"I was being light-hearted. I said something to the effect that the Italians chose the wrong side. It was nothing," Father Hofer said, in an arrogant tone.

"When I disagreed with you, what you said– when I told you my name, which is clearly an Italian name, you said, with a snicker and smirk on your face, you said, 'you're Italian. No wonder.' A lot of students will back me up on that," Marcello said, looking back to Monsignor Garrity.

Almost on cue, a faint chant began outside the Monsignor Garrity's window, in the courtyard below.

"Cello! Cello! Cello! Cello!" a group of some sixty students, many from Marcello's class were chanting. Monsignor Garrity rose to look out the window and survey the small group.

"Cello. Is that you they're referring to? Do you have anything to do with this?" Monsignor Garrity asked Marcello.

"Some people call me Cello for short. No sir, no Monsignor, I swear on my father's soul, I have nothing whatsoever to do with the students outside chanting. I only have a few friends here. I– "

"What about his shirt, Father?" Monsignor asked Father Hofer as he sat back down. The chant outside continued.

"Cello! Cello! Cello!"

"I was defending the honor and integrity of the university, and the Church as a whole. Yes, I grabbed him by the shirt and I held him up as an example of what I will not tolerate, nor should the university, nor the Church tolerate," Father Hofer said with commanding conviction and an arrogant belligerence. "No student has the right to disrespect me, the university, the pope, or the Church as this kid did."

"I was being honest, and your lecture that day was supposed to be about discerning between right and wrong. I was trying to do just that when you introduced Pope Pius' actions as being right– successful and prudent. I contend that he was wrong. And forgive me, Monsignor, but I respectfully contend that Father Hofer is wrong in this whole matter."

"We are never as close to God as we are when we are honoring the pope," Father Hofer said.

"I am never closer to God than when I pray, and when I attach my-self to the truth and what is right," Marcello said. Outside the chanting was getting louder.

"Cello! Cello! Cello!"

Monsignor pounded his hand on his desk as though it were a gavel, signaling the end of the hearing. He leaned back in his chair, closed his eyes, and deliberated in silence for a few very long minutes. Marcello squirmed in his chair. Sweat rolled down his spine. His breathing be-came short. Visions of telling his family, Chiano, and Father Finlay that he was expelled tumbled through his mind. That school of fearful fish returned to their slithery intrusion in his stomach. Finally, Monsignor Garrity broke his deliberative trance with a clap of his hands. He leaned forward on his desk.

"Father Hofer is right in terms of what is at risk here. I have an obligation to uphold the integrity of this university, the priesthood, and the Church at large. Father Hofer was also right when he said that we cannot tolerate disrespect in our university, and again, the honor of the Church, and the papacy. We can't. I can't." Monsignor Garrity said, as he rose and put both hands on his desk and leaned toward Marcello and Father Hofer. He peered into Marcello's eyes with a piercing clarity and steely strength.

"I must make a conscionable decision in the interest of all involved that this issue has offended– the entire university body, the priesthood, the Church, and the papacy. The only remedy I can implement is expulsion." Monsignor Garrity let the mass of that word sink in. Smelling victory, an air of vindictive achievement washed over Father Hofer's face, a conceit he could not hide. Then Monsignor Garrity continued.

"So, effective immediately, you are barred from this university, for life … Father Hofer." Monsignor Garrity's large head turned toward Father Hofer, and he leaned closer toward him. "Now get out of my office and be off of this campus by the end of the day," he demanded. Father Hofer began to speak but Monsignor cut him off at the knees.

"Leave!"

Father Hofer left Monsignor Garrity's office in silent shock and shame with his proverbial tail tucked deep between the crevice of his arrogance.

"It's OK to challenge authority when you are on the right side of right and wrong, Marcello." Marcello's heart sang. He was dancing on air. He was floating far above where any angels have been. A canyon-like smile spread across the monsignor's face and he opened his arms wide as he swayed around his desk.

"Now, come here, you," he said and took Marcello into his arms for a deep bear hug. "You're gonna be a great priest one day … Cello!"

Outside the chanting continued.

"Cello! Cello! Cello! Cello!"

Monsignor led Marcello to the window, opened it wide, and with Marcello at his side, and his gigantic arms waving out the window, his smile lit up the courtyard below, Monsignor Garrity vigorously chanted. "Cello! Cello! Cello! Cello!"

CHAPTER 15

Waves

"So, you want to be a rabbi," Rabbi Uhlmann said.

"Yes, sir, I do."

"'Yes, sir, I do,' better than the 'I think so,' answer I usually get. And what inspires Chiano Pratto to want to be a rabbi?"

"The ocean."

"The ocean," Rabbi Uhlmann said, amused. "Do you know that for the forty-five years I've been teaching, every time I ask a rabbi-wannabe what inspires them to want to be a rabbi, every single one of them says, 'the ocean.'" Rabbi Uhlmann enjoyed a robust laugh then continued. "The ocean. I am interested. Tell me how the ocean inspires a young man to want to become a rabbi." He moved to a cozy loveseat across from his desk. "I am going to need a comfortable seat for this story, and I am expecting a good story from you, Chiano Pratto."

Rabbi Uhlmann's office was plush by college professor office standards. Despite its location in a modest, nondescript, square building, his office was more traditional, softer, and more spacious than most professors' offices– a tribute to his stature at the university as a prized resource poached from Hebrew University in Jerusalem. It was decorated more thoughtfully with original art depicting art in motion: dancers spinning on clouds, an elderly woman passionately playing a cello in a formal garden, a vivid realism work of a violinist wavering with music you can almost hear, another sample of realism– hands poised over piano keys with the right hand depressed over a C Minor chord. His desk was clean.

A pair of brass bookends depicting sculptures of Plato and Aristotle held an Oxford dictionary, a five-volume set of the Torah, *Doctor Zhivago*, and a biography of Winston Churchill. That's it. But the wall behind his desk was filled with books from floor-to-ceiling. Generous corner windows welcomed light into the room while offering an inspiring view of students mulling about the courtyard outside. The rabbi sat in a cozy white loveseat with soft, rounded edges facing two matching swivel chairs; he motioned for Chiano to choose one to sit in.

"What about the mysterious ocean inspires Chiano Pratto to become a rabbi?"

"The waves. The ocean— the waves— they make me realize how short life is. They crash on the shore, leave their mark, and return to the sea, forever," Chiano said. "Yet, they're perpetual and they renew themselves. And since almost seventy-five percent of the earth is covered by water, it reminds me that seventy-five percent of my life is spiritual." Chiano waited for Rabbi Uhlmann to react but he just listened, waiting for Chiano to continue. "Maybe the seventy-five percent is not all spiritual, some of it is just unspoken thoughts, and inner dialogue, I guess. Kind of like the part of me you see is the surface of the water, and the rest is underneath, underwater. And kind of like the Torah ... you don't really see the meaning until you dig deep beneath the surface." Rabbi Uhlmann nodded, silently prompting Chiano to continue, to dig deeper into the ocean of his mind.

"I was watching the waves wet the sand, and it looked like it was enriching the land. It made me think that it could be enriching for me to enrich others. In the end, it's almost a selfish indulgence," he thought aloud. "And growing up in Rome, living through the Nazi occupation of Rome, I realize how unpredictable and precious life is ... it can end at any moment."

"Very true. What else, Chiano Pratto?"

"Well, I love the Jewish story and our way of life— our beliefs, our teaching, our traditions, and I want to perpetuate our story, and way of life ... like the waves perpetuate the tides." On impulse, Chiano rose from his chair and began pacing as he spoke. "I can see myself preaching, and teaching, and being a vital part of the community ... I can feel it. I can see myself looking up to the heavens and finding a connection from our past that inspires our future. I love being Jewish, Rabbi. I love our customs and rituals. Believe it or not, I love Yom Kippur ... My best friend is Catholic and he used to really appreciate going to confession and he got me to love Yom Kippur for the same reason he appreciated confession. It's so …" he searched the ceiling for the word, "cathartic, that's it. It's so cathartic to admit faults and weaknesses. It makes me feel cleansed and relieved instead of the cheap feeling you'd get if you swept your shortcomings and guilt under the carpet."

He paced in silence, then stood by the window looking down at the seeds of a vision for a college planted in the soils of noble ambition. He took stock of his peers bustling about, sewing ideas and bundles of optimism into the tapestry of their destinies. Then Chiano turned back to Rabbi Uhlmann. "I love our Rosh Hashanah custom of throwing bread, or pebbles, or twigs into the river to represent throwing our weaknesses and faults into the past. That ritual prepares me to be my best self." He sat back down on the edge of his chair and leaned toward the rabbi. "I can feel it, Rabbi Uhlmann, and I can see it; being a rabbi is all that I can see myself doing."

"Tell me, Chiano Pratto, where is the ocean that so inspires you, our Tel Aviv's beloved Mediterranean Sea? I want to drink from it as you have," Rabbi Uhlmann quipped. "Your thoughts are keen, not just for a young student, but even for a mature man. Your insight is a gift. Intuition and insight are rare blessings, and you have been sanctified with both these gifts," the rabbi said, then paused for a few moments, studying Chiano. "Let's talk 'Jew' for a bit … do you know what I mean when I say let's talk 'Jew?' I mean let's talk about what it means to be a Jew, a minority, envied by some, hated by many, praised only by ourselves," he chuckled again. "It is not easy to be a Jew and even harder to be a rabbi. We rabbis are perceived as 'instigators' and 'ring leaders' that inspire Jews to be Jews. Some people actually believe that we are born with horns growing out of our heads." Rabbi Uhlmann began prying himself from his cozy position in his loveseat. "You know, it is a beautiful day, and my doctor insists that I get off this couch more often. What do you say you and I take a walk and talk Jew," he said with humorous vigor. "Good?" Chiano hopped up from his chair to embrace the opportunity to spend genuine quality time with the professor and rabbi he admired so much.

Tel Aviv's tropical environment appealed to Chiano— and nearly everyone else who had stepped foot on it. Warm breezes tickled its palm trees and the ocean's refreshing air breathed an inspiring calm through the university's humble grounds. The city's clashing architectural hodge-podge of buildings competed for– even demanded– the eye's attention. After some time in Tel Aviv, and some conscious effort, the in-your-face style of the architecture faded into the atmosphere and played the supporting role of backdrop.

"This architecture agitates more than inspires, not like the gorgeous buildings of Rome, London, and the great European universities," Rabbi Uhlmann said. "Surprisingly, German Jews are responsible for this architecture. When the Nazis took control in Germany in 1933, one of the many things they closed down was the Bauhaus Art School where a lot of architects studied. Their design philosophy stressed modernism, minimalism, and ..." he paused for a breath. "Thousands and thousands of Jews fled to the area here and created a stupendous need for housing. Well, Chiano Pratto, they hired a bunch of architects, and as it turned out, a handful of the most influential of them were Jews from the Bauhaus School. They brought their modernism and minimalism philosophies here, and now we're inundated with all these undecorated white buildings all over Tel Aviv," he said waving at imaginary buildings. "And their obsession with new-new-new manifests as this hodgepodge in search of itself." Rabbi Uhlmann took another much needed breath of air before continuing.

"I suppose the intent is to look toward the future but looking at these buildings makes me want to run back to the past! I guess in the end, the style helps us realize that our purpose is not to admire buildings, but to build people to be admired, right?" Rabbi Uhlmann said. "So, like the university motto, *Pursuing the Unknown*, you are pursuing the unknowns of the ocean– and faith."

"I guess so. That's a good way to look at it."

"I have another unknown for you to ponder ... I think I would like you to address this subject in a paper for my class."

"That's great. What unknown?"

"Not what, but why?"

"Why?"

"Yes, why? Why are people antisemitic?"

"That's a big ocean."

"Indeed, it is, Chiano Pratto. But as we know, our mission is to pursue the unknown at Tel Aviv University, and this is an important unknown that will haunt every rabbi and every Jew until the end of time."

"Why are people antisemitic? Wow."

"I want to know your thoughts. Don't research this subject, just give me the thoughts of Chiano Pratto– Chiano Pratto. To know why people don't like us is a good place to start understanding how people can come to love us ... another big ocean, but the ocean is full of solutions, right? I made a funny joke," Rabbi Uhlmann said, sporting a tender grin and raised eyebrows.

"Why do you say my full name every time you refer to me?" "Because it's a beautiful name and to simply pronounce it brings a smile to my face. And I want to make you conscious of the notion of identity." Chiano Pratto and Rabbi Uhlmann wound up their walk in front of the library.

"So, Chiano Pratto, I forbid you to enter this building to research the assignment I gave you. It must come from your gift of insight, intuition, and your identity. This assignment will serve as a benchmark you can refer to for the rest of your life. And that, Chiano Pratto, is a very big, very deep ocean. But, you are a very deep young man, and I am looking forward to finding out what's inside here," Rabbi Uhlmann said, tapping Chiano's head, then his heart, before walking up the steps of the library. "Due in a week," he said over his husky shoulder.

"Rabbi Uhlmann," Chiano called out. Rabbi Uhlmann turned to face him without a reply.

"Thank you!" The rabbi saluted Chiano Pratto, smiled and continued up the library stairs. *A week to answer an age-old question. God, I wish Marcello was here now*, he thought.

Since the ocean was Chiano's inspiration and Batia had become his greatest source of comfort over his first two and a half years at the university, he tapped into her comforting presence and the ocean's invigorating spirit to find refuge from the rigors of his studies. He was comfortable in the big city of Tel Aviv, at the tiny, new university, and in his own skin. He was comfortable dating Batia, too. He loved walking with her with his arm over her shoulders and her head nestled into him. They left their shoes by the boardwalk and moseyed along the shoreline, soaking their tanned feet and warm souls in the welcoming waters of the Mediterranean.

"These are the guys– the waves– that moved me the most," Chiano said, kicking his toes into a wave. "They're amazing. They started miles and miles and miles away as a billion drops of water … and now, here they are … rolling into the shore as one wave. One by one, all integrated in this massive ocean, all individuals with their own purpose, their own identity, their own mark on the sand, and then, just like that," he said, clapping his hands, "their purpose is served, their lives over and renewed in the same moment. They drain back into the ocean unknown, with no form and no more purpose." He stopped walking and watched the waves greet, then retreat from the shore. "There are so many ways to interpret these waves. I was thinking …"

"What were you thinking, rabbi-to-be?" Batia said, with a smile and the twinkle of admiration in her eyes.

"I was thinking that I want to be more than a wave that crashes into the shore and leaves its mark, and melts back into anonymity. I want to be an ocean that creates the waves that touch the shore– I want to touch people and leave my mark." He pulled Batia closer to him. "The waves curl up on the surface and reveal all of the stuff of the soul beneath. It's like the ocean sends a sample of its entire being up to the top of a wave for us to see. But just like humans, most of our life is beneath the surface." They walked in silence for some time allowing all the thoughts below the surface to swell.

"It's a never-ending source of energy that perpetuates life over and over. It inspires me to want to perpetuate the Jewish story, the Jewish way of life. I want to make an impact, Bat," he said, rubbing her shoulder. "I want to change and grow and weather life's storms yet remain as a constant source of beauty and inspiration for people. I want to be someone who will always be there, no matter what– like the ocean." He heard his father's voice saying, *we must always be there for Marcello's family, no matter what.* "That sound crazy?" Chiano asked, knowing the answer.

"Far from it, Chiano. It sounds beautiful. Most people look at the ocean and just see water and sunlight's reflection on it. But you see the entire destiny of the life you want to create– a beautiful life … it's beautiful, Chiano."

"You're in that ocean with me," he said, running his fingers through her hair then kissing her forehead. Batia snuggled closer to Chiano, while retreating into the waves of questions diving below the tides of her own mind's surface. The sun that had risen in a brilliant yellow just fourteen hours earlier, now relaxed into languid melon-like orange tones, whisks of pinks, and streaks of lavenders that feathered into the proud, ever-reliable blue backdrop of the sky. Dusk dusted its fragile face across the shiny surface of the perpetual journey of the waves and winked a gentle good night to the world.

That glorious sky skirted its beauty into the closet that is night and drenched Tel Aviv in its dark caress. Chiano and Batia brushed the sands of romance from their feet and donned their shoes. They walked back to campus in a pronounced contented peace, closer still, with every synchronized stride. They kissed deeply at the bottom of the stairs leading to her apartment, a flat above a garage she shared with a roommate. Chiano held her and the pleasure of feeling a beautiful woman in his arms for several enchanting moments before he waved good night and headed home, into the fissures of his mind to search for explanations for why antisemitism?

Chiano spent the next four days almost exclusively pondering, preparing, and writing the paper assigned by Rabbi Uhlmann. He tried to think of reasons or rationale that explained why humans might fester hatred toward others, why humans committed vile and despicable acts against one another– for no apparent reason other than blindly hating Jews. He searched his mind for conditions, traits, or characteristics that might explain why Jews suffered the terror of the Holocaust and continue to encounter the indignation, cruelty, and dehumanizing injustices of antisemitism. The deeper Chiano delved into the question, the more his mind skidded into a sea of unknowns, a deep black hole of nothing. No answers. Another day without progress. No sense of command, no confidence. Nothing. He desperately hoped that his raw fear would evolve into a solid idea at worst, a legitimate answer at best.

A new day. New hope. Chiano walked Batia to her apartment after class scratching his head and listening to the echoes of his head-scratching tumbling off the walls of his mind.

"It's early. Take a walk on the beach. Let it go. Just get some space from it. Give yourself a break, and don't come back to it until you've forgotten about it," Batia suggested. "Believe in yourself, Chiano, and don't think about the deadline, enjoy the moment you're in. Just walk," she advised. "Go," she said, pushing him away. "Shoo. Go away," she urged. "Relax. Don't think. Let the thinking come to you." And so, off he went. As he walked away, Batia called out to him, "Chiano?" He turned, hoping … just hoping.

"When you wake up in the morning, just start writing and don't stop until you finish your paper," she hollered, knowing that Chiano would do just that. He smiled and turned toward his own apartment, which was actually just a small room in the rear of an elderly couple's home.

Chiano walked the beach, sat on benches gaping at the sky, the ground, the trees in search of answers. He enjoyed the air, the sights of the city, Tel Aviv's sea of twinkling lights flirting with the night. He walked and walked and just after midnight, he returned to his room, pleasantly tired but not exhausted. Relaxed. Calm. He undressed and slid into the cozy sheets and covers his mother had packed from his own bed at home. He rolled over onto his left side like he had every night of his life– even in *The Pulpit*– and clutched one cool pillow between his legs and another between his bent arm, shoulder, and chin. And like a child cuddled in a cradle of peace, he sank into a deep, restful sleep.

When he awoke, he felt alive, refreshed, and vigorous. He showered and dressed quickly and went to the student cafe and enjoyed a hearty breakfast. When he finished, he briskly marched to a stretch of breaker rocks jutting into the ocean, found a flat rock with a natural stone backrest behind it, sat down, took out a pen and spiral notebook, and started to write. And write and write and write until he progressed past a jumble of disjointed babel that eventually evolved into insight that became the context and content of the paper assigned by Rabbi Uhlmann, *"Antisemitism: Why?"*

He finished the paper on time. He was proud of the work and exhausted by the effort. He was relieved to hand in his work but anxious in anticipation of Rabbi Uhlmann's reaction to it. He addressed the question without concretely answering it, yet he did arrive at some worthy observations, theories, and conclusions. His anticipation and craving for a positive response– for validation from someone he considerably admired– was akin to a bloom desperately waiting for morning to sanction it to flower.

Rabbi Uhlmann was at his desk thumbing through a file of news clippings when Chiano knocked on the classroom door. It was a stark room with small windows in a row, well above the floor. Sunlight managed to find its way into the room in a diffused cast that was neither inspiring nor distracting, just a raw curtain of hazy light. The tile floor looked almost industrial, the desks, fundamental. A chalkboard behind Rabbi Uhlmann's desk covered the width of the wall. Semi-circles of chalk dust covered the blackboard with erased ideas and advice from another professor hoping to change the lives of the students who sat in the same classroom the day before. Rabbi Uhlmann looked up from his bland blonde desk. His beady brown eyes opened wider as he peaked over the top of half-lens reading glasses. A smile curled into his face upon seeing Chiano.

"Chiano Pratto, the ocean boy, good morning."

"Good morning, Rabbi," Chiano said as he proudly plopped his paper on the rabbi's desk. "It's finished, Rabbi," he said, feeling satisfied.

"From the look of liberation and gratification on your face, you are relieved to be finished or proud of what you've done. Or both."

"I would have to say you're correct, Rabbi. Both."

"Good. Gratification is a cousin of pride, which is a cousin of self-respect and self-respect is the uncle to dignity. It is a good family tree you brought to my class this morning." Rabbi Uhlmann picked up Chiano's paper and waved it up and down gently, as though he were about to guess its weight. "The ocean has not misled you? You have a good feeling about your work, Chiano Pratto?"

"I do, Rabbi." Rabbi Uhlmann shook his head and handed the paper back to Chiano.

"Good," the rabbi said. "We would love to hear it. You shall read it to the class this morning."

Chiano's face froze, as though he had just swallowed something far too large for his throat to accommodate. He felt suspended in an alternate plane for the moment, keenly apprehensive. His entire being was covered in a mist of nervous sweat. He turned cold, and for a moment, he could not hear, nor see, nor smell, nor feel anything within the room, within that moment, only the cool beads of nervousness that instantly encased his body. He tasted a pronounced tang of fear in his mouth. Chiano had to shake his head to snap himself back into the moment; he saw Rabbi Uhlmann's eyes peeling through the fright surrounding him.

"Are you OK, Chiano Pratto?" Rabbi Uhlmann asked. After a moment, Chiano gathered himself and was able to nod his head to signify his coherence. "Good," Rabbi Uhlmann said, "I'm looking forward to hearing your thoughts," he said, as Chiano took his seat two rows back. He started reading through his paper, rehearsing it in his head while his classmates filed into the classroom, one-by-one, and in random pairs. Eventually everyone was in class, about eighteen students stuffed into one-piece combination desks and chairs positioned in an inverted chevron pattern facing Rabbi Uhlmann. After what felt like a combination of an instant and an eternity to Chiano, Rabbi Uhlmann stood up, deliberately walked over to the classroom door, and closed it.

"Good morning, everyone," Rabbi Uhlmann bellowed, while returning to his desk. "This morning, we have two treats in store for you. One, I am going to keep my babbling mouth shut this morning. And two, we are going to hear one of your colleague's thoughts on a subject very close to our hearts, and very far from the grasp of our minds. A week ago, I was counseling your classmate, Chiano Pratto," he said, pointing out Chiano with the wave of his arm and an open palm. "I asked him to address a question important to all of us— important to us as card-carrying Jews, for some of us, as future rabbis, and for all of us, as members of the human race. So, without gratuitous and appreciatively preventable hesitation, Chiano Pratto, the floor and the room are yours."

Rabbi Uhlmann took a seat in the back of the class as Chiano approached the front of the room. Chiano propped his paper on a desktop podium on Rabbi Uhlmann's desk, cleared his throat, nervously shuffled his papers, then he spoke.

"Thank you, Rabbi Uhlmann. Thank you for this assignment and this chance to share my thoughts. Good morning, everyone," he said, and acknowledged the class's muttered, but polite response. Then he began to read:

"Antisemitism: Why?

"In considering the perplexing question, why has antisemitism always existed, we can thoughtfully speculate, but we will likely never definitively know why some people hate Jews. I find myself falling far short of any worthy rational answer to this inhumanely irrational phenomenon. Any legitimate answer to this question is laden with thinly veiled uncertainty. Antisemitism is at

worst, training in hatred, and at its best, a portrait of ignorance painted on a canvas of bias, and framed in bor-
ders of fear. Antisemitism is peculiarly historical, and
thus, inherently, culturally genetic. It is a dangerously
sinister, psycho-societal phenomenon deeply rooted in
what I suspect to be a combination of three major fac-
tors: primal envy, polarization through differentiation,
and ignorance through misconception.

"Primal envy breeds resentment. Jews are a vividly
defined people with fervent beliefs, values, divergent rituals, and practices. The Jewish lifestyle is rich, unique,
and at times, considered distinctly different from non-
Jews— sort of. Jews characteristically embrace their
faith— and their lives— with vigor and pride, and place
their Judaism front and center in their lives. In doing
so, and recruited by God as His chosen people, Jews
accept and behold the role of moral guardians of a righteous code of conduct for mankind. By proclaiming to
be God's chosen people, Jews likely prompted and amplified a degree of resentment for staking such a divisive
almighty claim."

Chiano stepped aside from the lectern to depart from reading from
his report.

"I don't want to try to explain or argue important
biblical references here, but the bible does reference
Jews as God's chosen people more than a few times. But
it was more of an assignment he gave us than a privilege— and a tough one at that: to be a light onto the
world. And we took it on. I won't call it a burden because I know He's listening right now, so I'll just thank
Him for this wonderful privilege of being a Jew."

A few of the students chuckled and Chiano relaxed back into the
lectern and continued reading.

"In addition, Jews value and practice a fierce commitment to education and often, to an unyielding will to do what it takes to achieve goals, and/or victory, and thus, they reap the enviable rewards of diligent effort. Jews have historically been extraordinary survivors and notable achievers in the sciences, arts, and commerce. Rather than emulate the Jewish model, antisemites, I suspect, have chosen and continue to choose, perhaps unconsciously and unknowingly, to envy and resent Jews. Jews are generally very proud to be Jews and very happy being Jewish. Non-Jews want what fortunate Jews have: fulfillment, to savor the fruits of education's nectar, to flourish in the warmth of strong family support, and to revel in spiritual awakening and personal enrichment through their faith. To find spiritual awakening and fulfillment in their faith, inspiration and solace in God, self, family, and community are truly enviable blessings. Granted, these virtues are equally available to non-Jews, but success evades the uncommitted, and it seems to me that religiously, non-Jews are more committed to dogma than the valuable personal and community values, and social services that we Jews commit to. Embedded into universal insecurities and frailties, an inherent envy or jealousy can simmer into a stew of resentment."

Chiano had shed the skin of fear and apprehension and glided into a valorous suit of confidence and inspiration. He dug deeper into the ocean of his mind and now, everything from below his mind's surface was out and on display, front and center. He continued, more confident, and more committed.

"Differentiation leads to polarization. Religious, cultural, and eventually national differentiation led to polarization, and that polarization intensified and festered and emerged as a pointed distaste for Jews– and all things Jewish. Jewish customs, rituals, language, and for some sects, dress and dietary habits, are distinctly different from non-Jews. Many of the shavings whittled from the foundation of antisemitism can be attributed to this differentiation. There is certainly some degree of psychosis among hate-filled people, and some people have exhibited outright hatred for what they do not agree with, and what they perceive as a threat to their safety or comfort. The perception of being distinctly different, and somewhat assumed to be intrinsically exclusionary, can fuel polarization, which can manifest as antisemitism. When a group of people zealously nourish an exclusive culture, it sets itself apart, and thus polarizes non-members of that culture. And when that group overcomes notable difficulties, and ultimately, heinous, catastrophic adversity beyond biblical imaginings, that group of people further distinguishes itself from others through its bond, which can trigger pronounced resentment among non-members. This is a tragically juxtaposed reaction to the respect and admiration one might expect when a group overcomes the supreme adversity Jews have overcome.

"Throughout history, inexplicable, unfounded hatred on the grandest scale despicably became accepted– without cause, explanation, or validity. And during World War II, that unspoken norm became a scream unheard amidst an ignoring world. Jews were being blamed for all the world's evils and shortcomings through insanely successful propaganda campaigns that created massive gaps between truth and lies, love and hate. Fear flourished, and people had to choose between aligning themselves with Jews, which endangered their lives. Snubbing and even turning against Jews, for some, became a means of survival. The world's people transferred their fears into associating Jews with horrendous consequences at the hands of a madman and his Nazi party. And much farther back in history, the birth of Christianity underscored a divide in religious convictions further distinguishing Jews from non-Jews. In what is perhaps history's ultimate irony, Jesus Christ, a Jew who was regarded as an extraordinarily charismatic rabbi, became the center of an enormously popular faith that harbors no small number of antisemitic hypocrites. Go figure! In the end, non-Jews simply feel and think, you're not one of us. That's polarizing."

The class was becoming more engaged than Chiano would have thought or could have hoped. So was Chiano. He had a flash of distraction thinking, *I wish Batia was here to hear this, to see me.* He paused, and inhaled a deep breath of achievement's gratifying pride before continuing.

"A portrait of ignorance. Ignorance can be most enlightening! Most non-Jews, I suspect, have little idea of what Jewish beliefs, values, and practices really are, and they dislike Jews without cause, explanation, or reason. That's ignorance. I often thought that if adults were to choose their religion as informed adults, and without the poisonous baggage of bias, a large majority would likely choose the Jewish faith. Through an erroneous perception of strength hiding behind hatred's mask, antisemitism is camouflage for what is, in reality, weakness. At best, antisemitism is a portrait of ignorance.

"I have learned that there are no rational answers or rational explanations for irrational thoughts or actions. I find antisemitism both irrational and inexplicable. Still."

Chiano looked up from his pages and peered at the class, his eyes asking *what do you think about that?* He straightened up tall. He looked polished, finished, and suddenly more mature than his classmates. More aware. He took a well-earned breath of relief and stood deeply proud of his work, and maybe even a bit closer to an answer to this perplexing question. He looked up at the class that had been somewhat ambivalent as to what was to occur when he bid them 'good morning' a few minutes ago. Now, he saw an attentive, engaged, and inspired room full of captivated faces. One boy seated close to the windows rose from his chair and looked Chiano in the eye with burning intensity. He stood up and he began clapping. Loudly. Firmly. And then another student stood up and clapped. And another, and two more and four more and another and eventually, the entire class stood, applauding Chiano Pratto with vigor, gratitude, and admiration.

"Bravo, Chiano Pratto, Bravo," Rabbi Uhlmann stood up and hollered from the back of the room with his hands cupped around his mouth forming a fleshy human megaphone. "Bravo!"

CHAPTER 16

Spiritual Advisor

The moment Marcello set foot on the curb at San Francisco International Airport, he felt at home, knowing that he was not at home. The climate on the California coast mirrors the summers in Rome, and the winters in heaven. A musky residue in the fragrance of eucalyptus and sage tempered the fumes of diesel buses and the chaos created by cars dropping off passengers with innate airport-urgency. California's perpetual sun seemed to smile with a subdued self-satisfaction, relishing in its ability to brighten the spirit as much as the day. Despite the business of the curbside frenzy, a universal orderliness and sense of placid respect prevailed. Marcello couldn't help but smile as he found his way to the area marked "Shuttle Van Pickup." He amused himself by observing the cars, buses, and limos buzzing before him until a green shuttle van displaying a "Menlo Park" sign pulled up.

The twenty-five-minute ride south on US 101 featured pleasing views of the San Francisco Bay drenched in the comforting blanket Marcello instantly came to know and embrace as California. He was going to like it here. He loved the lighting, the scent of ever-blossoming flowers that permeated even the foul exhaust expelling toxic vapors onto the highway. The bus pulled into its small terminal just north of the pristine community of Palo Alto, California, the home of the prestigious and heralded Stanford University. Marcello's new home for the next two and a half years is a ten-minute ride north at Saint Patrick's Seminary and University in Menlo Park. Yes, Marcello was going to like it here.

Marcello had prearranged a ride from Palo Alto to Saint Patrick's in a shuttle operated by the seminary. He had seen a few pictures of the campus but none of which did its stunning buildings and grounds justice. The pageantry of the stately brick building at the end of the majestic entrance stretched far and wide, rather than up. It presented a tempered opulence that read as distinctive power and well-preserved independence. Four sixty-foot palm trees placed in a circle equal distance apart seemed to crown a twelve-foot-tall sculpture of Jesus that rose from a stone pedestal. The sculpture stood at the center of an exceptionally well-manicured raised flower and shrub garden embraced by a three-foot-high circular stone wall. It was all the perfect complement to the building that served as an institution of training young men to portray the example and profess the values of Jesus Christ. A clear sense of pomp and intellectual fervor seemed to purr from the cadre of windows teasing one to inquire more intimately with the presumed wisdom inside. It was time for Marcello to do just that. The shuttle stopped at the double wooden and glass front doors of Saint Patrick's main entrance. Marcello gathered his duffle bag and the trusty suitcase Uncle Salvestro gave him when he left Rome for college four years ago.

"Here we are, fella ... best of luck to you," the shuttle driver offered.

"Thank you. Thanks very much," Marcello said as he maneuvered his bags from the van toward the building. A young Franciscan brother who was exiting the building greeted Marcello.

"New seminarian, hah? Welcome. Let me give you a hand," he said, holding open the door.

"Yes, I am. Thanks. Do you know where– "

"Father Kalkman's office," the brother said, finishing Marcello's sentence for him. "I do. Go all the way down the hall past the main office there, his office is the last door on the right ... the coveted corner office. They put him down there, so nobody has to talk to him," the brother joked. "Welcome and good luck," he said, as Marcello entered the building. He schlepped his bags down the long, immaculate tile floor hallway. Father Kalkman's door was closed. His name was written in gold gilt letters: 'Father Harold T. Kalkman, Dean of Students' on the door's frosted glass. The door was reminiscent of an old private investigator's office in a vintage movie. Marcello dropped his duffle bag and suitcase and wrapped on the door. The moment his knuckles touched the smooth glass for the third wrap he heard a gruff voice inside.

"You're gonna have to wait."

Marcello was about to turn the glass doorknob to open the door but froze at the command from the other side of the door. He stared at the door and tapped his fingers on his thighs. And waited. More than five minutes went by before the voice on the other side of the door spoke again.

"If you're still out there, come in." Marcello turned the glass doorknob to the left and pushed the door; it was stuck. He pushed harder and the door broke free and swung open briskly into Father Kalkman's tired-looking office. His desk was stationed before two large multi-pane windows offering a postcard-like view of the palm trees and sculpture of Christ at the grand entrance where Marcello had just arrived. Venetian blinds were drawn just slightly, splitting the sunlight into slats of warmth over the room. The same sun that brought a smile to Marcello's face throughout the ride to Menlo Park now forced him to squint. The wall around the windows was brick from floor to ceiling. The interior walls were paneled a third of the way up and painted white above the paneling, but years of pipe tobacco smoke had turned them a sickly yellow. The fresh, live floral air he so enjoyed outside was replaced by a stale stench of years of indifference, neglect, and the same pipe tobacco smoke that had turned the wall's white paint yellow. Father Kalkman did not look up from the magazine article he'd been reading to see who had entered his office. A straight stem pipe streaming ribbons of pungent smelling smoke rested in the corner of his mouth, with its bowl supported by his cupped hand, which in turn, was supported by his forearm which was supported by his desk. His hair was short and cropped close to his head in an unstylish rawness that signaled little more than an indifferent but recent haircut. An aura of uninspiring lifelessness hung in the air like a portrait of empty memories painted in dust.

"Sit," Father Kalkman commanded, still without looking up. He read the magazine for another two minutes before finally raising his head, revealing aged rosewood glasses with smudged, round lenses that seemed to confuse the light, absorbing it as a dull blur rather than reflecting it. "Who are you?"

"Marcello Luciari, Sir," Marcello said. He started to reach his hand out to shake the priest's hand but retrieved it quickly noting the priest had no intention of shaking hands.

"Luciari," he said, fumbling through a handful of folders until he found the one he was looking for and opened it. "Luciari," he said, scanning a page in the folder. "I presume your lofty Bachelor of Arts in Philosophy from Catholic University has trained you well enough to read the sign on my door identifying me as Father Kalkman, Dean of Students." He thumbed through a half dozen folders on the other side of his desk. He pulled one from the pile and slid it carelessly at Marcello. "You'll find your room assignment in there along with your schedule, and some general, practical information about the seminary: rules and regulations, operations, meal-time, campus map, and so on. Everything you need to know to get settled in and become productive here is in there," he said, pointing toward the folder with his pipe in hand. Assuming your tuition has been settled, your dorm proctor will issue your room key at the entrance of your building. You're in," he scanned a list on a clipboard on his desk, "Saint Thomas Hall. Advice: don't lose your key, don't procrastinate, and don't cheat. Questions?"

"Ah, yes, Father, I was– "

"Father Kalkman."

"Sorry, Father, I was wondering if– "

"It's Father Kalkman," he barked. "We don't wonder at Saint Patrick's, we know. We do as the bishop asks, and we adhere to the laws of the Church. We serve the bishop at all costs and we serve the Holy See. We serve the pope, adhere to the rules and governance of the country's 2,946 dioceses, uphold the values of nearly 220,000 priests, and serve as the face of the Church to over a billion Catholics. Understood?" Father Kalkman more affirmed than asked.

"Yes … Father … Kalkman … Ah, my acceptance letter stated that you are to be my spiritual advisor; will we– "

"You'll find your spiritual adviser in Marcelloel."

"Oh. Is he expecting me now?"

"He's always expecting you."

"Ahh, how will I know him– recognize him?" Marcello asked.

"He's the frail guy hanging from the cross," Father Kalkman said, looking through the murky lenses of his glasses without any detectable emotion. "As for my part as your spiritual advisor, here's my spiritual advice and assignment to you: I expect you to read each day's daily Mass readings– Old Testament, New Testament, and Gospel– then sit in front of your spiritual advisor on the cross, and contemplate how those readings are spiritually relevant and valuable. Then you're to write a homily based on your readings and contemplation every day that you're here. Clear?"

"Is that an actual assign– "

"Did I state that in a language other than the one you understand?" Father Kalkman asked abruptly. He looked at Marcello with degrading, condescending smugness that took much of the California out of the sunshine, and much of the sunshine out of California. "Now, as I said, your dorm, student center, chapel, cathedral, and everything else you'll need to find is on the campus map that's in that folder. You lose that, you lose yourself. You will live here on campus, but you will spend much of your time in one or more of the parishes in the community that we assign you to. You will live on site at a local parish in your second year here– as an attempt to give you a real-world perspective of parish life. Whatever you do, don't embarrass us at the parish or in the community." Marcello thought, "*I forgot more about parish life than this man ever learned about it.*" "Every Tuesday is a Day of Silence here, and it is rigorously observed, as is a devout respect for our bishop, Bishop Kearns. You will adhere to a fervent Saint Patrick's code of honor and unwavering loyalty to the priesthood, and the bishop," Father Kalkman said. "If you do as we say, study diligently, you can earn the Master of Arts degree in Divinity that you're here to pursue. Pay particular attention to the bishop's needs and requests and don't do anything too stupid," he said. He stopped talking and dismissed Marcello with a bland, unwelcome stare.

Marcello left Father Kalkman's office a little heavier and suddenly more tired than inspired. More aware of shadows than sunshine, but he was relieved to be out of Father Kalkman's office. He consulted his map and found his way to the dorm he was assigned to. The moment he got outside the main building, and onto the campus, his spirit lifted like a kite climbing the surge of a wind. He had already decided that no one, particularly someone as detached from humanity and spirituality as Father Kalkman appeared to be, was going to dampen his spirit, or temper his verve; the California in California and the Marcello in Marcello were far too rigorous and robust to be dampened at all, let alone by the likes of Father Harold T. Kalkman, Dean of Students.

Marcello's dorm was a bit bigger than the dorm rooms he lived in at Catholic University, and far more sunny, far more days. He spent as little time as possible in his room, favoring the glorious campus, Menlo Park itself, nearby Stanford University, and the Palo Alto area. He often rode a second-hand bike he found at a garage sale to Stanford University to study on its pristine campus, use its extensive library, and pray in its exquisite chapels. On Saturdays, when Stanford had home football games, Marcello and Raos, a Saint Patrick's custodian whom he befriended, would drive to the games in Raos' truck. Raos' brother was a security supervisor at Stanford and ushered his brother and Marcello onto the sidelines of Stanford football games, free. Raos often reminded Marcello how important it is to 'have friends in low places.' Marcello quickly continued to love watching American football, and learned to place shrewd, small wagers with money from a pittance he earned at his campus job as Raos' helper. He helped Raos set up for events, deliver A/V equipment, break down rooms after events, and whatever else needed doing. He also got a raise from the mystery monthly donor; he was now receiving envelopes from Rome that contained ten dollars every month– like clockwork.

Raos also often drove Marcello up to the prestigious University of California at Berkeley, an epicenter– if not the epicenter– of the 'Hippie movement.' It was 1965. The American culture was draped in a tapestry of turmoil, passion, rage, war, protest, civil rights, violence, sex, drugs, and rock and roll. It was a time of commitment amidst a blur of confusion. A time marked by the paradoxical union inherent in division. A time of raging discontent, intense disappointment, and the social darkness seeping from the acrid aftermath of the ghastly, world-changing assassination of John F. Kennedy two years earlier. It was a time when individual freedom reigned supreme. Women burned their bras and raised the bottom of their skirts to the tops of their legs to barely cover the bottom of their bottoms, a time when males grew their hair long in protest to the establishment's traditions and support of their peers' expectations. It was a time when young people spoke out, demanding honesty from our government and our institutions, and legitimate civil rights for everyone. A time when young people demanded the right to vote for the people who had the power to send them to war. For Marcello, it was a time of self-awakening and a deeper emergence into the 'Jesus movement' that professed love, peace, harmony, justice, goodness, sharing, caring, and more love and peace. It was a time when marijuana eased the collective mind of a generation into a euphoric comfort, and an occasional spark of synthetic insight. A time when LSD twisted the minds of many in many directions, some on ecstatic journeys, some on tragically terrifying twelve-hour nightmares, some on imaginative discoveries. It was a time when America's government sent 550,000 troops to Vietnam to fight an unworthy war, a time when 58,300 young Americans were killed there. Countless others returned mentally and emotionally maimed and riddled with cancers inflicted by chemical exposure to toxic defoliants. Our government, and the American chemical industry knew the chemicals, particularly a defoliant named Agent Orange, were deadly, and profusely harmful, yet they consciously and deplorably exposed our troops to these deadly chemicals. A time when hatred fueled by a humble hope for equality, a time when African Americans were beaten, hosed down by police, and attacked by police dogs with a viciousness that only the soulless can know. This was a time when music elevated its message, and its influence. A time of many voices shouting many messages with deep hopes of being heard. For Marcello, it was a time to observe, absorb, indulge, and process these intensely significant influences into impressions and reactions that shaped the foundation of his young life and the backbone of his adulthood. And it was a time to clutch onto the sacred robes of his spiritual advisor, Jesus Christ– with vigor.

A month into Marcello's second year at the seminary, he was assigned to Sacred Heart Parish in Menlo Park as an intern and a loose version of an apprenticeship. His objective was to learn the ins and outs of an active rectory and parish, but in truth, he was more of an errand boy and gofer for the tyrannical pastor, Father James Kerr. Also, in the name of truth, Marcello likely knew more about the workings of a parish than Father Kerr.

Father Kerr had a vicious temper attached to a very short fuse. Nearly everything annoyed him and nearly nothing pleased him except praise, either self-proclaimed or through disingenuous compliments that parishioners paid him. Father Kerr was also the figurehead principle of the parish's parochial elementary school, but it was Sister Patricia who managed the school, and she managed it exceedingly well. Sister Patricia's warm demeanor, youth, and devoted vigor reminded Marcello very much of Sister Volpinello. They were both conspicuously young among a sisterhood that seemed to be curiously almost exclusively made up of much older nuns. There were also two priests working under the tyranny at Sacred Heart: a comforting and mild-mannered, middle-aged priest who struggled through the challenges posed by a cleft palate, and a much older priest who was more committed to the spirit he found at the bottom of a glass of wine than he did at the altar.

One Saturday, just about six weeks after Marcello's internship began, he was cleaning up the rectory basement, which was used for Communion and Confirmation classes. As Marcello was loading folding chairs back on a rack for storage after a Catechism class, he heard yelling upstairs. When it became louder, he went up the stairs that led into the rectory kitchen. He stopped and stood by the kitchen table unsure of what to do. Father Kerr was in a rage, screaming at Sister Patricia.

"You have no authorization to speak to the newspaper without my approval! Who in hell do you think you are, making comments about our school to the press on your own? I can't believe how stupid you are, how stupid!" He was screaming in her face. "What is wrong with you? You fool! I swear, I could slap your face, I should slap your face. What did you expect to gain from shooting your mouth off with your unauthorized opinions?" He angrily grabbed the newspaper from the coffee table next to him and read from it.

"Assistant Principal Patricia O'Connell says if she had it her way, there would be a sliding scale on tuition so that every child would be able to afford a Catholic education, but I don't think Father Kerr would ever go along with that." Father Kerr rolled the newspaper into a ball and threw it viciously into Sister Patricia's face. "That's what you said to the press! You fool! This is what our parish and the entire city is reading right now. They'll be thinking of me as an insensitive monster." He grabbed Sister Patricia by the shoulders and shook her viciously. "What were you thinking, making derogatory comments about me at all, let alone to the newspapers!" he screamed. He did not know Marcello was watching and listening. Marcello's blood was curling with anger, his mind was quickly searching for answers, for what to do.

"Why? Why!" Father Kerr screamed, shaking Sister Patricia Moore viciously. His rage was escalating. "You made me look like a fool and a scoundrel, you stupid fool!" He ripped her veil from her head and threw it on the floor. He grabbed two fists full of her hair and shook her head violently and screamed in her face. "What in hell were you thinking! What in hell were you thinking!"

"Stop it!" Marcello screamed. "Stop!" Father Kerr released Sister Patricia from his vicious hold and spun around to see who had yelled. Marcello stood before him in a ready posture that sent a clear signal to Father Kerr to stand down. "What did you say! What did you say to me, you little punk?" Father Kerr said.

"Keep your hands off her!"

Father Kerr charged toward Marcello with both arms reaching out, but Marcello grabbed his arms and spun Father Kerr into a wrestling hold that he had seen while watching wrestling matches in Raos' basement office at the university.

"You disrespectful little shit. I will ruin you. You will never become a priest. Let go of me!" Father Kerr screamed.

"Calm down, Father, I don't– "

"Take your hands off of me, you punk!" Father Kerr screamed. Sister Patricia yelled.

"Stop! Let him go, Marcello. He means it– he will ruin you, Marcello."

Marcello felt the fight in Father Kerr's resistance diminish, so he released his hold on him. Father Kerr stumbled into a chair and clumsily landed in a sitting position. Father Kerr fought through a humiliation greater than the one he perceived in the newspaper article. He looked up to Marcello and Sister Patricia through a glaze of shame. His priestly collar had been partially torn from the slot where it was inserted into his shirt. His hair was in a rumpled mess, a sheath of anger's sweat dampened his red face. His breathing was rising and falling in exaggerated swells of regret in his chest. Marcello attempted to reason with him.

"I couldn't help it, Father, I– "

"Shut up! Get out of here– both of you. Now!" Father Kerr barked. Marcello stood in a puddle of confusion and regretful uncertainty.

"Do you mean get out as in– "

"Get out, as in pack your bags and don't ever let me see your guinea face, again," Father Kerr shot back. Marcello clinched his fist tight and stepped toward Father Kerr but quickly thought better of escalating an already damaging situation.

"Father, I'm sure we can– "

"Out!" Father Kerr screamed.

Marcello stood frozen, somewhere between regret and gratification.

"Are you okay, Sister?" Marcello asked.

"Yes," she said, as she crossed the room clutching her veil. She continued toward the door, drenched in humiliation and tears. Father Kerr hollered out to her.

"Don't let anyone see you coming out of the rectory like that."

Marcello packed his small duffel bag and rode his bike back toward Saint Patrick's. This was Marcello's second serious confrontation with a priest. This one felt more serious, but he also felt less apprehensive this time because he knew Father Kerr was dead wrong, just like Father Hofer had been at Catholic University.

When Marcello got back to Saint Patrick's, he immediately went to the president of the seminary's office, Father Daniel Patton's office, and told him exactly what happened at the Sacred Heart rectory in clear detail. Father Patton, a slender, polished man who looked more like a senator than a priest, listened intently without judgment and without discernible reaction. He ended the meeting by telling Marcello that he'll be hearing from him soon.

Two days passed. A week. Two weeks. Three. Finally, Father Patton met Marcello in the corridor when his *Scripture Interpretation* class ended.

"Let's take a walk," Father Patton said, taking a firm hold of Marcello's arm; it was more an authoritarian demand than a friendly suggestion. They walked to the end of the hall and outside to a courtyard garden. Father Patton led Marcello to a stone bench in a corner of the courtyard, a safe distance from other students.

"Well, young man, you are free to resume your internship at Sacred Heart Church," Father Patton said.

"Father Kerr is accepting me back?" Marcello asked in surprise.

"No, his replacement, Father Alverez, is accepting you back. Father Kerr has been reassigned by the bishop to a diocese in Seattle," Father Patton said. Marcello hesitated for a moment to swallow and digest what he had just heard.

"I see. So, when– "

"There is a condition attached to you being reinstated," Father Patton said. "It's kind of a legal settlement but more binding, from a higher court of sorts, it's a Church thing," he said, then paused to let the notion of 'legal settlement and the Church as a higher court' idea solidify in Marcello's mind. Then, Father Patton looked directly and sternly into Marcello's eyes and explained the condition: "You are never to speak a word about the Sacred Heart incident to anyone as long as you live. Clear?"

"But I– "

"That's the deal, Mister Luciari. If you want to become recognized as Father Marcello Luciari one day, you are never to utter a word about that incident to anyone. That's the deal, and it's a pretty good one as far as you're concerned," Father Patton said. He stood up and extended his hand to shake with Marcello. "Do we have a deal?" Father Patton asked. Marcello did not answer, but he did shake Father Patton's hand.

The formal aspect of Marcello's education followed traditional Catholic teachings and priestly training. He synchronously sought the purity of his purpose while contemplating and probing the wrangles of sacrosanct contradictions. He sat and kneeled for hours and hours before his hallowed spiritual advisor perched on the cross and spoke to Him, listened to Him, for Him. Adored Him, Confessed to Him, Thanked Him. and sought His help, guidance, and enlightenment. Marcello studied the daily readings and wrote homilies every single day at Saint Patrick's and attended Mass daily. He served hundreds of meals to homeless people, read books and the bible to people alone in nursing homes. He spent days in devotion and recollection. He studied, and excelled, he socialized, made valuable friendships and lifelong memories. He lived in a parish rectory for eight months and delivered his first homily and graduated two and a half whirlwind years after entering Saint Patrick's Seminary. He graduated at the top of his class, earning the Master of Arts in Divinity.

In his final days at Saint Patrick's, Marcello sat in Marcelloel where he had attended Mass virtually every day. He thought and reflected and wrote Father Finlay the most heartfelt letter he could pour onto paper. He thanked him for arranging yet another scholarship from unknown donors, and organizations such as the Knights of Columbus, and for favors he coordinated through his contacts within the United States Army ROTC program. Marcello remained uncertain about what that debt to the ROTC would be, but regardless of its form, he was ready and willing to repay it when called upon.

Marcello was grateful that Father Harold T. Kalkman assigned the best spiritual advisor possible, Jesus Christ. He was also grateful for being assigned to write a homily every day of his education at Saint Patrick's. By the time he had graduated, he had written over 700 homilies, an exercise and experience that would serve him well for the rest of his life. Marcello was also most grateful that he had never again stepped foot in Father Kalkman's office since his very first day at Saint Patrick's.

CHAPTER 17

Sabiches

Tel Aviv's weather drenched Chiano in a blanket of thick, wet heat. Late morning rain brought more discomfort than relief, dissipating into a suffocating temperature compounded by near 100% humidity. Men's shirts stuck to their chests like wet paper gummed to glass. Women's hair curled into tiny springs, constricted into little spirals coiled around their hairlines, and retreated from a persistent coating of dew dampening their foreheads. Dresses and trousers wrinkled under the steamy air, shirt sleeves rolled up to the elbows stopped the minute trickles of sweat winding down the arms beneath gauzy cloth. Rabbi Uhlmann and Chiano sat on a cement bench at a cement table under the grace of a towering eucalyptus tree, somehow ignoring the oppressive heat.

"One day, Chiano Pratto, we will look back on these little talks as big discussions. We discuss and resolve mankind's most pressing issues in our little talks," Rabbi Uhlmann said. "The major events of the day can be turned upside down from the outcome of what we say at this very table," he added, whilst shoving a hunk of pita bread teeming with roasted eggplant and hard-boiled eggs into his mouth. "This is such a delicious sabich. One of man's most precious privileges is the gift of food," he said, as he devoured his sabich. "Do you know the origin of pita bread, Chiano Pratto?"

"No, but I will in two minutes from now, won't I?" Chiano answered.

"Legend, otherwise known as the Rabbi Uhlmann tales of untruths, otherwise known as cock-and-bull stories … anyway, legend has it that at the Last Supper, they say that Jesus Christ said, 'Peter, pass the bread, please.' But Peter didn't hear him so, Christ spoke louder, 'Peter … Bread …' he said it while chewing a hunk of lamb, and the pronunciation sounded more like 'Pita.' So, from that day forth, this delectable grilled bread became known as pita bread," he concluded with a wide grin. He stuffed more food into his mouth. "So, Chiano Pratto, I can use your help on a small matter … well, not so small."

"Say the word."

"I heard of an opportunity for a graduate student to work on a project in Jerusalem this summer. They seek a bright young man, someone who can speak well, relates well to people, values the Jewish story and way of life, and has a BA in Jewish Studies from the prestigious burgeoning university we sit amidst. They also want this young man to have some familiarity with Rome, particularly the Nazi occupation of Rome. They prefer someone recommended by a prestigious and heralded professor and a rabbi named Uhlmann. Would you, by any chance, know of anyone that might fit the bill?"

"Well, I can scour my contacts, but that sounds like a very specific young man they're looking for. Tall order to find such a student."

"True. Maybe too specific. Maybe I should let the opportunity evaporate like this rain peeling from the cement all around us. Instead of talking of lofty opportunities, I will simply devour the happiness oozing from my sabich. But if you think of someone …" he said before diving back into his sabich.

"What's involved?" Chiano asked.

"Well, it is an experience that I am sure that this young man will find very moving. Maybe even life changing. Or life-defining." He paused to chew, then after swallowing most of his gigantic bite, he continued. "How would you like to be a tour guide at the Yad Vashem Holocaust Museum?" He let the offer hang in the airless air. "The wage is small but the exposure and experience is priceless. The in-depth immersion in the history of our people in a reverent atmosphere will help you translate the abstractions of disbelief into concrete understanding, and certainty," Rabbi Uhlmann said, pausing to dab dribbles of tahini sauce from his lips with the corner of a spent napkin before ripping another hefty bite from his sabich. He gave a nod and a look to Chiano that asked, "What do you think?"

"That would be amazing! What do I have to do? Is there an interview, an application?"

"You just have to say yes."

"Oh my God! Are you kidding? Yes! Absolutely! Yes!"

"Done." Rabbi Uhlmann dipped his sabich into a plop of hummus that dripped from the pita bread's pocket onto the wrinkled sheet of wax paper protecting the cement table from the oozing runoff of his sabich. "There are details we must address ..." he took another forceful bite ... "transportation to Jerusalem, housing, meals, all of the minutiae that goes with such things ... but all very pleasant minutiae. And there is one other requirement, Chiano Pratto." The rabbi looked at Chiano with the serious look he often kept hidden behind the shimmering eyes of a rascal pulling a prank. "In the Yad Vashem, you will find a magnificent dome called the *Hall of Names*. It is magnificent not just for its beauty, though its design is exquisite, but what makes it magnificent is that this dome portrays photographs of Holocaust victims to honor their memory, a personal tribute to all those who perished. It is a very sobering reminder of their being murdered in the most callous, cruel, and calculated acts in the history of the human race. It is a memorial to every Jew that died, most of them murdered, in the Holocaust. What I ask of you, Chiano Pratto, is to spend much of your time at Yad Vashem under that dome, absorbing the cries of those people and their families, and saturate your soul with the tears of their incalculable sorrow and injustice. Make them a part of you and make the perpetuation of their story the core of the rabbinical exploration you plan to pursue after graduating from Tel Aviv U."

Rabbi Uhlmann continued eating in a more somber silence than Chiano had ever seen in him. The weight of the rabbi's words pierced Chiano's emotional armor, like a bull goring a matador into alarm's clarity." A new urgency permeated into Chiano Pratto's twenty-two-year-old mind, heart, and soul.

"I ... how do I thank you, Rabbi?" Rabbi Uhlmann reached his chunky hands across the table and held both of Chiano's hands beneath his.

"Some things we are thankful for, some things we are grateful for. A fine line distinguishes the two. Many nuances in life cast ambiguous shadows over that cryptic fine line dividing understanding from the unknown. This is an experience that you will be more grateful for than thankful for. You will understand what I mean by this one day. Hopefully, I will understand what I mean, too." He paused to wipe the residue of his sabich from his cheek. "But with gratitude, comes appreciation, and they are the seeds of peace and contentment. These are good things, Chiano Pratto." He began packing his used napkins and wax paper into a humidity-softened paper bag as he rose from the bench. "Now, the sabiches have faded into happy vapors of satisfaction ... Do you know what that means?" Chiano shrugged not knowing what that could possibly mean. "It means we must have ice cream to close the book on our meal." Rabbi Uhlmann revisited his hearty laugh, and they vacated the cement table and pitched their paper lunch bags into a trash bin. The impalpable vision of what was to come developed on the canvas of Chiano Pratto's mind, like a Polaroid photograph developing from a black blur into a colorful image reflecting reality.

Chiano's first thought was to try to express his thanks and gratitude for the deep appreciation he felt for Rabbi Uhlmann's belief in him. His second thought was to rush over to Batia's apartment to tell her, what was at least to Chiano, very good news. He sliced his way through the heat and humidity saturating Tel Aviv in discomfort and ran to Batia's apartment.

With his heart pounding beneath the rumpled, damp pocket on his shirt, Chiano ran up the stairs leading to Batia's apartment and rapped on the door. He rapped again before anyone could answer. A few moments later, the dead bolt latch tumbled free within its housing and the chain lock on the door chinked and jingled. The worn door knob turned and the door opened just enough for a shard of lamp light from inside to leak out. Batia's roommate Rachela stood in a posture that blocked Chiano from entering.

"She's not here. But she expected you later. She left something for you. Wait here a minute," Rachela said. She closed the door, and locked the deadbolt, leaving Chiano standing on the landing puzzled and anxious. He heard her footsteps inside the apartment, the deadbolt mechanisms turned again and the door opened again– just a crack. Rachela handed Chiano an envelope.

"Batia asked me to give this to you when you came," Rachela said, sheepishly. She handed Chiano an envelope. She rolled her soft brown eyes upward from the envelope toward Chiano's eyes and locked onto the urgent anticipation peeling from his face. She peered through the wispy fringe of hair that arched over her forehead and locked onto Chiano's eyes. She handed Chiano the envelope through the sliver of space between the door and the door jam, then quickly closed and locked the door, separating pity from vulnerability, and happiness from sorrow. Chiano opened the envelope with a knowing unease dousing his stomach with fear. He felt apprehension's sweat pasting his shirt to his body, his damp pants stuck to his legs like bark on a tree. He read the letter while still facing the door that had just closed on his moment of joy.

> *Dear Chiano:*
>
> *I am sorry not to tell you this in person, but I just didn't have the heart to see the sadness in your face, the face that always wears a smile and helps me find mine. I have to move on, Chiano. You want to be a rabbi, and I want to be a biochemist. You want a sacrosanct life, and I want a secular life, free of the inevitable restraints inherent in being a rabbi's wife. I know I am jumping way ahead but I think it is important for me to know that this is the best decision for me now, and in the end, for you, so that we can both enjoy other partners while we are lucky enough to be young. I know it is hard to believe, but I do love you, but we want different things in life, Chiano, and we should both set out to find those things before we have regrets that are hard to undo. I know you will be a wonderful rabbi and a wonderful husband and father one day. I wish you nothing but the best.*
>
> *Love, Batia*

The euphoric glee and joy Chiano was steeped in just moments ago crumbled like shattered glass tearing into the walls of his gut. The air in his emotional sails collapsed like a heap of risen dough jabbed with a pointy knife. *No*, he thought to himself. *No!* He turned and walked down the stairs with his lungs filled with shock's chilling precursor to grief. How could his new opportunity be exciting or enjoyable now? How could his possibility be a possibility without Batia to share it with? He moved through the streets of Jaffa leading back to the campus unaware, unconscious, and incoherent. His autonomic magnetic field drew him to Rabbi Uhlmann's office without comprehending time, space, sound, sight, smell, or taste. Just heartache and the sadness that precedes sadness with sadness. He stood at Rabbi Uhlmann's door unable to speak. He entered the rabbi's office in a trance of sorrow and sat down staring without seeing and handed Rabbi Uhlmann Batia's note.

Rabbi Uhlmann read the crushing words that were couched in residual affection. He laid the note on his desk and sat and looked at Chiano in silence before speaking.

"Nothing feels as good as love, Chiano Pratto, and nothing feels as bad. I am sorry, my friend. I am truly sorry."

"She told me in a note ... she couldn't even face me."

"It takes a lot of courage to say what you feel and believe to someone's face. Some people don't have it. They say the hardest things to say are the things that most need saying." He stretched back into his chair and looked at the ceiling as though consulting some cosmic source. "People are often afraid to be judged poorly as bad people, or thought to be foolish, so they pretend, live behind the façade of hollow compliments, or write letters instead of delivering unpleasant news face to face," Rabbi Uhlmann said. He scanned the letter again.

"She has done you a favor, my friend. She has saved you many years of emptiness that decline into an agonizing quagmire of disappointment. And without ever enjoying the vigor of the fire, you find yourself dusting the ashes of discontent from your days, and you realize you have wasted precious years." He slid the letter back to Chiano. "Tuck this pain into some corner of your brilliant neshama– your soul– Chiano Pratto, and use what you are feeling right now to someone's benefit someday. How? Who knows, but one day, your pain in this moment will serve you, and someone who needs your help. You'll know when that time comes." Rabbi Uhlmann rose from his chair and picked up the waste basket stationed next to his desk. He held it up toward Chiano. "Come, throw this note into this waste basket, and thank God for the time you will never waste. Come, throw this pain and this note away for good." Chiano dropped the note into the wastebasket and found a trace of the smile he always wore.

"As God once said to Moses, this is one ass-kicking you're gonna have to take," Rabbi Uhlmann said, and stood next to Chiano with arms wide, offering a heartfelt hug and a caring smile.

CHAPTER 18

Names

Rabbi Uhlmann's promising words that conjured up notions of enthusiasm, excitement, and even adventure, morphed into feelings that moved Chiano at his very core. Rabbi Ullman's words *'Holocaust Memorial'* certainly struck an emotional chord when he spoke them, but a sense of perceptibly safe distance protected Chiano from reliving the tragedies of the past. Now, thinking of a Holocaust memorial made him feel noble and inspired. The day had come to be in the presence of horror's haunt. Chiano felt an unfamiliar and disturbing apprehension as he approached Yad Vashem, Israel's memorial to the Holocaust, and all its heartbroken families of its victims. He felt like a feather blown into the turbulent winds in the canyons of a dreadful unknown.

The museum reflected a tempered coat of grief compassionately comforted by time's soothing balm. Yad Vashem's brilliant sheen of honor seared through the horrific lesions of the Nazi's calculated mass massacre like a determined dawn burning through the scars of history's darkest night. The Holocaust.

Death lives eternally in a paradox of the perpetual moment ablaze in the Holocaust victims' haunting eyes peering from behind the severely geometric walls of Yad Vashem. Chiano was uncertain and uncomfortable about what he would experience inside. Everyone was.

Entering the main glass and marble-rich entrance, Chiano was instantly absorbed in an ether of reverence mixed with an empathetic torment anticipating what was inside. He was cordially greeted by Sarida

Goren, a tall, slender woman with a lippy smile and bright eyes lit by optimism's strength, and knowing's comfort.

"You must be Chiano," Sarida said, extending her hand to welcome and comfort him. "I'm Sarida Goren, welcome to Yad Vashem. We're happy to have you join our team."

"Chiano Pratto. I'm very happy to be here … and to meet you," Chiano said, through a parched tangle in his throat.

"Come with me. I'll show you around and fill you in on the job," Sarida said, as she whisked Chiano across the expansive gleaming floor. "It won't take you long to learn the tour guide training material, but it can take a lifetime to absorb the spirit of the memorial," she suggested, as her smile unconsciously dissolved into the solemnity of the museum's content and purpose. "Rabbi Ullman speaks very highly of you," Sarida said.

"He's a great guy. He was like a father to me at University," Chiano said. "He's the one that recommended me to you … but you know that, of course," Chiano said, tripping over his words, distracted by admiring Sarida, and his anxiousness in his desire to impress her.

"The memorial is a very emotionally trying experience, Chiano. There's really no way to prepare for it, so we're just going to get to it, if that's ok?" Chiano nodded a gesture of agreement and Sarida led him out of the entrance where visitors buy tickets and press their hips through turnstiles to enter the museum. It was before public visiting hours and no guests were in the expansive reception area yet. Thousands of scuff marks from footsteps across the entrance the day before had been washed and polished away to make way for this day's thousands more.

Sarida led Chiano to the first exhibit, an utterly sobering memorial devoted to children who fell victim to the horrors of the Holocaust; one and a half million Holocaust victims were children. One and a half million! Children. Killed. In the Holocaust. They lost their lives long before they were able to enjoy being children, just shortly after their families had filled their hearts with love. All these precious and innocent lives so horribly destroyed by a madman's cruelty.

"Yad Vashem was established specifically to personalize and individualize the Holocaust. When people speak of the Holocaust, this tragedy takes on a sense of singularity, but it is about the six million individual people– people within a people– that perished," Sarida said. "We memorialize each and every one of them here– both the Jews, and Gentiles that fought for, and helped Jews during that horrible time," Sarida explained. "We preserve their identity and their integrity." She stopped walking, turned to Chiano with her eyes searing into the core of his soul. She took firm hold of his arms. Her fingers pressed hard into the muscles of his biceps and triceps. She unconsciously pressed harder as she spoke, transferring the urgency of her inner rage into Chiano's whole being.

"It is their names that matter, Chiano. They were killed for their label– Jews! But they will be remembered here forever, by their names."

She held her piercing stare into Chiano's eyes for a long moment, then slowly reeled her passion back into her own body through the cyclone of fervor in her eyes. As they descended down the stone step ramp leading to the Children's Memorial entrance, Chiano noticed Sarida's smile and happy demeanor melting like warm wax hardening in reality's chill, settling on the shaft of a candle. He followed behind her, registering her graceful, confident stride as it waned into cautious, tentative steps, like veneration preparing for homage. Her fluid grace merged with a respectful commemoration, a perpetual mourning that sustained perpetual life. Chiano followed Sarida thoughtfully down the entrance ramp that was lit by a generous serving of sunlight distributed through openings between a pergola made of bulky beams. The mixture of light and shadow mirrored the very contrast between the brilliant life Chiano was granted, and the unconscionable torment cast upon the innocent children memorialized in the darkness inside. As they arrived at the exhibit's entrance, Chiano stopped to absorb a sculpture of a little boy's face carved into stone on the entrance wall. The boy's cheeks swelled into two little round apple-shaped circles resting on the crest of his smile. His hair neatly groomed, and even in the cloudy ill-defined softness that is sculpture, Chiano saw– and felt– the shine of life in his eyes. His smile will glow from his sweet face forever; he lives on the outside. Chiano looked deep into the eyes of this eternal little boy for a long time before moving inside. The splendor that is the sun took its place behind Chiano's shoulders in its drifting seat in the sky, quietly watching and waiting with God.

Inside, a peaceful, thoughtful dark surrounded the circular room, forming its own surreal world in a mysteriously thick curtain of black uncertainty echoing death's whispers. Photographs of children floated in the dark room, unattached to this world. Mirrors reflected their tiny faces, evoking symbolic encouragement that soulfully reminded Chiano that these faces belong to children– with names– to people, to Jews whose stories we must reflect on, preserve, and retell. Their images hanging from mirrors suspended in mid-air enabled these innocent victims to live in three worlds– their memorialization within the Holocaust's agony, the bliss of the afterlife, and in the very moment, the very place Chiano stood, observing their faces and absorbing their pain. He wondered what their stories were. Who were they? What would they have contributed to our world had they lived? They would be young forever, reflecting a screaming message in their silence, encouraging us to look at ourselves far beyond the mirror, into our hearts, and our souls. Chiano clutched firmly onto a rail to hold himself up under the weight of considering their monumental torment. He stood and held his eyes locked on the children's eyes, hearing their distant cries. He gazed at their photographs and wondered, *Who gave that child that hat? What was that little boy laughing at? What made that other boy smile? What is this little girl's name? I would name her Hanna,* he thought. A single flame burns in the background behind the children's pictures to honor each person killed in the Holocaust as an individual. The minuscule flame tempers our sadness with compassion's comfort and exposes our silent petition for immortality.

Sarida progressed slowly, allowing Chiano to move at his own pace. A recorded male voice in the background called out the names and ages and countries where the murdered children were from, as Chiano and Sarida purposely progressed around the room.

"My God, this little girl can't be more than two. Children. My God, they murdered children. Nine. Four. Six. Six. Twelve. Eight. Fourteen. Seven. Five. Nine ... Poland. Russia. France. Italy. Poland. Italy. Poland. Holland. Russia ... *What kind of human being can kill children– for any reason,* he thought. *How? Why? Twenty-five percent of those killed were children. My God,*" he thought. Chiano couldn't get that number out of his mind. One and a half million. Twenty-five percent. He took one more look around this solemn room, and thought to himself, *Rabbi Uhlmann didn't tell me about the children. How is it that I am not with them? Marcello's family saved our lives. I am just now beginning to realize what that truly means,* he thought.

Sarida ushered Chiano outside for a view of Mount Herzl, and a breath of fresh air, a much needed respite from the sadness and sorrow inside. She stood in silence, allowing Chiano to gather his thoughts and his emotional equilibrium.

"When you first mentioned the notion of names, it didn't dawn on me how powerful that foundation– names ... identity– is to the human being. Our names. Our identity," Chiano said.

"'Yad Vashem' literally means a memorial and a name," Sarida said. It was very insightful of the memorial's founders to latch onto the importance of names as a connection to individual people. The name 'Yad Vashem' is taken from a verse in the Book of Isaiah. 'To them I will give within my synagogue and its walls a memorial and a name better than sons and daughters; I will give them an everlasting name that will endure forever,'" Sarida quoted. "That's about the only quote I can recite from the Torah ... and that's only because I work at Yad Vashem," she said, recapturing her smile. "But it's a quote so worth knowing."

Sarida led Chiano to another section of the museum. Gratitude beamed from his face in thanks for the privilege of seeing this monumental pillar of his Jewish history, in an absolutely private tour.

"I can't tell you how thankful I am for you showing me the museum this way," he said.

"It is a lot to take in, we will have lots of opportunities to absorb the museum in private," Sarida promised. She led him to an exhibit inside a long corridor that housed several small exhibit rooms off the main foyer. These smaller rooms featured photos, videos, and artifacts of horror. Chiano stopped at an exhibit of hundreds and thousands of pairs of shoes, shoes that were ripped from the feet of Jews hauled into concentration camps, stripped of clothes, human rights, and dignity. Their lives. Their shoes, soles emptied of their souls helped the Nazis tally the murdered victims, as well as intimidate and demoralize the already demoralized victims of a war, a war they had little stake in, but paid the highest price. Chiano moved slowly up the length of the exhibit with his eyes fixed on the shoes ... thousands of empty shoes. He knelt down and touched a child's shoe. He pet it as though he were comforting a puppy that had returned home after being lost. He touched it all over, every side, every angle. Inside. Outside. He sat down and rubbed the sole of the shoe to the sole of his own shoe and closed his eyes.

"May the sole of your soul lead the sole of my soul to a road that pays you honor," Chiano whispered. "And may all the souls be heard." Sarida led Chiano deeper into the depths of the hallowed history of the journey of the Jews. They moved on to the memorial's *Hall of Names*, the Jewish people's memorial to every individual Jew that perished during the Holocaust. They had no headstones, no manicured, bucolic gravesites gracefully embracing eternal rest, no artifacts recalling or explaining their lives, but they had the Hall of Names at Yad Vashem to honor their memory, preserve their legacy, and humanize the inhumane. Their poignant photographs and *Pages of Testimony*, one-page summaries of their lives on earth, cataloged the footprint of their lives and provided a dignity due all human beings. Chiano's face grew older as each photograph seized him, arresting his heart and mind, demanding, as much as inviting his attention. Names raced through his mind as he read their faces. Children, mothers, fathers, sisters, brothers, uncles, nieces, nephews, aunts, friends, neighbors, professionals, teachers, merchants, statesmen, paupers, clergy, artists, tradesmen, shopkeepers– Jews. People from all corners of life now perched on the wall of a dome, they look down upon us forever, silently pleading for another day. And now, looking at their faces fixed in eternity's moment, we hope with earnest sentience, that we will never be as powerless as they were. He moved from photograph-to-photograph, page-to-page, person-to-person, bowing his head and silently promising each person whose image is honorably affixed to that wall that he would do as Rabbi Uhlmann asked. He heard the rabbi's voice dancing in his mind saying, *make them a part of you, and make the perpetuation of their story the central core of your rabbinical exploration.* And deep within the emotional stew simmering in Chiano's soul, he vowed to do just that.

CHAPTER 19

Homily

A brilliant September day bathed San Gregorio church and all of Rome in sunlight and warmth. It was Sunday. The bells of San Gregorio chimed and boomed in a pleasant alert, calling the faithful, the hopeful, and the sinful into God's home. The parishioners filed into the church as they had been doing all their lives, greeting each other, dipping their fingers into Holy Water pooled in an ancient bowl carved into a marble pillar. They blessed themselves with the sign of the cross, and in how they cared for one another. The church's magnificent pipe organ flooded the church with a medley of chords of worship that seeped beyond the walls of the church into the open air of the piazza. Inside, in the sacristy, Marcello prepared for the most ceremonious day of his life: he was about to serve his first Mass as an ordained Catholic priest. At exactly 10:00 a.m., the organist transitioned from a random mesh of pleasing chords into the formal playing of this day's Mass Entrance hymn. This was the cue for the congregation to rise, and the procession of altar servers and the priest to enter from the rear of the church and march to the altar. Today's procession was different, bigger. On this day, the procession included two priests as altar servers– Father Frischetti– Marcello's Uncle Salvestro– and Father Finlay. The organist and the organ were a bit sharper this morning, and the choir a bit more vibrant and moved by the verve of the occasion.

Marcello's mother Giuliana, his sister Mia, Chiano, and the entire Pratto family, including Uncle Jewels, took their seats in the first pew of the church. The procession marched into San Gregorio's center aisle under a canopy of music and singing one of Father Marcello Luciari's favorite hymns, *Let There Be Peace on Earth.*

"Let there be peace on earth,
And let it begin with me.
Let There Be Peace on Earth,
The peace that was meant to be.

With God as our Father,
Brothers, all are we.
Let me walk with my brother,
In perfect harmony.

"Let peace begin with me,
Let this be the moment now.

With every step I take,
Let this be my solemn vow,
To take each moment and live,
Each moment in peace eternally.
Let there be peace on earth,
And let it begin with me."

Marcello scattered clouds of incense from corner-to-corner on the altar before taking his place in the center, where he kissed the altar, and began the Mass, as all Catholic Masses begin, with a blessing he voiced with verve and veneration.

"In the name of the Father, the Son, and the Holy Spirit, Amen," Marcello proclaimed, almost chanting, while making the sign of the cross. The congregation uttered a collective 'Amen.' Pride and exhilaration glowed from Marcello's face like red from an apple. He chose the readings and hymns for the Mass and reveled in every moment, every gesture, every word, every detail of the Mass. The homily— the sermon— that is presented after three bible readings, was to be Marcello's golden moment. Before beginning, he savored a moment at the pulpit in silence, relishing knowing he was about to deliver his first homily as an ordained

Catholic priest. He dove in with ease and vigor.

"Today is a day I will remember for the rest of my life … the day I served my first Mass as an ordained Catholic priest. The day I entered the seminary in San Mateo, California, I entered this majestic building at Saint Patrick's Seminary. I immediately went to my spiritual adviser's office. I expected him to share wisdom and insight and fan the spiritual fire already burning in me. Well, without so much as looking at me he said, 'Your spiritual advisor is in the cathedral; he's the frail guy hanging from the Cross.'"

A gasp murmured throughout the church as reaction to the callous reference to Christ crucified, especially when considering the source of that reference.

"I had a similar reaction … my gut turned upside down. Then, he assigned me to pray on my knees before that Crucifix and meditate on the daily Mass readings– everyday– and write a homily for the daily Mass based on the day's Gospel reading. That was the extent of his spiritual advice. No wisdom. No insight. No personal counsel.

"In the end, his advice turned out to be very valuable to me. His assignment enabled me to dig deep into my spiritual essence, and find the grace to interpret, and articulate the Gospel readings in the most honest, the purest terms possible. It enabled me to learn to listen for the Holy Spirit to whisper His words into my ear, to understand those words in my heart, and act on them with my life. Each and every one of more than 700 homilies I wrote as a seminarian reflects a striking reminder that the best spiritual advice we can receive comes from the personal conversations we have with God. When we sit or kneel in silence, and allow God into our hearts, we are drawn so much more deeply into our relationship with Him."

Marcello stepped down from the pulpit and stood at the center of the altar facing his family and friends in the first pew. Then he knelt on the altar for several seconds praying, before returning to the pulpit.

"Yes, my spiritual advisor is on that cross, but my life advisors are in the front pew today. You all taught me how to live. My mother. Mama, you taught me what a wonderful feeling it is to be loved. To be secure, even at the most threatening times, to stand up to bullies as a means of sitting them down, to serve others, even at great personal cost and risk. I love you, Mama. And I thank you. My sister, Mia. You are what sweet is to sugar. You taught me how to cry through the agony of grief, and that I would awake on the other side of anguish feeling loved and never alone.

"Uncle Salvestro. You taught me to be a priest, and to be a man … to listen to God, to love, to care, to nurture, to take action. You taught me that serving God and His people is more vital than serving the organization of the Church.

"My uncle through adoption of sorts, Uncle Jewels, you taught me the value of time and that enrichment is not through what you acquire but through what you give and share." Marcello raised his arm to show off his new watch. "People often receive a watch when they retire. Uncle Jewels has given me this handsome watch on my very first day on the job. He says it's the best of both worlds: Italian design and Swiss engineering. I love you, and I thank you, Uncle Jewels.

"Monsignor B., you taught me that life should be joyful, that laughter is not only the best medicine, but the best teacher, and how to find warmth in the human spirit while standing in an icy mountain stream, and how to smile through my pain. You gave me the very pen that I used to write this homily, and all those that will follow. I love you, and thank you, Monsignor B.

"Chiano Pratto. My best friend, and my mentor. You taught me to be a good friend through your being a great friend, and the joys and wisdom in Jewish rituals, beliefs, and practices. You are my second soul and the ink in my pen, Chiano, and as I write my life story, you will be the words that help define and articulate it. I love you very much, my friend.

"The Pratto family. You taught me that despite the Nazis occupying the Roman streets, they could never occupy the Roman mind. Your friendship with my family taught me the value of community, and how the strength of friendship endures, even amidst the unimaginable. I love you all so very much.

"And Father Finlay. Father Finlay, you gave me the opportunity to build my life work by opening the door to the Catholic University. You gave me the foundation that I will build my life upon. I thank you with every fiber of my being.

"Yes, the savior so cruelly nailed to our Cross is the light of my spiritual world, but you, my family and dearest friends, are the beacon that lights my way. I love each of you very, very much. May God bless you all. I thank God for the faith that I had in knowing that I would become a good seminarian, and one day, God willing, a good priest. Today, my life begins as a priest. I vow to make my life as a priest about seeking God, practicing compassion, and exercising faith. And I vow to use the pulpit to do more than speak."

Marcello couldn't help but sneak a peek, and a knowing look to Uncle Salvestro and Chiano, recalling the valuable role the pulpit physically played in hiding Chiano's family.

"I will use the pulpit as the catalyst of action. I will look up to that Crucifix every day of my life, and I will see, not a frail guy hanging from a Cross, but the strongest, most vibrant God floating on the wings of eagles, instilling strength, courage, and compassion in me, as His righteousness guides me to actions in His example, to make our world better."

Marcello stepped down from the pulpit and crossed to the center of the altar where he bowed in a deliberate genuflection and kissed the ground at Christ's feet. He turned and faced the congregation from the center of the altar with his arms raised outward.

"I invite all of you to join me in a few minutes of silent conversation with God. If you have nothing to say, I promise, he will have something to say to you. Let our conversations begin," he said and knelt on the altar floor. The entire congregation followed his lead and knelt in their pews. There was some shuffling, a nervous cough here and there, and then silence. Marcello maintained this silent indulgence in prayer for nearly five minutes. The veins in his forehead bulged with intensity's tension as he prayed, conversed, and communed with God. He eventually rose from his knees and after a moment, raised his arms, prompting the congregation to rise to their feet. He blessed the chalice that was filled with Communion hosts, symbolic of Christ's body, and another chalice filled with wine, symbolizing the blood Christ shed on our behalf, and a drop of water, symbolic of Jesus' body being pierced with a spear, drawing blood and water from his heart. Marcello prayed silently with passionate urgency, clutching the holy chalice in his hand, then raising a host to the heavens, he prayed aloud.

"This is the body of Christ, blessed are those that are called to his supper," he prayed and genuflected with worshipful devotion. He hesitated, head bowed, knees bent, holding the altar, and squeezed full, round tears from his eyes. In this sacred moment, Father Marcello Luciari, was one with his Lord more than ever before. Moments he beheld, feared, loved, hoped for, and prepared for all his life flashed through his mind like shooting stars flaring through an August night, forcing tears of joy, sorrow, and gratitude to roll down his cherry cheeks. He rose, blinked, wiped the tears from his eyes, and his smile reflected the bright light of the very core of his soul.

The congregation came forward and kneeled in a row before the altar, prepared to accept the symbolic body and blood of Christ. The first person that Father Marcello Luciari administered Communion to was his mother. He moved to her, tears in both their eyes, savoring this moment like no other. He stepped up to his kneeling mother with a host between his index finger and thumb.

"Mama, this is the body of Christ." He placed the host on his mother's extended tongue, and the tears streamed more readily down both their cheeks. He reached into the gold chalice and retrieved another host, and reached toward her again, his hand shaking just enough to notice. "Papa, this is the body of Christ." He placed the second host on his mother's tongue, and held his hand on her head, and silently blessed her.

He moved to his left to serve his sister Mia, and placed a host on her tongue. "Mia, my loving sister, this is the body of Christ." He and Mia were both in tears now, too. He turned and retrieved another host and laid it on Mia's tongue saying, "Gaia, this is the body of Christ." Marcello laid his hands on his sister's head and prayed in silence.

Chiano remained seated in the front pew; only Catholics (in good standing) were allowed to receive Communion. Marcello looked over to Chiano and blessed him silently with a pronounced sign of the cross, his eyes locked on Chiano's. He then moved on to distribute Communion to the co-celebrants and Mass servers, and then he turned to the remainder of the congregation while the choir sang another of Marcello's favorite hymns, *On Eagles Wings*. He continued administering Communion and blessing the congregants one-by-one as the choir sang:

> "You who dwell in the shelter of the Lord,
> Who abide in His shadow for life,
> Say to the Lord,
> My refuge, my rock in whom I trust!

"And He will raise you up on eagles' wings,
Bear you on the breath of dawn,
Make you to shine like the sun,
And hold you in the palm of His hand.

"The snare of the fowler will never capture you,
And famine will bring you no fear,
Under His wings your refuge,
His faithfulness, your shield.

"And He will raise you up on eagles' wings,
Bear you on the breath of dawn,
Make you to shine like the sun,
And hold you in the palm of His hand.

"You need not fear the terror of the night,
Nor the arrow that flies by day,
Though thousands fall about you,
Near you it shall not come.

"And He will raise you up on eagles' wings,
Bear you on the breath of dawn,
Make you to shine like the sun,
And hold you in the palm of His hand.

"For to His angels He's given a command,
To guard you in all of your ways,
Upon their hands they will bear you up,
Lest you dash your foot against a stone.

"And He will raise you up on eagles' wings,
Bear you on the breath of dawn,
Make you to shine like the sun,
And hold you in the palm of His hand ..."

Father Frischetti and Father Finlay returned the altar to its original state in preparation for the next day's Mass.

"I wish to thank you all for being part of this most special day. I also want to thank whomever it was that sent me those much needed, and deeply appreciated envelopes of money throughout my education." He peeked at Uncle Jewels.

"Finally, I wish to thank Father Finlay who nearly single-handedly made my entire preparation, education, and entry to the priesthood possible. And now, I want to announce that after spending some time with my spiritual advisor who is looking over my shoulder right now, I have come up with a way to thank not only Father Finlay, but the United States of America ROTC program for all they have done for me." He paused and swallowed before continuing.

"Throughout my education, I often asked Father Finlay what my obligation to the United States Reserve Officer Training Corp program would be. He always said, 'Don't worry about that; just study.' When I graduated, he said, 'You owe them nothing but thanks.' Well, as I said, my spiritual advisor who stands behind me, came up with a way to express those thanks." He paused again as though to assure himself.

"I understand that the United States of America is increasing their military presence in Vietnam. I owe that ROTC program a significant debt. So as a means of repaying that debt, in two weeks' time, I will follow the footsteps of Father Finlay; I will be leaving for training to prepare to serve the United Nations Forces, and the United States Army as a Chaplain in Vietnam."

Shock burned through fear's dread and spread across Giuliana's face. Tears rolled down her eyes as the thought of losing her son immediately clashed with pride in supporting his decision. Father Finlay turned in surprise, so did Uncle Salvestro. Marcello nodded to them, then turned back to face the congregation.

"The Mass has ended. Go in peace to love and serve the Lord. In the Name of the Father, the Son, and the Holy Spirit, Amen," he said, and led the procession down the aisle toward the back of the church, as the choir sang "Through *the Mountains May Fall*."

"Though the mountains may fall and the hills turn to dust,
Yet the love of the Lord will stand.
As a shelter for all who will call on His name,
Sing the praise and the glory of God.

"Could the Lord ever leave you?
Could the Lord forget His love?
Though a mother forsake her child,
He will not abandon you.

"Though the mountains may fall and the hills turn to dust,
Yet the love of the Lord will stand.
As a shelter for all who will call on His name,
Sing the praise and the glory of God.

"Should you turn and forsake Him,
He will gently call your name.
Should you wander away from Him,
He will always take you back.

"Though the mountains may fall and the hills turn to dust,
Yet the love of the Lord will stand.
As a shelter for all who will call on His name,
Sing the praise and the glory of God."

Marcello greeted the well-wishing congregants one-by-one on the church steps with a never fading smile, warm handshakes, and hugs with the hymn still playing inside the church.

CHAPTER 20

The March

"I think I want to go, Uncle Jewels," Chiano said. "I can make it the focus of my independent study project for the semester," he said.

"Why something so dangerous? It is a powder keg, Chiano. Why get in the ring against so many enemies? Cheer for your side of the fight from outside the ring," Uncle Jewels said.

"That's just the point– to get in the ring, to be up close where I can see the truth, to make an impact," Chiano declared. "If I'm going to be a rabbi, I want to be a champion for peoples' rights, and what's more fundamental than the basic civil rights these people are fighting for?" Chiano reasoned, as he maneuvered yet another watch in an already robust collection of watches displayed in the window of his uncle's new store, Pratto Jewelers– in the United States. This new store was a brave new venture into retailing for Uncle Jewels, but he had an eye for knowing what it took to make any venture a good one. Uncle Jewels chose to locate his new store in the small hamlet of Rye, N.Y., just a twenty-minute train ride into Midtown Manhattan, the heart of New York City, and the heart of the world. He chose Rye in order to capitalize on a wealthy and discriminating clientele that prospered from Wall Street salaries and enabled them to indulge in suburban luxuries. He also chose Rye for its proximity to Hebrew Union College– HUC– where Chiano was enrolled in his second year of rabbinical school, just two blocks from Washington Square and New York University ... and light years away from much of the universe. Chiano lived in a small flat with a roommate from HUC but visited his Uncle Jewels in Rye frequently. And Uncle Jewels was frequently in the city doing business in New York's renowned Diamond District.

"Why so many watches, Uncle Jewels … do you really sell this many watches? You've always had a ton of watches on display in your store. Marcello and I used to think you were a little coo-coo," Chiano said, unable to resist the tempting pun. The eye-catching display of watches he was building reflected a sense of symmetry and simple elegance. A collection of handsome men's watches rose on three levels of shelves over the brilliant light of backlit white-milk glass shelves. A complementary collection of women's watches was similarly positioned on the right side of the men's watches. There was a short aisle-like entrance to the store with display windows on both sides. Small black and white tiles served as the entrance floor. Customers were able to view a glittering inventory of watches, necklaces, bracelets, rings, and pins under dazzling lighting showering both sides of the entrance. A sense of welcome allure drew the eye to the stark black canopy above the entrance of the store bearing the words 'Pratto Jewelers' written in smart silver script. The stunning display presented in the windows elevated every store near it, and drew the attention of passersby because it was new and impeccably designed.

"Watches are the lifeblood of the store– as far as you and Marcello are concerned, young man. Watches behold the most precious of all precious gems. Time!" He proposed his proposal with the deliberate lifting of his left eyebrow, and a very subtle, self-affirming nod of his head. "The watches present every second. Time, Iano, is everything. It is perpetual, imperceptibly fusing the past with present and future in immeasurable, microscopic capsules of existence that we call 'Now!' And it is gone before we're able to perceive it, let alone acknowledge it. Yes, 'now' is the ultimate gift. It is gone, lived, and renewed in the very same instant. You can watch time in many ways, Chiano," he said, setting Chiano up for a dose of his exclusive Uncle Jewels wisdom.

"For instance, as you display these watches, we can say that you are 'watching.' It is a twist on the verb, to watch, yes? When we take a watch from the case, we say, 'watch out!' I hope you're watching that watch so no one steals it. Not on my watch," he said, chuckling. "If I give you a watch, am I 'watching' you? And look," he said, pointing at two different watches, one after the other. "We have a day watch, and a night watch," he said. "And you know what, when I went to the bank or post office, or for a walk, you and Marcello would watch the store ... do you know what that means?"

"Hard to tell," Chiano said, humoring his uncle.

"It means you used to put watches in the window ... you were watching the store ... and when you were little, I used to watch you!" Uncle Jewels laughed his good-natured laugh and patted Chiano on the back. "Please, watch out while I squeeze past you," he said, giving in to the attraction to one more watch joke.

"I gotta watch out for you," Chiano added. And they both had an easy laugh.

"Just take my word for it, you and Marcello will come to appreciate watches as much as I do one day," Uncle Jewels said, as he unpacked more watches to be displayed. "You just watch," he said, again, unable to resist the chance to be silly. He handed Chiano another watch to display. "So, tell me, why is it so important to you to go to Alabama to march over a bridge with people you don't know, to protest against people you don't understand?"

"It's about people I want to help, people I care about, Uncle Jewels. I want to show my support for Negroes, and Civil Rights. I want to show my opposition to the white people that are cruel and suppressive to Negroes. We all deserve civil rights. It's no different than the Nazis suppressing and terrorizing Jews, Uncle J."

"I see. What you say is true. Noble. Your father will be as proud of you as I am. But I am worried about your safety, Chiano. These people who are suppressing the Negroes are filled with hatred, and venom, and they will go to extremes to hold the Negroes down. Hateful people will go to extremes to protect the power that they fear losing, Chiano. I don't want you to be a target of such hatred just by being there."

"Uncle Jewels, we're Jews. We have been the victims of hatred's arrows throughout history," Chiano countered. "It's almost our way of life, it's as Jewish as gefilte fish and horseradish." Uncle Jewels' jovial light-hearted demeanor vaporized instantly like lights going out in a room.

"Don't ever think of yourself– or Jews– as victims, Chiano. We were survivors of the Holocaust but in the end, we are not merely survivors, we are, and always will be, achievers." Uncle Jewels relaxed his hold on tension and breathed a little easier. "I love you too much to see you exposed to danger, Iano. I think you should find another way to show your support to the Negro people, and your opposition to their oppressors," Uncle Jewels said.

"I want to show my support and opposition authentically, Uncle J. I want it to count ... for real," Chiano reasoned. "There are a few leaders in this movement that I'm really inspired by ... especially Reverend Martin Luther King Jr.; he gives me goosebumps when he speaks. He's a tremendous speaker with amazing insight and such an innate sense of spirituality. He preaches peace, Uncle J. He's so right in demanding rights and insists on demanding those rights peacefully," Chiano said. "And there's another guy, a guy just my age, Arturo Lewis, he's the chairman of a non-violent student committee who's one of the leaders fighting for Negroes to have the right to vote. And there's a guy named John Lewis, he's Chairman of the Student Nonviolent Coordinating Committee– he has such a grip on what's right and wrong. He lives in this kind of quiet courage and wisdom that you just have to get behind. I want to be exposed to these people, Uncle J. I want to fight for what they're fighting for. I want to be counted in, and counted on. I care about these people ... as a Jew, as a prospective rabbi ... as a person ... I care about them and believe in what they're fighting for. It's like the Nazis and the Jews all over again, Uncle Jewels. I can't just stand here and watch," he maintained.

"Ah, there's that watch thing again. You have to watch out for that ..." Uncle Jewels said, less jovial than before. "I'll tell you what, you promise me that you will do what you have to do in order to remain safe while showing this authentic support you speak of, and I will stand behind you– not literally, but I will stand behind you. And I will provide you with what you need in order to go on this march. But you must promise me that you will be very careful."

"I promise, I will pay– " Uncle Jewels covered Chiano's mouth with his hand to silence him before he could finish speaking.

"Just promise me that you'll be careful. Promise to remember how ugly hatred can be and how some people do not value all human life like you and I do. Don't give hatred's monsters the opportunity to prey on you. Promise me you'll be careful."

"I promise, Uncle Jewels," Chiano said. "I'll watch out for myself."

Two days later, Chiano boarded a bus organized by a civil rights activist committee at HUC. Chiano's excitement in committing to a cause he believed in clashed with his apprehension about the potential danger Uncle Jewels, the national media, and the event organizers warned him about. He stuffed his duffle bag into the rack above a seat toward the rear of the bus hoping to sit alone and stretch out over the 1,100 mile, sixteen-hour ride to Selma, Alabama. He got his wish for a solo seat and then some: a slender, attractive young woman with shiny, light-brown hair enriched by natural blondish highlights that attracted sunshine, made her way down the aisle of the bus, scanning for a strategic seat. Chiano prayed vigorously to himself. *Please sit here. Please sit here. I hope she sits here,* he pleaded to himself. Her smile was wide, and her eyes bright with a twinkle of calm happiness. She appeared intelligent just through her posture and relaxed air of confidence. A far-reaching passion was couched in the fabric of her casual demeanor, and approachable manner. She was cute, beautiful, and pretty all at the same time. She wore a shade of classic reddish lip gloss and just a hint of eyeliner that created an intriguing effect of subtle radiance that meshed into the background of her sharply defined features.

"OK if I sit here?" she asked Chiano.

"Please. Of course. Here, I'll help you with that," Chiano said, motioning to her hefty duffle bag as he got up from his seat to help her.

"That'd be great. Thank you so much." Chiano dutifully wrestled her bag into the stingy rack above her seat as she dumped another large leather bag, and a three-quarter-length black sweater onto her seat. When Chiano finished tucking her bag into the skimpy luggage rack, she extended her hand in greeting.

"Avigail Cooper."

"Chiano Pratto," he said, with a smile, accepting her solid handshake. "Nice to meet you. Avigail with a 'v'?" he asked.

"Yes. My parents were not exactly conventional." Her smile was magnetic. Chiano instantly felt comfortable with her.

"That's really pretty."

"Chiano Pratto is, too. You're Italian."

"Yes, I grew up in Rome." Her face registered that she had instantaneously did the math and made the connection that Chiano had grown up during the Nazi occupation of Rome.

"Oh. Lucky you ... right?"

"Yes, and no. You're very perceptive," Chiano said, knowing that she was referring to wartime. She acknowledged the compliment with a smile that she tucked behind her innate humility. "It was mostly good after the Nazis left," Chiano said.

"It's Rome, right," she said. "I've never been, but it's high on my list."

"Yes, it's Rome. It's really amazing, even if you've grown up there, you can't get enough of it. How about you, where did you grow up?"

"Wisconsin– Madison. My parents both teach at the University of Wisconsin there."

"Wow. That had to be an advantage through school."

"It was. They taught my brother and I to love learning and how to study. It really was an advantage."

"What'd you major in?"

"I did a double major in Political Science and Journalism."

"Nice. Impressive."

"Scheduling and my interests just happened to work out," Avigail said.

"Are you at HUC now?"

"No, no, I'm at NYU for a Masters in a Public Policy program. Are you at HUC?"

"Yes. I'm training– or studying– to be a rabbi."

"An Italian Rabbi. I like that."

Avigail also liked Chiano. And Chiano liked Avigail, instantly. Just thirty-five minutes into the drive, they gave up their coveted solo seats and sat side-by-side. Well into the bus's 1,100-mile roll toward Selma, Avigail fell asleep on Chiano's shoulder, and he fell asleep under the blanket of her magnetic allure. They spoke about their families, friends, fears, dreams, hopes, aspirations, wonders, careers, politics, and why they were sitting on a bus to march across the Edmund Pettus Bridge in Selma, Alabama, to show their support for Civil Rights, and to oppose the atrocious injustices inflicted upon African Americans. The time, and the ride, was passing with little notice by Chiano and Avigail as they completely engaged in conversation and occasionally, a comfortable silence, and catnaps.

After two long days on the bus, separated by an overnight stop in Wytheville, West Virginia, they arrived at The Tabernacle Baptist Church in Selma, Alabama. The church looked more like a courthouse from the rain-dotted bus window Chiano and Avigail were peering through. The church's yellow-gold bricks formed a half-block-long rectangle. Four two-story-high Roman columns were supported by square brick pedestals. The pedestals were built into the top of wide concrete steps that led to the church's wooden French doors. A large white pediment trimmed in crown molding rested upon the pillars to welcome all who entered below. An intriguing circular glass dome rose from Marcelloel behind the pediment, like a missile silo poking out of the earth. The bus came to a long awaited, and much needed, complete stop in front of the church, its tired motor tumbled to silence, and its doors squeaked open. Comforting traces of fresh, humid Alabama air dressed in a jacket of rain flowed into Chiano's parched nostrils, and hungry lungs. He gathered the tattered and tightly hitched discs holding his spine in place and stretched upward to relieve the discomfort in his body and prepare his backbone and gut to march with courage and conviction the next day.

Outside the bus, a small group of Black church members greeted the busload of mostly young white Jews, four Catholic nuns, and three priests with open arms and broad smiles. Chiano felt welcome the moment his eyes met a Black man wearing horn-rimmed glasses, and a brilliant smile that lit up the dreary sky. He heard none of the other voices, only this man's well-deep baritone voice.

"Welcome to Tabernacle Baptist, son. I'm Reverend Grady Moore. Welcome son, thank you for being here with us," Reverend Moore boomed. His gratitude flickered through a certain twinkle and tiny, little tears welling up in the corners of his eyes. "Come on inside," he said, ushering Chiano, Avigail, and the others up the church steps. "Come get yourselves some sweet tea, sandwiches, banana puddin', Alabama Caramel Cake ... the ladies fixed up a feast for y'all. Come right in ... welcome, come in, come in ..." Reverend Moore urged from behind his radiant smile. He created an atmosphere of warmth and welcome that sprinkled optimism's herbs into the solemn soup souring the entire south. The march was to begin in the morning, but tonight was all about the vibrant spirit permeating throughout the church.

After a welcome meal and two pieces of Alabama Caramel Cake, Chiano wandered from the meeting hall into the dome, the church itself. He stood at the back of the church marveling at the uniform stained-glass windows containing the spirit inside, and inviting the gray light and energy from outside in. An ingenious theater-like circular balcony surrounded the main floor in a soft swirl of light that seemed to smile down at the altar filled with the choir's folding chairs. Yellow Alabama wild-flowers surrounded the pulpit on the altar where Reverend Moore voiced his vision, and sang his inspiring message of faith, love, and worship every Sunday.

"You've found our cathedral," Reverend Moore said, never departing from that infectious smile as he entered the church. "We love our church, I can tell ya, love it real deep," he said.

"I can see why," Chiano said.

"The trick is to see *how*," Reverend Moore suggested, with a hardy pat on Chiano's back and even heartier laugh. "I'm just playin' with you, son. But we sure do love our church. One of our own built it. "Brother by the name of David West was a deacon at the Tab, as we like to call it. He was an architect and a contractor. Did the whole thing for us ... gotta be ... forty years ago. Looks a lot different from outside, don't it?" He laughed again. "Looks like a bank or something from outside ..." he mused. "But inside, inside, this is God's house, and we treat it as such," he said, then paused to admire and absorb the powerful spirit whispering in the stillness of the church. In the Tab.

"We're glad to have you here, brother," Reverend Moore said with a friendly hold on Chiano's shoulder. "Means a lot to us to have white folks with us. Means a lot."

"I'm glad to be here, Reverend, it means a whole lot to me, too," Chiano said, looking soulfully into Reverend Moore's eyes, as Avigail entered the church beaming.

"Wow! This is absolutely beautiful, Reverend. I'm Avigail," she said, shaking Reverend Moore's hand.

"Reverend Grady Moore. Nice to meet you, Mam. Thank you for joinin' us. I was just telling this young fella how much the march means to a whole lot of people," the reverend said, shaking his head. "Whole lot o' people. A march is way more than a walk, you see. We are on the march, and God's truth is marching right there with us," Reverend Moore declared. "I'll leave you two here to enjoy the spirit of the Tab," he said, patting Chiano's back once more. "Very nice to meet you all." He left Chiano and Avigail in The Tab to soak in the rain of God beading up on the stained-glass windows outside, and on the souls of Chiano Pratto, and Avigail Cooper inside.

The morning of the March was chilly and gray, temperatures vacillated in the low forties. Most of the marchers were Black men, some were white priests and ministers, some white nuns, and there was Chiano and his HUC colleagues, simple people who cared and dared enough to show up to pit compassion against primal hatred. They showed up to support Black American's right to vote, express their opposition to policies designed to suppress Blacks, and to protest the shooting of Jimmie Lee Jackson, a deacon and activist shot to death by state trooper, James Bonard Fowler, during a peaceful rally several days earlier in Marion, Alabama.

The mood on the morning of the march was somber. Apprehension cut through the armor of the marchers' raincoats and invaded their guts with tension's bile, but that vile bile was seized and demolished by resolve's raw grit. The profound will to elevate wrong to right energized the marchers. Their march began on their knees at The Tab with a prayer and a plea for hope's help. Their steps scuffed along as a muffle of muted scratches of leather soles scraping along the pavement. The scent of a briny mist peeling off the Alabama River below the bridge soured the stomach and turned the gray air more opaque.

Arturo Lewis, the non-violent leader that so moved Chiano, and the 600 marchers behind him, stepped onto what Reverend Martin Luther King Jr. described as the 'Highway of Freedom,' The Edmund Pettus bridge. They were intent on delivering their grievances to the doorstep of Alabama Governor George C. Wallace at the state capitol in Montgomery. The marchers approached the hump of the bridge two-by-two. They couldn't see beyond its crest, but they imagined– they knew– what to expect on the other end of the bridge: a band of violent racists made in the mold of the man the bridge was named for, Edmund Winston Pettus. Edmond Pettus was a senior Confederate officer who became a leader of the Alabama Klu Klux Klan after the Civil War and callously retrained and imprisoned Black people long after the war. Like Pettus, the 150 men bearing arms on the dark end of the bridge, stood at the ready, eager to release their harbored hatred by unleashing powerful fire hoses, ferocious dogs, and the cruel clubs of racism over the bodies of peaceful protesters hoping to claim the basic human rights due them.

Chiano and Avigail positioned themselves toward the front of the line of marchers. The marchers were orderly as they proceeded. Most were solemn, some scared, some inspired, all were intent on standing up for the same rights white Americans enjoyed: the right to vote, the right to live with dignity, to savor the fruits of the same freedom and liberty that one and a half million African Americans fought for while serving in the United States of America's armed forces in World War II. They simply sought to be free of the consequences and taint of prejudice, free of bigotry, free of bias, freed from the cruel shackles of hatred's choke hold. Free to become. Free to be.

There was no hesitation when they got to the crest of the bridge. The apprehension escalated as a line of state police, local police, and a posse of hate-filled men on horseback formed a defining line of defiance. The angry mob posted on the Selma side of the bridge aimed to preserve the racist values beheld by many whites in power in 1965 Selma, Alabama, and tragically, in much of America's south. Their stand was as much about deprivation as it was about preservation.

Chiano could see Reverend Moore immediately behind Arturo Lewis and James Bevel, the Southern Christian Leadership Conference Director of Direct Action, and the man who called for three such marches that spring. Mr. Bevel had been working on securing Alabama voting rights for Blacks since 1963. Chiano heard Reverend Moore's voice in his mind saying, *It's more than a walk, son, it's a march.* Chiano passed over the crest of the bridge and saw the line of defiance more clearly. He could see the helmets on police officers. They were patting their billy clubs in the palms of their hands; they reminded Chiano of *that day,* as a scared little boy, watching a Nazi lieutenant pat his billy club in his palm the exact same way, before he beat and killed Marcello's father. Most of them wore gas masks. Uncle Jewels' voice ran through Chiano's mind: *Don't give hatred's beasts the opportunity to prey on you. Promise to be careful. Too late now,* he thought. As the front line of marchers got closer to the end of the bridge, the police and the posse moved into position, like an American football team's lineman approaching the line of scrimmage after breaking their huddle.

The marchers marched forward, collected and determined, despite the wall of hatred eager to expel their wrath upon them. As Chiano and Avigail got to that wall of white hatred, they saw that the police and their posse were armed to the teeth with rifles, tear gas, billy clubs, and hatred's might. They marched forward, not tentatively, not timidly, but not bold either. They were intent. Chiano saw patches of white faces peeking through the frightening gaudiness of gas masks. The state policemen's bulky, boxy grey pants underscored the belligerence of their stance. Their dark blue shirts ironically resembled the blue Union Army uniforms that the southern states fought so bitterly and futilely in defeat in the American Civil War. The Alabama police and their posse were prepared to beat Negroes because they did not want Negroes to have the right to vote, to speak, to voice their opinions. They did not want Negroes to live equally, to have the same opportunities that they had enjoyed by the simple virtue of being born into white families, families that raised them to hate Negroes. This was in fact, bigger than a walk, this was a march, a march that would march far beyond Montgomery, Alabama.

As the marchers approached the battalion of heavily armed protectors of bias and hatred stationed at the foot of the bridge, one of the state troopers lifted a bullhorn to his mouth and spit out a muzzled message.

"I am Major Addison. This is an unlawful assembly. You have been banned by the governor. I am going to order you to disperse. This march will not continue," Major Addison barked into the bullhorn. The marchers stopped, unsure of what to do. The leader of the march was a man named Hosea Williams of the Southern Christian Leadership Conference. Hosea addressed Major Cloud.

"Mr. Major, I would like to have a word. Can we have a word?" Hosea asked.

"No. I will give you two minutes to leave."

Again, Hosea Williams asked, "Can I have a word?"

"There will be no word." Just one minute and five seconds after Major Addison's two-minute warning, he ordered his troops to advance and the toxic social hell that was 1965 Selma, Alabama broke loose. State troopers thrashed the marchers with billy clubs, fired tear gas canisters and a wall of helmeted, gas-masked policemen charged the marchers. Panic. Violence. Chaos rolled into the 600 marchers like wrecking balls bashing into buildings. Violence smashed into peace, hatred into love, racism into equality. Chiano saw Reverend Moore take a blow to the head from a billy club and fall to the ground. Another policeman drove the butt of his billy club into the reverend's ribs– again and again and again. John Lewis took a similar harsh blow to the head. Chiano heard his skull crack. The sound of the billy club smashing John Lewis' skull carved a permanent impression in Chiano's psyche and a lasting sickness in his stomach. He ran toward John Lewis to help him, hold him, drag him away, do anything he could to protect him from hatred's brutality. He took three quick steps, never feeling the Selma pavement beneath him, when a thick, dull thud whacked the back of his head. He went down hard and fast. A policeman hovered over him. Chiano could see the eyes of rage almost bursting through his military gas mask. He looked at Chiano like the Nazis looked at Jews just before they killed them– with an inhuman, unimaginable, unfounded, intense hatred. He saw the man draw his billy club across his body and began a downward backhand stroke that Chiano was able to blunt with his arm. His head was hot with pain, confusion, and shock, and wet with blood. He heard Avigail yelling. The man bashed his billy club over Chiano's head again. Just before he lost consciousness, he heard the angry snarl of an attack trained German Shepherd tearing into the skin of the woman who served him Alabama Caramel Cake the night before in the peaceful sanctity of The Tab. Then he heard Avigail's desperate pleas.

"Stop! Stop!" She screamed to no avail. A posse member not wearing a uniform or facemask smacked her from behind with a hard backhand that knocked her to the ground. The policeman beating Chiano stepped on his chest and kicked him in the ribs before running off to inflict pain upon another unarmed, innocent marcher, an American citizen who merely wanted his due right to vote. Chiano tried to roll to his side, to raise his feet to attend to Avigail, but he was too dizzy, too weak. He fell back to the ground and his eyes fixed on John Lewis trying to find cover under the flimsy shield of his raincoat as a policeman beat his head unmercifully, shattering his skull with vicious blows of his billy club. Chiano's vision seemed to be moving back and forth as though he were looking through a camera being shaken side to side. He tried to focus, tried to comprehend. He saw a deputized posse man beating yet another Black woman senseless with yet another billy club. She lay unconscious just a few feet in front of him. He recognized her face as Ameilia Boyton, a vocal, courageous Civil Rights activist he had seen in newspapers and had come to admire. Through the blur of his blur, he discerned the image of Avigail running toward him. He tried again to rise to his feet to come to Ms. Boyton's aid when a tear gas canister landed just two feet in front of him. His eyes swelled almost instantly. Tears flowed. A burning stream of fluid ran from his nose. His mouth burned. His throat felt like it was closing, constricting; he was choking. He struggled to his knees but fell again. Uncle Jewels' voice tripped through his mind again: *Don't give hatred's beasts the opportunity to prey on you.* He reached up for someone to help him, screaming out:

"Uncle Jewels! Uncle Jewels. Help me!"

CHAPTER 21

Saint Saveus

The engine's roar in the Bell Helicopter Company's UH-1 helicopter, the HUEY, was deafening. The rattle and jerking couldn't be detected from the ground as it zipped across the sky above the jungle, but it was more than noticeable rattling the teeth of the troops inside it– and in the pit of Marcello's stomach. The thick stink of JP-4 aviation fuel smothered the oxygen in 'The Box,' the designation U.S. Army helicopter pilots assigned to the crude area behind the cockpit. Troops sat in The Box on 'benches' made from canvas seats and backrests tied to a frame of metal pipes. This was drop day– the day Marcello was to be dropped into the thick jungles of the la Drang Valley in Vietnam's Central Highlands, 3,000 miles from his home in Rome, and a million miles from the world. Marcello, now in cooperation with the Army ROTC program and the United Nations, was an official United States Army Chaplain who quickly attained the moniker 'Chap.' He enjoyed the nickname, it made him feel accepted as one of the troops, one of the guys. Marcello was a non-com– a non-combat troop. He joined some 185,000 troops deployed to Vietnam in 1966; 1,928 of them never returned home.

A few soldiers shouted nearly indistinguishable phrases of contrived bravado as the HUEY carrying them nearly shaved the treetops as they dipped into valleys. Most troops remained silent. They were all younger than Marcello, who was twenty-eight. The boys surrounding him were still in their late teens, two just hit twenty. There was a sergeant in The Box, too; Sergeant Bostic; he was twenty-four but looked more like forty-four. War's scars were etched on his face and its memories burned behind his lifeless eyes, refusing to be dismissed and refusing to be acknowledged. His focus locked in on survival and the safety of these eighteen- and nineteen-year-old kids pinned to the blood- and mud-stained canvas seats beneath their rumps. As the HUEY descended, Marcello closed his eyes, clutched a crucifix hanging with his dog tags, said a silent prayer, and made the sign of the cross. He could see the HUEY in front of the one he was holding onto for dear life as it dropped its troops. He saw green figures loft out of the chopper's doors on both sides. It was like watching a car in front of him on a ride in an amusement park, foreshadowing what thrill or terror was to come. Very, very soon. The HUEY descended lower and faster now; the chopper ahead made its quick drop, and even quicker dust off. Marcello's drop was next. Now.

"Listen up. When we go, it's heads down, eyes on your landing target. Jump away from the chopper's skids. Watch out for rocks. When I say 'go,' we go," Sgt. Bostic shouted over the engine's roar. He pointed at a soldier in the back of the chopper and hollered, "You're first. You're next," he shouted at the terrified looking boy next to the first boy … "Then the rest of us down the line will follow," he shouted, then he shuffled to the other side of the chopper to give the same instructions to the troops on that side.

There were six soldiers on each side of the chopper. The elephant grass sprouting out of the jungle like a shag carpet under a microscope got closer and closer, waving, and curling under the force of the chopper's whirling blades. The heat of the ground bounced off the heat of the HUEY in a combative, defiant opposition, an attempt by the land, and the country to challenge the physics of the chopper, gravity itself, and the mechanics and politics of war. Marcello was fourth in line to jump when the order was given.

"On your feet, men. Get ready," Sgt. Bostic shouted, his voice muffled by the roar of the HUEY's engine and its ferocious blades. The Huey got close to the ground and tipped forward to remain parallel to the slope of the hill hovering six feet above the ground. "We're going to that tree line at two o'clock," Sgt. Bostic said, pointing in the direction of a line of trees to the east. "Stay low. Hit the ground and run like hell to those trees," he shouted. "If we take on fire, hit the deck, fast!" Closer to the ground, a vision of Marcello's father, Vieri, cranking up the Victrola flashed through his mind. A smile warmed him from the inside, taking him away from war's moment to embrace a moment of his own. For the next twelve months, all his moments will belong to the United States Army.

"Go!" Sgt. Bostic shouted, shattering Marcello's moment of peace. "Next guy, go!" He yelled until everyone was out of the chopper and dangerously landed in Vietnam. Marcello hit the ground hard but upright. He had to wait for the soldier in front of him to recover from a clumsy landing. Marcello grabbed the boy by the arm to help him up and they ran to the tree line crouched low to the ground. They got to the tree line and found a squad of American troops with weapons poised, protecting the newbies. Their eyes and weapons were fixed on the HUEY landing area and the perimeter around it. The guys Marcello just flew alongside looked much younger now than they did five minutes ago. And Marcello was feeling a little older, too. The bright, humid days of Vietnam's tropical sunshine flushed into the toilet of night's war, all too quickly.

The U.S. Army Chaplain's core mission was to conduct services, and provide counseling and moral support, but the purpose and practical value reached far deeper and broader into the thick tangles of Vietnam's violent jungles. Marcello soon found himself holding babies while South Vietnamese mothers searched for belongings among the rubble of their burned-out villages. He prayed with local dignitaries and taught children to tango, cha-cha, and waltz. He discussed local traditions over crooked pottery cups of potent portions of pungent rice wine that, on one occasion, nearly induced him to forget his name. Since Vietnam was fought under guerrilla warfare, Marcello had to be as mobile as the troops he was there to comfort. He delivered medical supplies into remote bases and conducted services in tents, open fields, helicopter hangers, and nearly anywhere else he set foot. Despite being a faithful man, a man of God, Marcello learned to be skeptical as a means of survival. Was the cheerful young man that cut the troops' hair and cleaned their fatigues in the morning the same guy perched in a tree all night taking pot shots at soldiers moving about the base? Was the little boy delivering what looked like a bowl of rice really carrying a bomb under the towel covering the bowl? Is that soft patch of grass that appears as an inviting place to lie down and rest covering a lethal punji trap? Is that branch twisting in the river current a fallen branch from a tree, or a cobra on the hunt? Marcello learned to suspect such hazards because he had witnessed them more than once.

Marcello liked the close contact he had with the soldiers and local villagers; they became his parishioners as he moved about under the canopy of vicious and perpetual jungle warfare. One of his pet civic projects was to serve as the spiritual core and practical leader of the Sacred Heart Orphanage just outside Da Nang. He offered Mass every morning and his warm spirit all day at the orphanage. The orphanage was supervised by the Sisters of Saint Paul de Chartres whose purpose was to teach, provide nursing, and care for the poor, the orphans, the aged, and the mentally ill. These devout and miraculous nuns have been serving this purpose since their inception– 3,000 years ago!

Marcello held, rocked, coddled, and fed children on picnic tables on the orphanage grounds. He sang songs with the nuns and the children. Despite the language barrier, Marcello read picture books at night in English and Italian, and often in a silly language he invented to engage and entertain children. He wept on more than one occasion as the reality of these children's hardships and terribly unjust circumstances took command of his mind. One boy in particular named Mihn Vong, an eight-year-old with cowlicky hair, sad eyes, and a magnetic smile, stole Marcello's heart. Confusion, sorrow, and innocence spilled from Mihn's eyes. Love and warmth melted from minute fragments of hope burning in his sad, little-boy heart. Marcello liked to pick Mihn up, sit him in a chair, look deep into his eyes, and then take his two index fingers and form Mihn's mouth into a smile. Then Marcello would mirror Mihn's smile with his own. He would then hold Mihn's head in his hands and pull the boy close to his heart, release the boy, then touch his hand to his own heart, then Mihn's heart. After three times going through this routine, Mihn smiled upon site the moment he saw Marcello, and he would touch his hand to his heart and wave to Marcello.

"I love that kid so much," he told one of the nuns who often witnessed this routine. "He stole my heart, and I don't think I'll ever get it back," he said. Being touched by a child like Mihn was one of the few rewards of a chaplain's job. He loved the children but loathed how bad he felt for them, and he loathed how injustice was so unjust, so unfair, so cruel. He made it a point to touch the head of every child that he saw every day as an affectionate gesture to help God touch the children who needed His touch most. Adults in Vietnam desperately needed God, too. And Marcello was committed to bringing God wherever he walked.

Soldiers in Vietnam were just boys. They were assigned to the ghastly task of killing people, subject to the grisly experience of seeing friends being killed and maimed almost daily. They were exposed to the risk of death most days and nearly every night. They suffered from guilt, suppressed their fear, yet they mustered extraordinary courage. The hideous human toll imposed by war inflicted deep emotional lesions and substantial mental damage upon these soldiers, these man-boys. Marcello was often their only source of consoling, and often their only means of preserving ever-evasive threads of evaporating sanity. His training in philosophy, psychology, and divinity often fell short of the task of effectively counseling the men, women, and children who so desperately depended on such counseling. The ineptness he felt when he knew he could not soothe the deep wounds of war left Marcello in need of counsel himself. But there was none. He longed deeply for a talk with Chiano, Uncle Salvestro, his Mom, and Uncle Jewels. He turned to the spiritual advisor he had always depended upon– the strong, silent man hanging from the Cross. And the answer was always the same: offer genuine compassion, encourage quiet contemplation with God, find a way to be part of the solution, and take action to provide it. The advice seemed to work. He also enlisted the gracious counsel and open ear of many blank pages of paper wherein he captured and neutralized the chaos disrupting his calm and tempered the impact of discouragement.

10 Oct 66

Dear Chiano:

I am finding some solace amidst war's inherent carnage in the open arms of blank pages, so I thought I'd share some of my pages, my thoughts, my feelings, and my observations about what I suspect is hell, with my best friend. And I say this out of a somber reality that I fear I might never shed. There's a little boy here that I have come to love. His name is Mihn Vong. He's eight. He's very sad all the time— with good reason. Like me, he watched his father being shot and killed. The sadness in his eyes makes me cry, Iano. His sadness is so deep and so lasting. But I have taught him to smile. Now, every time I see him, even though he doesn't understand a syllable of what I'm reading, he comes running to me, smiling. It is one of the deepest rewards I have ever felt. He keeps me from falling into an inescapable darkness. I sit him on my lap and just hold him and read to him. And we smile. Here's what he taught me:

Child's Play

Seeing the world
from a child's perspective
teaches us all we need to know:
to enjoy, to smile, to live—
even amidst the
cruel machinations
of war.

His bright eyes
urge me to ignore
the fence, the boundary
called war.
I smile for his delight
in his pure elation;
I smile in my delight
in knowing
there was not a bomb
strapped under his shirt
when he came to greet me.
I feel only the warmth
of his pounding heart
and elated lungs, the genius
of his pure innocence.

To him, this gentle boy,
we're watching a magical
metal bird soar through the sky,

exciting, happily soaring
in a whirl of wind and power,
lights and noise and exhilaration.

To me,
I'm seeing a plane
bringing boys,
now men,
back to the world:
I so wish I were
in that plane.

So thankfully
we hold this moment of
peace.
I hold this sweet child
and we smile.
That's what this little guy taught me.

Here's what I learned on my own, as they shaved my
hair off, a small installment on my debt to the ROTC pro-
gram.

Who Was I

I wasn't sure who I was
but now, whatever identity
I lived within or under,
is being buzzed away
by a stranger's hands,
shearing who I was
into strands and locks of
yesterday's forever
onto tomorrow's floor.

The prickly reality

of human indifference
slashes my independence
into a sheer insignificance
that paradoxically elevates me
to a precious commodity:
I am valuable
because I am dispensable.

So shave my head's hollow
Who,
and I will permeate
from mine to yours –
U.S. Army–
to order as you please,
even if I never knew
who I was,
or who I am.
Now,
I do:
Yours.

That's what I took away from the worst haircut I will
ever have.

No Return

The land below
my tenderfoot boots
appears alien and averse
to our landing on it.
Our leap from tenuous security
crouched behind the chaotic clatter
in our precarious Chopper 39,
to the murky clarity of the unknown,
progresses as a frozen moment

locking time behind
perception's door.

We see the earth's armor
as a blurry mosaic
framing a crisp image of
our boots
suspended in gravity's hold,
like hard fixed to a stone.

The blasting whir from 39
dominates the moment
in its stirring urgency.
We drop
without knowing, without feeling,
into a surreal uncertainty
where human will must disable fear.

Our new truth
hastily outwits our naïve delusions
as this eternal moment
between the soles of our boots
and the terrain of an
unwelcoming world
marks the point
of no return—
the moment our lives
change forever,
our only recognizable truth
is fear.

Our only means of
courage
is hope's faith
sewn into faith's hope.
God.

That's what I was thinking as they moved us deeper into what they call, 'the Shit' here; it's when you know you're going into an ugly fire fight. It stinks bad, thus the name. I'm sure God will forgive my profanity amidst these most vulgar conditions imaginable. Don't you agree? That's all for now, my friend. I feel so much better having talked to you, if only on the fiber of this bare page. As I said before, you are the ink in my pen. I love you, Pal.

Love, Marcello

The troops' silent call for comfort often led Marcello into the field with combat soldiers, especially when 'A Big' was coming, and the boys knew they were going to be 'In the Shit.' Marcello often pulled wounded soldiers out of the line of fire, assisted medics by holding bags of intravenous filled with false hope over dying boys' heads, applied pressure to legs blown apart by shrapnel and spewing blood from femoral arteries. He held wounded soldiers' trembling hands while these man-boys squeezed the last drops of life from their bullet-riddled cores, as futile drops of morphine trickled into their veins in vain. And he served Mass amidst the mayhem of attacks, almost daily. His judgment in insisting upon repaying his debt to the ROTC program was becoming questionable, but Marcello decided it was a fair price for the opportunity Father Finlay and the program provided.

One rainy Saturday night, Marcello was serving Mass in a tent turned chapel that the troops named *Saint Saveus.* Two candles converted from sterno cans wavered shaky flames over a makeshift altar made of a door salvaged from a burned-out village. The door was supported by four empty Agent Orange barrels and sandbags. A crude hand-carved cross hung behind the altar from rope tied to a bamboo pole that supported the tent's roof. The platoon was preparing for a mission that evening. Some sought solitude, leaning on the base of trees behind the tent, some sought distraction in a game of cards, or a few hits on a joint, some slept, six of the soldiers pursued support and courage at Marcello's nightly Son Set Mass. They hoped to find strength, reassurance, protection, solace, forgiveness, and any emotional and mental nourishment possible.

It was near the climax of the Mass. Marcello raised his hands to the heavens, clutching a morsel of a cracker as an improvised communion host. He said, "Behold, this is the body of Christ. Take this, and eat of it all of you, this is …"

BOOOOOOOOMMMMMM! Mortar fire tore through the tent and exploded. Two men were killed instantly. Marcello dove to the ground behind the altar as it absorbed a deluge of shrapnel. Marcello took a load of shrapnel in the lower torso and hip. Blood erupted from his hip on contact. The Agent Orange barrels burst open. Soldiers hit the deck. A barrage of mortar shells assaulted the tent creating a dizzying chaos. Soldiers in and around the tent dove to the muddy ground for cover. The mortar fire continued. A grenade exploded at the feet of a soldier and blew his feet off his body. One instant that changed his life forever. Screams and shrieks in the windy rain were swallowed up by the assault. Another grenade explosion ripped into another soldier's neck and entire left side. He was pinned between the altar and the earth, between life and death. He was bleeding profusely from his neck and chest. Hopelessly. Marcello crawled to him and dragged him behind the sandbag altar hoping to find elusive safety. They crouched behind the sandbags ducking another barrage of firepower flying all around them. Hours disguised as seconds seemed to stop time. The soldier in Marcello's arms looked up at him with the most innocent, most hopeful, most childlike eyes, searching for answers, explanations, and conclusions. His eyes closed, shut, locked in death's hold. Forever. Marcello held the soldier tighter in the surreal terror in knowing this moment is not surreal at all; it is Vietnam. Chaplain Luciari rocked uncontrollably, holding the dead soldier. Somewhere between now and forever.

"Whyyyyyyyyyy!" He screamed. "Whyyyyyyyyyy do we do this to each other! Whyyyyyyyyyy!"

Nearly two seemingly endless, relentless hours later, the attack ended. The jungle dripped its noisy silence over the makeshift base. Marcello laid against the blood-wet sandbags still clutching that boy, shaking until shock's sleep rescued him from the unbearable consciousness of the hellish place he was in. Vietnam.

Six weeks after that horrible night in God's tent, *Saint Saveus*, Marcello's hip was healing faster and more thoroughly than the wounds in his mind. But that would all hopefully change very soon; Marcello was going home, after sixteen months serving in Vietnam, four months longer than the average tour and his enlistment required. His debt to the United States Army ROTC program had been paid– with interest. As he was packing the last of his gear into his tattered Army issued duffle bag, a soldier carrying a handful of letters and a small package approached Marcello. A smiling, and deliriously happy Mihn Vong was packing a bag, too.

"For you, Chap. Catch," the soldier said, as he tossed Marcello the parcel, which he juggled before securing the catch. Marcello looked the package over.

"Thanks, pal."

"You got it, Chap … happy home. I'm under a hundred days, but I'm not countin' 'em. All the best to you, Chap," he wished Marcello, and shook his hand. "The kid helpin' you pack?"

"He's coming home with me. We're gonna give my pal here a new life in Rome," Marcello said, nodding his head toward Mihn.

"Lucky him. Lucky you, Chap. Have a good dust off," a soldier's term for taking off in a chopper.

"God Bless you. Come home safe," Marcellolain said. He and Mihn turned their attention to the package. It was plastered with a collection of Italian stamps. He grabbed a knife from his duffle bag, cut the string wrapped around the package, and tore the brown paper open. Mihn was wide-eyed and still smiling. Marcello was now holding a watch box that he opened with a smile, as a vision of Uncle Jewels flickered in his mind. The box contained a folded, hand-written note.

> *Dear Marcello:*
>
> *I know for a fact that you already have a watch, but I also know that every man needs more than one watch. I am holding the watch that belongs in the box you just opened in my left hand as I write this note. I will hold the watch for you as a gift to celebrate your return, and in honor of your service.*
>
> *I thought it best not to trust this watch to the fate of the United States Army trying to find you deep in the jungles of Vietnam. A good idea, right? So, Marcello, I will watch your watch until the time you arrive home. Until*

that time, have a good time, all the time, every time. My time is up now, so I bid you a safe trip home. In the meantime, watch out!

Love, Uncle Jewels.

PART III

CHAPTER 22

300 Steps

The 'Sanctuary of Santa Maria dell'Isola,' was named 'sanctuary' for good reason. It is a stunning Catholic church crowning a rock cliff in Tropea, Italy, overlooking the Tyrrhenian Sea, also deservedly known as 'The Coast of Gods.' This magnificent hilltop basks in its privileged proximity to the sea and the spectacular beaches of Tropea, one of the Calabria region of Italy's most cherished, most beautiful locations. It is a cathedral for prayer and worship, and a sanctuary for observing and absorbing the crystal blue skies that color the pristine waters of the Tyrrhenian Sea. There are 300 steps carved into solid rock shaping the climb to the Sanctuary of Santa Maria dell 'Isola; this is where Marcello has been gratefully celebrating Mass for the past 10 years. Each odd number day of the month, at the specific moment of sunrise, Marcello offers daily Mass to those faithful who are moved enough to climb those 300 steps to pray, worship, and give profound thanks for being on that spot at that moment. Mass starts at exactly the moment the sun is scheduled to rise, so in addition to being faithful and fit enough to climb the steps, the worshipers must be cognizant of the exact time the sun will rise, and thus, what time Mass will begin.

Marcello loved celebrating Mass outdoors because he says, "there is nothing between us and God when we're outdoors." Marcello also celebrates Mass on the spectacularly beautiful beach at the foot of the rock where the Sanctuary of Santa Maria dell'Isola has been sitting since the 9th century. He loved to begin Mass at sunrise because there is little in the world as beautiful, as inspiring, and as spiritually magnificent as worshiping God as the sun rises over the horizon announcing the first moment of the day. Marcello has dubbed his sunrise Masses, the Son Rise Mass, and his daily sunset Masses, Son Set Mass.

Bishop Soniorelli attended the Son Rise Mass every other week. He also spent the weekends attending Mass here, secluded with his extraordinarily clandestine female companion in private quarters above the rectory of Santa Maria. The bishop likes to participate in the Son Set Mass on Friday evening, then disappear into the seclusion of seclusion for the weekend, then furtively escape in the pre-dawn shadows on Monday mornings. But this Monday, instead of disappearing, he celebrated Son Rise Mass with Marcello and joined him for breakfast in the rectory.

The sizzle of homemade breakfast sausage from Ronivicci's Butcher Shop snapped and popped, filling the air with the disarming allure of tasty local sausage. Notes of fresh baked Italian bread toasting in a small brick oven aroused the appetite and cuddled the moment with homey goodness. Traces of the acrid aroma of robust coffee pierced the anticipation of an enticing breakfast. Marcello and Bishop Soniorelli pulled out thick-legged wooden chairs over a simple, beautiful pattern of large, white tiles with a crackled background trimmed in cobalt blue and lemon-yellow ribbon lace pattern. The skylight high overhead lit the table in a soft curtain of light that added a cozy clarity to the room; Marcello was always conscious of this light, and all light for that matter, a warm connection to his days admiring stained glass with his Uncle Salvestro. He referred to this light as 'the haze from God's gaze.'

"I'm thrilled that you're able to join me, Your Excellency," Marcello said.

"Me too, Marcello. Me too. I have to do this more often."

"I'd like that, I always enjoy having you join me," Marcello said. Sensing there was more purpose for his staying other than merely sleeping in, and the allure of Mrs. Moltovecchio's cooking. Mrs. Moltovecchio was a legendary cook. She volunteered to cook breakfast and dinner on Sundays through Thursdays for Marcello. She shopped, cooked, served, cleaned up after every meal, did Marcello's laundry, tidied up the rectory, and did it all with a silent smile that only pride's inner delight can prompt. She was a small woman with her hair pulled back in a tight bun. Her print dresses were always crisp and clean. Marcello could not remember ever seeing her without an apron covering her dress, and a smile defining her face. She convinced the proprietors at Ronivicci's Butcher Shop, Arcononi's Fish Market, and Benovono's Market to climb the 300 stairs to Santa Maria's to deliver their goods and bill the church for the purchases. She always added a generous tip, and they all universally always refused it. As Mrs. Moltovecchio served Marcello and Bishop Soniorelli, she quietly hummed a tune that faded to a respectful silence when they spoke.

"Marcello, later this morning, your phone is going to ring and you are going to hear the annoying voice of a lackluster man who serves as the assistant to Cardinal Falanzzano; his name is Father William Boyen. We call him 'the lump' because he's got his nose so far up Falanzzano's rear end that he creates a lump under the cardinal's cassock. I also call him the little prick because that's what he is. Everybody ignores him, but he's a persistent little prick … like a gnat … even buzzes like one."

"I know him well. We were assigned to the same parish in Cosenza for a while. He edited a newsletter for a right-wing faction of the Holy See. He's a very antisemitic twerp with a malicious Napoleon complex. Yes, I know Boyen well. I physically pulled him off of a nine-year-old boy in a Catechism class once. He was beating the kid with such ferocious venom because the kid didn't answer him fast enough. Boyen was slapping the kid across both sides of his face, back and forth, screaming at him, 'Respond! Respond!' The kid couldn't hear the question because he was almost completely deaf. And couldn't read Boyen's lips because Boyen's head was turned away from the class," Marcello said, biting back his anger. "I pulled Boyen off the kid and shoved him into the hall, and pinned him to the wall. I was furious. I wanted to slap him like he was slapping that poor little kid. I made him go back in the class and apologize." Marcello was turning red with anger while recalling the incident. "Yes, I know him. And he knows me." He took a deep breath to calm down. "What does Cardinal Falanzzano want?"

"Whatever makes Cardinal Falanzzano more money, gives him more power, or lessens his responsibilities," the bishop answered. Mrs. Moltovecchio presented their dishes bearing three links of sausage, three perfectly over easy eggs, three perfectly toasted pieces of home-made bread with a small scoop of whipped butter on the side, and three thin slices of fresh oranges. They each thanked her verbally, with smiles, and grateful nods. Bishop Soniorelli leaned into Marcello and whispered:

"What's her name?" he asked, as she turned back toward the stove.

"Mrs. Moltovecchio."

"Mrs. Moltovecchio," you have outdone yourself. This breakfast looks exceptional. Thank you very much," the bishop said.

"Thank you very much, Your Excellency. I did everything in threes," she said, holding up three fingers. "The Holy Trinity," she said.

"God bless you, this looks fantastic," he said.

"She's the best, Your Excellency. She treats me like a son ... and spoils me like a grandson," Marcello said. Mrs. Moltovecchio smiled, bowed her thanks, and left Marcello and the bishop to discuss whatever they needed to discuss and enjoy a superb breakfast. Marcello and Bishop Soniorelli jabbed into their sausages and forked their eggs. Dipping the perfectly toasted, buttered bread into his eggs, Bishop Soniorelli said,

"Who lives better than you?"

"You," Marcello answered without missing a beat.

"Let's not spoil this glorious breakfast; we'll talk about Falanzzano after we eat," Bishop Soniorelli suggested. Marcello nodded in agreement, and they devoured the delectable breakfast.

Not quite an hour after sopping up the last bit of egg yolk with a crispy wedge of toasted bread, Bishop Soniorelli disappeared like a vapor evaporating into a cloud, and not long after that, Marcello's office phone rang. He looked at it, knowing it was the call the bishop warned him would be coming.

"Father Luciari, can I help you?" he said into the phone. A nasally voice squeaked into his phone.

"Father Luciari, it's Father Boyen. I'm calling to- "

"Father," Marcello offered, indifferently."

"Cardinal Falanzzano and I will be visiting your parish. You'll need to make some arrangements," he declared. "Lodging, meals, local transportation; that sort of thing," Father Boyen said. Marcello didn't respond, he just listened to dead air. After a few seconds Father Boyen asked, "Are you still there?"

"Yes," Marcello said, then just listened in silence again.

"We'll need to be picked up at the train station," Father Boyen said. "Then- "

"The parish doesn't own a car, but taxis are plentiful at Tropea Station."

"Do you understand that I'm calling on Cardinal Falanzzano's behalf?"

"Yes," Marcello said, in a deadpan response.

"I would expect a sense of urgency from you knowing who I'm representing." Marcello just listened again. He sensed that his subtle taunting was annoying Father Boyen, and he was enjoying it. "We'll be arriving in three days' time; arrangements need to be made," Father Boyen demanded.

"The cardinal is welcome to stay in our guest room; It will be ready when he arrives," Marcello said. "In terms of getting him from the train station to Santa Maria's, I suggest a taxi. As for meals, he is- "

"I'll be accompanying the cardinal. I will need a room for myself as well," Father Boyen said.

"There is a hotel just a few minutes' walk from- "

"I need to be with Cardinal Falanzzano, and you will need to make sure such accommodations at the rectory are in order by our arrival on Thursday," he said. "Or do I have to tell His Eminence that there's a problem accommodating him?"

"Not at all, we'll have lovely accommodations for His Eminence, the problem is in accommodating you- unless His Eminence is willing to have you bunk with him. We can arrange for a cot to- "

"We'll both need a room. Figure it out! Also, I have some dietary requirements you'll need to address for His Eminence, and- " Marcello calmly hung the phone up before Father Boyen finished his sentence. He held his hand on the phone knowing it was about to ring again. It did. He answered.

"Father Luciari. Can I help you?"

"You disconnected me; it's Boyen. I was about- " Marcello hung up the phone again, smiling broadly. He watched the cradled phone, waiting for it to ring again. It rang. He let it ring and ring and ring and ring and ring and ring, many, many times before it stopped. His smile had evolved into a mischievous laugh. After a very short silence the phone rang again. This time, Marcello picked it up on its very first ring.

"Father Luciari, can I help you?" he said, squelching his snicker. "Luciari, it's Father Boyen! What's going on? The- " Marcello couldn't resist hanging up one more time; nor could he suppress his outright laugh.

Mrs. Moltovecchio came into the office to be sure the pastor was OK. He got up from his desk and spoke through a lingering laugh.

"Mrs. Mo, my phone is going to ring in a second; please pick it up but don't say anything. Let the nasty little man on the other end blow off some steam for a bit, then, interrupt him, tell him that I am not in the office and you don't know when I'll be back," he said, still enjoying a good laugh. The phone rang again. Mrs. Moltovecchio picked it up and just listened. Marcello could hear Father Boyen screaming into the phone from across his office.

"What kind of shit are you trying to pull, Luciari? Do you know who- "

"This is Mrs. Moltovecchio, Father Luciari's cook and housekeeper," Mrs. Moltovecchio said into the phone. "Father Luciari is not here, and I don't know when he will be back." There was a sharp, silent pause for a long moment while an embarrassed Father Boyen was presumably stuffing his proverbial foot into his mouth.

"I am so sorry, mam, I am so very sorry. I will try back later. Goodbye," Father Boyen timidly whispered as Marcello bit his finger to keep from laughing in the background. Mrs. Moltovecchio hung up the phone, and she and Marcello shared a laugh. He lovingly twisted Mrs. Moltovecchio's cheek like he would his mother's.

"Perfect, just perfect. Thank you," he said and left the room still laughing.

Father Boyen made good on his plan to call back. This time, Marcello attentively recorded Cardinal Falanzzano's requirements and put the arrangements in motion. There was actually little to do to prepare the rectory guest room- Bishop Soniorelli's room- since Mrs. Moltovecchio kept the room in perfect order. The most critical detail was to be sure there were no traces of evidence of a woman accompanying the good bishop eight nights a month in that room- for the past several years. As for Father Boyen, Marcello found a perfect solution in a corner of a riser in the rectory attic. Despite the lack of air conditioning, the attic did have good ventilation with gorgeous views through the thin slats of the air vents. And once the sun set, Santa Maria's caretaker, Remigio's two dozen racing pigeons settled into their coop and cooed directly above Father Boyen's cot.

Three days later, His Eminence and his subservience arrived nearly an hour past the planned 10:15 a.m. arrival. Marcello had one of Santa Maria's altar boys call his office from a cafe by the foot of the cliff supporting the church when he saw His Eminence's car arrive. When he got the call, he took up a perch at a corner of the terrace in front of the church and watched an empty-handed Cardinal Falanzzano struggle up the 300 steps to the church. His subservience, Father Boyen, struggled behind, dragging two pieces of luggage, and two briefcases, much to Marcello's amusement. When they finally completed the arduous climb, Marcello reached out to greet them with a robust handshake and a satisfied grin.

"Welcome to Santa Maria, Your Eminence," he said, while shaking the cardinal's hand. "Father," he said, nodding indifferently, to Father Boyen, who was thoroughly beaded with sweat from his luggage-hauling climb. Cardinal Falanzzano was a tall thin man with a stern expression drooping from his long face that seemed to form as a drip collected at the bottom of his extensive chin. It was a look more comparable to secular arrogance than spiritual reverence.

"Let me show you to your quarters, Your Eminence. I'm sure you'd like to freshen up and settle in." He led Cardinal Falanzzano to the rectory's guest room almost exclusively reserved for Bishop Soniorelli and his companion. The two outer walls were finished in artisan stonework, the inner walls awash in a soft textured, ashen tangerine that mimicked a late afternoon sun caressing the puffy cheek of the sky. The floors were well-worn, wide planks with a traditional rectangular Italian Mediterranean rug under the bed that sprawled its multiple colors beyond the bed's perimeter. A circa 1880 Venetian Louis XIV Rococo Walnut Burl veneer credenza with a matching dresser, mirror, and headboard embraced the room in comfort and beauty's echo. Stunning ocean views poured into the room's oversize windows with diffused light filtering in like a blanket of white peace. Upon seeing this spectacular, though simple room, Cardinal Falanzzano's annoyance with the hot, steep climb up the 300 steps to the sanctuary, washed into the view of the placid sea below.

"Make yourself at home, Your Eminence. Get comfortable. What do you say we meet for lunch in the dining room at say, 12:30? Sound good?"

"That's fine. From the looks of this room, I think I should have planned more than an overnight; it's absolutely charming," Cardinal Falanzzano said.

"I trust you'll be comfortable. See you at 12:30," Marcello said. He motioned for Father Boyen to follow him.

"Would you like me to unpack you, Your Eminence?" Father Boyen asked the cardinal, who dismissed him with a curt wave. Father Boyen followed Marcello out of the cozy guest room to the end of the hall. At the very end of the hall, Marcello opened a narrow door. There was no room behind the door, just steep, narrow steps into the attic.

"You'll be up here," he said to Father Boyen. It's not as well appointed as Cardinal Falanzzano's room, but then again, he's a cardinal, and we are mere priests, right?" he quipped.

"You're kidding, right?"

"Not the lap of luxury, but it's dry, and if you peek through the slats in the vents, you'll have a beautiful view of the bay," Marcello said, and stepped out of the way and gestured for Father Boyen to climb the stairs. "There's a bathroom downstairs that you're welcome to use and an outdoor shower behind the building. You'll find a towel on your cot– it's in the corner, you'll have to unroll the mattress and put the sheet on it" he said. "There's a lamp on the floor, you can plug it into the outlet on the light bulb fixture on the ceiling." Father Boyen climbed the stairs to the oppressively hot attic in disbelief and anger's steam. He found an overhead light fixture splattering a faint dusting of light onto the tired mattress that he rolled out onto the cot. There was a towel and pillow as promised, at the top of the cot that was wedged into the eve of the attic beneath Remigio's cooing pigeons.

Mrs. Moltovecchio volunteered for double duty, serving lunch and dinner to accommodate Cardinal Falanzzano. She formally set the dining room table for three. Just before they all sat down, Marcello brought up a point of warning.

"Your Eminence, I saw a black car at the base of the steps of the church; is that your car?" Marcello asked. "It might be parked in a restricted spot."

"Yes, Father Boyen parked it at the foot of the steps. Is it safe there?" Cardinal Falanzzano asked.

"Safe? Probably not. Illegal? Absolutely. The polizia are zealous about ticketing cars ... with steep fines for parking in 'No Parking' zones by the beach. They will– "

"I'm sure the polizia will understand that this is a cardinal's car,"

Father Boyen said. "A personal blessing from a cardinal will get them to turn their heads the other way," Cardinal Falanzzano said.

"I'm afraid they worship lira more than the Church, Your Eminence," Marcello said. "And if they tow it, which they routinely do, it's very expensive and cumbersome to get your car back, and it's not guaranteed– or even likely to be returned in one piece," Marcello warned. "I suggest you have Father Boyen move it."

After contemplating for half a second, Cardinal Falanzzano decided against the risk.

"Go find a safe place to park the car," he commanded, nodding in Father Boyen's direction. "In fact, you might give Father Luciari and I a few hours alone before you return. We have matters I want to discuss, and we could use the time. Get something to eat by the beach," Cardinal Falanzzano said. Again, he waved Father Boyen out of the room with his demeaning style of dismissing him. Father Boyen left like an obedient puppy, deliberately avoiding eye contact with Marcello, camouflaging his anger, and shielding his shame behind a pathetically artificial smile.

"I was going to suggest exactly that, Your Eminence," Father Boyen said as Mrs. Moltovecchio entered with a huge tray of food, her happy demeanor brightening the room.

"I am serving you the catch of the day– branzino in my special garlic, lemon, white wine sauce, stuffed with sausage and broccoli rabe. Roasted potatoes and carrots," Mrs. Moltovecchio said, while proudly placing a soup terrine on the table. But first, a fresh gazpacho to start off."

"We are in for a treat, Your Eminence. Mrs. Moltovecchio is as good a cook as you'll ever find."

She served Cardinal Falanzzano first, ladling out gazpacho. She placed three pieces of grill-toasted bread from Benovono's Market onto his plate, and drizzled local olive oil over the bread. She set a plate teeming with chunks of sharp parmesan cheese, and poured a glass of the Lamezia region's prize rosé, and bowed her head to the cardinal. Then she served Marcello. Cardinal Falanzzano picked at the cheese first, then sipped the wine, savoring its surprising depth for a rosé. He nodded to Marcello and looked to the glass of wine in unexpected approval.

"Few appreciate, or even know how versatile and enjoyable a good rosé can be– and not only in the summer months" Marcello said. "My uncle taught me to seek out a wine that seeks me out rather than follow a rote, habitual recommendation," he said. The cardinal merely shook his head and continued eating cheese and sipping the rosé. He dipped his spoon into the gazpacho and closed his eyes. "We need to nominate this woman for sainthood," he said, raising his rigid eyebrows to Mrs. Moltovecchio. She bowed her head in appreciation in return.

Marcello coyly let Cardinal Falanzzano direct the conversation, the meeting, and the meal. After a near awkward silence, the cardinal dipped his bread into the soup, chewed, then spoke– without lifting his cold greenish-brown eyes up from his soup.

"Two weeks from tomorrow, I have an audience with the Holy Father. One of the matters we'll be discussing affects you," he said, using bread to catch a dribble of soup drizzling down his chin. "It's a proposal I am going to make to the Vatican." He dipped more bread into his soup then stuffed it into his mouth, and shook his head with appreciation. "I'm going to propose we convert Santa Maria into a retreat for retired cardinals, and I suppose a few select bishops. My plan is to– "

"What?" Marcello asked in disbelief.

"My plan is to complete the conversion within a year's time," the cardinal announced, mopping up gazpacho from the side of his bowl with bread in a smug air of authority.

"What!"

"A year's time."

"I'm not talking about the when, I'm talking about the why? The how. Why would– how could you want to take a thriving parish and convert it into a vacation home for retired, and with all due respect, inactive cardinals? Over 2,000 parishioners depend on Santa Maria. We have– "

"I understand your reaction; I expected it. Who would want to give up the cushy assignment you have here?"

"I resent that re– "

"No offense intended. Listen, I wouldn't want to give up this gravy assignment either. But you have to appreciate that we need a means to reward clergy who have given their entire adult lives to the Church. And … you have had an exceptionally long joyride here in this paradise. Be grateful for– "

"You have to appreciate that this church– the cornerstone of this church, is its 2,000 parishioners. You want to take away their connection to God and the Church so a dozen … dormant clergy can meditate?"

Cardinal Falanzzano's jaws clenched with anger.

"Watch yourself," he commanded, glaring at Marcello.

"Your Eminence, I mean no disrespect, but I will defend Santa Maria's parishioners' church with vigor. I will not- "

"You will do as you're told. You have no influence. You have no voice. You're a parish priest. Accept that for what it is. Be thankful that you've had this picnic here for ten years. You'd be well advised to go with the flow and take advantage of a potential opportunity. If you cooperate and play your cards well, we might consider keeping you around to administer our needs."

"If it's a bellhop you're looking for, call the jackass you just sent to move your car. And I am proud and honored to be a parish priest. I thank our Lord every day for the privilege to celebrate Mass every day and night for these faithful people dedicated enough to climb those 300 steps to get on their knees and pour their hearts out to God! Yes, I am a parish priest and I thank God for that every day. When's the last time you served someone other than yourself?" Cardinal Falanzzano pounded the table, rattling the silverware, dishes, and glasses.

"How - dare - you - speak - to - me - like - that! You will do what you are told!" He paused, scowling at Marcello, his nostrils bent upward, spit wadded in the corners of his mouth. "I'll see to it that you're relieved of your holiday here within a week," Cardinal Falanzzano shouted. He turned his ire-drenched face to Mrs. Moltovecchio. "You," he shouted at Mrs. Moltovecchio, who was entering the dining room proudly presenting her tray of branzino. "I'll have dinner at 6:30. Alone!" He rose quickly, knocking his chair to the floor. He pounded his fist on the table and threw his napkin on the floor. Marcello leaped out of his chair and grabbed the table with both hands, his eyes bulging with fight's rage.

"You can say what you want to me, but do not speak to her like that!"

"Or what!" Cardinal Falanzzano burst out of the room and tore down the hall. He disappeared behind a slammed door.

Marcello gave Mrs. Moltovecchio the hug a son would give a mother. "I'm so sorry about that."

"It means nothing to me. He's a brute. He's the one who has to stew in the poison of anger, not me, right," she said. "Sit, don't let this beautiful branzino get cold."

"Join me, please," Marcello said, and he and Mrs. Moltovecchio sat down. They toasted and indulged in a most treasured privilege– enjoying a wonderful meal, overlooking the picture of the paradise that is Tropea, Italy. Laughing.

The moment Father Boyen completed his second trip up the 300 steps, Cardinal Falanzzano summoned him to collect his luggage and unceremoniously left the beauty of Santa Maria dell 'Isola.

CHAPTER 23

The Letter

After the congregants dispersed from the Son Rise Mass, Marcello re-entered the empty church and sank to his knees before the crucifix and prayed for a long time. His head was bowed but his heart and spirit raised. He was intense in his prayer and calm in his openness to God's word. After some time kneeling, he rose and sat in the first pew, looking upward through closed eyes. He often claimed that he saw his clearest vision when he closed his eyes. He rocked slowly, easing himself into an elusive peace. He sat for a time this way then eventually rose and began a very slow and graceful waltz with an imaginary partner. His head gently swayed and his body moved into the supple slides and sways of a graceful waltz. The music in his head grew louder and more distinct and it reflected in Marcello's lithe dancing. His head tilted backward, swaying as he danced across the altar; a slight smile creased his lips, then a broader one. His arms became more animated. His steps more defined, more punctuated. He was dancing as his loving mother taught him, hearing her voice in the chasms of his memory. *It is impossible to feel anything but happiness when you dance, Marcello.* He danced for several minutes on the altar, then eventually danced his way outside to the courtyard and back to the rectory, a much more light-hearted man despite the distress introduced by Cardinal Falanzzano.

Marcello entered his office and took his seat behind his desk, dialed the phone, and waited. Uncle Salvestro picked up on the other end.

"Uncle Sal, how are you? Retirement agreeing with you?"

"Marcello, my boy. I'm fine. How are you," Uncle Salvestro said, in a voice softened by the years.

"Fine, Uncle Sal. Fine. Mama OK? And Mia, and the kids?"

"Everybody's great. They'll be happy when I tell them you called. So, what's new?"

"I have a situation to deal with, Uncle Sal. Is your friend in the Vatican still there?"

"He is. Why, what's up?"

"Any chance he can get me before the Holy Father?"

"Get you before the Holy Father? Wow. That's quite a request. A tall order. What's going on?"

"Remember Cardinal Falanzzano?"

"Of course."

"He wants to convert my parish into a retreat for retired cardinals."

"Son of a biscuit."

"Yeah. He's proposing it to the Holy Father in two weeks. For some reason, the Holy Father seems to tolerate Falanzzano. I'm afraid he'll approve it."

"Let me call my friend and see what he suggests … see if he can help."

"Thank you, Uncle Sal. I'm sorry to ask but it's– "

"No need to say another word. I'll let you know what I find out as soon as I can. In the meantime, you better get busy writing some notes in case we're able to make this happen."

"You OK, Uncle Sal? You sound a little faint."

"I'm fine. A little tired, that's all."

"Alright. Thank you, Uncle Sal. So much."

"Don't mention it. I'll do what I can, as soon as I can. Why in God's name would cardinals need a retreat after they retire, they don't even do anything before they retire?" Uncle Salvestro said.

Marcello spent the rest of the morning and much of the day preparing notes for an unlikely, but possible, meeting with the Holy Father. Late in the day, Marcello's phone rang. Before he could speak, Uncle Salvestro spoke.

"Marcello, I spoke to my friend. He said he can't arrange a meeting with the Holy Father but he's still trying. In the meantime, he did promise if you write the Holy Father a letter, he will get it before his eyes. That's exactly how he said it," Uncle Salvestro said.

"That's a great start. I've been thinking about it all day; I'll convert my notes into a letter. I'll work on it tonight and get it in the mail in the morning. It has to be there before Falanzzano's meeting in two weeks. I'll get it there within a week. Where do I send it?"

"To me. I will hand deliver it to my friend and we'll go from there."

"Fantastic. It'll be on the way to you tomorrow morning."

"Good luck, Marcello. I love you."

"I love you, Uncle Sal. Thank you so much. Kiss everybody for me."

"I will. You knock 'em dead with that letter."

"I will. Don't forget to kiss everybody for me. Ciao."

Marcello spent the rest of the night writing and rewriting and rewriting and rewriting his letter to the Holy Father with the highest hopes; he was utterly unconcerned about any offense to Cardinal Falanzzano. His letter read:

> *Most Holy Father:*
>
> *On Wednesday, 28 August 1977, Cardinal Sergio Falanzzano plans to make a proposal to you requesting to close and convert the thriving parish of Santa Maria in Tropea in Calabria from an active and heralded parish serving nearly 1,000 plus members, to a retreat serving just ten to twelve retired cardinals. As pastor of this parish, Holy Father, I humbly ask, with profound urgency, that you reject this proposal to close this wonderful parish.*
>
> *Each morning, I celebrate a Mass we have named the "Son Rise" Mass. And each morning, some twenty to thirty parishioners climb more than 300 steps up a steep cliff to worship God here. Every evening, I celebrate a "Son Set" Mass and another twenty to thirty parishioners attend that Mass. Each Saturday, another forty to fifty parishioners climb those same steps to confess their weaknesses, seek for-*

giveness for their offenses, and sins of omission. And every Sunday, Holy Father, some 250 to 350 Tropean parishioners climb those 300 stairs to express adoration for our Lord, further confess their weaknesses, thank God for their blessings, and put their humble pleas before God.

Santa Maria dell'Isola nourishes and inspires the vital spiritual fervor these 1,000 loyal parishioners seek and need. It is the zenith of beauty, enjoyed by more than thousands of faith-filled tourist visitors each year. The Santa Maria dell 'Isola has been at the soul of faith in Calabria for hundreds of years, and shines as an icon of the church in its humble grandeur and inspirational vigor. I am quite sure that our Lord God prefers this glorious church, the first church in Italy dedicated to the Blessed Mother, to remain as it is, serving thousands of followers, rather than a dozen retired cardinals who have completed their active mission in the name of God.

I plead with you, Holy Father, to reject Cardinal Falanzzano's forthcoming proposal to convert this rigorous mecca of Catholic faith into a silent hideaway for a mere few.

Respectfully, Yours in Christ,

Father Marcello Luciari,
Pastor, Santa Maria dell'Isola
Tropea, Calabria, Italy

Immediately following the Son Rise Mass the next morning, Marcello tucked the letter safely inside an envelope addressed to Father Salvestro Frischetti. He walked his letter addressed to the pontiff not to the postal office but to Ettore Benevicci, a grocer and produce distributor who delivered fresh Sicilian and Calabrian produce to Rome every Monday, Wednesday, and Friday. Ettore operated out of the back of his overstocked market that offered local everything: produce, olives, olive oils, cheeses, fish, breads, charcuterie, baked goods, condiments, and all things Tropean. Ettore's wife Antonella operated the store and Ettore ran their distribution business. They were loyal parishioners for thirty-five years and willing to do anything Marcello would ask.

Marcello entered the tiny shop, savoring the scents of subtle, yet sharp cheeses, produce, breads, and coffees. The salty water at the surface of a barrel of Castelvetrano olives reflected the gleam of the early morning sun. Four brands of three-liter tins of local olive oil were stacked outside the door next to pyramids of canned tomatoes, sacks of flour, and crates of fresh tomatoes, lemons, broccoli rabe, lettuce, and other varied produce. Antonella was stacking boxes of macaroni when the tiny bell on the door jingled and Marcello entered. That little bell always reminded him of Uncle Jewels.

"Hmmm, I love the smells of the meats and cheeses and breads in here," he said sniffing deeply. "How are you this morning, Antonella?" Marcello asked. "Beautiful as always," he said, kissing one of her cheeks and then the other. "Ettore in the back?"

"Of course. Hiding in the back all the time while I'm up here doing all the work," she said with a grin.

"He's a lucky man. Mind if I go see him?"

"Of course not. Be careful, he has boxes all over the place back there. It's a mess," she said, at the exact moment Ettore entered from behind a tower of jarred roasted peppers next to a barely visible door at the back of the shop.

"What's a mess?" Ettore asked in a good-natured way while raising his right hand to meet Marcello's hand. His tough left hand gripped Marcello's shoulder. "How's by you, Father? Everything's good?"

"Everything's good, Ettore. I just need to ask you a favor."

"You name it, you got it, Father, you know that."

"I know it, and I appreciate that, Ettore. I really do."

"What do you need?"

"I need this delivered to my Uncle Salvestro in Rome on your next trip up there. Can you do that for me?" Marcello held up the envelope and waved it.

"Of course. Piece of pie. No problem, I'm happy to do it."

"It's very important to me, and honestly, to all of us at Santa Maria dell'Isola. Can I count on you?"

"Of course. I'm going to Rome tomorrow and I'll have it in your uncle's hand late in the afternoon … before you take your first spoon of Concetta Moltovecchio's soup." Marcello handed over the envelope and hugged Ettore and Antonella.

"You're the best, both of you. Thank you very much, Ettore," Marcello said. "Mrs. Moltovecchio knew I was coming here so she gave me her grocery list."

"Smart woman," Antonella said. "Let me see what's on there." Marcello handed her the list and Ettore headed toward the back of the store.

"Let me put this in a safe place where I won't forget it tomorrow," he said, while patting the envelope containing the letter. It's in good hands, Father." Ettore disappeared into the cave of groceries behind the store.

"The best," Marcello said. Antonella buzzed around the stuffed aisles of the store picking Mrs. Moltovecchio's order while Marcello stepped outside to enjoy the sunshine and greet people passing by.

Not long after, Marcello climbed back up the 300 stairs to Santa Maria toting three sacks of groceries and a world of hope. Despite the challenge of the stairs, there was a happy hop of optimism in his step. Now all he could do was pray and hope. And he did. Vigorously.

Three days passed. Then four. Then five. Then six. Then, on the seventh day, as in Genesis, the phone on Marcello's desk rang.

"Marcello, you must have my room ready a day early, can you do that? Can you have it ready for tomorrow morning? I must speak to you in person," Bishop Soniorelli pleaded into the phone.

"Sure, of course, is everything OK?"

"Everything is fine, but I must see you tomorrow morning."

"Yes. Your Excellency, do you want to hear what Cardinal Falanzzano wants to do?"

"I know all about it. Never mind that for now, we will talk in the morning. I must go." The phone went dead. Marcello hung up the phone and stared into the paradise that is Tropea, Italy. And wondered. What was so pressing on Bishop Soniorelli's mind? What beyond writing a letter could he do to stop Cardinal Falanzzano from destroying the sanctity of Santa Maria?

The day passed agonizingly slowly. What else could he do? What's going on with the bishop? Why wouldn't he talk about Falanzzano's plan to destroy Santa Maria? Marcello walked the grounds, savoring every step of the dry, dusty earth caking on the soles of his shoes, the protruding roots he stumbled on, every angle of every view. He inhaled the invigorating scent from the juniper bushes, the savory salty Calabrian air, and admired the endless blue sky that defied perception as it stretched beyond all boundaries. He embraced every chirp from every bird, the acrid taste of the dew cast by lemon trees sprinkled about the precious two acres Santa Maria sat upon. He wondered, as he wandered, what was to come, what was to be, but mostly he pondered what else he could do to thwart Cardinal Falanzzano's plan.

The next morning's Son Rise Mass concluded and Marcello devoured one of Mrs. Moltovecchio's excellent breakfasts. He spent an hour in the church praying with rosary beads squeezed between his fingers. He glided around the altar in a freeing dance. Several minutes later, the doors to the church opened and a sweaty and anxious Bishop Soniorelli tottered down the center aisle of the church.

"Pack your bags, Marcello, The Holy Father wants to see you and I in Rome on Monday. He wants you at the meeting with Cardinal Falanzzano.

CHAPTER 24

Piping Plovers

The Holy Father sat behind his desk immersed in reading a document that an assistant and he were reviewing. Another assistant ushered Marcello and Bishop Soniorelli into the office. The pope looked up and cordially greeted them.

"Good morning, gentlemen. I will be with you in just a moment. Please, sit," he said, gesturing toward three seats in front of his polished cherry wood desk trimmed with an intricate thin molding depicting rope. Marcello's eyes scanned the volumes of books squeezed into the matching cherry wood shelves behind the pontiff's desk. He examined the tall pewter crucifix on the desk thinking it was out of scale, it appeared to be too big, *but could a crucifix ever be out of scale, too big,* he thought. A single candle stood tall at one corner of the desk and a handful of smaller books were pressed between blue and white marble bookends with a depiction of the Virgin Mary carved into them.

"OK," the pontiff said to the assistant, who collected the document from the desk and left the room. "Gentlemen, welcome. Thank you for making the trip," the Holy Father said. "Father Luciari, I read your letter and thought it would be productive to have you and Cardinal Falanzzano in the same room so we can all discuss his proposal together. He should have been here by now," the pope said, barely hiding his annoyance. "What have you got there?" the pontiff asked Marcello, motioning to a framed oil painting he was carrying.

Just as Marcello was about to show the pope the painting, the same assistant that showed Marcello and Bishop Soniorelli in, knocked on the door and entered the office.

"Holy Father, the others have arrived." The assistant was followed into the office by Cardinal Falanzzano who was toting a large portfolio case. Upon seeing Marcello and Bishop Soniorelli, the exuberance beaming from the cardinal's tan face dissolved like wet clay melting from the foundation of an unfinished sculpture. His face turned a color that can only be described as 'apprehension white.' His cheeks and jowls quivered like jello jiggling in a bowl. Father Boyen remained seated in the outer office.

"Your Eminence," the pontiff said and waved his hand toward the empty chair next to Marcello.

"I apologize for being– "

"I invited Father Luciari and Bishop Soniorelli here to discuss your proposal. Father Luciari has written to me to voice pointed opposition to your plan, so let's discuss it," the pontiff said, as he leaned back in his chair. "Tell me, Cardinal Falanzzano, how many cardinals will this retreat you propose serve?" Cardinal Falanzzano fumbled through his portfolio case and pulled out several boards of an artist's rendering of the proposed retreat. "Save the art show for now and just explain your answer," the pontiff said, holding his hands up as though to block his view of the boards.

"We will accommodate twelve to fourteen at full capacity. Each– "

"Just twelve to fourteen." The pontiff paused and nodded as he thought. "And how will this retreat be funded?"

"The guests will pay a nominal fee, tourist receipts will– "

"You have sketches there. That implies that you are proposing renovations, and construction."

"Minor cosmetic changes, Your Holiness. Decorating, small layout changes, things along those lines. I'm happy to show you," the cardinal said. The Holy Father waved him off again.

"What about the legal rights to the property; have you checked into that?" the pontiff asked.

"The Franciscans lease us the property. I expect they would be willing to continue its terms for the ret– "

"You expect?"

"I would have to confirm that– "

"What exactly is the purpose this retreat will serve– and for whom?"

"It will provide a place for retired cardinals, and presumably some bishops, to meditate, to reflect. Relax."

"Reflect and relax. And these cardinals are retired?"

"Yes, Your Holiness. It's a reward for a lifetime of service. A perk. We have a detailed PR plan to– "

"A perk. And a PR plan?" the pontiff asked with an undertone of sarcasm couched in a mock curiosity. "I thought worship was the Church's perk, and service was its PR plan," the pontiff said, rubbing a finger over his upper lip as though to prompt thinking. "You mentioned tourists' receipts. Where does that revenue go today?" the pontiff asked.

"To the Vatican, Holy Father," Bishop Soniorelli answered.

"We will eventually do the same, Holy Father. As soon as the obligations for cosmetic changes have been met, we will return to sending proceeds to the Vatican."

"Father Luciari is concerned for the 1,000 parishioners that will in essence be thrown out of their church. How will you accommodate these people?"

"I'm not certain that it's actually 1,000 members, but our plan is to build a new church at the north end of Tropea," Cardinal Falanzzano said. "We have been– "

"At the far end, a long walk. Most of our parishioners walk to Mass, Holy Father," Marcello explained. The pontiff raised a hand to silence Marcello for the moment.

"Just how do you plan to fund buying land, and building a new church? And honestly, Your Eminence, how can you justify taking a beautifully functioning church away from the parishioners that love, need, and support it?"

"Holy Father, the retreat is a reward for men that have given their lives to the Church. Men like you, Holy Father. Cardinals that have come up through the ranks as parish priests, bishops, and officers of the Holy See. It's a reward," Cardinal Falanzzano professed. "They've earned this. You have earned this. We all have. After all, our retirement age is seventy-five. Surely it isn't too much to ask to create a place for these men to spend a few weeks a year at a pleasant retreat. These men have dedicated their lives to serving the Church. They deserve a reward. And there's no worry about money, financing's already in place." The cardinal remained silent as he thought for a moment, then looked to Marcello. "And with all due respect, if Father Luciari's parishioners can climb those steps up the mountain the church sits on, they can walk to the end of the town to Mass."

"What do you have to say, Father– beyond what you've said in your letter?" the pope said, sliding the letter over to Cardinal Falanzzano to read.

Marcello stood up and placed his framed painting on the desk so the other three men could see it. It was a painting of an endangered species of little birds named piping plovers. They are little, white-bellied birds with light grey feathers that fuse into darker grey as the color progresses down their backs. They don a jet-black ring around the area that appears as their shoulders and necks. Their prominent black eyes contrasted against their orange and black beaks, create a simple, and pleasing natural color symmetry. Their quick, brisk waddle across the sand is cartoon-like and instantly wins one's affection. Marcello's painting shows them pecking into the beach's sand to snap up morsels of insects, marine worms, crustaceans, and beetle and fly larvae before their little bodies are overtaken or even washed away by rushing waves. A large, overfed seagull in the photo is about to bully the piping plovers out of his way and steal their food.

"One of our parishioners painted this and gave it to me as a birthday gift. I keep it on the wall in my office. I find a rich metaphor in it." Pointing out the details as he spoke, he explained what the photo meant to him. "I see the sea as spirituality nourishing these endangered little birds with hope, inspiration, and faith, wave after wave, day after day. Each wave washes in a banquet of nutrients onto the shore. These little piping plovers run to retrieve whatever nourishment the waves leave behind. In the same way, Holy Father, our parishioners at Santa Maria seek spiritual nourishment from God. God is our sea, Holy Father. The Mass, our sacraments and prayers are the waves carrying the Church's spiritual nutrients to our spiritual parishioners. Just like the sea provides these little piping plovers with nutrients, wave after wave, the Mass renews our parishioners' faith and spiritual health, Mass after Mass. Then one day, this big bird," he said, pointing at the bully-like seagull then glancing to Cardinal Falanzzano, "comes bursting onto the scene and chases the defenseless piping plovers away so it could feast on the nourishment the little birds need to survive. Cardinal, with all due respect, you and the retreat you propose are no different than the seagull– the big bully stealing nutrition from the little birds– the Santa Maria parishioners." Marcello returned to his chair, content with his plea. The pontiff enabled the ringing silence filling the room to do the talking. He contemplated with his face propped up by his hands in a praying position.

"Well, that's a cute little story about these dirty little birds, but these men I propose to reward are not bullies, they are Cardinals in the Catholic Church," Cardinal Falanzzano said, raising his voice and jamming his index finger into the pontiff's desk to amplify his words. "They are life-long servants of the Church. Our Holy Father is keenly aware of the service demands cast upon these men, and how taxing it can be," he said, looking down his nose at Marcello. "How dare you refer to us as bullies and compare life-long servants of the Church to birds pinching morsels of worms from the ocean," Cardinal Falanzzano said, nearly shouting. "They have earned a reward!" He shoved Marcello's letter at Marcello.

"Bishop Soniorelli, you're shuffling in your seat like a race car driver waiting for the green flag to drop; what do you have to add?" the pope asked.

Bishop Soniorelli placed a manilla folder on the desk and paused for dramatic effect and to silently ask for God's help. *Let go and let God*, he thought to himself, a supportive phrase he often relied on. Marcello leaned forward, sensing news and the bishop's support.

"A few months ago, I got wind of a plan to build a church in the northwest corner of Tropea. Finding little merit in the idea and knowing– believing– that no one would discuss building a church without first consulting the diocese's bishop, I dismissed it as a dumb rumor; I ignored the idea, I blew it off. But just two weeks ago," Bishop Soniorelli said, leaning forward toward the pontiff in an air of confidence and assumed comradery, "A surveyor called me assuming that as bishop of the diocese, I would be at the center of this project." He gave a quick nod to everyone around the desk. "At this point, I was thinking this is a real project, but how could that be? How could anyone expect to build a new church in my diocese without my blessing so to speak, let alone without me knowing at all?" he said with a lilt of surprise in his rising voice. "Well, during that conversation with the surveyor, I found that a company named *Senior Breezes* recently purchased the property at a discount and was issued a mortgage– "

"Let me guess: The Vatican Bank?" the pontiff interrupted.

"Yes, Holy Father, and the terms are most generous, and Your Holiness, the loan issued was for more than three times the value of the property. I can show you here," Bishop Soniorelli said, opening his folder to show the pontiff. He glanced at the paper on top of several pages in the bishop's folder then looked back to Bishop Soniorelli as a prompt to continue.

"It gets quite upsetting, Your Holiness," Bishop Soniorelli said, feigning profound concern to camouflage his joy in revealing a juicy scandal. "The company– *Senior Breezes*– Your Holiness, is owned by two partners. I got all this information from an officer at the Vatican Bank in the interest of ethics," the bishop said parenthetically. "The company is owned by," he paused again for dramatic effect, "Mister Nunzio Corsetti and Mister Buto Falamino." Bishop looked directly at Cardinal Falanzzano with a stern, accusatory authority. Cardinal Falanzzano's jaw quivered. Guilt and anger sucked the color from his face like a thirsty towel soaking up a spill. The pontiff looked to the cardinal then back to the bishop for an explanation, for the payoff.

"These two men are actually three men in one, Holy Father. These names are aliases used by Cardinal Falanzzano, Your Holiness. The Vatican Bank accepted these names on official loan documents, but, as you know, the Vatican Bank always secures its loans and buried deep within the legal papers, the loan is tied to Cardinal Falanzzano." The pontiff's face turned into an angry snarl and as red as his red leather papal slippers. He breathed deeply through his nose as his blood pressure steamed into a near boil. Bishop Soniorelli used the moment as an opportunity to finalize his pitch. "I am so very sorry to bring this news to you, Your Holiness," Bishop Soniorelli said, in a tone of poorly concealed insincerity. "There is one last item, Your Holiness." The pontiff looked to the bishop through blank eyes. "There are three officers listed on the loan application: Misters Corsetti and Falamino– that is Cardinal Falanzzano– with Mister Corsetti listed as beneficiary, and Father Boyen … he is listed as the treasurer."

"How special," the pope said. "Is there more?" After an unpleasant pause, the pontiff broke the silence. "Last chance, anything else ... anyone?" the pontiff asked from behind a wave of scorching anger saturating the room with a heavy silence.

"I have something to say, Holy Father," Marcello said. The pontiff gave him the floor with a nod of his head. "Many of those 2,000 parishioners are children. I beg of you to leave their chance for hope, their fountain of faith and inspiration as it is today, and allow them to climb those sacred 300 steps to bow before God, partake in the body and blood of Jesus Christ, and experience the glory of feeling the Holy Spirit vibrantly living within them. I plead with you, Holy Father, to allow Santa Maria to continue on– forever– as a vital organ of life in the community of Tropea, and within the body of the Church. I beg of you, Holy Father."

The Holy Father held his chin between his folded hands and contemplated for several minutes. He closed his eyes and thought and prayed, rocking in his chair to soothe his ire, then after what seemed like several long minutes, he nodded his head, apparently arriving at a conclusion. He opened his eyes and expelled a deep breath of tension's destructive air.

"Your Eminence, I am trying very, very hard to move the anger I am feeling toward you in the emotional fury in my right brain to a rational calm in my left brain. I am trying very, very hard. There is little point to lecturing a grown man, yet a senior cardinal who is entrusted with trust as a vicar of integrity in the Church. But I will take swift and rigorous action. "You will work with my office, beginning immediately, to return this property to whomever you bought it from. Is that clear?" the pope demanded rather than asked, continuing without waiting for a response. "What's your most valuable skill as a cardinal?" the pope asked.

"Administration– organizing, managing." The pope opened and scanned a page in a folder on his desk as Cardinal Falanzzano spoke.

"And this Father Boyen waiting for you out there, what about him? What's he good at?" he asked while continuing to scan the papers in the folder.

"Father Boyen ... I would say his strengths are obedience and discipline," Cardinal Falanzzano answered.

"And you, Father, you, as a priest, what are your strengths?" the pontiff asked Marcello.

"Inspiring the people of my parish to open their hearts, souls, and minds to the Holy Spirit," Marcello answered without hesitation. The pontiff closed the folder.

"Bishop Soniorelli?"

"Faith, friendship, and forgiveness."

The pontiff shook his head, digested the answers, spun his thoughts through a succession of possibilities while wrapping his fingers on his desk. He closed his eyes and thought in silence again. He prayed. Thought more. Prayed more. Finally, he held his hands together in a gesture of affirmation but paused before speaking as though to assess one last thought. He looked to Marcello.

"Father Luciari. I would like you to suggest some names for your replacement at Santa Maria." Cardinal Falanzzano squirmed in his chair like a worm wriggling through a puddle of confusion, hope, and bewilderment. His eyes glimmered with a misplaced glint of hope. "We need to replace you, Father, because I am invoking my pontifical power to declare that effective on the first day of November of this year, in five weeks' time from today, I am appointing you Cardinal Luciari. You will report directly to me– here in Rome– as special advisor to the pontiff."

Marcello's eyes widened. Beamed. Happiness and uncertainty danced across his face like fireworks sizzling in the night sky. "And effective on that same day, you, Bishop Soniorelli, you will be elevated to Cardinal Soniorelli. You will replace Cardinal Falanzzano and assume all his duties and enjoy his privileges in the diocese. "And you, Cardinal Falanzzano, you will be taking your penchant for real estate development, administrative, organizational, and management skills to develop a new parish in Zaire. You will take Father Boyen with you; his obedience and discipline will prove valuable. And remind him, as a decree issued directly by me, if he ever lays a harmful hand on a child, as his record reflects he has in the past, I will excommunicate him and have him prosecuted," the pontiff declared. All color retreated from Cardinal Falanzzano's face as regret flooded his gut and balled up into a fiery glob of lead-spewing acidic explosions of dread. The Holy Father leaned forward on his desk toward Cardinal Falanzzano. "I am insulted and infuriated by your avaricious and sleazy scheme and by your expectation for me to entertain a proposal to convert a thriving parish serving 1,000 parishioners into a resort for a handful of retired cardinals. You will assume your new responsibilities in Zaire as a parish priest at a priest's wages in accordance with local standards and your pension will be based on a Congolese parish priest's salary. Or you can resign– right now." The pontiff sneered at Cardinal Falanzzano then looked away as a means of dismissing him as he said, "Assuming you don't resign before leaving this office, Father O'Meara from my staff will be in touch with you to fill you in on the details of your transfer and demotion."

Cardinal Falanzzano collected his sketches and left the pontiff's office in silence wrapped in the pasty-white skin of a sick and broken man. He closed the door behind him, leaving the privileged life of a Catholic cardinal indulging in the fine life in Rome behind. Turning back to Marcello and Bishop Soniorelli, the pontiff continued. "I would like the two of you to remain for a bit." The pontiff rose from his chair and extended his hand and Marcello and Bishop Soniorelli each kissed his ring.

"Cardinal Luciari, Cardinal Soniorelli, congratulations! We will put this nightmare behind us by enjoying a celebratory lunch, then we will tell your families the good news."

Marcello squeezed out a tear and Bishop Soniorelli pressed out a rascal-like smile with grateful surprise. The Holy Father embraced them both and bowed his head in prayer. With his eyes still closed, he blessed them with the sign of the cross as Father O'Meara quietly entered the room unnoticed, his face clouded with concern.

"Father Luciari. It's your uncle, Father Frischetti." The warm, vibrant joy radiating from Marcello's face drained into an alarm of frozen dread.

CHAPTER 25

The Father, The Son

Marcello stared at his Uncle Salvestro, oblivious to the machinery, bleeps and beeps breaking the silence, and the tubing surrounding his uncle's bed. He sat in the reek of hospital smells: futile antiseptic attempts at sterility competing with the stench of bacteria, stale urine, and decomposing feces so intrinsically embedded in a hospital room. He saw only his uncle's pasty frailty propped up in a once sterile bed turned soiled with the fluids and invisible shroud of sickness preceding death.

"Did you have any warning, feel it coming on at all?" Marcello asked.

"Not really, Cello. I've been feeling tired lately, but I just chalked it up to my age and I've been busy lately, but none of the heart attack signs that they speak of," Uncle Salvestro answered.

"What's your doctor say?"

"It's what he doesn't say that matters. He's got me on pain relief but, honestly, Marcello, that's just to keep me comfortable and quiet," Uncle Salvestro spoke in more of a whisper than speech. The once vibrant voice commanding the Mass from the altar sounded feeble and meek. The oxygen tube positioned over his nose seemed more a source of discomfort than an instrument of relief. "There's really nothing they can do for me, Cello," Uncle Salvestro declared in the faint breath of concession. But I'm at peace with that."

"Uncle Sal." Marcello reached out his hand and held his uncle's hand in his and rubbed it with tender affection as the ache of sorrow swelled in his throat. the thought running through Marcello's head was, "*You can't die, Uncle Salvestro. Please don't die.*" But he said nothing. He rubbed his uncle's hand for several minutes as mortality's indifference began closing the imperceptible door separating faith from doubt, light from darkness, and life from death.

Marcello finally spoke again, "What can I– " Uncle Salvestro shushed him with a silent gesture, bringing his finger to his parched lips. After several elusive breaths, Uncle Salvestro spoke in a weak whisper.

"I've been a priest for almost sixty years, Cello. Now, I am about to be embraced by the God I served and lived for all those years. I am cautiously eager, and I am grateful," he said, pausing to grasp for morsels of air. "But my embracing God comes at the great cost of leaving you, my sweet boy, the boy and the man I have loved so much, and lived for all these years." Uncle Salvestro's eyes seemed to lose definition. A soft brown glaze engulfed his pupils and washed all traces of life from his expression.

"My faith is strong, Cello, but it is overshadowed by the pain I am feeling in leaving you in this life." Tears surged up in Marcello's eyes and rolled down his cheeks, attracting the dull fluorescent light from above Uncle Salvestro's bed. Tears Uncle Salvestro could not see but felt. "You have defined my life, Marcello, and now, my death by making me feel complete. Fulfilled." Marcello buried his head next to his uncle's side. "You are everything to me, Uncle Sal. Everything. Everything." They both wept quietly, squeezing each other's hands.

"And you … " were the only words Uncle Salvestro could muster while struggling to breathe. His once strong chest laid nearly still as he gasped for evasive air. His eyes closed but it wasn't he who had closed them. The force of life slowly seeped from his being. He was losing his battle with the weight of sedation, pain, and weakness. He dozed off for several minutes before opening his eyes again.

"As men of the cloth, you would expect we would have more clarity on matters of our preaching," Uncle Salvestro said. He paused for air then continued in a faint whisper, "But I can honestly say, I know little more than a child." He laboriously turned toward Marcello. "I believe so deeply, and faith, Marcello, is a far more powerful force than mere knowing. Any man can know what he has been taught and learned," he managed before needing to regroup, needing to rest. "But faith is an entirely different power than knowing. Not all of us are capable of great faith. And I can tell you– " an intrusive cough overtook Uncle Salvestro's speech and breathing.

"It's OK, Uncle Sal. It's Ok. Try to relax."

Uncle Salvestro eventually stopped coughing but barely found his breathing.

"I can tell you, Cello, I know more deeply through what I believe than through what I know." A calm settled in, even a slight moment of energy. Nephew and uncle, father and son continued to hold each other's hands.

Questioning the question in his mind, Marcello remained quiet, giving his uncle a chance to say whatever he could, whatever he wanted. Sensing his uncle's need for a prompt, he asked, "What do you most want to tell me at this moment, Uncle Sal?"

"That you and I and all of our family will rejoice together in heaven. I know that life is very, very precious, and despite the number of years, it is very short, Marcello." His eyes closed for a few moments and he faded into another place before returning. "It is so very important to use, to cherish every moment in this life, Cello. So precious. We are the lucky ones," he said, before needing to rest, needing to breathe before continuing. "Family is the greatest treasure. No one loves you like your family. It is the fiber we are made from and I am so grateful to have our family as we have."

"You have been the core of our family, and the core of my life, Uncle Sal. As I said to you once before, you were not my dad but you were the best father I could have ever hoped for." Marcello bent forward and leaned into Uncle Salvestro's feeble body. "I love you so much, Uncle Sal. So, so much." Uncle Salvestro instinctively wrapped his intravenous laden arm around Marcello's head.

"And I love you, Cello. So much." Uncle Salvestro's breathing became more labored. He rested, seeking a reprieve from the exhaustion in dying. "You are a fine priest, a fine man, a credit to the Church. As long as you serve God and the people as you have all your life, you will be a model priest. And there are few more noble callings, Cello." Uncle Salvestro managed to capture a solid breath of air. "The Church is so lost in its service to itself and its self-centered dogma … please don't let that happen– don't let yourself get tangled up in the Church's self-service to the organization. Serve the people as you have been doing," he said, and closed his blank brown eyes. Minutes later, his eyes slowly opened again.

"My life was made rich by being so close to you, Marcello. It is so fitting that you are with me now." He grasped for his last breaths of air.

"I am ready to receive my final Sacrament, Cello. And so glad it is you to administer my Last Rites." His throat gasped, seeking the final few breaths he needed to form and power his final words.

"I am ready to receive my Last Rites, Cello. I am ready to meet God. Now." A dry gurgle tumbled in his throat. "I love you, Cello, my sweet boy. I love you."

Cello buried his head in his uncle's body and wept like a child. He performed the Sacrament of Last Rites in a mechanical, rote stupor, choking on his words, drowning on the sorrow of his own tears as he paid the painful price attached to the immeasurable joy of loving someone: Uncle Salvestro.

As Marcello placed a sign of the cross over Uncle Salvestro's forehead, the uncle, the father he loved so deeply, died under the touch of his thumb.

CHAPTER 26

Now

Four men were about to be consecrated Catholic cardinals. The pontiff himself would serve the Mass with joy and pride; he hand-picked these men, including Marcello and Bishop Soniorelli. The new cardinals were about to receive their scarlet red hats and sacred rings – beautifully designed by Uncle Jewels – and pronounce their vows. The vibrant red symbolized the cardinals' willingness to shed their blood for their faith. Their rings were designed by the pope in a spirit of rich symbolism. The bands were made of eighteen-karat-gold, symbolic of the precious gift of love given Jesus. Three gold miniature Roman columns symbolizing the Blessed Trinity supported a rectangular, faceted-cut amethyst stone, symbolizing the liturgical season of Lent and Jesus' suffering for our sins. The perimeter of the stone was secured to the supporting posts by a silver hoop, fashioned in the form of a crown of thorns, as reference to the crown of thorns thrust upon Christ's head before his crucifixion.

The pontiff celebrated a touching Mass grounded in simplicity's grace amidst a backdrop of glory's grandeur that is Saint Peter's Basilica. It was a heartfelt spiritual sharing wrapped in the configuration of Catholic tradition. For the new cardinals and their families, it was a leap into God's embrace and an assignment into the service of their fellow men and the Church. In short, it was a very big deal. Chiano flew in from New York where he had been serving as a rabbi in a Reformed Synagogue for the past ten years. Avigail stayed behind to watch their two daughters and son. Giuliana, Mia, and Mia's husband and two boys attended. Uncle Jewels sat in the first pew with his wife, Tessera, and their adopted son, Mihn Vong-Pratto, the little boy Marcello brought home from Vietnam. Monsignor B. was there. Sister Volpinello was there. God was there, too. And Uncle Salvestro was certainly looking down from the heavens with great pride and gratitude.

The altar at Saint Peter's Basilica was an ocean of red roses flanked by waves of white roses. The Vatican orchestra saturated the basilica with glorious music that lifted the spirit while moving the soul. Incense draped the air with its pleasant, smoky musk wafting its haze over the still air, and the light pouring through its stained glass. The echo of the pontiff's voice circling the basilica settled in the congregants' ears like understanding settling into knowing.

After reciting a *Profession of Faith* and the *Cardinalic Vows*, the Holy Father officially introduced Cardinal Marcello Luciari. There was no spectacular moment of triumph or revelation like one might feel scoring a winning goal or nosing out the field to break the tape in a foot race. But there was a profound sense of peace and spiritual euphoria running through Marcello's veins. More than turning a page on a chapter of his life, he was about to open a new book filled with blank pages to be written, a new life to be lived.

Just days after the celebratory Mass, Marcello was formally assigned to serve the pontiff as a Special Advisor on a broad array of pontifical and spiritual issues. He was summoned to the Holy Father's office to discuss his new purpose just days after his settling into an apartment owned by the Vatican. It was a small, aptly appointed apartment with furniture defying description beyond a generous classification as 'eclectic.' But it was an apartment close to the Vatican, and the buzz that was Rome, and that was more than suitable to the newly appointed Marcello.

"Come in, come in, Cardinal Luciari. How's it feel to hear your new name: Cardinal Luciari?" the Holy Father asked while moving from behind his desk to join the new cardinal. He extended his ring for Marcello to kiss and motioned for him to take one of the two chairs facing one another near a large window overlooking the papal gardens. He extended his hand again, this time for a handshake as congratulations and welcome. They shook hands and sat down. "The cardinal vestments suit you well," the pontiff said. He poured two short glasses of Nocino, a walnut-based Italian liqueur, from a decanter, and offered up his glass in a toast. "To Cardinal Luciari. May you live a long, spiritual, and graceful life." They cordially clanged their glasses and downed the Nocino. "I salute the monks that make this Nocino, and I salute you, and I treat myself to something special. And it's good for the gut and helps control blood pressure. It's a good thing, right?" the pontiff said. He refilled their glasses and clanged Marcello's glass with his, and they sipped again.

"Cardinal Luciari, when we met some weeks ago, you said your strength was to inspire. I want to put your gift to work," the pope said. I want to address the cardinals. I want to start a spiritual fire with a message that permeates into the whole Church," the pontiff said. "I will host a Mass at the Conference of Cardinals in January, I would like you to develop a theme and the message for the conference. I want to make a splash we'll all remember," the pope said. "Take some everyday truth and elevate it to universal application. I want a simple, but poignant message," the pontiff said. He paused to sip his Nocino. "Something that blasts through that forty-foot wall of stubbornness and preconceived notions they live behind."

"I am honored, Your Holiness. I am more than happy to," Marcello said, wading through surprise and humility's humility.

"I am leaving it completely in your good hands. Let's give them something they will not forget, agreed?"

"Agreed. Yes. Certainly" They clanged glasses once more and sipped the dark, syrupy, invigorating, walnut-based liqueur. Nocino.

"And I want to commemorate the event with a meaningful memento, something significant, something of value, luxurious but not excessive– but something they will value, and use often, something that will remind them of this event– and your message of course. I'll leave the selection of this memento up to you, as well," he said. "We have a Cardinal's Fund that's subsidized by contributions from financial companies courting the Vatican; you can use that fund for the memento you choose; let's say up to 500,000 lira per gift. That should buy a nice gift, something special, OK?"

"Certainly, Holy Father. I will find a relevant and memorable gift. That is very generous of you." The Holy Father rose from his chair, sipping the last of his drink; the meeting was over.

"I'm confident that you will serve us well, Cardinal Luciari," the pontiff said, raising his hand for Marcello to shake, rather than kiss his ring.

"Ask Father O'Meara how to access the funds. I don't know the first thing about those procedures," the pontiff said, while patting Marcello on his back, politely guiding him toward the door.

Marcello took a long walk into the tranquility of the Vatican gardens. Its plush green carpet of manicured lawns and sculpted shrubbery indulged the eye in a festival of shape, form, texture, and scents that soothe the soul and clear the mind. He strolled calmly, hands clasped behind his back, absorbing the peace and beauty of the gardens' profusion of flowers: lavender amaryllis, larkspurs, bellflowers, irises, white lilies, dangerously poisonous but beautifully textured baneberries, spectacular white roses, and peace lilies. Yellow daffodils, a garden of stars-of-Bethlehem, black-eyed Susans, and floppy daylilies. Orange lily of the Incas, common sunflowers, and poppies. Pink peonies and twinspurs. Red carnations, laceleafs, sweet Williams, crane's-bills, and petunias. And tulips of every species and color imaginable. This treasure of color, form, shape, and scent filled Marcello with inspiration's vigor.

This colossal array of flowers emerged from the earth in various arrangements, and from ornate planters in perfect complement. Meticulously groomed and trained boxwood shrubs were miraculously arranged in the form of the papal seal. Fountains sprinkled peaceful trinkets of water into a soft soothing splash, spraying comfort over worn stones of the fountains' floors. The subtle yet intense beauty of a particular fountain stopped Marcello in his tracks. It was a tall, narrow structure framed in marble. It featured a large oval opening in its center where a gold sculpture of a man standing on a small cylindrical stone platform played a violin. Figures of men and women and angels were sculpted into each side of the fountain's frame. There was a certainty about its romantic, even sensual appeal playing in the figures in the sculpture. The entire sculpture commanded not only Marcello's attention, but his engagement, as well. It struck Marcello that the one note being played by that golden man playing the violin in that very moment, would be playing forever. One note, one perpetually renewed moment in time to be played forever. Neither the past nor future existed, just this perpetual now. It is always now. Marcello had his theme for the pontiff's Mass: time. And he instantly knew what the gift had to be. He left the papal gardens inspired and eager to begin working on his project for the pope.

It was early afternoon when Marcello tinkled the little bell attached to Uncle Jewels' jewelry store door. A young couple was looking at wedding rings as he entered.

"Cardinal Luciari– who will always be Marcello to me. This is a beautiful surprise. Come in, come in. Let me hug this man of God," Uncle Jewels cried out. He embraced Marcello in a loving bear hug.

"Uncle Jewels, how are you!"

"I am wonderful as always. Come, sit, and I will make you an espresso. Would you also like an espresso?" he asked the couple that was browsing. They shook him off politely and returned their attention and aspirations to the case of wedding and engagement rings gleaming in a perfectly-lit jewelry case.

"None for me, either," Marcello said. "Believe it or not, I am here on official business– in addition to coming in for a hug, of course," he said.

"Business? I am happy to help you. What would you like to see?"

"Watches. I need 185 watches!" Uncle Jewels' eyebrows arched, and a tiny smile spread across his lips. He shook his head, assuring himself that Marcello was serious and that he could accommodate the request.

"One hundred and eighty-five watches?"

"Yes. In six weeks. Can you do– "

"Of course. But you only have two wrists; what will you do with the other 183 watches?" Uncle Jewels inquired, peeking over the top of his reading glasses and under the curve of arched eyebrows. A deliberate blink of his eyes awaited Marcello's response.

"They are gifts for cardinals who are coming to the Vatican for a conference." Uncle Jewels took a peek to check on the couple who were looking at rings.

"Anything you want to see in that case, you just let me know," he offered the couple. Turning back to Marcello he said, "Nice gift. How much are you looking to spend on watches for these 185 cardinals'?"

"I can go up to 500,000 lira per watch," he said. "And can we do something special on the face of the watch?" he asked.

"It depends on the something," Uncle Jewels answered. Marcello took a folded piece of paper from his coat pocket inside his cappa magna, the long black cape-like garment cardinals wear, and handed the paper to Uncle Jewels. He examined the paper and looked up at Marcello, then back down at the paper. He shook his head, pursed his lips, and shook his head some more. He thought. He bobbed his head. He thought some more. Shook his head from side to side, weighing the possibility. Finally, he looked up at Marcello, then again back at the paper before nodding once more, this time with a conviction of affirmation. "I think I can do this for you. If you will give me one day's time, I will give you your answer with certainty," Uncle Jewels said.

"Perfect," Marcello said.

"Cardinal Marcello," Uncle Jewels said. "This is a very nice order for me. Very nice. I thank you very much. I appreciate it deeply," he said.

"You always told me that watches were very important to Chiano and me, right? Uncle Jewels, I can't tell you how happy I am to bring this order to you. You have showered me with kindness and generosity all my life. This makes me so happy. So happy," Marcello said.

"Come here, you. I must give you another Uncle Jewels hug," he said, and he did.

Marcello busied himself in the Vatican Library developing the message for the conference. He kept the Holy Father abreast of his progress in weekly updates in the pontiff's office. The more the project progressed, the more it became an extension of Marcello, who became more of an extension of the pontiff. Time passed quickly and sooner than later, the day of the conference arrived. A Mass was to be celebrated by the Holy Father at Saint Peter's Basilica as the kickoff for the event to set the tone for the conference. A week before the conference, the Holy Father asked Marcello to select the readings appropriate for his theme and, to Marcello's surprise, delight and honor, the Holy Father asked him to deliver what he referred to as an "inspirational homily that would call the cardinals into action." Marcello savored the opportunity and the resounding vote of confidence from the pope.

The morning of the Mass at which Marcello would make his mark on the College of Cardinals and the Church was crisp enough for a coat and sunny enough for sunglasses. Cardinal after cardinal proceeded into the church dressed in full Choir Dress: white mitres as headdress; scarlet mozzettas– short, elbow-length capes with twelve silk-covered buttons that represent the twelve apostles, covering rochets– white lace garments draped over the shoulders, and full length, scarlet-red silk cassocks, with thirty-three buttons to symbolize the thirty-three years of Christ's life. Symbolism and reverence flowed through Saint Peter's Basilica like oxygen and blood flowing through the body, and through the body of the

Church. As is often the case for special Masses at Saint Peter's Basilica, scarlet-red and snow-white roses adorned the altar, and the Vatican choir filled the world with a Gregorian chant sure to arouse the sleeping angels from divinity's slumber. Then, as the entrance procession began, a female soprano delivered a heaven-blessed version of *Ave Maria*. The procession included several bishops, Marcello, and the Holy Father. The cardinals in attendance stood and faced the center aisle, bowing as the pontiff passed them. The procession approached the altar in reverence and veneration. Something sacred was about to begin: The Catholic Mass.

The singing of *Ave Maria* saturated the cardinals in a stirring glory from the top of their minds to the depths of their hearts and souls. The first two verses were sung by an angelic soprano in concert with the Vatican orchestra. A violin assumed the role of human voice in the third verse, then, that angelic soprano's gloriously stirring voice returned. At its conclusion, the Holy Father closed his eyes and paused for a very long moment to savor the beauty of the moment. He prayed in silence, then bowed reverently to the singer who had just honored God and man with her beautiful tribute to Mary, the mother of God.

The Mass progressed in the formal order of the Catholic Mass. The Holy Father read the First Reading of the Mass from the Old Testament and the Second Reading of the Mass from the New Testament. The Third Reading, the Gospel Reading, was read by Marcello. After reading it, he moved to the pulpit to present the homily that the Holy Father assigned him to deliver. He was excited, not nervous. He had rehearsed the homily he had written several times, and developed a heartfelt attachment to the message, and a deep appreciation to the Holy Father for this honor of addressing the College of Cardinals.

> "Good morning. Welcome to the glorious Saint Peter's Basilica, and welcome to Rome. My name is Cardinal Marcello Luciari. I am deeply honored to be asked by the Holy Father to address you this morning to celebrate the Mass initiating this conference we have entitled, *The Hands of Time*.
>
> In the spirit of *The Hands of Time*, I would like to take a minute of time to distribute a commemorative memento from the Holy Father as a gift to each of you.

I ask that you please wait until all of you have received your gift before opening it."

On that cue, a group of young Franciscan Brothers marched down the aisle and distributed small black boxes adorned with cardinal-red ribbon and bows to all the cardinals in attendance. There was a stir of almost boyish excitement as the cardinals examined their gift boxes. Some were stoic, some childishly anticipatory, some nearly giddy, and some suspicious. But all were engaged. After all the gifts were distributed, Marcello continued.

"Gentlemen, please open your gift from the Holy Father."

There was a stirring of bodies as the sound of paper being unwrapped and torn from the boxes echoed throughout the magnificent cathedral. 'Wow's' and 'Ooo's,' and 'Ahhhs' resounded as the cardinals opened their gift boxes and discovered a very pleasant and unexpected surprise: a ruggedly handsome watch with a dramatic rendition of Michelangelo's *Hands of God and Adam* on the face of the watch. The face of the watch was enclosed in a scalloped, white-gold bezel. The hands were ivory-white slender arrows with Roman numerals in the same color. The band was a sturdy dark-tan leather with a gold buckle. A spontaneous resounding applause erupted, and the entire flock of cardinals rose from their seats and applauded vigorously in thanks to the Holy Father. They applauded for well over a minute. The pontiff bowed in return and looked to Marcello and winked, smiled, and clasped his hands in prayer and thanks as he mouthed a 'thank you' to Marcello, who bowed in return and mouthed back his own 'thank you' then returned to the pulpit.

"I'd say we're off to a good start ... When the Holy Father asked me to work on today's theme, I shook my head to be sure I was hearing correctly. After the honor and privilege sunk in, I took a walk through the Papal Gardens to collect my thoughts and savor the honor of the Holy Father's confidence. I walked through the beauty and peace of the gardens trusting that God would help me come upon an idea for a theme ...

something to get my mind around and build a message on. As I walked, and thought, and looked, and hoped, I felt like I was somewhere between anxious and hopeful, somewhere between apprehensive and faithful, doubt and confidence. But the one thing I was sure of, was that God would be guiding me.

"As I came around one corner, a gold statue stopped me in my tracks. It was a statue in tribute to Johann Strauss– the King of Waltz. The sculpture captures Strauss poised with his violin bow fixed on a single note. It occurred to me that the King of Waltz will never play that note and yet, at the same time, I thought, he will play that note forever, fixed in that beautiful setting in the Papal Gardens, fixed in a perpetual state of 'now.'

"That moment united me with my past. You see, my mother was a dance teacher, and she taught my friend and I every dance known to man. My favorite was the waltz. To this day, I dance the waltz alone, as a means of soothing myself. That dance has brought great comfort to me in the most trying times. And now, in that very moment we know as 'now,' the King of Waltz was before me, playing a waltz in a way that lasts forever.

"I would like to recognize my mother and thank her. My mother taught me the pleasure and healing powers of dance when I was emotionally crippled. She taught me how to rise and move on with strength when I was emotionally paralyzed. She taught me how to be a man when I was just a little boy. And yet, she enabled me to be a child, despite having my innocence stolen from me in a cruel act of war that forced me to carry many burdens a child should not have to bear. My mother taught me that every single beat of a song, and every move in a dance is a source of, and cause for joy, as this watch will remind us that every second of our lives is so very precious. She taught me to live, and to love … all people, all the time. Thank you, Mama, so very much."

Marcello bowed to his mother who was seated in the front pew, and the pope instinctively motioned for Giuliana to stand; she did, and the Holy Father began to applaud Giuliana, and the cadre of red-drenched cardinals instinctively followed his lead. Giuliana wiped tears from her proud cheeks and blew a kiss to her son, and he blew one back to her as she sat back down. Marcello continued:

"Now.

"Now is the most important time of all. The beautiful watch we were just given so generously by the Holy Father ticks with relevance. When I was so graciously and appreciatively appointed to become a cardinal, honestly, my first impulse was 'ahhh, thank God, what a wonderful reward ...' but when I consulted my spiritual adviser," he said, gesturing to the crucifix, "I quickly realized that yes, it is a profound privilege, but more importantly, it is a vital calling, and it is underscored in the rich visual metaphor in the brilliant Michelangelo painting, *Hands of God and Adam*, that we see replicated in the face of the watch that our Holy Father gave us.

The hand of God perpetually reaches for Adam's hand– the hand of man. And Adam's hand, perpetually reaches for the hand of God. Perpetually. It's always 'now.'

"Take a look at your new watch for a moment. Go ahead, have a look."

Marcello waited several seconds to assure that every cardinal actually took the time to look at their watch. He consulted his own watch before continuing.

"What do those hands that are perpetually reaching out telling us? Why did Michelangelo portray the hands reaching out but not touching? Why did he choose to feature the index fingers?

"No one knows for sure, but could it be that God's sacred hand is reminding us that He will always be reaching out to us, and that we must always be reaching out to Him? Could it be that those hands that are not actually touching can be a sign reminding us that our work is not yet done? And could it be that those index fingers are pointing to us, choosing us to do His work? Can these dramatically portrayed hands be a timely reminder to us to answer this higher calling, a divine calling? Is this wonderful depiction of an attempt for God and man to touch telling us to touch the hearts and souls that depend on us to lead, inspire, and guide them? To serve them? The face of this watch reminds us that the time for us to act is now.

"Now is all we have, and now is the time to use each of our very own hands to do something important. Our lives are very, very short. Just check your watch, and you'll see that time is passing every single second. How much time does each of us have? Our time is ever changing, ever running out. But we do have now.

"Now is the time we must reach out to each other, to our congregants, to our world, to do God's work. We must use our very hands to make God's world better, to make our lives and all the lives we touch better for our being here.

"The Holy Father has given us the wonderful gift of time. Every time we look at the face of this watch, its hands will tell us so much. The hands of God, and Adam, and the hands of the watch itself call out to us, telling us that the only time we will ever have is now. It is now, and now is the time to use our own hands to serve and heal the world. Because it is later than we think. Time is running out.

CHAPTER 27

Homage

It had been twelve years since Marcello and Chiano were together face-to-face. Their careers– their lives– had taken shape and direction down the same road on different paths; Marcello became a Catholic cardinal in Rome, and Chiano became a Reformed Jewish Rabbi in a suburb of New York City, but home– Rome– had been tugging at Chiano's heart strings for some time. When a job as the senior rabbi at Tempio Maggiore Synagogue in Rome became available, Chiano worked feverishly to secure it. Through fate, effort, and good fortune, he got the job, and now, in their early sixties, Marcello and Chiano were reunited in their childhood backyard. Distance had never tempered their friendship but being back together day-to-day brought them closer than ever. The years that physically separated them deepened their love for, and attachment to, one another.

They sat side-by-side in captain's chairs wearing matching captain's hats at the edge of a large pond in the Vatican Gardens, manning the joysticks of remote-control sailboats. Marcello's boat had the name 'Holy Water' painted on its stern, and Rabbi Chiano's boat was named 'Jew-belee.'

"It'll be a fantastic book, Chiano. I can't wait to read it. I know you poured your heart onto every page, and people will feel every word you write. I'm so proud of you for accomplishing this," Marcello said. He mussed the top of Chiano's hat like an affectionate uncle rubbing a child's head.

"There's something I have to tell you ... about the book, Cello."

"All ears."

"I hope you won't mind … and if you do, I am happy to change it– but I don't think you'll mind," Chiano said.

"Shoot."

"I dedicated the book to your father and your family." Marcello turned to Chiano in surprise. His hands fell from his remote control as a smile and gratitude spread across his face.

"Wow. You did that?" He paused and absorbed the charity of Chiano's gracious act. "My family will be thrilled, Iano. My father would have been thrilled. You really did that? That's amazing?"

"I did. I had to. Who else would I dedicate a book to? You risked your lives for us, Cello, we'll never forget that. How could we?"

"I'm overwhelmed, Iano … I really am …" Marcello said. He rose out of his chair to embrace his friend in a warm hug. "You're the best, Iano … the absolute best," Marcello said, and kissed his friend on both cheeks. "Thank you … so much."

"Second best. To you," Rabbi Chiano whispered in Marcello's ear.

"And I love the title: *Homage to the Righteous*," Marcello declared. "It demands to be read, you know?"

"I hope so," Chiano said, as they both sat back down to man their controls.

"You know, this is a great hobby. I love watching these boats rip through the water, responding to our commands as we respond to the wind, the current, the surface of the water," Marcello mused as he maneuvered his boat. Its sail was white and majestic with a graphic of praying hands printed on it. Chiano's sail was white, too, with a Hamsa, the Jewish symbol for the Hand of God, printed on it.

"Interesting how we both chose symbols related to hands on our sails, without ever discussing it," Chiano said.

"Must have something to do with touching people with our work– I should say God's work," Marcello reflected. "You're really dedicating the book to us? I can't get over that."

"Yup."

"Avigail and the kids and grandkids must be really proud of you. Their dad's an author; that's huge."

"Same as you. Just a matter of putting in the work," Rabbi Chiano said.

"So, let's hear about it."

"It comes out of an experience a long, long time ago ... from the days looking up from that pit that your dad and your uncle dug under the church. *The Pulpit*. I'll never forget my family being cuddled together in that dark hole, praying that we'd be OK. And we would hear your uncle's footsteps. He would kick the side of the pulpit three times, very distinctly, to let us know it was him, and that we were safe. My father would tell us to pray for you and your family all the time. We would each lead a prayer dedicated to a different member of your family. We would pray you'd be safe, and we'd pray to thank you. I was always assigned to pray for you," Rabbi Chiano said.

"I hope you still do," Marcello joked.

"Count on it. It's so odd; that dark, dank hole began to feel safe. I can't say comfortable, but maybe comforting, because we were there together and we had a strong sense that your uncle was looking out for us, and somehow, we really did believe we'd be OK. Or at least I did. I never doubted that. And I remember hoping, 'today is the day'– everyday. Then the morning they hustled us off to *Schools* was like a rescue line from God. I had no idea you were going to be there. I was so afraid that you guys had been discovered."

"All we ever thought about was how *not* to be discovered," Marcello said.

"I can't imagine," Rabbi Chiano said, shifting his attention to his boat for a moment. "Anyway, when I was at the synagogue in New York, on more than one occasion, people would say how lucky I was to be here, and I would always say that I have a lot of people to thank for that– meaning your family. Without you and your family, Cel, me and my entire family would have been on one of those horrible trains." He reached out and rubbed Marcello's arm. "I'll never be able to thank you enough. Never. My book is a small attempt to thank– "

"You would have done the same for me ... for my family."

"I know it's hard to believe, but I have to say, we would have. We would have, Cel."

"I know." They sat in silence for a few minutes thinking about what they were trying not to think about: *that day.*

"How badly does it haunt you?" Chiano asked.

"It's always there. I guess that's bad, right? But I've never let it own me, or stop me from living. I'm able to dismiss it, or at least shove it to a back corner in my mind. But it's like being hungry after you eat; like background noise that never goes away. It's an emotional tinnitus that never stops. I try hard to focus on gratitude and serving others. That's mankind's best guarantee of fulfillment, right? Gratitude and serving others."

"I feel bad for bringing it up, but as your best friend, I feel like it's up to me to bring it up once in a while. I can't let you swallow all that pain alone." Chiano touched Marcello's arm again. "I love you too much for that. I would do anything to take on some of that pain, Cel," he said through such earnest eyes. "I so would."

"And I'd do anything to keep it from you, pal. So, we're even. Fair enough?" Marcello rubbed his hand over Chiano's hand and they shook hands with a lifetime of affection and conviction in their grip.

"So, the book?"

"Well, when I was still in college, remember when I had that job at the Yad Vashem Holocaust Museum in Jerusalem? One section of it's dedicated to the Righteous– all the people that put their lives on the line, risking death so Jews could live. I was really moved by that memorial, but I thought the only people who are aware of those righteous people that helped us, are the people who are lucky– or cursed– enough to get to the Yad Vashem. That stuck with me all these years. I always wanted to do something significant to honor people like you and your family, so, this book is it."

"How'd you approach it?" Marcello asked.

"My synagogue had a small, very private group of survivors that used to meet regularly at the synagogue for special services I created just for them. We would talk, read the Torah, share stories. Every single one of us had someone help them avoid or survive the camps. Every single one of them said, more than once, 'I wish I had a way to thank that guard who snuck me food, or that priest that hid me under the organ, or that butcher who let us hide in his freezer, that coworker that shoved me under the counter, that cabinet maker that built a trap door in our floor, or that tailor that hid me among his racks of clothes, the grocer that hid my baby in an empty bean sack ... or in my case, those wonderful people–

your family– that built a fake door to enable my family to hide in their attic. And then there's your father and uncle, who so cleverly converted a church pulpit into an escape hatch leading to the bunker they built to hide us, and God knows how many other Jews. It goes on and on like that, Cel," Chiano said. "I also interviewed a lot of people who were the Righteous that helped us. I got a lot of material from the Yad Vashem and kept these files and notes for years and years until I felt I had enough for a book, and the time and energy to write it," Chiano said.

"That's amazing, Iano," Marcello said, shaking his head. "I am so proud to be your friend."

"And I'm so thankful to be yours."

"So, when's the book actually coming out; when can I buy it?"

"Six or seven weeks, it'll be in the stores and on newsstands, as they say."

"You gonna do a book tour like the big shot writers do?"

"A small one. That takes so much time and a lot of money that I really can't spend right now, and the publisher won't spend much on this kind of book from an unknown writer. But honestly, I'm happy to have it done and if a few people read it, great. I'm just thrilled to have it done and out," Chiano said. "I'm basing my Yom Kippur sermon on the book next month. The message– the book's message– goes beyond atonement. My intent is to motivate people to actually do something– to take action, especially as it relates to what you guys call sins ... what we Jews call the glorious opportunity in discovery and recovery from mistakes. And I hope to motivate people to correct offenses of omissions," Chiano explained. "The Yad Vashem is buying two dozen copies for their gift shop."

"I love the whole idea of Yom Kippur and atonement. We have Confession in the Church, but it isn't that formal, it's really lost its relevance over the years, it's an individual act that doesn't have the punch that Yom Kippur packs." He paused to attend to his boat. "I'd like to do something about that someday." They sailed in silence for a few minutes, shifting sails, managing rudders, changing directions, picking up speed, and adjusting to the ever changing wind.

"The biggest difference between Yom Kippur and Confession is practicality. We encourage people to make amends for our sins directly with the people they've offended. Make a call to the people we've hurt or neglected to apologize and ask for their forgiveness. Only the people we've hurt can forgive us," Chiano said. "With all due respect, my cardinal friend, and this is not a judgment, but if a priest simply absolves a person's sins, what impetus does that person have to correct it, or really make tangible amends for it? Again, no knock on Confession, but one of the things I like most about Yom Kippur is the encouragement to undo wrongs you've done in concrete ways," Chiano explained.

"No argument from me, Rabbi."

"Charity's an important aspect of Yom Kippur too; not just donations, but volunteering time, or donating goods, acts of kindness. Honestly, I love Yom Kippur in its purest form," Chiano said.

"I'd love to incorporate some of those practices into the Church one day."

"More importantly, it helps us teach our young their history and encourages them to help people that need help. Look at the risk and potential cost to people like your family. We can't let anyone ever forget that."

"How do you deal with Pope Pius XII in the book?"

"I had an open mind, I even wanted to give him the benefit of the doubt, but after digging into some of his history and documentation, and my own memory, I wrote a chapter titled *Silence in the Screams*. It sheds light on his approach to the Nazi occupation of Rome. The point– do you want me to tell you or let you read it?" Rabbi Chiano asked.

"Give me the gist of it."

"The point was that he remained silent while people were in the street– literally under his window, as so many have written– being hauled away like animals and put on trains to be murdered. And his action was to remain silent. He professed to have ordered priests and bishops to aid Jews, but his choice to remain silent and attempt to engage in diplomacy with a madman proved catastrophic. If he had taken a stance– a clear, strong stance against Hitler and the Nazis, I am convinced tens of thousands of lives would have been saved," Chiano concluded.

"But he didn't. A cardinal sin," Marcello said. They sailed in silence again, their boats shearing through the water like knives through cake, carving paths in the water's plane and memories into the sailors' souls.

"I have an idea," Marcello said. "Tell me what you think of this: what if we gave the book out to a handful of cardinals, bishops, priests, rabbis, all kinds of religious leaders, as material for inspiration? We can send it with a letter that encourages them to use *Homage to the Righteous* as a base of discussion. This could get the book out to more people and get the message more widely distributed. I think I can get the communications office at the Vatican to get behind it, and we can create an event around Yom Kippur to feature your book. How about that– the Catholic Church promoting Yom Kippur," Marcello said, full of enthusiasm's vigor.

"You think that's possible? You really think they'd go for it? Honestly, I haven't thought about all that; I was just focused on finishing the book."

"Let me look into it. How soon can you get me fifty copies?"

"As soon as it's out."

Time flashed by and six weeks later, Marcello arrived at Saint Cecilia's in Trastevere with fifty copies of *Homage to the Righteous*. The new pastor at Saint Cecilia's who loved and respected Uncle Salvestro agreed to allow Marcello address his congregation as a guest at Sunday Mass. The homily was based on an excerpt he read from a chapter named *The Pulpit* from Chiano's book; the theme was *Sins of Omission*. He read to the congregation:

> "So many people could have said no. So many people could have turned their heads and ignored our Jewish brothers and sisters cry for help, their need for help to survive. To live, to save their children from the terror and evil inflicted upon them by the Nazis. So many could have turned away and let those people die, let those six million– six million– innocent people be murdered. And so many did turn their heads. So many let those desperate pleas for help to save lives fall on deaf ears. So many said no. Even many leaders in our own church said no. They turned their heads away from a desperate, crying human need.
>
> "But the book I just read from is about the people that said yes. The people who heard the screams for help and responded with open hearts, open arms, courage, and compassion. They risked their lives, they risked their families' lives to save others' lives, many whom

they never even knew.

"My father was one of the ones that said yes. He found a way to hide our Jewish friends, a way to protect them from the Nazis, and because he said yes, that Jewish family is alive and well today, and one of the members of that family wrote the book I just read from. To this day, he is my very best friend. And he always will be.

"The Nazis found my father and they shot him dead in front of our family ... inches from my very own eyes. Why? Because he helped save Jews from being murdered! His reward was punishment. His sentence was death. It's no wonder so many said no. But what if we all said no? What if no one stood up to Hitler and the Nazis?

"Imagine what the world would be today if those six million people were spared. Good, loving, warm, happy, smart people. Imagine the contributions to our world they would have made. Imagine the friendships, the families, the weddings, the celebrations, the joy of six million lives.

"Saying yes to people in need, despite catastrophic risk, is not about courage, it is about values. It is about caring. It is about standing for something, about believing in something enough to step into the winds of fear and danger in order to protect yourself against the very danger you fear. Is saying no to people in dire need a sin of omission? Is turning your back on the screams for help a sin of omission? The conditions the Nazis imposed were tragic. Cataclysmic. It was easy to say no to those screams for help. But my father and others like him found the strength to answer the call when people needed it most. It cost him his life and our family unimaginable suffering. But he did what he believed was right, what was moral, he did what Jesus would have done.

"I beg of you, when you hear even the most simple

pleas for help, or desperate screams for survival, do what Jesus would do, and what he did do, for you, and for me."

Not only could one hear a pin drop, but you could hear its echo as it bounced on the marble floor of the church, like the boom of a bass drum being pounded in the rumble of a parade. A sense of guilt mixed with inspiration's sway. Some heads bowed in timid shame, some jaws thrust outward in denial's arrogance, some perked up, answering the call, some stared straight ahead, burying the secret good deeds they did in their memories' hidden vaults. Chiano wept, alone, in the balcony of the church. As the Mass ended, and Marcello and the procession left the church, he craned his neck to spot his friend in the balcony, winked, and blew Chiano a kiss.

CHAPTER 28

Letters of the Cloth

Dawn bathed Saint Peter's Square in intense splendor, and its gentle caress-like hue on color. The Basilica rose in the shadow of the imposing Egyptian Obelisk standing in stately divinity as the centerpiece of the square. Bernini's eighty-eight seventeenth-century pillars rose up beneath the pedestals supporting 140 statues of saints, casting their eternal watch and perpetual blessings on Saint Peter's Square. A man clutching a briefcase nearly outran his own hat, as he scurried anxiously across the square. Despite being far too early to be late for anything, he was apparently late for something. Three stories above a set of bronze doors, a light glowed from a third-floor window. The muffled music seeping from the window's gentle glow conflicted with the clumsy cadence of this hurrying man's shoes as he scampered across the stones in Saint Peter's Square.

The interview with Stefano Zurentino from *Vestments* magazine, the briefcase toting man who just dashed across Saint Peter's Square, was scheduled for the early hour of 6:15 a.m.. Mrs. English, Marcello's longtime devout assistant greeted Zurentino and showed him into the office waiting area. Marcello met Mrs. English, an obvious nickname he gave her based on her origin, while he was filling in at Saint Cecilia's when he volunteered to step in as the temporary pastor after his Uncle Salvestro's death. He counseled Mrs. English and her husband through the sorrow and horrors of their battle with cancer, a battle her husband eventually lost after a noble and difficult struggle. Soon after, Mrs. English threw herself into the Church, prayer, God, religion, and serving the parish, which equated to serving who was pastor at that time. Marcello and Mrs. English developed a very warm and productive relationship that served them both well, and he was eventually able to put Mrs. English on the parish payroll. He became her savior on earth, and she became his. They got along like an ideal couple who were born for each other, but not meant for each other.

Zurentino noted the faint scent of cedar and books in the office, not a musty book scent, but a cozy, welcoming one. He admired the sheen in the marble floor surrounding the thick Persian rug beneath the cushy, pale-blue wingback chair he was nestled into. The light was soft and tamed Zurentino's tired eyes, the overtaxed eyes of a reporter who often worked long hours zipping around the Vatican and the cryptic annals of the Church like a picnic fruit fly buzzing about, harvesting secrets and gossip. The most prominent impression he gained while sitting there waiting, was from what he heard: Charleston music and men laughing on the other side of the door. As a good reporter would do, he snooped around.

He went to the wall of photographs first. It was a reflection of Marcello's career and his life. Zurentino carefully examined photograph after photograph: Marcello with his arm around his great nephew, Gio, a moppy-haired twelve-year-old holding a football; Marcello with the Holy Father on the altar of Saint Peter's, Marcello dancing with his mother at Mia's daughter's wedding, Marcello and Chiano standing in a mountain stream holding up a huge, largemouth bass, Marcello hugging Gio while holding his sailboat's remote controls, Marcello and Chiano seated arm-in-arm in a gondola sporting ear-to-ear grins, Marcello with his hands on Chiano's son Moses' head, with eyes closed in prayer, blessing the boy, Marcello, Chiano and Uncle Jewels seated at a café table enjoying pastry and espresso, Marcello with arms raised in praise at the altar at Saint Cecilia's with Uncle Salvestro at his side, Marcello in front of Mia's Christmas tree with his arms around Mia and her daughter and her two boys. Zurentino made some notes then poked around the bookshelves, his hands grazing over several titles written by Marcello, and one written by Chiano. He returned to his seat and made more notes, looking up every now and then at the door separating him from the Charleston music and apparent happy ruckus going on in the office on the other side of the door. The music finally faded and succumbed to the sound of the men inside still laughing. Zurentino was more than curious. The laughing faded and he heard the men's voices but couldn't decipher what they were saying, he would ask soon enough. Finally, the door opened and Chiano appeared.

"Stefano, good morning. He'll be right with you … he's picking out a hat," Chiano said, stumbling through a hardy laugh. "He'll just be a minute," Chiano added. Stefano Zurentino raised his eyebrows in a polite gesture of agreement and smiled out a 'thank you.' Mrs. English entered, and he rose from his seat.

"No, no, sit, sit. I just want to ask you if it's OK to conduct your interview while on the move?" Mrs. English asked, in her disarming British charm. "He has a Mass to celebrate for a nun who is retiring after seventy years of service to the Church. You'll have a few minutes before he has to leave but is it OK to continue talking while you walk to Marcelloel?"

"Of course," Zurentino answered, covering his disappointment behind a practiced forced smile.

"You can chat here until it's time to leave, I'll let him know when it's time," she said. "Espresso, Mr. Zurentino? Chiano?" They both declined and as they did, she went back to her office and Chiano retreated behind the music door. Zurentino did more snooping about, searching for details and texture he could include to help shape the story he was here to write. He went back to the bookshelf to the books Marcello had written over the past twenty some years: a trilogy, *In the Name of the Father's* three books, *Son Rise, Son Set, Spiriting;* then a few standalone books, *Symbols Cymbals, White Lies, Nun of Your Business; A Handbook for Parish Pastors; The Privilege of Confession.* He chuckled as he thought to himself, "An author's books are an open window into the man; they make him an open book." Zurentino opened *White Lies* to a random page and read a random line.

> 'Sadly, in too many cases, the white priestly cassock serves more as a shield to hide untruths as opposed to serving as a reminder of, and a commitment to purity. But more often than not, the white cassock mystically transforms secular standards and expectations into a concentrated service to God and clarifies our purpose.'

Zurentino shook his head, pondering the thought. He returned the book to its spot on the shelf and flipped open *Nun of Your Business* and read from a random page.

> *'My gratitude for nuns serving the Church reflects my gratitude for my mother. I hope one day to be in the position to give more stature to nuns. The sisters serve such a vital purpose in Catholic education and they do it with unassuming humility, dedication, and grace. They are the worker bees making priests' lives infinitely easier and far more productive than priests would be on their own. Few will admit this truth but all are profoundly aware of it.'*

Zurentino put the book back and wrote a few more notes, and at that moment, the office door opened, and a sheet of pure white papal vestment moved into the room. Zurentino turned and saw the recently, newly-elected pope: Marcello Luciari had become Pope Boniface X. But to his family, Chiano, and Mrs. English, he would always be Marcello.

Pope Boniface is a spry maverick at seventy-nine. He was affixed to honor and compassion like hope on prayer. He was followed into the room by his ever-present dog, a little black and white Boston Terrier named Bravo, and Chiano, also seventy-nine, and a pillar of happiness and wisdom who supported his lifelong friend with warmth and a silly disposition.

"Holy Father, it is such an honor," Zurentino said, bowing to kiss Pope Boniface's ring.

"A handshake is fine, Stefano," Pope Boniface said, shying away from the formality and pomp with a man he had known professionally for many years. "Thank you for getting up early with us. Our days are very full so every minute counts, right?" He led Zurentino to two face-to-face wingback chairs finished with soft, tufted, oatmeal-colored upholstery where he took a seat. Chiano sat to the side and began reading a newspaper. Zurentino instinctively pulled a notepad and pen from his inner jacket pocket and flipped to a blank page. "Rabbi Chiano promised to be quiet as we talked. Did Mrs. English tell you we'll have to continue as we walk?" the pope asked.

"Yes, Holy Father, she did," Zurentino answered.

"Good, good. Now, what can I tell you?"

"I'm intrigued by your books. Now that you are our pope, will you still be writing books?"

"I hope to, but my time is more in demand now. I treasure the written word. I might not have the time to complete book manuscripts, but I will certainly make good use of the written word," he answered. "Writing gives me time to think and edit what I might regret saying out loud before thinking," the pontiff said with a good-natured grin.

"Bad enough to have to put your foot in your mouth, let alone when it's in a red slipper," Rabbi Chiano chimed in.

"As I said, Rabbi Chiano promised to be quiet while we talk," Pope Boniface quipped.

"Do you have a favorite ... book?" Zurentino asked. "I loved your trilogy."

"Me, too," Pope Boniface said with a smile. "They're all my favorite."

"Were you surprised to be elected our Holy Father?"

"Of course. Some of the conservative cardinals don't like me, but enough of them to elect me like me, I suppose," he said, still smiling as he paused to pet Bravo. "I think every pope is surprised when that possibility becomes your reality. Once it becomes a possibility, you can't help but hope and pray that it's God's intent for you, but you fear it a little bit at the same time."

"What is it you fear?"

"Letting people down."

"If some conservative cardinals don't like you, do you expect those cardinals to sew division in the Church?"

"I am only focusing on unity."

"It took eight votes to elect you. Does that imply– "

"It denotes that we were careful and that we've elected a pope, Stefano."

"There's talk that Cardinal Heimreich was the conservative wing's choice. You've butt heads with him in the past. What are the major differences between you?"

"Well, as I said to Cardinal Heimreich– to his face, he has an agenda, I have a purpose. Cardinals take a vow to serve. It's not a position of entitlement or privilege."

"Have you always had the ambition to be the Holy Father?"

"Once in a while at a ceremony or during a discussion, honestly, I would fantasize that could be me one day, or I would think, 'If I were pope, I would do this or do that ...' sure ... I thought about it a little."

"Now that you are the pontiff, what are some of the 'this or that's' that you would like to do?" Zurentino asked.

"At this point, I am just planning my planning, so we'll have to wait on that answer. I will tell you this though, Stefano, I am very eager to resurrect the Church's integrity and make our faith more about unity and social action than it has ever been."

"Can you elaborate on that?"

"I'll give you this, I'll give you an acronym that's going to guide my papacy. The acronym is C.H.U.R.C.H. The '**C**' stands for Compassion. The '**H**' stands for Honor. The '**U**' stands for Unity. The '**R**' stands for Responsibility. The second '**C**' stands for Courage, and the second '**H**' stands for Helping people."

"Can I quote you on this?"

"You can use it as your headline." Almost on cue, Mrs. English entered the room holding a folder.

"Marcel– Holy Father, it is time for you to leave," Mrs. English said, crossing the room and handing Pope Boniface the folder. "Here's your homily and a few notes on Sister Lorraine. My apologies for interrupting Mister Zurentino."

"Quite alright. We can talk as we walk," he answered and rose to follow Pope Boniface out of his private quarters.

"Rabbi Chiano was making fun of my hats in there," he said, while taking a mitre from its case to show Zurentino the ornate headdress. "I'll stick with the zucchetto." He put the white skull cap on his head and returned the mitre to its case.

"I heard the music you were playing. American Big Band?"

"Charleston. My mother was a dance teacher and she taught my dance partner and I," he said, nodding at Chiano, "the Charleston as kids, and we loved it. Still do. Now, here we are at seventy-nine years old, doing the Charleston at 6:30 in the morning in the Papal Palace," Pope Boniface said.

"Who knew," Chiano said. "I'm thrilled to be vertical at seventy-nine– anywhere– let alone doing the Charleston in the Papal Palace," Chiano added, with his patented smile. "I thank your sweet mother every day for teaching– for insisting that we learn to dance when we were just pups," Chiano said. "What do you think, Bravo," he said to the dog, who looked up at the rabbi expressly unimpressed.

"Just don't make fun of my hat anymore. It's hard to believe people will take me seriously in this hat."

"They won't," Chiano chirped in, again, from behind that smile.

"Any rabbinical words of wisdom for this wonderful nun's Mass?" Marcello asked.

"Yes, tell her it's later than she thinks," he said.

"She's ninety-four, Chiano. She knows it's later than she thinks," the pontiff quipped. "Any *uplifting* wisdom?"

"Tell her it's never too late."

"I'll be sure to include that. See you at the pond later," Marcello said, and made his way toward a papal chapel with Stefano Zurentino in tow.

In addition to his papal vows, Pope Boniface self-imposed a vow to see his great nephew Gio often, and to allocate a meaningful amount of leisure time to being with Gio. After the Mass for Sister Lorraine, Pope Boniface went to meet Gio at a park nearby, a logistically tricky security feat for a security team protecting a pope who enjoyed the pedestrian aspect of Rome. He traveled as inconspicuously as the pope might hope to travel by seldom announcing where he would be when on personal business and in a nondescript, but chauffeur-driven car. And Mrs. English protected his schedule like a hen nesting her eggs.

The park was dotted with kids, one of whom was Gio. As the football in his game was kicked astray, it was suddenly booted back with vigor– off the foot of his Uncle Marcello– Pope Boniface. Bravo seemed impressed.

"Hey, Uncle Cello," Gio happily shouted.

"Holy Father!" His friends yelled out, excited and proud to occupy the pontifical inner circle through the virtue of being friends with the great nephew of the pontiff. Gio ran up and hugged his uncle, and Pope Boniface instinctively bent down and kissed the boy's head.

"Bravo boys, bravo," Pope Boniface greeted the kids. Bravo recognized his name being called by The Holy Father, which warranted a few short barks of approval. "Who wants gelato? Let's all go to get gelato. Good?" They all approved of the idea and crowded around Pope Boniface in a circle as though they had just won a championship and he was their star player. "If your mothers ask you if you had gelato before your dinner, you tell them that it was sacred gelato from the pope, and it's OK. OK? I don't want anybody's mama mad at me, OK? Bravo, you can have gelato, too," Pope Boniface promised. The boys and the big boy, the pontiff, and three security officers from the Swiss Guard left the park in a jubilant herd bound for the gelato shop located on the southwest corner of the park. It would be a moment these boys would remember fondly for life.

As always, Pope Boniface kept his best friend in mind: after sharing a gelato with Gio, he brought Chiano a cup of pistachio gelato to the pond. They sailed their remote-control boats there a few times each week as a means of reflection, meditation, discussion, and premeditated, as well as impromptu horseplay. Chiano had the sailboats in the water ready to sail; he brought a gift-wrapped box with him that he stored under his chair.

"Thanks for the gelato, Popo," Chiano's new nickname for his friend turned pontiff. Pope Boniface waved his coffee gelato spoon to acknowledge his friend. He spooned out another bite and savored it for a minute.

"What's in the box?" Pope Boniface asked.

"A surprise."

"For who?

"You."

"Me? Nice. How come?"

"Birthday present."

"Next week. Both of us. Can you believe it? We're going to be eighty. I have a present for you, too; I'll show you after we sail a bit. Are you giving me my present now?"

"Right after I finish my gelato."

"It's melting; you should hurry up."

"It's better if you savor it.

"Not what the gelatorian said. You're supposed to eat it before it melts. It's better."

"My sources say it's better to savor." Chiano sat his gelato on the ground and they each prepared their sailing controls.

"I have a higher source, right from the gelato maker's mouth. You should eat it right now then give me that gift, or do I have to play the 'God' card?" Pope Boniface said. Then changing subjects, he said, "Gio tells me he's bored by his Confirmation class. He says he means no disrespect, but it feels like the only important thing to him is to get it over with."

"That's not a surprise, is it? I'd be bored as a twelve-year-old, too," Rabbi Chiano said.

"I told him his adopted Uncle Chiano and I would come up with a way to make it more interesting. Even meaningful," Pope Boniface said. "So, we're on the hook."

"OK, we're on the hook."

"Are you finished with that gelato? I should've gotten you a smaller one."

"Savor. Savor," Chiano said.

The remote controls were ready and boats rigged, the wind soft but supportive– good for sailing these scale-model boats.

"The wind is so much like faith. Invisible, no detectable form, no color, no shape, no discernable depth. Nothing's there, yet it's everywhere, and man, is it powerful," Pope Boniface observed. He nodded toward the gift-wrapped box again, trolling for a response but Rabbi Chiano didn't give in to the pontiff's curiosity. Turning back to his thoughts beyond the gift, he continued his reflections on faith.

"Its power pushes and pulls you, and dictates your direction, your choices. You can't see it but it's always there … it's like light on day," Pope Boniface said. Unimpressed, Bravo lifted his leg and poised himself to leave his mark on the gift-wrapped box. Chiano quickly pulled the gift out of harm's way just in time, and Bravo scooted under the pontiff's chair.

"Little sssssshhhhmuck," Chiano said.

After sailing for just a short time, Pope Boniface decided to embark on another activity.

"I'm going to take a break and plant some tomato plants," Pope Boniface said, resting his controls on his chair. "Come with me, say hello to Amodeo, he's starting a stonewall today."

Amodeo looked more elderly than he was. His hair was soft and grey and wisped in the wind. His face was traced with distinct crevices etched by the sun, like the bottom of a lake gone dry. His smile was bright and toothy, but not an enviable toothy. He was slight in build, but his arms were disproportionately large for his body, the result of a lifetime of lifting, chiseling, and positioning heavy Roman stone into flawless stonewalls with artistic perfection. His hands looked like dusty leather.

"Amodeo, my good man, I marvel at how your hands and knowhow create such beauty," Pope Boniface said.

"Thank you, Holy Father. I promise, on the day you pick your first tomato, I will show you your finished wall," he said, casting an arm toward the pontiff's tiny tomato plants.

"Perfect, we'll sit on the wall and celebrate," Pope Boniface said. The pope patted Amodeo on the back, then he and Chiano moved to a short round table that held photo albums, a bottle of chilled Fiorano Bianco, one of the Lazio region's favored white wines, three wine glasses, a plate of assorted cheeses, and a large vine of white grapes. Before sitting down, Chiano presented his small, vertical gift-wrapped box to Pope Boniface, along with a warm hug.

"For you, my friend. Happy Birthday." The pope embraced Chiano with heartfelt warmth and appreciation, then, like a child at Christmas, he unwrapped the present. He laid the wrapping paper on the table and opened the box from the top and gingerly pulled out a potted sapling planted in a wooden chalice. "It's oak," Chiano said.

"Oak?"

"Yes. Oak."

"Oak." Pope Boniface observed. "It's superb, Chiano. Look at that," he said, turning the chalice in a circle, examining the plant and the chalice. "Oak."

"Not just any oak. The chalice and the sapling come from the most famous English Oak tree in the world. It's a thousand years old, and thirty-three feet around, Popo. A thousand years old!" Rabbi Chiano exclaimed.

"A thousand years?"

"A thousand years ... thirty-three feet around," Chiano affirmed. "Oak's the traditional gift for an eightieth birthday, you know. In eighty years from now, this little sprout will be 155 feet tall and thirty-three feet around. This is no everyday house plant, Popo. This is oak." Pope Boniface continued to admire the sapling.

"No, not every day by any means. It's oak. Impressive little guy. Well done, Chiano. Thank you ... thank you very much." The pope lifted two brochures and a photo album from the table and handed them to Chiano. "My gift to you is really for both of us. Take a look, we can choose it together." Chiano looked at the brochure but before looking at it, he hugged Pope Boniface.

"Whatever it is, Cello, thank you very much. Your friendship's the only gift I'll ever need," Chiano said. He raised the brochure to his eyes, and surprise glazed his face like icing coating a cake. "A river cruise. Thank you, Cello," he said, hoping to shroud his aversion to boating with a show of genuine gratitude. "What a nice gesture," Rabbi Chiano said. After an awkward pause, he continued. "But do we want to be trapped in a room half the size of a closet for ten days? What about a lake vacation," Chiano proposed. "Mountain-fresh air, beautiful scenery, serenity. Peace and quiet." Chiano suggested.

"Look at this," Pope Boniface said, handing Chiano a photo album. "We can cruise from Paris to Prague ... we'll see gorgeous mountains, magnificent castles."

"Popo, you live and pray in an exquisite castle. You serve Mass before the most revered frescoes in the history of mankind. You pray in the Sistine Chapel, for God's sake! You need to see castles on vacation?" Chiano light-heartedly reasoned.

"Picture it. Drifting in the breeze, sliding over the water."

"I picture two unshaven old goats trapped in a floating box, choking up gefilte fish and hard-boiled eggs. You want that?" Chiano countered.

"Come on, we can go in mid-September, the weather'll be perfect. We'll go right after I present my first Encyclical Letter."

"The Jewish High Holy Days are in the middle of September; we can't go then. And why are you presenting your Encyclical Letter, they're well-educated grown men, let them read it," Chiano argued.

"It's perfect timing. There's a Bishops' Synod in September, and the subject is momentous. I want to present it to them in person– for the impact."

"What's so momentous?"

"Cardinals from the right wing of the Holy See are using this synod to push a movement to canonize Pope Pius XII. But I'm going to deliver my first Encyclical Letter at that synod and denounce the cowardly son of a biscuit."

"Ah, Pius XII, Hitler's pope. Well, good for you, Cello. I remember the day your mama marched to Saint Peter's Square and screamed at him. 'You coward! You coward!'" Chiano chanted, cupping his hands around his mouth.

"She's still screaming at him from heaven, God love her."

"Amazing: despite all the technical advances, and our obsession with technical communications, the best way to make a point is still a good letter," Chiano said. Pope Boniface poured two glasses of the Fiorano wine and they clanged the glasses in a toast.

"To letters– Letters of the Cloth," Pope Boniface toasted.

"To Letters of the Cloth," Chiano affirmed.

"What are you toasting?" Mrs. English asked in her polished British appeal, as she entered the garden, understated, yet with a distinct sense of purpose.

"Letters of the Cloth," Chiano said.

"I'll toast to Letters of the Cloth, too," she said, taking the lone empty glass and holding it toward Rabbi Chiano to fill. "Holy Father, I just called Cardinal Heimreich's office to request the agenda for the Bishops' Synod as you asked, Marcello," she said, slipping into an informality reserved for the pontiff's closest friends, "Cardinal Heimreich didn't include you on the agenda."

"He omitted the pope from the agenda!" Pope Boniface asked, in shock. "That's like omitting music from the dance."

"Omitted as in oversight, or omitted as in left out?" Chiano asked.

"Just omitted. Not included. His office expressed regret but they said the schedule is chock-a-block full. There's just no room."

"I know Heimreich would love to omit me, but he can't omit the pope! Good God, Judas betrayed Christ, but at least he gave him the floor at the Last Supper."

"Is it scheduled for mid-September? Cello's free in mid-September," Chiano said.

"I know he prays for me to die every day, but does he really think he can get away with omitting the pope from a Bishop's Synod?" Pope Boniface said, rising from his chair. "He's trying to silence me. He knows I'm dead against canonizing Pius."

"He should have been arrested, let alone canonized," Chiano said.

"He was Hitler's puppet for Pete's sake," Pope Boniface added.

"This is not right, Popo," Rabbi Chiano said, between sips of wine and nibbling cheese and nuts. Indignation and purpose materialized on Pope Boniface's face like heat radiating from fire. "What are you going to do?"

CHAPTER 29

Agendas

Cardinal Ryker Heimreich's office was a cluttered mess. Even its staleness smelled stale. He was a physically imposing man of sixty-eight. His craving for power curled into a furled tension between his eyes as he continually flexed the muscles in his forehead into tightly wound cords of stress. His hairline receded deep on both sides of his head but came to a peninsula-like rounded point in the front. His grey-white hair was wiry, as though it were objecting to being on his head and smelled of yesterday's ashtray. His desk teemed with yellowed files, newspapers, unopened and opened mail, notepads, and his enormous hands. A cigar burned between the index and middle fingers of his right hand. He was scanning a piece of paper held in his left hand. Father Gerard Baines, a balding priest in his fifties, dwarfed by hideously oversized glasses, waited obediently, not to be confused with patiently, on the visitor's side of Cardinal Heimreich's desk. Eventually, Cardinal Heimreich looked over the top of his gold-plated reading glasses at Father Baines with the fire of threat flaming in his eyes.

"I don't want any glitches with flights, ground transportation, hotels … no glitches. This synod is gonna be an example of German precision, not typical Vatican chaos," Cardinal Heimreich said.

"What is the Holy Father's role?" Father Baines asked.

"To wish he had a role," Cardinal Heimreich barked. Father Baines's face reflected surprise, a lot of surprise.

"You expect me to give him time on my stage to derail our agenda with his obsession for lambasting Pius XII, and every conservative value we fight to protect? Not a chance," Cardinal Heimreich declared. "Not a chance."

"Much of the Holy See's sentiment is in your corner, Your Eminence," Father Baines said.

"The Holy See follows where I lead it, Gerard. And so will the pope." He shoved a folder at Father Baines. "Make sure every bishop on this list receives a gift, something nice. Send it with their invitation. And figure out how to charge all of it to one of the pope's budgets." Cardinal Heimreich spun his chair to the side of the desk and grabbed his phone. He dismissed Father Baines with an indifferent wave of his humongous hand.

While Cardinal Heimreich plotted ways to keep Pope Boniface from participating in the forthcoming Bishops Synod, or worse, influencing it, Pope Boniface was at prayer in the glorious Saint Peter's Basilica before it opened to the public. He cherished Saint Peter's and used it alone as often as he could without taking time from the faithful who were so eager to experience its splendor. He was settled on a kneeler in prayer at the center of the basilica, bathed in the light of its magnificent dome, the third tallest dome in the world at 448.1 feet. The inside diameter is 137.8 feet, and the outside diameter is 193.7 feet. Its scale is measurable, but its exquisite beauty is not. The divine-like light it casts cannot be comprehended, only felt. There were two chairs opposite the kneeler: one was occupied by Bravo, the other, empty. A small side table was placed next to the kneeler. There were two empty sterling silver chalices, a crystal cruet filled with wine, and a large, sealed envelope on the table. Pope Boniface often chose this spot at the center of the basilica to pray and to absorb what he called 'the light of God.' His head was bowed in deep meditative prayer as footsteps approached the ring of solitude that the pope was immersed in. The Sistine Choir chanted in a divine mantra in a far-off corner of the basilica.

The approaching footsteps belonged to Brother Arturo Nordino, Pope Boniface's youthful, yet tested confidant. Brother Nordino was like a polished stone; his smooth and gentle aura shielded the rock-hard man inside. He wore the label of an ex-boxer who learned to duck far too late and far too slowly. But as a young man growing up in the alleys of Naples, he learned to land a punch when he had to, and to take one when one caught him. Pope Boniface met Brother Nordino eight years ago when Brother Nordino was a researcher in the Vatican Library. Despite his rough core, Brother Nordino was a skilled researcher and gifted communications director that Pope Boniface hoped to poach from the Holy See to direct papal communications. The pope rose to meet Brother Nordino with open arms, and responding to Brother Nordino's instinctive sense of reverence, he offered his ring to be kissed. Pope Boniface shooed Bravo from his chair and motioned for Brother Nordino to take a seat opposite him.

"Brother Arturo, my friend, sit, sit. How goes the wordsmithing?"

"I'm two verbs and a synonym short of perfection, Your Holiness," Brother Arturo said with a smile. "How are you, Holy Father?"

"Two smiles and an omelet short of wonderful."

"Perfect." Brother Nordino said, as he looked around the glorious basilica, waving a hand over its magnificent panorama. "I love what you've done with the place," he said, prompting a chuckle from the pontiff.

"Beautiful, right? So holy. I treasure this space," Pope Boniface said, reaching out to tap Brother Nordino's knee. "Just like I treasure you, my friend."

"Thank you, Your Holiness. Thank you." Brother Nordino said. He opened his hands to welcome the Holy Father's anticipated request for help. "How can I help you?" The pope edged his chair closer and sat knee-to-knee with Brother Nordino and bowed his head a moment to retrieve his thoughts. He sat up straighter but remained bent toward Brother Nordino.

"The year I was born– 1939– five significant events occurred." He counted each event on his fingers. "First, I was born, second, three days later, Rabbi Chiano was born three doors down. Third, Mahatma Gandhi was born, fourth, Hitler invaded Poland and started World War II, and fifth, Pope Pius XII issued his first Encyclical Letter."

"*Summi Pontificatus, The Unity of Human Society,*" Brother Nordino recalled.

"Precisely. So, what does all that have to do with you and me sitting here in this glorious basilica, seventy-nine years later?" Brother Nordino was charged with anticipation's call; he instinctively opened a notebook to take notes. "I'll tell you. I want you to serve as my Communications Director. Will you accept? I know that I'm shamelessly pilfering you from the Holy See, but that's OK," Pope Boniface said.

"Of course, of course … I accept. But isn't that role typically reserved for a cardinal."

"It's a new day in the Church, Brother."

"Count me in, Holy Father. A hundred percent, count me in. Tell me what you need from me." Pope Boniface rose from his chair. He underscored his words with an emphatic pumping of a clenched fist.

"Arturo, I want every Catholic cardinal, bishop, priest, nun, altar boy, deacon, parishioner, and every Christian, Jew, Buddhist, Muslim, and atheist to feel a vibrant, new spiritual honesty and sense of courage from the Church. And I want them to expect nothing less than honor from us," he said, then he slid into his comfort zone– a deliberate waltz, saturated in the pure, white gauze of the dome's glorious light.

"I like to use acronyms, Brother. My papacy will stand on three ideologies seated in the acronym H.A.S. The **H** stands for **H**onor ... the **A** for **A**ction ... and the **S** for **S**incerity." Still dancing, Pope Boniface lifted the silver chalice from the table and admired it as though it were his dance partner. "This was once raw metal, tarnished, and rust covered– just like the Church's reputation is now. But I will confess the Church's deplorable sins, Brother, and convert our tarnished reputation, and the rust of shame into a shining, sterling pride we call honor– the first pillar." He became still. He admired the sterling silver chalice, then returned it to the table and resumed dancing.

"Next, Arturo, like a spirited dancer moving with purpose and grace," he said, stepping up his tempo, "we must take action to transform our vain, stagnant, ecclesiastical dogma into proactive, compassionate action toward human service: action, our second pillar. The world is our vineyard, Brother. Despite the contaminants in yesterday's soil, the grapes of tomorrow's wine will grow in a new sun– today's sun." He danced up to the table like a hockey player swishing up to the side boards and picked up the crystal cruet. He held it against the backdrop of Saint Peter's brilliant, mystical, divine light, then resumed dancing, the cruet of wine, his fluid partner. "Then, Brother, we will operate under the light of a definitive transparent clarity," he said, still dancing, still admiring the beauty of the crystal. "I will transform the Church's tolerance for a murky hypocrisy into a forceful insistence on a sincerity as clear as this crystal: sincerity, our third pillar," Pope Boniface declared. He danced back to the table, ceasing his dance long enough to empty the wine from the cruet into the silver chalices. He returned the cruet to the table, then returned to dancing with graceful assurance.

"There you H.A.S. it. Honor, Action, and Sincerity. He continued his waltz for a few moments then returned to his chair and locked eyes with Brother Nordino, eager to hear his reaction. After pausing to think, to process, to absorb what he had just heard, Brother Nordino responded.

"Holy Father, you are the grape and the wine of the Church's spirit, and you are today's sun. I am very eager to help you."

"Great. Then let's get started." Pope Boniface handed the envelope from the table to Brother Nordino.

"Pope Pius XII's first encyclical, *Summi Pontificatus*. The original," he said, registering Brother Nordino being moved by the historical weight and significance of the document. He opened the envelope and moved his hands over it, seeking a connection to history.

"The cowardly silent voice echoing in the cries of the Holocaust," Brother Nordino said. "It was criminal."

"As you know, Brother, many mistakenly believe Pius should be canonized for allegedly helping a handful of Jews escape the Nazis. Many others scream for his head for enabling the murder of thousands of Roman Jews who were taken from under his nose as he sat in silence," Pope Boniface declared.

"If I had a voice in the matter– "

"You will soon have the loudest voice in the Church, Arturo– my voice. And I am blessed with a license to pontificate, to be heard by all. Pope Pius is called Hitler's pope for a reason. So, in the spirit of the very voice I feel compelled to exert, from the pulpit I have been chosen to affect, I promise you that a new torch will light the spirit of the Church. And, Brother, Pius' silence will roar." The pope moved closer to Brother Nordino, sitting knee-to-knee with him again.

"In two months, eighty years to the day after Pius released his first Encyclical, on the very day that the Holy See launches its campaign to canonize him, I will release my first Encyclical, *In Chordus de Silentium, The Aftermath of Silence*," Pope Boniface said. He rose again and began pacing, then dancing.

"Pius' *Summi Pontificatus* was presented as a dissertation on the unity of human society, but it was couched in the language of deceptive vagaries, and his policy of neutrality and silence. It amounted to tolerating and enabling Hitler's unthinkable murdering of six million innocent people, simply because they were Jewish, and five million non-Jews!" He pounded on the table. "My *Aftermath of Silence* will publicly condemn Hitler's atrocious crimes and admonish the Church's unacceptable silence– once and for all. And in that same Encyclical, I will chastise our Church's appalling practice of condoning deplorable sexual abuses through more cowardly silence and criminal cover-ups. God's voice will not be silenced by any man, especially the immoral," Pope Boniface declared.

"You could very well be the first pope to use the most powerful pulpit in the world as it should be used," Brother Nordino said. Pope Boniface grabbed Nordino's shoulders.

"And despite the certainty of a battle with Cardinal Heimreich and his conservative reprobates in the Holy See– that contaminated and piteous hundred-year-old obstructionist bureaucracy that governs the Church– I am going to set the Church back on the right rails with my campaign. Honor. Action. Sincerity." Pope Boniface released his hold on Brother Nordino, then handed him a chalice of wine and raised his own chalice.

"*In Chordus de Silentium!*"

Brother Nordino clung his chalice to Pope Boniface's chalice.

"*The Aftermath of Silence.*"

CHAPTER 30

Food for Thought

Marcello's and Chiano's public roles– their lives– became more formalized; as Marcello became publicly recognized as Pope Boniface, Chiano became publicly recognized as Rabbi Chiano, Chief Rabbi of Rome. Privately, they remained the little boys they always were: Marcello, aka Cello, and Chiano, aka Iano.

While Pope Boniface and Brother Nordino partook of the symbolic wine in the splendor of Saint Peter's Basilica, Rabbi Chiano busied himself preparing and serving nourishment of his own making. The synagogue meeting hall was bright, the dividends of several tall windows and a corner location in the rear of the building, complemented by an excess of overhead lighting. A commercial-size kitchen served as the control center for many of the synagogue congregants' special events: anniversaries, birthdays, bar and bat mitzvah parties, even an occasional wedding. But its most important value was its daily function as a soup kitchen that served dinner every night of the year to a dozen to two dozen people in dire need.

Rabbi Chiano and eight bar mitzvah and four bat mitzvah candidates stood in a line behind a long buffet table serving food to hungry people. They served generous helpings of split-pea soup, baked chicken, green beans, bread and butter, tossed salad, and cherry pie.

"Dip the bread in the soup? It's the only way to go," Rabbi Chiano urged one of the patrons.

"I always do, thank you, Rabbi. You got a lot of good helpers here," he said, gesturing toward the kids.

"They're great kids. They're all candidates for their bar and bat mitzvahs ... we're training 'em to be good Jews by being good people," Rabbi Chiano said.

"It's workin, Rabbi, thank you for doin' all this for us."

"It's a privilege," Rabbi Chiano said, in genuine humility. "Forks, knives, spoons, napkins– everything you need is over there. Take a piece of pie ... we have cherry today."

"It's so impressive. You're the Chief Rabbi of Rome, yet you are right here 'in the soup with us– everyday," a young girl volunteer said.

"I say inspire by doing what you want others to do," Rabbi Chiano said. "Our purpose is to contribute to others, and this is a great way to do that."

"What a great purpose," the young girl said.

"Looks like everybody's been served; let me serve you." Rabbi Chiano filled a bowl of soup for the volunteer and one for himself, then they sat among patrons. Rabbi Chiano immediately addressed a man named Sergio. "How ya feeling today, Sergio? Breathing better?"

"Pretty good during the day, not so good at night. Thanks for askin', Rabbi," Sergio said.

"I want to see you here to get plenty to eat every day, OK?"

"I promise," Sergio said.

"How 'bout you, Biaggio; everything OK with you? Shoulder back in action?"

"Almost, Rabbi; my arm moves pretty good now. You make the soup today?"

"Depends. You like it?"

"I like it, I like that little zing in it," Biaggio said.

"Little dash of cayenne pepper. Glad you like it. Where's your pie?"

"I don't like cherry pie ... but thank you very much. You seeing the pope today? I like his sermons ... the words."

"I see him every day. I'll tell him. Your kind words are as nourishing as that soup."

"Words can change the world, right," Sergio piped in.

"Especially when they create action," Rabbi Chiano said.

"You have a good word for today?"

"Compassion," Rabbit Chiano said, without missing a beat. "Take care of that shoulder."

Pope Boniface was seeking his nourishment through prayer that evening. But not just anywhere, he prayed in the Sistine Chapel. He cherished his rare privilege to pray amidst this gallery of mankind's greatest art, let alone being able to pray alone. Pope Boniface knelt in prayer as the comforting chant of a Gregorian Choir purred in a chamber nearby. He prayed:

> *"Dear God, please accept my adoration for you in the reverence in which I kneel before you. Strengthen my faith, Father. Bless me with vision in the deep, dark of my closed eyes.*
>
> *Dear God, help me inspire goodness. Help me find the strength to walk my journey in your name, help me find the power to forgive.*
>
> *Bless me, Oh God, with deeper faith, unwavering certainty and clarity in discovering your purpose for me. Help me to see how your blessed son became a catalyst of division as opposed to a staff of unity. Help me, Oh God, see what you need me to see, hear what you need me to hear, say what you need me to say, and, Dear, God, please help me discover and do what it is you need me to do.*
>
> *Forgive me, Oh God ... for I cannot find the strength or will to forgive despite my professing that we all need to forgive."*

After an earnest session of prayer, Pope Boniface returned to his apartment to indulge in one of his favorite, happy pastimes: cooking for friends, specifically Rabbi Chiano and Mrs. English. He was busy preparing a meal as Mrs. English played soothing piano chords in an adjoining room; Rabbi Chiano served as a quasi sous chef.

"Fava bean soup, Dover sole stuffed with crab meat, steamed asparagus, a garden salad from vegetables grown in my holy soil, a beautiful Piedmont Cortese wine, orange walnut cake, fresh ground espresso ..."

"What a shame you became the pope, you could have been a fantastic chef," Rabbi Chiano kidded. "I like asparagus but I can't trust any food that you smell in your pee ten minutes after you eat it. Something wrong about that. And the name, 'asparagus?' Come on."

"These recipes come from a fantastic chef— a chef on a cruise ship."

"Your persistence is a blessing, but a cruise is not in our future," Rabbi Chiano promised, as Pope Boniface enjoyed a robust swallow of wine.

"I could listen to her play forever," Pope Boniface said, waving his glass toward the room where Mrs. English was playing a piano.

"It's beautiful."

"She plays like an angel." They continued enjoying the notes saturating the moment in a peaceful grace and the crisp white Cortese wine arousing their spirits.

"It's romantically melancholy. Like a lost soul that finds itself," Chiano suggested, referring to the music Mrs. English was playing.

"Mysterious. Ethereal. Secretive and stirring," Pope Boniface said.

"The music or the wine," Rabbi Chiano jibed.

"Both."

"Her music– that melody– sounds like a summary of life's song. Struggle– succeed– fail– adjust– struggle– succeed. Enjoy. Live. Enjoy," Rabbi Chiano suggested.

"I struggle more than I expected I would at this point in my life, Iano," Pope Boniface said.

"This doesn't really surprise you, does it? You have a world to inspire and lead out of the dregs of wickedness. Divisiveness at every turn, climate change, soulless, corrupt, immoral leaders creating a perception of reality even lunatics find offensive, hideous conspiracy theories," Rabbi Chiano said, then paused for a savory sip of wine. "We're hypnotized by technology sucking us into a dumbing, numb trance, our environment's under siege, and there's a shortage of Prozac for dogs. So, what's the struggle about?" Rabbi Chiano asked, good naturedly, as Pope Boniface swirled wine around his glass.

"My struggle– one of them– is living up to the values I expect of myself and ask others to live by." He took another thought-provoking swallow of wine and looked to his glass with admiration and gratitude for the soul-quenching gift– wine from Cortese grapes. "I just can't forgive the Nazis, Iano. And I just can't forgive the murderer that killed my father, and my sister. I can't fathom forgiving him, and the thought of praying for him makes me sick to my stomach. I just can't forgive– " Rabbi Chiano put his hand over Pope Boniface's hand, interrupting him.

"Popo, no one can forgive that. It's beyond human strength or even expectation to forgive an act like that. But you can forgive yourself for not forgiving the unforgivable. You have to. You have to embrace our imperfection– not as a crutch or excuse for weakness, but as an act of accepting reality's truth, Cello," Rabbi Chiano suggested.

"But that makes me the very hypocrite that I denounce and detest. I preach and beg for forgiveness every day, yet I'm not willing to forgive that Nazi officer. Or Hitler. Or any of them for that matter," Pope Boniface admitted.

"Who can? Who would? You can't punish yourself for an unrealistic shortcoming you imagine and impose upon yourself, Popo. What they did to your family and six million Jews is far beyond forgiveness ... in anyone's eyes. God included," Chiano suggested.

"I was chosen to lead 1.2 billion Catholics to spiritual goodness and honor, yet, I have no willingness, strength, or even an intention to forgive the Nazis. And I don't have the courage to admit this to anyone but you. And God," Pope Boniface said, from the bottom of his conflicted heart as he emptied the bottom of his glass of wine into his haunted mind.

"The most courageous thing you have done is to admit the truth and confront what you misguidedly consider a fault. Popo, you and your family were the victims of the most unimaginable savage cruelty. Human brutality far beyond forgiveness. The only one who would even consider the inconceivable possibility of forgiveness is you," Rabbi Chiano said, then refilled Pope Boniface's glass.

"I preach that forgiveness frees the soul more than faith itself, but I can't bring myself to forgive him. I'm consumed in this anguish, I swear, it has my soul locked in shackles," Pope Boniface said. Rabbi Chiano took Pope Boniface's hands in his own.

"Cello, he killed your sister before your eyes. He forced a gun into your six-year-old hand and shot your father! Who could forgive that? Who would?" Rabbi Chiano paused long enough for the pope to absorb his words. "You are by far the most honorable man on this planet. I won't allow you to be burdened by groundless guilt." He squeezed the pope's hand. "Look into my eyes, Popo. Look into my eyes. The one you have to forgive is yourself. Forgive yourself, Cello. You have to forgive yourself ... you have to." He squeezed and gently shook Pope Boniface's hands as he spoke. "You're the bravest, most courageous, and most honorable mensch ever born. You'd make a great Jew! You're a combination of Jesus

Christ and Moses– on their best days," Rabbi Chiano said. He took Pope Boniface's face in his hands.

"Popo, you are the antithesis of a hypocrite. Release yourself from this noose of over-pious expectation. You are the pope, Cello, not God. And I have to believe that God himself has no willingness to forgive what you are asking yourself to forgive," he said as he released his hold on Pope Boniface's face. "You are the voice of God to Catholics and they could find no better voice than yours. Believe this. Please believe this," Rabbi Chiano said, looking deep into the pope's eyes. "My dearest, dear friend, I beg you to forgive yourself. Just focus on giving the world a healthy dose of whatever God whispers into your ear and etches onto your soul." He pinched Pope Boniface's face with affection. "You cannot ask for the impossible of yourself … Forgive yourself, Cello. Please … forgive yourself." Chiano pleaded.

"It gets harder every year," Pope Boniface said.

"But easier every day, right? Food for thought?" Rabbi Chiano said.

"Food for thought," Pope Boniface said, shaking his head in affirmation. Pope Boniface touched his glass to Rabbi Chiano's. They sipped, and Pope Boniface tapped Rabbi Chiano's glass again.

"You ease the burden of the curse and sorrow I subject myself to. Thank you. I love you, my friend. I love you very much."

"And I love you, Popo. Very much." They clung their glasses once more in an unspoken toast and sipped a savory taste of their bond. Rabbi Chiano put his glass down and clapped his hands together sharply, happily, lightening the mood. "Now, as any good Jew would say at this point … mangiamo, 'Let's eat!' Mrs. English's piano notes blanketed the room in warmth. Pope Boniface's meal was the perfect end to the day and the perfect transition into a sound night's sleep.

The next morning, as always, Pope Boniface rose early to celebrate Mass in his private chapel. As he was offering Holy Communion to a line of cardinals during the Mass, Cardinal Heimreich was next in line. Pope Boniface held out a host to Cardinal Heimreich's opened hands.

"The Body of Christ," the pope said, reverently, then whispered into Cardinal Heimreich's ear. "Come to the sacristy after Mass." The cardinal nodded, suppressing his annoyance at being summoned, an annoyance that Pope Boniface noticed.

Despite his irritation, Cardinal Heimreich made his way to the sacristy after Mass where an altar server was helping Pope Boniface remove his vestments. Cardinal Heimreich impatiently waited.

"I need twenty minutes to address the bishops at the synod," Pope Boniface said while lifting his chasuble, his cape-like, sleeveless outer garment, over his head. The cardinal began to respond but the pope cut him off. "I'd like you to get the agenda to Mrs. English this morning for my review."

"Your Holiness, the agenda has been finalized; it's already over-ambitious and full. It's been– "

"The agenda might be full, Your Eminence, but it's incomplete."

"With all due respect, surely I can convey any– "

"With all due respect, Your Eminence, you should have included me in your planning for the synod agenda from the beginning– despite your personal agenda," he said, pausing from removing his white robe. "You can't serve wine without nurturing the grape, Your Eminence. With all due respect, Sir, the pope is the grape, and the wine" Pope Boniface said.

"Your Holiness, I'd be happy to– "

"You'd be happy to silence my opposition to canonizing Pius XII is what you'd be happy to do. But the Church's days of silence and secrecy about its sins are over. This is my message and my mission, Your Eminence. Either buy in or back off." Pope Boniface turned away, clutched his stomach, and reacted with a grimace to an apparent sudden pain. He sought comfort in dancing slowly. "At the synod, I'll be offering an official apology from the Church's silence– Pius XII's silence– during the Roman occupation and the Holocaust."

"You want to do what! You can't– "

"I'm not seeking your endorsement, and I don't need your sanction, Your Eminence."

"Pope Pius XII's silence was vital to– "

"Pope Pius' silence was an act of cowardice and it led to an implied endorsement of Hitler's murdering six million Jews," Pope Boniface said.

"His silence protected against an escalation of arrests– "

"Arrests? Arrests for what? Being Jewish is not a crime!"

"Pius' silence assured keeping diplomatic ties intact," Cardinal Heimreich argued.

"His diplomatic ties were a smoke screen that attempted to persuade Catholics that he was doing something. What he was really doing was appeasing Hitler."

"He instructed Catholics to help Jews and– "

"He was whispering in a closet to himself when he should have been out on the street screaming to the world."

"His Encyclical condemned– "

"His Encyclical couched any hint of condemnation in a sea of ambiguous, vague, legalistic language that he touted as diplomacy, but in reality, Your Eminence, it was a weak attempt at camouflaging cowardice, and I'd go as far as to say antisemitism. His diplomatic ties were an extension of his close relations and allegiance to Germany, not an honest attempt to protect Jews."

"The deportations stopped. Bottom line. Diplomacy worked," Cardinal Heimreich insisted.

"The deportations– your word for abductions with intent to murder– stopped because the Nazis finished their mission, not because of Pope Pius XII's silence. How many more Jews were even left in Rome?" Pope Boniface said, stepping forward, just inches from Cardinal Heimreich's face. "Saintly life is a not matter of uncertainty, Your Eminence. It's black and white, judged by a clear distinction between right and wrong. Pius' refusing to confront Hitler's atrocities and turning a deaf ear to the pleas of innocent people being senselessly murdered under the cowardly claim of neutrality was not neutrality, Your Eminence, it was an endorsement, and it was wrong," Pope Boniface claimed in a raised voice. "He never even had the guts to speak up after the war. You call that an act of a saint? Not in my book and not in my Church." The two men stood amidst the echo of a booming silence. Finally, Cardinal Heimreich mustered a thought.

"Are you supposed to judge? You're supposed to preserve our culture, our way of life, not the Jew's way– "

"I'm supposed to lead us to spiritual fulfillment. I'm supposed to set an example of honor and ignite spiritual verve, and a genuine apology to the Jews is in order and long overdue." Pope Boniface began peacefully dancing and Cardinal Heimreich understood that the meeting was over.

"This is not gonna happen!" Cardinal Heimreich shouted, slamming the door on the way out. Pope Boniface blissfully continued dancing.

"Yes, it is," he said, with a peaceful smile.

CHAPTER 31

Bondfire

At 7:30 p.m., Pope Boniface and Rabbi Chiano assembled Gio's Confirmation class, Bravo, and the rabbi's bar and bat mitzvah classes in a courtyard in the papal gardens. They sat in a circle around a temporary fire pit holding an enormous heap of wood with several candles burning around the pit. Rabbi Chiano stepped onto a bench and began leading a 'Simon Says' game that he punctuated with emphatic motions.

"Simon says close your eyes and tap your hands on your heads." Most of the kids followed him. "You know why we're doing this? To remind ourselves to use our heads to make smart choices in our lives." He placed a hand on his heart and one over his head. "Now, rub your belly." A few kids rubbed their bellies, most didn't. Pointing out three kids, he said, "You're out … you're out … you're out." Some of the kids giggled. Rabbi Chiano continued. "Simon says pound your hearts with one hand– gently, gently … and leave one hand on your head … Simon says say 'why?'" The kids answer with a spirited, "why?"

"To remind us to be compassionate and honest and to make our choices with our heads and our hearts." Rabbi Chiano put his hands over his eyes. "Hands over your eyes." Some kids covered their eyes, most didn't. He pointed out the ones who covered their eyes and gave them the 'you're-out-of-here' signal with his thumb. "Simon says put one hand over your mouth and stand on one foot," Rabbi Chiano said, covering his mouth with his hand and standing on one foot, surprisingly gracefully for a seventy-nine-year-old. "Whyyyy? To remind us to stand up and speak out for what's right and against what's wrong … to speak out for those who can't stand up for themselves." Then, Rabbi Chiano raised his arms and signaled two of the kids to climb onto the bench with him. He took the kids by the hand.

"Simon says put your leg back down, hold hands, and raise your arms to the sky ... look to the heavens," he said, gesturing to solicit a collective "why" from the group. "Because Simon's boss is God, and God says because it reminds us to reach out– to God in prayer and reach out to help others who need help." He nodded to Pope Boniface, "and what does Pope Boniface say?"

"The pope says to use our arms to hug and love people of all races, all religions, all people. And to use our hands and arms to hold up the weak and the poor." Rabbi Chiano stepped down from the bench and emphatically marched throughout the group and prompted them to join him.

"Simon says march like this," he said, cupping his ear to hear a "why." "To remind us to walk the path of honor, the road of good choices." As the kids marched around the fire pit, the Vatican Choir approached the fire pit and formed a circle behind them, filling the courtyard with the glory of their voices. They began singing and continued as the rabbi, the pope, and as Mrs. English distributed hymn books and small sticks. The sticks were whittled clean on one half, and still covered by bark on the other half. When they finished their song, a male and female cantor took over for the choir. They sang a heart-capturing Jewish Shabbat song, as the kids continued marching around the fire pit. Rabbi Chiano stopped marching, held up a raised candle, and pointed to the whittled end of a stick.

"Let's have some fun. The clean whittled end of these sticks represent our inner purity and all the good things in our lives– our families, our loved ones, God, our friends, and ourselves. Our candles represent love, warmth, and enlightenment," Rabbi Chiano said. Pope Boniface and the rabbi lit the whittled end of their sticks, then used them to light shards of kindling wood placed at the bottom of the wood pile. "Let's all use these candles to light the clean end of our sticks, then use our burning sticks to light our fire." The kids all followed their lead and lit their sticks, then the kindling at the bottom of the wood pile. Then, Rabbi Chiano raised his flaming stick up high.

"Our fire will burn away the bark– all the crummy, ghastly things that trouble us, things that twist or hide the truth, or keep us from being our best, and our happiest ... our fire will burn away all the bad things."

He tossed his flaming stick onto the pile of wood, and all the kids followed his lead, placing all their flaming sticks onto the woodpile. The fire came to life slowly at first then began to rise, and rise, and rise, engulfing the wood in its blazing grip.

"This is a very special fire– a *Bondfire*! Not a common bonfire, but a *Bondfire*. It symbolizes and strengthens our powerful bond with each other." The pope moved to Giorgio and affectionately held him from behind.

"Gio, remember when I said 'Uncle Chiano' and I would figure out a way to make your Confirmation special?"

"I do."

"Does this feel special to you, and important?"

"Sure does, Uncle Marcello. It's so cool." He hugged his uncle. "Thank you." Pope Boniface turned Gio around and squatted down to speak to him eye-to-eye.

"Remember this fire as the moment the Holy Spirit lit its fire to strengthen your life. This is what your Confirmation is all about, my sweet boy, feeling the Holy Spirit alive within you." The fire's flames climbed high, lighting the courtyard with its glow as the ecstatic children and the choir sang, arm-in-arm-in-arm-in-arm … in a ring of unity around the raging *Bondfire*. Pope Boniface then turned his attention to the whole group.

"Now, Simon says for each one of us to hold our hands together in a sign of our unity as Christians, Jews, Muslims, Buddhists, and even the non-believers," Pope Boniface loudly declared. The singing resumed, the holding of clenched hands strengthened, and the *Bondfire* raged higher and higher into the night like faith emerging from hope. Pope Boniface and Uncle Chiano delivered on the pope's promise to make Confirmation feel special and important. It now had more meaning and purpose than to merely 'get through it.' Gio and his classmates, all the kids from Rabbi Chiano's bar and bat mitzvah classes, and the choir embraced the notion of the Holy Spirit and the pure joy of unity. A night they'll all remember as special.

CHAPTER 32

Sour Grapes

The heat steaming from Cardinal Heimreich's forehead veins was more scalding than the espresso he and Father Baines were sipping at a street café. The cardinal hunched over his cup like a storm cloud surrounding an impaired sailboat that drifted farther out to sea than planned. His demitasse cup looked like a child's toy in his meaty hand, and when he dropped his hands to the table, he crowded Father Baines' little vessel holding the black liquid jewel that is espresso, made blacker by the contrast of the curl of lemon kinked over its rim.

"There's no way on earth I'm going to stand by while he apologizes to the Jews and that Jew-bastard rabbi he parades around with. No way."

"What does the Canon Law say?" Father Baines asked.

"It's not a legal issue, Gerard, it's a Catholic issue. It's a pope issue. It's religious tyranny. He's the friggin' pope, he could do whatever he wants," Cardinal Heimreich said, stuffing the majority of an entire biscotti cookie into his shark-like mouth. He continued his tirade, spewing dry cookie crumbs in Father Baines unprotected space, even spewing a few sizable crumbs directly into Father Baines' defenseless cup. "I'm not gonna have it. He'll have to find a way around me because he's not going through me."

"Well, there are a few avenues we can pursue to block him," Father Baines said, considering options. Cardinal Heimreich took out his phone and began texting, ignoring Father Baines for the moment. He finished his text and slammed his phone down on the café table.

"Pardon my foul Ecumenical French, but you know what that son of a bitch had the, the, the fucking audacity to do? Not only did he make this ridiculous declaration and demand time at my synod– my synod– the son of a bitch broke the news to me with his back to me … while he was dancing one of his asinine dances. He dances all the time … Some people smoke, some listen to Mozart, some have a drink to relax; he dances! All the time! Dances more than he fucking walks!" Cardinal Heimreich pounded his fisted hand on the table hard, spilling a precious gulp of espresso from Father Baines' cup. "No way will I let him interfere with our movement to canonize Pope Pius. He deserves to become a saint." Father Baines waited a moment for the cardinal to simmer down before speaking.

"I was about to say, I have a few ideas about how to deter Boniface. Could get a little dicey, but I think you have the stomach for it," Father Baines said. Cardinal Heimreich lit a cigar and laid his lighter on the table, a chrome lighter with a worn logo embossed onto it. The logo was surrounded by the word 'Dundesnachrichtendienst.' Cardinal Heimreich noted the curiosity spark in Father Baines' eyes.

"Dundesnachrichtendienst," Cardinal Heimreich said, pronouncing the tongue twisting word with ease. "It was … the German Secret Service," he said, flicking the swanky lighter, his eyes confronting yet hiding intruding memories. "It was my father's. Now the son's guilt wrestles with the father's pride. Keeps the old man's fire burning, I suppose," Cardinal Heimreich reflected with a snicker of self-admiration for his pun. He spun the small metal wheel pressing against the lighter's flint with his thumb and a flame rose. He lit a napkin on fire and watched it burn. "No doubt he's burning in hell right now."

While Cardinal Heimreich spewed hatred for Pope Boniface, Rabbi Chiano, and implicitly for all Jews, Rabbi Chiano was pouring love into his wife Avigail's eternally resting soul through the cold barrier of her tombstone, through the mysterious network that connects the living with the dead: the human mind. He was alone but refused to acknowledge his loneliness. He picked up a stone, kissed it, and placed it on Avigail's tombstone next to several others he had left on recent visits.

"Hi, Avi, precious. You would love the way the sun is warming your face right now … and my heart. It always does when I'm here, with you. I'm trying hard to be strong, Sweetie. Really trying. Trying not to cry again … but I miss you … so badly. I miss us so badly." He carefully crouched down on one knee. "I looked at our pictures from our trip to Barbados this morning … that might go down as the best week of my life," he said, petting the ground. "Remember the morning we saw the big monkey on the roof? And how 'bout our breakfasts? Staring at the ocean, shaking our heads, thanking God for such a beautiful life. And all that sea glass we collected? Remember, my pockets were full of sea glass and sand. I brought you one of your favorite pieces." He placed a piece of cobalt blue sea glass on the tombstone next to the other stones. "I keep one in my pocket all the time, and one on my desk. They bring me back to those wonderful walks we took on the beach every morning … collecting all that sea glass," he said, choking back the ache in the back of the roof of his mouth and behind his eyes, that ache, that ball of sorrow hardening in his throat and heart, at the core of lost love. He began crying more openly. More easily. More fluidly. "I love you so much … I miss you so much, Angel." He caved under sorrow's weight and heartache's wrenching crush squeezing his heart, his mind, his life. He fell to both knees and bent over her grave, waiting– not trying– but waiting to collect himself, or for God to intervene and soothe him. He wept for a few long, surreal minutes. "I'm OK, Sweetie. I'm OK now," he said, finally dismissing his tears, slowly gaining his composure. "I can't wait to be with you … but I won't rush," he said, prompting a much-needed laugh, comic relief bringing a smile to the dark face of deep grief. "But for now, Cello needs me for now; we have important work to do, then I'll join you, Sweetie," he said, rising up to one knee. He was silent for a moment, touching the sea glass he had just placed on her tomb. "I love you so much, Avi. So much." He bowed his head for several minutes. He didn't pray. He didn't speak. He didn't think, he just felt. He just missed Avigail.

That evening, Chiano sought out the most assuring comfort he knew. He and Pope Boniface spread blankets on the Sistine Chapel floor and indulged in an innocent escape. They often found solace and grace in the peaceful glory of the Sistine Chapel, alone, amidst the gently anesthetizing euphoria of cannabis' amusing trance.

"I miss her so much, Popo," Rabbi Chiano said, through the echoes of his sorrow.

"I know you do, Iano."

"Cannabis gives me some relief," Rabbi Chiano said, drawing in a deep vapor of smoke. "So do you … cannabis tempers my back pain, too," he said, holding the vapor of relief deep in his lungs. "So does lying on this hard floor. Go figure."

"I'd do anything to help you feel better," Pope Boniface said.

"I know you would," Rabbi Chiano said, inhaling again, and gazing upward. "Do you think Michelangelo knows we're here right now?"

"I think Michelangelo and God are talking right now … watching us, and Michelangelo is telling God how to chip away at us like we were raw marble, and he keeps chipping away until he exposes our souls … in their purest forms," Pope Boniface suggested. "And when he's finished, we'll know who we are. He'll immortalize us in pure, cold, beautiful marble. Our new undeniable essence will be shown to the world."

"I know Avigail feels us. I know she's here, too; she's inside that one– Delphica," Rabbi Chiano said, pointing up to the painting of Delphic Sibyl, a celebrated prophetic priestess, who lives amidst the glorious frescoes that adorn the Sistine Chapel ceiling. "Look how beautiful she is. That strong but somehow feminine nose, innocent and gentle, but fiercely strong, too. Look at those big, beautiful, courageous eyes, her long neck, perfect lips. What engaging eyes. She's so magnetic. So strong and beautiful."

"She's what any man would want in a woman …"

"I betcha Michelangelo was intimate with Delphic," Rabbi Chiano said, handing the vape pen to Pope Boniface. "I marvel at your restraint," he said within the grin tumbling over his face. I think it's stupid but, ehh … tweech his own … to each … tweech … tweech his own," Rabbi Chiano said, amusing himself by experimenting with the words. Pope Boniface was lost in a puff of thought.

"I have thought of Gillian as a wife of sorts at times," Pope Boniface pondered aloud. "She takes such good care of me. She's been with me for more than forty years, and I have never heard a cross word, a complaint, nothing but sweetness from her," he reflected.

"Gillian? I don't think I've ever heard you call her by her name– our sweet dear friend, Mrs. Gillian English. You and Mrs. Gillian English would make quite the couple."

"If only we could …" Pope Boniface mused.

"Hey, you're the Popo, you can do anything you want. Why not let priests marry; it'll solve a lot of your problems," Rabbi Chiano said. "And bring in the nuns; let them be priests while you're at it."

After reflecting in silence for a few minutes, Pope Boniface curled his lips and in the spirit of consideration, he simply said, "Hmm."

By then, Chiano was onto a more historical question he discovered in the paintings on the Sistine Chapel ceiling.

"These people must have had great eyes," Rabbi Chiano said, pointing to the artistic marvels on the ceiling. "Ever notice that none of them wear glasses? You should commission an artist to paint glasses on some of their faces. Give 'em haircuts, too," Rabbi Chiano suggested.

"Wouldn't it be amazing to be in one of those paintings?" Pope Boniface wondered.

"How do you know we're not in one right now," Rabbi Chiano mused. "Maybe there's a hundred people staring at us and a tour guide is telling them a BS story about who we are and why the painter put us on the floor instead of the ceiling. Maybe we're the rejects." They laid quietly for a time thinking of such things as how to define nothing, and everything, whether the leaves on a tree communicate with the branches and the trunk, if blades of grass in a field feel claustrophobic, why electricity is silent, what if importance and irrelevance were a married couple? Chiano eventually broke their surreal silence. "Know what I found out?"

"This is going to take a long time to tell, isn't it?"

"Well, not everything I ever found out."

"What did you find out?"

"I ran into the old postman who used to come into Uncle Jewels' shop." They exchanged possession of the vape pen again. "Remember those envelopes with money we both used to get in college?"

"I'll never forget them. They were a Godsend."

"Well, what I found out, what the postman told me, is that one night, he and Uncle Jewels were at the wine bar, and I mean they were 'at' the wine bar," Chiano said, then paused for a laugh. "Well, the postman, Marino, was his name. Marino told me that he and Uncle Jewels spent a good part of the night with their heads tilted backward, staring into the bottom of wine glasses, and after their third barrel or so of wine, Uncle Jewels got pretty comfortable with him. Anyway, Marino asked him about all those mysterious envelopes that he sent to the two of us every month, and you know what Uncle Jewels told him?" Pope Boniface waved a lazy hand to welcome Rabbi Chiano's answer. "He told him that since we were little kids, he put the profits from every single watch he'd ever sold into a special savings fund ... all the profits from every single watch he'd ever sold, all those years, from all those watches ... he gave you and me the profits. That's how he paid for my college tuition and sent us both money all those years."

"Wow," Pope Boniface said, after a long silence. "That's amazing. Uncle Jewels, when we get up there with you in heaven, we're going to have a great time," he said. "Pun intended."

"That's why he always told us that watches were the most important item in the store as far as we were concerned. I always wondered why he said that, but I never asked him," Rabbi Chiano said.

"Me, too ... Now we know," Pope Boniface said.

"Remember, he would say, 'all time is free time ... a watch is the best gift because time lasts forever ... the best gift for the price.' Remember, he always said that." Rabbi Chiano said. Pope Boniface winced slightly and took hold of his stomach. His eyebrows involuntarily scrunched toward the bridge of his nose in pronounced apprehension. He shut his eyes, seeking comfort he hoped to find. More indulgence in the comfort of cannabis soothed his discomfort and enabled him to return to his apartment for a good night's sleep.

The new morning approached in the hush of sunlight whispering goodbye to the tailing fringe of night. A visibly annoyed Cardinal Heimreich paced back and forth over the steps of Saint Peter's Basilica as the sun fulfilled its promise to rise. A curtain of light filled the morning with glory, and a feisty step in Pope Boniface's gate as he crossed Saint Peter's Square, clearly beyond the stomach pain that impinged his peace and comfort the night before. He sauntered toward Cardinal Heimreich, carrying a rolled-up scroll and a large bunch of grapes.

"Invigorating, isn't it? I relish this glorious church," he bellowed to the angry cardinal, who didn't answer. "So, why did I want to meet you here, why at the wonderful moment of dawn? Look at this magnificence, this glory," he said, delighting in looking over the columns, statues, and the obelisk towering over Saint Peter's Square. He ignored Cardinal Heimreich while savoring the view of the square for several moments as the cardinal stewed in annoyance's resentment and resentment's annoyance.

"I wanted to meet here, at this most sacred and sanctified corner-stone of our faith, as a reminder that we're called on to conduct ourselves in a most sacred and sanctified manner, Your Eminence," Pope Boniface declared. He was patently enjoying the moment, the setting, and being the pope. "Why dawn? To underscore a new day in the Church." He handed Cardinal Heimreich the scroll. "This is a copy of the *Roman Catholic Spiritual Doctrine*. You are presumably familiar with it, and you likely know that it describes and underscores my power as our pope," he said, tapping the scroll. "In short, Your Eminence, it says the pope– by reason of his office as Vicar of Christ, as pastor governing all Catholics– is infallible." He handed the scroll over to Cardinal Heimreich. "As pope, the *Roman Catholic Spiritual Doctrine* regards me as infallible, Your Eminence."

"Beneath the cloak of our positions, we're merely old men," Cardinal Heimreich snapped.

"But I'm the old man chosen to lead the Roman Catholic Church, Your Eminence, and I'm leading us into a new dawn," Pope Boniface said, waving an arm toward the new day's rising sun.

"Are we finished here?"

"One more thing– another reminder," Pope Boniface said, handing Cardinal Heimreich the large bunch of grapes. "You can't serve the wine without nurturing the grape. The pope is the grape, and the wine, Cardinal." Heimreich stormed off, tossing the scroll and grapes to the ground. Unmoved and unaffected, the pope raised his arms and welcomed the day with vigor and jubilance, and he slid into a satisfying waltz.

Later that morning, as Mrs. English happily organized papers at her desk musing in the afterglow of the *Bondfire's* joyful experience. She tapped her desk with a leftover half-whittled stick that they used to light the *Bondfire*. Then, something occurred to her. Concern invaded her face and sickness rolled in her stomach, sensing– knowing– something was amiss. She dropped the papers she was working with and headed into Pope Boniface's office. He wasn't there. His restroom door was closed. Mrs. English moved quickly to the closed door and knocked. Marcello? Your Holiness? Are you ok?" She listened for a moment then knocked again. "Cello?" No response. "Marcello, are you OK?" She waited but nothing happened. No answer. No response. No noise. "Marcello!" After several agonizing seconds, Pope Boniface opened the restroom door. He was pale and looked anxious. Sickly beads of sweat dotted his face.

"My God, what's wrong?"

"I have blood in my urine. A lot."

Before he knew what had happened, Mrs. English was helping him out of a side exit of the Papal Palace. Rabbi Chiano's car swerved to a stop at the door. He got out and he and Mrs. English helped a sluggish and weak Pope Boniface from the building to the car and sped off.

CHAPTER 33

Preparations

Saint Peter's Basilica was cordoned off to the public for 'Official Vatican Preparations.' Cardinal Heimreich supervised the delivery of flowers, the positioning of candles, music selections, the order of the entrance entourage, seating assignments, and everything but the weather for the day of the Bishops' Synod kickoff Mass. Cardinals, bishops, and priests ambled about, absorbing and admiring the basilica and talking in small groups. Cardinal Heimreich directed workers dry-mopping, dusting, and primping the basilica like a frenzied theatrical director preparing for opening night. Father Baines approached Cardinal Heimreich and ushered him behind a nearby pillar so as not to be heard.

"What do you think the press would do if they were to get wind of a story questioning the pontiff's mental health?" he asked.

"Go on."

"I think it would be of vital concern if the press were to hear that behind official doors, the Holy See is addressing an important and discrete matter regarding the pope's sanity. What if stories were circulating around the Holy See suggesting that the mental health of our pontiff presented cause for major concern?" Father Baines asked Cardinal Heimreich. "Despite the assumed infallibility inherent in the papacy, what if suspicion and evidence of human frailty– the inevitability of aging– has suddenly besieged our Most Holy Father?" Baines led Cardinal Heimreich deeper into the basilica for privacy and secrecy. "I can produce a petition signed by several bishops requesting a formal inquiry into the pontiff's mental health because they think he's nuts. The bishops will never know what they're signing, and it's a perfect explanation to the press why the pontiff isn't on the agenda." Heimreich cast Baines an approving nod through a coffee and tobacco-stained smile, a taxing and unfamiliar feat for Cardinal Heimreich.

"This is good. I approve. Get the petition in the works and leak it to the press … and put something out on all those phony websites you run. You have somebody we can trust?"

"I think so."

"Don't think, know— for sure," Cardinal Heimreich demanded.

While preparations were getting underway at Saint Peter's, Pope Boniface was at Mercy Hospital, unknown to anyone but Chiano, Mrs. English, and the attending medical staff. Rabbi Chiano was rifling through magazines, pacing, playing with the window's blinds in a waiting room. Mrs. English was worried sick, too, but she was managing better than Rabbi Chiano. The room reeked of tension and smelled of sickness, bedpans, and food that festered over that fine line distinguishing food from garbage.

"Did he eat asparagus," Rabbi Chiano blurted out. "Five minutes after you eat them, your pee smells just like them. There's something wrong with that." Mrs. English shook her head, considering what the rabbi had said, then she broke into a hearty laugh. And the rabbi couldn't help but follow. After their laughter diminished, a question occurred to Mrs. English.

"Chiano, how did you two meet? I have no idea how you two met," she said.

"You don't know? He never told you?"

"No. I don't. I never asked him, and it never came up."

"Wow. That's surprising. Well, I'll tell you," Rabbi Chiano said. They both instinctively sat on the waiting room's stiff couch and leaned toward one another. "We were born three days apart, and three doors down from each other. Not long after that, my family moved in across the hall from Marcello's family's flat. We were the best of friends from the moment we could see. Marcello's family and mine were together all the time. Our fathers and mothers were friends, our sisters were friends. When the Nazis were rounding up Jews during the occupation, Marcello's family hid my family in the attic of their apartment. They hid us, fed us, protected us. His family saved our lives. Marcello's father and sister gave up their lives to save ours." Rabbi Chiano said, choking on sorrow peppered with survivor's guilt swelling in his throat. "And even if it weren't for that, we would still be this close," he said, crossing his fingers. "I was there when they killed his father and his sister. I watched it from his attic. They forced him to do it," Rabbi Chiano said, struggling to maintain his composure. "They forced Marcello's hand onto the gun and pulled the trigger, killing his father." Rabbi Chiano abruptly shut down.

"Oh my God. How awful. I had no idea. You poor dears," Mrs. English said, then hugged him with earnest empathy. "You poor dears. You poor dears."

"We have been attached to each other like a song and music ever since."

On the other side of the waiting room wall, Pope Boniface drifted like a stick in a stream between fear and courage, determination and optimism, maybe even between life and death. The pope was seated on an examining table, his stately white cassock traded for a humbling backless hospital gown. The doctor that entered the room surprised the pope; he expected to see Dr. Ernesto Moniorelli, his personal and official Vatican physician. Instead, a man with very black, very greasy, slicked-back hair entered. His moustache was scruffy, unruly, pointing straight outward. His square-framed green glasses created odd shadows on his face, they were too green for fashion, too soiled to see clearly through. Pope Boniface was at the mercy of mercy itself.

"Your Holiness, I am Dr. Kajackas; Your doctor, Dr. Moniorelli is at Lake Como for a family wedding this weekend. I am your attending physician on call on his behalf," Dr. Kajackas said, in very loud, deliberate speech, emphatically punctuating words in an Eastern European accent. He stopped and nodded awkwardly after nearly every sentence. He kissed the apprehensive Holy Father's ring. "Holy Father, when we see urine in the blood we experience concern. Much concern."

"I don't scare easily, doctor; what are you telling me?"

"This could be very, very serious, Holy Father ..." he said, then nodded.

"What do you– "

"But ... but it could be something else, not too serious. We will see."

"What are– "

"Tests. We will perform tests," he said, interrupting the pope again, which was quickly becoming an annoyance to the Holy Father. Dr. Ka-jackas stared at the pope, nodding. Pope Boniface tried to get a word in again.

"What– "

"Tests will identify the problem, of course. A cystoscopy, urine cytology, ultrasound. We want to collect a biopsy, examine your urethra. CT-Scan. Tests, Holy Father, we must do tests ... to discover the problem."

"What do you think it– "

"Maybe ... it could be, maybe cancer ... in the bladder. But note that I say maybe," he said, staring and nodding at Pope Boniface who was now shaken and trying to grasp what he was hearing. "Then, maybe not. Maybe it could be a kidney infection, maybe a kidney stone."

"Do you think–"

"I don't trust thinking, Holy Father. It is important to know these things instead of thinking ... guessing. What will we discover there? Kidney stone, gallstone, horrible tumor? Who knows?"

"A horrible tumor!" Pope Boniface burst out.

"Holy Father, we will see. I recommend to you that we operate rapidly to collect a biopsy. We perform this procedure. We see. We discover. We know. We address. Hopefully we discover the benign ... not the other. But we are wise to act rapidly."

"It's going to have to wait. I have very important work to do," the pontiff declared.

Pope Boniface dressed and returned to the waiting room to Rabbi Chiano and Mrs. English. He looked more puzzled than worried. Rabbi Chiano and Mrs. English looked to him for an explanation.

"Was it asparagus?" Rabbi Chiano blurted.

"There's something wrong with my bladder. He wants to take a biopsy. Soon. They were all swallowed by fear's horror into the unsettling belly of the unknown.

Through either divine intervention or just raw luck, Pope Boniface managed several days with little or no discomfort, but there was a price to pay: Cardinal Heimreich's all-out effort to produce the Bishops' Synod without the pope's involvement was making notable progress day-by-day, and the event was just two days away. Bishops from all over the world were descending on Rome, the Vatican, and Saint Peter's Basilica. Father Baines was working the crowd mulling about the basilica, assertively pulling unsuspecting bishops aside one-by-one to secure their signatures on a page pinned to a clipboard. One after the other, Father Baines made the same hurried pitch to the bishops.

"Your Excellency, Cardinal Heimreich and many of the cardinals in the Curia are circulating a petition to lower bishops' retirement age to seventy; sign here, and you'll be taking the first step toward getting the pontiff to agree to an earlier retirement for you," he said. He repeated the pitch over and over to several bishops, and one-after-another, the unsuspecting bishops signed the page. "Perfect, Your Excellency. Perfect. Enjoy yourself. See you in retirement," Father Baines repeatedly said. He approached bishops throughout the day and generated over 150 signatures. Cardinal Heimreich remained at the center of activity orchestrating the preparation details. He condescendingly directed a boys choir to a section of pews to the left of the altar. Workers delivered and placed flowers on the altar wherever the cardinal's fat finger pointed. Bishops and cardinals meandered about as a less than peppy Pope Boniface approached Cardinal Heimreich. The scarlet trimmed cardinals and subordinate bishops closest to him parted their sea of clergymen and bowed to the Holy Father as he passed, blessing them.

"Your Holiness, we are about– "

"You never showed me the agenda," Pope Boniface snapped, cutting the cardinal off.

"Your Holiness, as I told you earlier, the agenda is jammed full; showing it to you would be a waste of time– at a bad time. And as you see, we're– "

"People won't look up to you or respect you merely because you're center stage, in charge of an event, Your Eminence. They will look up to you and respect you when you develop a noble vision and lead them to it," Pope Boniface contended.

"This is ridiculous!"

"This is disrespect! It's irresponsible! You're making an exceptional mistake," Pope Boniface warned. The cardinals and bishops within earshot stepped back out of respect for the pope and embarrassment for Cardinal Heimreich.

"I don't think so," Cardinal Heimreich said.

"You're assuring yourself embarrassment," Pope Boniface snapped again, then he abruptly turned and left the basilica. Those same near-by cardinals and bishops parted the way again, bowing to the pontiff, searching thin air to find answers drifting in the hanging tension.

Pope Boniface returned to his office where he peered out the window, rocking in a subdued dance as he thoughtfully pruned the flourishing oak sapling Rabbi Chiano had given him as a birthday present. Looking out the window, the pontiff watched Amodeo placing stones in his wall; he had made significant progress, so have the pope's tomato plants near the wall, they were tall enough to be staked now, and little pointy green leaves with tiny yellow flowers cuddled the little tomatoes-to-be in their soft folds of green. Pope Boniface danced toward another window and peered out at the bishops and cardinals bobbing about Saint Peter's Square; Brother Nordino entered with his omnipresent notebook and pen.

"You sent for me, Holy Father."

"Yes, Arturo, I need your help," the pontiff said without breaking stride in his dance. "I need you to pick fifty bishops down there– at random– and invite them to a private luncheon with me tomorrow. And Arturo, you know Father Baines, don't you?"

"We call him 'Father Weasel,' yes, I know him."

"Good. He's in the basilica politicking and who knows what else. Make sure that he overhears you inviting a few of the bishops.

"Consider it done, Your Holiness."

"Thank you, Brother. Mrs. English has the particulars. We will invite several of the nuns from the diocese, too. And let's make it seventy-five bishops. I'd like you to be there, too, of course, Brother." Brother Nordino turned to leave the room but the pontiff stopped him.

"Arturo," Pope Boniface called out, ending his dance.

"Holy Father?"

"How did you come to be a brother?"

"Well, it's a bit of a story, Your Holiness." Pope Boniface motioned for Brother Nordino to take a seat next to him to tell his story.

"Well ... I guess all stories start in the beginning, don't they? He paused to swallow a bitter pill of the past before continuing. "I'm told that my mother left me on the altar of the Church of Girolamini and Convent in Naples when I was just a few days old. The nuns took me in and raised me in the Saint Joseph's Orphanage. The nuns were great teachers ... not so nice sometimes, but very good teachers. One of the nuns, Sister Giosetti, took me under her wing for some reason. She taught me everything. Reading, how to write, math, history, everything. We read the newspaper every morning and books every night. Her father was an opera star of sorts and she was a huge opera fan. When I was a little older, she introduced me to the opera house, and to singing opera. I had a pretty good voice– we used to sing in class and we were all required to be in the choir– and she encouraged me to pursue singing. Somehow, she got one of the singers at the Teatro di San Carlo Opera to give me voice lessons." The pontiff was absorbing Brother Arturo's story and enjoying it.

"I'm loving this. Please, continue, Brother."

"Well, the opera lessons were good and bad. In the end, it led to trouble. I loved singing but I was beginning to catch heat from some of the bullies around the orphanage as the teacher's pet. Opera boy, they called me," he said. "They assumed I was a pushover or a sissy of some kind because I liked singing opera," he said, shrugging his shoulders. "Anyway, I sang more and more and I was getting pretty good– thanks to the singing lessons. I learned how to breathe, project, control my tone, and clarify my timber. They asked me to fill in at rehearsals sometimes at Teatro di San Carlo, and in exchange, I was admitted into the opera rehearsals and performances for free. I loved it, really loved it– the passion, the talent, the staging, costumes, intensity, all of it. But like I said, I was an easy target for bullies– or at least they thought so– without really thinking," Brother Arturo said, taking a moment to pause and peer into his memory.

"The priests at Saint Joseph's were good to me, too. There was a Father Diorello at Saint Joe's. He was worried about us, Naples being the rough and tumble city that it was, so he brought in guys to teach us how to box and to protect ourselves, which in my case, led to trouble."

"Fascinating. A writer who sings opera and boxes becomes a Franciscan brother in the Vatican," Pope Boniface said. "Sorry for interrupting. Tell me, how'd this lead to trouble– and how did that lead to becoming a Franciscan Brother?"

"Not the typical path to the Franciscans, right," he said, and cleared his throat. "So, I was about sixteen or seventeen. One night after a rehearsal at the opera, I was walking back to the orphanage's teen hall when

I saw a guy slapping a woman around, really giving it to her. I assumed it was his wife, I'd say they were in their mid-30s. Anyway, I instinctively jumped into the middle of it and got into a pretty nasty fight with the guy. We both got pretty lumped up, but at least I stopped him from beating this woman anymore."

"Now you're a hero to boot," Pope Boniface said.

"Well, this, too, was good and bad for me. I ended up giving the guy the beating he deserved– out of her defense and my own. That's the good part. The bad part is that this guy was a middle level boss in the mafia, but high enough up to have their goons come after me … as you can see," he said, pointing to his notably bent nose. "But as that turned out, I ended up lucky again. Thanks to Father Diorello's boxing lessons, I was able to beat the two gorillas off me– I hurt one of them pretty badly. I broke his nose and jaw, and I got the other guy pretty good, too, but the good luck-bad luck seesaw came into play again." He paused to smile at his fortunate misfortune. "These guys had me arrested– me, the one who helped the woman! They attacked me, but I was the one arrested! That's Naples, right?" They both shrugged their shoulders. "And of course, the judge assigned to my case was as crooked as my nose. He was one of them. But in the end, Holy Father, I thank that judge."

"Fascinating. How so?"

"At my sentencing, the judge– Judge Gaetano Taglieri– that's his name. Judge Taglieri gave me three choices. One, he said, I could go directly to jail for eight years. Two, I could enlist in the Italian Army for eight years. And before he told me the third choice, I said, 'I'll take number three.' Number three was to become a priest and work for him. He had a twisted fantasy about tapping into the corruption at the Vatican Bank and he wanted me to become his inside puppet in order to access fraudulent wealth. But listen to this: three weeks after I entered the seminary, Judge Taglieri was found shot in the back of the head in his closet." Brother Nordino raised his eyes and shook his head affirming the peculiarity in his story.

"There were a lot of Franciscan brothers in and out of the orphanage that I kept in touch with. One of them, Brother Kimura, a Japanese guy, encouraged me to pursue the brotherhood instead of the priesthood. I really didn't want to take the celibacy vow, so I switched from pursuing the priesthood to become a Franciscan brother … so, here I am."

"What a fascinating story. I'm so glad I asked. And what about the writing and public relations background? Where did that come from?"

"The opera. Sister Giosetti got me into college, then after I graduated, she helped me convince the Teatro di San Carlo to hire me to do their public relations. Between college and what Sister Giosetti taught me about writing, and I learned on the job, I became pretty good at it. So, again, here I am."

"And I'm so glad that you are, Arturo," Pope Boniface said, rising from his seat, prompting Brother Arturo to do the same. The pontiff embraced him with a warm hug and a wide smile. "God bless you, Brother." Pope Boniface patted him on the cheek and watched him go off into the task which he had assigned.

Brother Nordino wasted no time delivering invitations to bishops milling about the basilica; each was curious and honored, including a handful he selected based on their being within earshot of Father Baines, who quickly bit the bait.

"What's this about a luncheon with His Holiness?" Father Baines asked Brother Nordino, as he handed a bishop the invitation.

"The Holy Father is hosting a private luncheon for several– seventy-five– bishops tomorrow."

"Which bishops? Does Cardinal Heimreich know about this?"

"The bishops are being chosen at random. As for Cardinal Heimreich, I have no idea what he knows and doesn't know," Brother Nordino answered.

"Selected at random?" Father Baines asked in search of validation.

"Yes."

"Well, I hope all goes well. Carry on, Brother. Don't let me hold you up," Father Baines uttered from behind a snide smile. He was still trolling for signatures for his phony petition as he made his way to Cardinal Heimreich near the basilica steps.

"It looks like the Holy Father has accepted defeat in securing a spot on your agenda. He's hosting a luncheon tomorrow for seventy-five bishops– desperately selected at random," he said, gloating. "It appears he's using this pitiable luncheon to save face with at least seventy-five of the bishops attending; he'll have an audience of seventy-five out of almost 4,500," Father Baines said. "What's that, two percent?"

"I guess his earlier tantrum with me was more a concession than a protest. He's laughable," Cardinal Heimreich said, struggling through his contorted effort at producing a smile as Stefano Zurentino approached.

"Here comes our man," Father Baines said.

"Zurentino? Can we trust him? He's on our side of this?"

"I think so."

"You think? Jesus Christ. What do you know for certain?"

Stefano Zurentino was too close for Father Baines to respond without the reporter hearing him. He smeared a phony smile across his face and stepped toward Stefano.

"Stefano, good to see you," Father Baines forced out as he reached to shake hands.

"Father," Zurentino said, shaking Father Baines' hand. "Your Eminence," he said, reaching for Cardinal Heimreich's hand and reading their respective faces. Cardinal Heimreich barely offered his hand to shake and offered no words, just an apprehensive nod.

"Come with me, Stefano, I have much to tell you," Father Baines promised as he led Stefano on a deliberate stroll into the basilica, far away from snooping ears.

"The conversation we're about to have is not a conversation, it never happened, understand," Father Baines said. But Zurentino didn't acknowledge the prompt. Once inside and out of earshot, Father Baines dropped his sham of a story. "There's a disturbing matter developing relating to the Holy Father's mental health," he said, pausing to send a look into Zurentino's eyes. "It's why we couldn't include him on the agenda for the synod. It's a shame," he said, "Just elected, and now this," he said, shaking his head in fraudulent pity. Members of the Holy See and several bishops are very concerned," he said, waving his clipboard full of pages with bishops' signatures. "They're circulating a petition demanding a formal inquiry. Of course, you understand that because of the sensitive nature of this matter you can only quote 'a source close to the pontiff' on this. I know you understand the critical need for the public to know …" His voice trailed off as they walked deeper into the basilica to sew propaganda's weedy seeds. "A shame, just two days before the synod and I have to tell you this news," Father Baines said.

As Father Baines prayed for his lie to take root, one day before the synod, the curious bishops filed into an opulent papal banquet room for a private lunch with the Holy Father. Pope Boniface, Rabbi Chiano,

Brother Nordino, and Mrs. English sat at the dais before a huge 'U'-shaped table arrangement where several nuns and the bishops sat enjoying a jovial lunch with the Holy Father. The mood was light, the meal, not so much. Brother Nordino clanged his water glass with a fork to summon Pope Boniface's guests' attention.

"I guess we religious can't curb our appetite for symbolism; even the arrangement of these tables has meaning beyond practicality," Pope Boniface said, gesturing appreciatively to Rabbi Chiano. "My dear and best friend, Rabbi Chiano, and I are very much inspired by the notion of union. The 'U'-shaped table arrangement is a subtle gesture to underscore our sense of unity." The pope and Rabbi Chiano raised their glasses to toast, and all the guests followed.

"To unity," Rabbi Chiano declared, and they all clung glasses and sipped their wine. "And here's to Your Holiness, my best friend for seventy-nine years, and the best man I will ever know." Rabbi Chiano draped his arm around the pontiff, who leaned close to him and whispered.

"Can you finish up for me; I'm not feeling well," Pope Boniface murmured meekly.

"Of course," Rabbi Chiano answered as the pope rose from his chair.

"My good people, I must leave you in the good hands of my dear friend and colleague. Please– chat, philosophize, inquire … but no pontificating … that privilege is reserved for me," he said, prompting a few chuckles. "As an adjunct to our lunch today, I'm inviting each of you to be active participants in a special aspect of tomorrow's Mass: can I count on you?" The guests offered back a universal chorus of 'yes' and 'of course,' "That's great." Pope Boniface continued. "Thank you. My treasured comrades, Mrs. English and Brother Nordino will fill you in on the details," he said as Mrs. English and Brother Nordino waved to identify themselves. "I must ask for your absolute silence and absolute confidentiality. Please, do not mention a word of our plan to anyone. I am counting on you," Pope Boniface said in a no-nonsense, but polite tone. "Now, let me leave you with a brief story."

"I recently asked a very, very wise man what my message should be to my congregation one day, and without batting an eye, he said, 'tell them it's later than you think.'" He paused deliberately for effect. "I asked him if he had any more positive– upbeat advice, and again, without missing a beat, he said, 'tell them it's not too late.' So, I leave you with his simple but wisdomatic words as it relates to our Mother Church. It is later than we think ... but it is not too late. The future is not in what we believe, but in what we do. And we have to do it now." He offered a silent blessing ending with the sign of the cross and left them to digest the meaning of his thoughts. Once the pope was out of the room, one of the bishops raised a hand to get Rabbi Chiano's attention.

"Rabbi, before we get into the matters of tomorrow, I have a trite but curious question," the bishop said.

"I probably have a trite and disappointing answer," Rabbi Chiano said.

"We hear that the pontiff dances all the time: what's the history behind that?"

"Well, maybe my answer won't be so trite: Pope Boniface's mother was an accomplished ballroom dancer and dance teacher. She taught the pontiff– and me along with him– to dance, every day of our childhood. Today, he dances for fun, and in a small way, for exercise. But the real reason he dances is to soothe himself and pray. It's how he keeps himself grounded– at peace." Rabbi Chiano paused, waiting for the thought to clear. "He likes to say, 'in order to find grace, one must be graceful.' The gracefulness he finds in dancing permeates into the rest of his life." Another bishop raised his hand.

"Sir?" Rabbi Chiano said, recognizing the bishop.

"We hear that there is a bit of tension between The Holy See and the Holy Father over this petition going around to lower the retirement age, and tension over this synod in total for that matter. We hear the Holy Father isn't on the agenda at all. Is there friction among Church leadership?" the bishop asked. Brother Nordino stood up and waved to Rabbi Chiano.

"I'll take this one, Rabbi," he said and stood up. "I'm Brother Arturo Nordino, the Director of Communications for the Holy Father. I can tell you that there are differing opinions and will always be different opinions when goals conflict. Every pontiff will have strong feelings about the many issues related to the Church. Every one of us in the human race has strong feelings on different matters. But the one unwavering principle that the Holy Father adheres to and will insist on all of us adhering to, is to embrace, and in fact exemplify honor, action, and sincerity. We are the stewards of a Christ-like example, and the integrity of Catholics the world over. The Holy Father expects all of us to be on the same page when it comes to integrity. As for the petition regarding early retirement, I can tell you that the subject has not been raised with the Holy Father, I recommend you ask the source of the petition you're speaking of to authenticate it. In fact, as the Holy Father's Communications Director, I sure would like the name of that source, and if anyone has the letter supporting the petition, I'd like to have that, too," Brother Nordino asserted. He sat down and a puzzled buzz hissed around the room.

"Thank you, Brother," Rabbi Chiano said. "If there are no further questions, let's get into the plans for tomorrow."

Several hours later, Pope Boniface and Rabbi Chiano were lying on blankets on the Sistine Chapel floor, sharing a vape pen packed with cannabis.

"Your bishop friends are kind of a stiff bunch, but they're OK," Rabbi Chiano said, exhaling smoke." You feeling any better?"

"A little better. Thanks for taking over the luncheon this afternoon. They liked our talk about union. What a funny word …Uuuuuuunnn yun. You yun. Spell it: Y O U N Y U N. Uuuuunn yun," Pope Boniface mused.

"It could be an entrée on a Chinese menu: Yun Yon. I'll have the Chicken Yun Yon and fried rice. Maybe that's the name of the place. Yun Yon Golden Kitchen." Rabbi Chiano joked as they relished man's most coveted masterpieces above.

"Just look at the genius on this ceiling," Pope Boniface said, after inhaling.

"I love the fusion– the uuunion of the Old Testament paintings' stories with New Testament paintings' stories. That's us. Me and you, Popo," Rabbi Chiano said.

"Listen … hear it?" Pope Boniface asked. "It's the chanting … I love that chanting," he said, referring to a choir's Gregorian Chanting not far from Marcelloel. Rabbi Chiano considered the peaceful, melodious, calming chanting.

"Whose voice do you hear when you think? Or pray? What voice do you hear in your Inner Voice? And when you pray … whose voice does Pope Boniface hear?" After careful reflection, the pope answered.

"Yours."

"Nice," Rabbi Chiano answered. Then they laid in silence. Pope

Boniface made motions with his hand as though he was painting the Sistine Chapel. Rabbi Chiano gently moved his head in slow flow with the chant he was hearing. After some time of silence, he asked, "Why Boniface? What made you choose the name Boniface? Why not Rufus, or an American name– like Pope Jimmy– or Pope Billy," he said, stirring himself and the pope into a laugh. "Pope Jimmy, I'd like you to meet Pope Billy," Rabbi Chiano said, laughing harder.

"Unfinished business," Pope Boniface eventually answered, almost too long after the question was asked for Rabbi Chiano to remember what he had asked.

"You're going to explain that, right?" Rabbi Chiano asked.

"Pope Boniface IX ruled under the duress of what they called the Great Schism, it was tearing the Church apart ... a horrible rift, similar to the kind of damaging polarization stirring now."

"Schism. It's like Uuuion but with a Schizzz," Rabbi Chiano digressed into another laugh. "How did Boniface IX resolve the schism?" Rabbi Chiano asked again, playing with the word, pronouncing it several different ways. "Schism," he said very quickly. "Shisssss um. Shizz UM. Schism!"

"He didn't resolve the shizzzzum, it went beyond his reign. But I won't let others' agenda divide the Church during my papacy," Pope Boniface said, pausing to take a hit from the vape pen. "And Boniface was just a good guy; tough, but a good guy," he continued. Following a random thought he asked, "Iano, how can something get easier every day but harder every year?"

"Don't know."

"OK. So, back to Boniface IX. He treated his mother, brothers, and nephews well," He exhaled and paused to admire the ceiling's masterpieces more deeply. "And being brought up very much under the influence of a priest, my Uncle Salvestro– who loved Boniface IX's spiritual vigor– what he liked to call piss and vinegar," he said, then gave way to another laugh before being able to continue. "Uncle Salvestro liked how Boniface IX fought for what he thought was right. That inspired me to become Boniface X. Plus, I like the number ten. But you can still call me Marcello, Cello– or Popo." Pope Boniface returned the vape pen to Rabbi Chiano, who took a long hit. A knowing smile trickled across his face, an inspired sparkle glittered in his eyes as he savored the euphoria filling his lungs and mind.

"Popo, I have a great idea," he said, handing the pen back to the pope, and just as their hands touched and their eyes met, the rabbi cackled out a cloud of smoke.

"What's your great idea?" Pope Boniface asked. After a dramatic pause for affect, Rabbi Chiano answered.

"Joint-Venture!" He smiled, cuddling his idea like affection embraces love. "Catholics merge with the Jews. It'll be amazing. We'll be Jewthlics!

"Joint-Venture," Pope Boniface said. "What a brilliant yuuu yun."

CHAPTER 34

The Mass

The day has come.

Several cardinals and bishops filed into Saint Peter's Basilica in orderly veneration. A stiff pompousness saturated the air. The synod's grand ceremonial opening Mass was about to begin. Back in the papal apartment, Rabbi Chiano and Mrs. English were helping Pope Boniface get decked out in full papal splendor.

"You look good and ready, Popo," Rabbi Chiano said.

"I'm excited, this is going to be great," Pope Boniface said, relishing a self-willed reprieve from whatever ailment was recently hindering his health.

"It is going to be great. Everything's in place."

"If you were me, what would you be thinking right now?" the pontiff asked.

"I'd be thinking that I'm so happy that I'm Pope Boniface X and not Rabbi Chiano Pratto!" They enjoyed a good laugh and continued helping the pope dress.

"Honestly, I'd be thinking I'm the luckiest man in the world to be praying and teaching, and leading people into the grace of honor from the most powerful pulpit in the world," Rabbi Chiano said. Pope Boniface joined hands with Rabbi Chiano and Mrs. English.

"I'm thinking I'm the luckiest man in the world to have you two as my best friends," Pope Boniface said. "Let's go."

Outside Saint Peter's, several small busses and vans carrying the bishops and nuns that attended the pope's luncheon arrived. Giorgio and his

Confirmation class arrived. The rabbi's bar and bat mitzvah students and several volunteers and clients from Chiano's soup kitchen arrived. Inside the basilica, some 4,500 cardinals and bishops rose as a procession of priests and bishops deliberately led the celebrant, Cardinal Heimreich, into the basilica, up the central aisle, toward the altar. The organ blasted out a dissonant entrance hymn and a boys choir and small choral group mechanically joined in, laboring to be heard over the howling organ. Cardinal Heimreich was in his glory, sopping up the attention and stature of celebrating a special Mass in the most celebrated basilica in the Catholic Church. This was the moment he craved– to immerse in and remember forever, what he hoped would be many moments of fame. He imagined himself as the pontiff. He always had. The euphoria of power burned through his veins and infested his mind with an intoxicating elixir of self-serving emotional gluttony.

The congregation took their seats and Cardinal Heimreich waved a ceremonial thurible of smoking incense around the altar. In addition to symbolizing prayers being transported from earth to God through the smoky musk, the visual impact and sense of control over the ritual inflated Cardinal Heimreich's starving ego like helium filling a balloon.

The exuberant choir director and orchestra leader widened her already wide brown eyes and arched her brows. She looked up into the magnificent dome, and beyond, to heaven with thanks as the organ faded to a quiet hum; the entrance hymn was clearly not her choice, not to her liking. She found a comforting smile in Brother Nordino's eyes in a nearby pew. Brother Nordino was surrounded by reporters and photographers, including Stefano Zurentino, in a section of pews on the right of the altar. Cardinal Heimreich milked the moment to garner and preserve the attention fixed on him. He took a second, then a third exaggerated swagger around the altar, spreading musky, pungent clouds of holy incense.

As the Mass progressed inside, all the bishops, nuns, and others who had just arrived in buses and vans methodically assembled at the steps of the basilica outside. Well into the progression of the Mass, Pope Boniface, Rabbi Chiano, Mrs. English, and Bravo arrived in Pope Boniface's official Popemobile– a signature turquoise and white 1957 Chevy Bel Air convertible driven by Rabbi Chiano. Mrs. English rode shotgun, and the pope sat atop the backseat waving and smiling. Bravo hung out the back of the car at the pope's side. They were all smiles, a picture of radiance.

Inside, the Mass had progressed to the point for the homily to be delivered by Cardinal Heimreich. He relished being the center of attention, happily full of himself, teeming with a zeal to deliver what he hoped would be a compelling and convincing pivotal homily that would advance the canonization of Pope Pius XII, Hitler's pope. Cardinal Heimreich approached the pulpit in deliberate devotion, savoring his moment. The moment he was about to step onto the sacred pulpit, Brother Nordino texted the word 'NOW' into his phone and pressed send. Three seconds later, the glorious bells of Saint Peter's erupted into an urgent clang of alarm announcing something vital was about to occur. The bells thundered above the basilica sending Cardinal Heimreich into a befuddled shock and instant anger. The thunderous clamor of the bells was the choir director's cue to launch the choir into song. A small orchestra inconspicuously positioned around the perimeter of the front of the basilica went unnoticed– until this moment. They followed the choir director's lead and supported the choir. Brother Nordino rose from his seat and the orchestra, choir, and choral group supported his booming voice as he broke into singing a stirring version of *Let There Be Peace on Earth*. Cardinal Heimreich's faced twisted into a puzzled sack of alarmed flesh distorted further by involuntary surges of adrenaline and cortisol blasting anger into his veins. Brother Nordino stood on the thin rail kneeler attached to the pew and waved his arm to direct the congregation's attention to the rear of the basilica. All heads turned toward the back of Saint Peter's as the singing continued.

The bishops and nuns from the pontiff's luncheon, the kids from the *Bondfire*, and the Vatican Choir entered as a procession into the basilica. They were all carrying several copies of a thin bound book. They distributed the books to the congregation as they made their way up the center aisle, proceeding their leader, Pope Boniface X, in the pageantry and treatment due royalty. Bravo brought up the rear.

Positioned immediately before Pope Boniface in the procession was Gio decked out in altar boy vestments. He was carrying a tall banner that read, "*In Chordus Silentium, The Aftermath of Silence. Pope Boniface X.*" That same title was printed on the cover of the books the members of the procession distributed to every cardinal and bishop in the congregation.

Cardinal Heimreich was a caricature of rage gone awry. The congregation was surprised, apprehensive, amused, moved, and captivated as the lengthy entourage lined the basilica's center aisle. Pope Boniface smiled broadly, waved, and blew kisses to the congregation from under the glow of a gold gilded miter trimmed in jewels. He blessed the congregation with robust flicks of a holy water-soaked aspergillum as he proceeded toward the altar, beaming with papal, divine, and human joy. The bishops' veneration for him was unmistakable and universal, even most of the reluctant ones appeared to be moved. Each pew of the congregation bowed in reverence as the pontiff passed them. The music and singing continued to fill the basilica.

The music wound down as Pope Boniface stepped onto the center of the altar. He approached Cardinal Heimreich who was seething mad, straining and struggling to temper and mask his anger. The members of the pope's procession took seats surrounding the rest of the congregation that Brother Nordino had roped off early that morning without Cardinal Heimreich's knowledge. The effect of surrounding the congregation with the pope's supporters was functional and symbolic. Pope Boniface approached Cardinal Heimreich and put his hands on his shoulders.

"Bow," he whispered to Cardinal Heimreich. The pope offered the kneeling cardinal his ring to kiss, looking down at him with sternness. "Here we are: you evaporating in the heat of shame in God's spotlight, as the rest of us shine in the clarity and purity of good intention." Cardinal Heimreich kissed the pope's ring, grudgingly– drenched in regret, humiliation, and bitterness, struggling to save face. Pope Boniface blessed Cardinal Heimreich with the sign of the cross, and the humiliated cardinal rose at the pope's command, more obedient than Bravo, who peaked out from behind the pope's cassock.

Pope Boniface waived for Giorgio to approach the altar. He brought two bunches of grapes in a silver bowl to the alter. Pope Boniface gestured for Cardinal Heimreich to sit by the altar servers, and intentionally kept his eyes– his attention, and every eye in the basilica focused on the upstaged cardinal until he took his seat on a cushion of humility.

"I thank my great nephew Giorgio for presenting the good Cardinal Heimreich with two bunches of grapes, symbols of our need to nurture the fruit of our spirit: one bunch from our very own region of Lazio, and one bunch from the cardinal's home in the Weinbaugebiete region of Germany." Gio purposefully presented the bowls of grapes to Cardinal Heimreich, who accepted them in a puzzled discomfort mixed with rage. "As they say, Your Eminence, you cannot serve the wine without nurturing the grape, yes?" Pope Boniface said. He genuflected before the crucifix then stepped up to the pulpit and turned to the congregation in an official air.

"I stand before you as the grape of salvation's wine, and a chalice filled with faith and God's joy," He paused often as he spoke in order to enable the congregation of clergy to absorb his many thoughts.

"Welcome to all of you. Today, I want to introduce a movement. Despite my love of words, our Church and our world needs more than words. We need action. As my dear friend Rabbi Chiano Pratto reminds me often, we must not merely discuss the virtues of our dogma but must act to strengthen the weaknesses of our deeds– we must act, to serve those in need, we must act, to perfect God's world. Our world."

Father Baines stewed in a sickening shock and foul regret. He absorbed Cardinal Heimreich's furious glare like a kick in the gut from a vindictive mule. Stefano Zurentino smiled at Father Baines displaying a face shining with integrity's reward: he had refused to nibble on Father Baines deceptive bait. Pope Boniface continued.

"To take action, we need unity. We need sharing. We need compassion, intellect, and spiritual verve. And we must understand and embrace the notion that the pursuit of honor is the cornerstone of strength." The pope's eyes scanned the congregation as his message steeped into their minds. "Ironically, strength often begins with acknowledging imperfections, admitting weaknesses, and mustering fierce resolve to overcome them." He took an ear-piercing silent pause before continuing.

"First, I pledge to you that beginning this very moment, we will start to transform our shameful actions of our past into the honor of our tomorrow," he said, shaking his fists in genuine ire and determined conviction. "Second, we will transform our rote, passive dogma into compassionate action!" He paused again. "And third, we will transform our vile hypocrisy into sincerity". An awkward silence hung for several moments before being broken by a single clap. Then one-by-one, more bishops applauded. More clapping followed. Then more and more and more, and before very long, most of the congregation erupted into rigorous cheers and applause. The congregation eventually rose to its feet in a boisterous standing ovation. Several cardinals looked to Cardinal Heimreich for their cue, and eventually, even he reluctantly rose and applauded to avoid further embarrassment. Cardinal Heimreich's stomach spun in a vortex of anger and rage while Pope Boniface reveled and relished in the encouraging positive reception to his message. He prompted the congregation to return to being seated with his pontifical hands moving downward.

"My brothers and sisters, we cannot think we are doing God's work by remaining silent when the world needs us to speak out. We cannot be seated when the world needs us to take a stand. And we are not doing God's work when we serve ourselves and our organization, rather than serving our people." He moved from the pulpit to the center of the altar with his thin book– his first Encyclical Letter– in hand. He comfortably immersed himself in the purity and power of the deluge of light pouring from Michelangelo's celebrated dome. An altar server set a microphone and stand before the pope. Cardinal Heimreich's face turned as red as his cassock, his neck bulged with a river of anger he choked on more than swallowed. Pope Boniface summoned two bishops that attended the luncheon to wheel a large church bell fastened to a wooden frame onto the altar.

"At this time, I invite my best friend and spiritual advisor, Rabbi Chiano Pratto, to come forward." Surprised, Rabbi Chiano joined the pope at the center of the altar. "I think I can safely say that I am the first pope in history to have two Jewish rabbis as spiritual advisors; my friend Rabbi Chiano Pratto, and a fellow we all know," he said, pointing toward the crucifix behind him.

"Rabbi Chiano, as an official means of a formal apology for the Church's silence during the Holocaust, I present you with this bell from the bell tower at Saint Daniel's Church in Calabria. Much of Saint Daniel's was destroyed by an earthquake thirty-five years ago, but its bell survived. Its voice survived. Its message survived." Pope Boniface rested his hands on the bell and silently blessed it. "Daniel is the patron Saint of Courage. Courage is the foundation of hope. I present this bell to you as a symbol of the Church's need to exemplify courage and to speak up loud and clear with the clarity of a church bell to distinguish between right and wrong. And let me say with exact clarity, the Church's silence during the Holocaust was wrong. We are sorry. I am sorry. On behalf of the Roman Catholic Church, I officially apologize to you, to all Jews, and to all the world for that silence when the voice of the Church was most needed."

Gasps rose from the congregation shocked by the pope's audacity and his courage. Pope Boniface paused for several seconds again, eying the congregation that was stunned by his honesty, his candor, and willingness to speak out so clearly against the Church that instinctively swept its own sins under the carpets of cover-up. He looked upon them not with an eye of judgment, but with the conviction of a courageous leader fixed on the right side of right juxtaposed against wrong, like a persuasive fresco saturating a cathedral wall.

"And let me also say with exact clarity, I am sorry, the Church is sorry, for harboring criminals under the camouflage of a maze of reassignments. I am referring to bishops who protect and hide child molesters behind a cloak of scandalous silence while children and their families are being terribly harmed. This is wrong!" Again, Pope Boniface paused in a notable silence. "Today, we acknowledge the aftermath of silence!" He clenched both of his fists. "Today, I introduce a new day in the church. Today, I present my first Encyclical Letter– *In Chordus Silentium– The Aftermath of Silence*. It is the blueprint for my papacy, and the beginning of a new era of honor, action, and sincerity in the Church." He allowed the gravity of his message to resonate and sink in. Then Pope Boniface yanked the bell's rope with pointed force and its ring shook the basilica with reverberating vitality. "I ring this bell today with clarity and conviction as a ringing proclamation of truth and honor." He rang the bell again– forcefully and dramatically. Then he rang the bell a third time and allowed its ring– its message– to resonate deep into the congregations' minds and souls. Pope Boniface continued.

"Yes, today, we acknowledge *The Aftermath of Silence*. In addition to an apology for our silence during the massacre of six million Jews, let this bell ring out as a loud call to action. The pope handed Rabbi Chiano his bound Encyclical Letter. "I am presenting you with my first Encyclical Letter, *The Aftermath of Silence*, as written testimony of my official apology for the Church's silence when Jews, and the entire world most needed the Church to respond with a vigorous voice of opposition. And this first Encyclical Letter is testimony of the Church's commitment to a loving fellowship with our Jewish brothers and sisters." He held up the bound copy of his Encyclical Letter and waved it for all to see. "And my first

Encyclical Letter clearly and explicitly details profound and expansive reasons supporting exactly why Pope Pius XII is unworthy of canonization– irrefutable reasons."

Rabbi Chiano was about to succumb to tears. The pope summoned two bishops to bring out a beautifully carved wooden chair; Pope Boniface gestured for the rabbi to sit in it.

"This chair is symbolic of that same silence we must confront. We must not sit in silence as Pius XII did at tables of invisible diplomacy, we must take a seat at the table of the world and make our voice and our values heard." Pope Boniface turned to Rabbi Chiano. "Rabbi Chiano, we are happy to present you with this oaken chair, carved from wood from the Sherwood Forest in England, the most famous oak tree in the world. The tree is a thousand years old, Rabbi. A thousand years old! It's oak!" Pope Boniface placed his hands on Chiano's shoulders. "This chair is a symbolic reminder that Jews will always have a seat at our Catholic table. It is also an ironic reminder that our work is not accomplished in the comfort of chairs but in the forests of the world." The rabbi rose from the chair and endearingly embraced the pope. Two bishops approached the altar and placed the chair next to Cardinal Heimreich as the pope raised his arms to absorb the light and fervor of the Saint Peter's Basilica.

"I stand in the grandeur and purity of this holy light embracing the clarity and sincerity of this new day in the Church. I hope my message and my intentions are as clear and pure as this very light. Look at it," Pope Boniface said, directing the congregation's attention toward the miraculous fountain of soft, white light bathing the basilica with God's warmth. The congregation remained stunned and intrigued. Cardinal Heimreich remained on the brink of losing his mind to anger's rage. Rabbi Chiano smiled broadly through joy's tears.

"As we fuse the Old and New Testament messages at every Mass, we must go beyond merely reading words, we must live the words and ways our Jewish savior Jesus Christ lived– honorably, sincerely, and compassionately. And we shall never silence the voice of God or avoid the call for the Church to be the voice of justice and the voice of the oppressed. If we do not uphold honor we attract and endure disgrace. And if we are not an example of integrity we endorse corruption. The choice and responsibility rests on our shoulders." He paused at length again, enabling silence to speak.

"I pause to remind us how loud silence speaks." He paused again before continuing. "You shall hear a roar from the new Church in this *Aftermath of Silence.*" The pope gave the choirmaster a nod and she stirred the choir, choral group, and orchestra into a rousing presentation of the hymn– *Let There Be Peace on Earth* … and the entire congregation joined in. The pope ceremoniously proceeded down the center aisle of the basilica sprinkling the congregation with holy water. When he reached Brother Nordino, he affectionately embraced him and whispered in his ear, "It's a new day in the Church, Brother. I'm so glad you got arrested."

"Me, too. And I'm so glad that now my life is all about sentences," Brother Nordino jested with a pun. Most of the congregation was jubilant, some confused, but all were engaged, and all were in awe of Pope Boniface. Cardinal Heimreich was consumed by the angry bile he was wallowing in, as the pope triumphantly enjoyed a procession around the basilica, blessing the congregation once more. The basilica teemed with pageantry, pomp, reverence, and spiritual verve. Truly a new day had begun in the Church. The entire congregation sang:

> "Let there be peace on earth,
> And let it begin with me.
> Let There Be Peace on Earth,
> The peace that was meant to be.
>
> "With God as our Father,
> Brothers, all are we.
> Let me walk with my brother
> In perfect harmony.
>
> "Let peace begin with me,
> Let this be the moment now.
> With every step I take,
> Let this be my solemn vow,
> To take each moment
> And live each moment
> In peace eternally.
> Let there be peace on earth
> And let it begin with me …"

CHAPTER 35

The Last Dance

The midnight blue of night wrapped its sprawling arms around Rome like a cozy oversize sweater snuggling its owner in security. This day, so well lived, left Pope Boniface and the many he so thoroughly inspired at the Bishop's Synod Mass, committed to genuine righteousness and peacefully revived. The pontiff relaxed in the contentment inherent in a best effort and achievement's blessings. Mission accomplished.

After a delicious meal of the pope's favorite dish, ravioli with meatballs and sausage, a tossed salad finished off with devil's food cake topped with fluffy cream cheese icing, Mrs. English played the piano. Pope Boniface was in his sleepwear: blue silk pajamas, a navy-blue silk robe bearing the papal seal, and black leather slippers with an open heel. He danced ever so lightly, so gingerly, peacefully, soulfully while taking occasional snippets to prune the still-flourishing oak plant Rabbi Chiano had given him. He carefully snipped the plant as though he were fingering the hair of a dancing partner. His face reflected contentment, fulfillment, and a satisfying soothing peace. He was complete.

He danced toward his window and he heard the music– the piano playing– stop. He looked back to Mrs. English and she softly smiled at him. Her kind smile warmed his soul. It always had. She crossed the room and took a record from a shelf beneath a table that served as home for an antique Victrola, much like the one Pope Boniface's mother used to play in the piazza. Like the one his father was manning the day he was murdered. Mrs. English wound up the Victrola and placed its needle arm on the record and a scratchy sound skipped into the recording. The sound became music, clear and sweet. A waltz. Mrs. English crossed the room waltzing. She took Pope Boniface by the hand and they instinctively melted into a graceful waltz. Looking into her eyes, he found warmth and joy and a deep spring of happiness. They danced as though they had been partners all their lives. In many ways, they had been. They swayed and moved with the lightness of air. They closed their eyes and smiled and wondered. A lot. It was a long dance, a memorable dance. A beautiful dance, a long overdue dance, for both of them. When the music scratched to a stop, Mrs. English kissed Pope Boniface gently on both cheeks.

"I love you, Marcello. I really love you."

Pope Boniface held her very close to him, then kissed her on both of her cheeks.

"And I love you, Gillian."

"Good," she said, and smiled in warm contentment.

Bravo snuggled against the pope's leg and sat at his feet; looking up at the pope, he whimpered, a plea to be pet. The pope lifted Bravo gently, and tenderly held him in his arms.

"We love you, too, Bravo." Bravo showed his appreciation with a series of licks over the pope's cheeks. Pope Boniface carried Bravo over to the window with him and the three comrades stood together– the pope of the Roman Catholic Church, Mrs. Gillian English, and Bravo– looking over Saint Peter's Square.

"I am forgiving myself. It's time to forgive myself," Pope Boniface declared.

The night sky seemed to serenade the pope's private window with its soft hum, too.

With morning's call for a new day, the peace of night yielded to the organized frenzy of Mercy Hospital. Today was the day for Pope Boniface's exploratory surgery. A nurse and an intern wheeled Pope Boniface down a sterile hospital corridor on a gurney. Giorgio's soccer ball was at his feet; it was signed to Uncle Marcello by all of Gio's pals. Bravo was perched at the bottom of the gurney like a hood ornament leading the way. Rabbi Chiano and Mrs. English walked alongside, each holding one of the pope's hands. Mrs. English was failing at trying to keep herself together. Rabbi Chiano was too terrified to speak. The pope squeezed their hands to comfort them.

"Don't look so worried, Iano," the pope said to Rabbi Chiano.

"I have to worry, it's in my DNA. And I love you," Rabbi Chiano said. "Lucky for you that you have a Jewish doctor raised in Rome and educated in Israel. But I'm still worried."

"Oh God, Marcello, so am I," Mrs. English said. He patted her hand, then raised it to his lips and kissed it. He looked up at Chiano and they instinctively reached their hands toward each other and exchanged the same marble they had exchanged as six-year-old boys some seventy-four years ago in the piazza that terrible day. They examined their marbles and their lives in that poignant moment, seeing the world's clarity and its color in the glass marbles in their palms. Their escape into their own private world was interrupted by hurried footsteps approaching from behind. The nurse and intern stopped the gurney. It was Amodeo running down the hall toward them carrying an enormous basket filled with grapes with a note card attached to it. He was also carrying a small placard.

"This was delivered this morning for you, Holy Father." He handed Pope Boniface the card. He opened the envelope and read the card aloud.

"'Under the cloak of your position, you are far more than a mere old man … you are the pope, the nourished grape that inspires the spirit of the Church. My prayers are with you. Cardinal Heimreich.' Pope Boniface looked to Chiano and Mrs. English through the jagged uncertainty of a puzzling thought. "Well, what do you make of that," Pope Boniface said.

"Sour grapes …" Rabbi Chiano asserted.

"Maybe let's hope God doesn't hear Cardinal Heimreich's prayers related to me today," Pope Boniface said, in a spirit of humor with a wink.

"Holy Father, I brought these, too," Amodeo said, holding up two perfectly ripe tomatoes. "And the wall … the wall is finished. And this, too," he said, showing Pope Boniface a bronze plaque. It read, 'Pope Boniface X. Courage. Honor. Integrity. Compassion. 1939– Eternity.'

"Amodeo, this is just beautiful. And you grant me eternity. Beautiful. Thank you, Amodeo. Thank you."

"You will live forever in the wall, Your Holiness."

The pope squeezed Amodeo's hand and blessed him.

"Thank you, Amodeo. So very much. As soon as I get back, you and I will celebrate with wine and cheese and tomatoes next to your wall." The nurse and intern resumed the trip to the operating room. They stopped just before entering it in order to allow the pontiff a final word with his friends, and to remove Bravo from his perch.

Rabbi Chiano and Mrs. English kissed the pope's hand and his forehead. The pope took a brochure from under his blanket and handed it to Rabbi Chiano.

"Iano, you'll be happy to know that I booked us– the three of us– a vacation on a lake, in the mountains: fresh air, heavenly scenery, serenity– "

"I'm afraid I can't make it, Popo; none of us can. We have other plans." Rabbi Chiano placed an envelope on the pontiff's chest. Pope Boniface pulled three tickets from the envelope.

"We're going on a cruise, Popo. The three of us. So, you do well in there because we're going on a river cruise."

"Let's hope."

Pope Boniface removed his watch.

"Please give this to Gio. Tell him it's the best gift– for the price. Time." The pontiff squeezed Rabbi Chiano's and Mrs. English's hands, closed his eyes, and danced with a waltz playing in his mind.

The End

Made in the USA
Middletown, DE
05 October 2021